RHETT C BRUNO
TITAN'S FURY

TITAN'S FURY

©2019 RHETT C. BRUNO

Published by Aethon Books LLC.

Cover Art by: Jasper Schreurs

Cover Design, Print and eBook formatting and cover design by Steve Beaulieu.

CHILDREN OF TITAN

Pick up the whole series.

PROLOGUE

"GET AWAY FROM ME, FREAK!"

Another student at the Phobos Youth Academy gave Zhaff a shove, sending both him and his lunch tray flying into the wall. Zhaff said nothing; he never did. For as long as he could remember, he hated talking to others. There was too much to think about—too many ways a response could be formed to impart meaning.

Zhaff merely stared.

That seemed to make the bully angrier. "You want to say something?" he said, friends behind him smirking.

Zhaff didn't. After a year at the Academy, he still wasn't sure why his peers harassed him so often. It was illogical. Everyone in the program had top scores on entry exams and came from affluent, reputable clan-families who could afford the astronomical tuition meant to set them on a path toward USF administration or corporate directorship, except Zhaff only had one of those. He had been an illegitimate bastard from the Martian underworld, enrolled on a special outreach scholarship funded by Luxarn Pervenio—the man he now knew to be his biological father.

"Answer him, freak!" another boy shouted.

"He can't," the bully said. "This piece of sewer trash probably never learned how to talk. That right, Zhaff?" He grabbed Zhaff by the collar and lifted him against the wall with ease. Like most offworlders, Zhaff had grown tall, but his stringy limbs had yet to fill in.

"Would you say something!" The bully shook him.

"Something," Zhaff replied. Speaking was easier when his conversant gave direction, like how Luxarn had when he'd met with him to award the scholarship. No use of slang or local colloquialisms. *Why do others insist upon making speech so difficult?*

A few of the bully's friends burst out laughing.

"You some sort of smart-ass, freak?" the bully said, cheeks flushing red as he squeezed Zhaff's collar tighter.

Zhaff tilted his head. "Surely you know the rear-end is not the region from which human intelligence derives?" he said.

"That's it." The boy reared his hand back, revealing his intent—and his intended target point—far too early. He went to punch Zhaff in the face, but malnourished as Zhaff was, he was also exceptionally agile. He ducked his head just in time, causing the bully's fist to slam against the metal wall. He howled in agony as Zhaff slipped under his grasp.

Walk away. That was what one of Zhaff's instructors had told him on his first day when another over-hormonal student pushed him for staring. Ever since, he'd handled every altercation in the same manner. Except this time, one of the boy's friends stepped in his way.

"Where do you think you're going, freakshow?" he asked.

"Please, move asi—" Zhaff couldn't finish the sentence before the bully grabbed him by his shirt and threw him to the ground.

"Am I a joke to you, Zhaff?" he screamed. His voice resonated with a fury in no way suited to the situation. His fist slammed into Zhaff's cheek. In the moment, it barely hurt, however, Zhaff instantly recognized he'd suffered an orbital fracture. The onslaught wasn't finished.

"To ensure the safety of human propagation. Right, Zhaff?" the bully asked. Only the bully had suddenly aged sixty or so years, his skin scarred and craggy, his beard gray as the Earthen sky. His voice spoke of ash and whiskey. And behind him was no longer the burnished metal and wood-trimmed walls of the Academy, but stormy, orange-hued skies wrapping a frozen cliff-face.

The bully punched Zhaff again and again, pounding into his face until all Zhaff could see was blackness and blood. The others peeled the bully off before Zhaff's skull was crushed, but not before his right eye was rendered useless.

"Family," the bully said as he was carried away. "I hope you understand, Zhaff!"

Only he didn't. Zhaff never could figure out why he'd done it. He hadn't insulted him, hadn't injured him. Perhaps a bad day had led to an explosion of rash behavior. Stress or past trauma could have that effect on people with weak constitutions. Luxarn always said sometimes people are born rotten, and that was why he ordered the bully thrown out of the Academy before Zhaff could ask him...

"Agent Zhaff," a nearby voice echoed. "Agent Zhaff!" Someone shook his shoulder, and Zhaff had the man's sleeved wrist gripped within his new synthetic fingers even before he turned his head to face him.

"By Earth!" Pervenio Director Barret Ulnor yelped.

Zhaff released him. After that day at the academy, when Luxarn invited Zhaff to his quarters and revealed who he really was, Luxarn also told him never to let another person harm him, no matter what.

It used to be easy to tell who meant him harm. His eye lens

revealed all. Through it, Zhaff simultaneously saw the rush of heat to Ulnor's chest and every detail of the man's face, down to the fibers of hair coating his too-soft cheeks. He could see his lips twitch from one hundred meters away. Every subtle alteration on a man's face revealed intent, only, since Zhaff had woken up from a coma, something in his mind wasn't working properly. He wondered if it was the experimental, cerebral implant which had helped stimulate his brain function. It started as a Venta Co. prototype after all, and his father's corporate rival never had been the most reliable.

Regardless, Zhaff's mind kept wandering off to that day as a child when he was so senselessly beaten. Kept distracting him with flashes of his final moments on Titan. Flickers of Titan's sky crept into the corner of rooms. Gunshots booming like thunderclaps. He couldn't remember exactly what had happened after he and Malcolm Graves entered the Children of Titan's secret hideout, only that the enemy had gunned them both down. Now the enemy had Malcolm prisoner and the Ring in its grasp.

An image of an old, bloodied man pounding on his face rushed through Zhaff's head again and made him stagger. His synthetic fingers raised toward his barely-human temple to try and drive out the sudden pulsing pain. His eye-lens struggled for focus.

Focus, he told himself. *Mission first.*

"What is it with you Cogents?" Ulnor said, still shaking his bruised wrist. "Luxarn said you were the best."

Zhaff drew a deep breath, feeling the pull only on one side of his chest. Exposure to Titan had left him with only one working lung; the other had been replaced by a new 3D-printed elastic polymer model. His throat, ravaged by cold, had been rebuilt with synthetic weaving and a respiratory aid that hummed every time it helped Zhaff inhale. Half his heart had required microelectronic augmentation to maintain optimal performance.

Zhaff knew all of the changes within his body but could feel so little of them. He was a puzzle with pieces that fit together but formed disparate images. Connections without connecting.

"We're almost there," Zhaff said. He shook his head and turned his attention to the lift's floor counter.

"Thanks for letting me know." Ulnor brushed off his formal tunic and checked his hair and teeth on the chrome doors. He appeared satisfied by the sight of himself. Zhaff knew little about him, only that he had connections to a wealthy clan-family.

"All right," Ulnor said. "Once we get up there, I want you right outside the door. You aren't coming inside and scaring them away from making this deal with what's left of your face."

"That is agreeable," Zhaff said.

"And you—oh, good. I pull this agreement off, Mr. Pervenio might start taking me more seriously. I didn't spend a year at Phobos Academy to wind up a farming director on Earth."

"You went to Phobos?"

The man chuckled. "Who here didn't?"

For a moment, Zhaff wondered if he was the one who'd beaten him—he had trouble remembering any names from that time due to the brain trauma. Then he cursed his faulty mind. That wasn't logical. He'd learned enough about his father to know the bully was somewhere terrible, or dead.

The elevator doors opened. Zhaff stepped out into the hall, his Pervenio-labeled boiler suit worn proudly. His pulse pistol hung at his hip. The floor of the Red Wing Assembly Hall was busy. Aides, dignitaries, security officers; they all waited outside the conference room where a pivotal deal allowing Pervenio Corp to supply engines for all Red Wing vessels was to be negotiated.

Director Ulnor was to serve as Luxarn's representative, and the service bot hovering behind their backs his proxy. Zhaff stood silently, ignoring the stares of so many as Director Ulnor was greeted and invited in. Luxarn bid them all hello from a screen on the service bot's lens—his first semi-public appearance since the enemy stole the Ring.

"Thank you for the escort, Zhaff," Luxarn said through a private com-link set within Zhaff's ear. "You know what to do."

"Yes, sir," Zhaff replied. That was the code-phrase indicating their operation was green-lit. It wasn't easy smuggling what they needed to into the Red Wing headquarters. They didn't have a central headquarters in a city like Venta or Pervenio—instead, theirs was aboard a luxury cruiser in constant rotation of Mars. The Red Wing, true to their name.

Zhaff left Director Ulnor behind and hurried toward the restrooms. He had to push through the crowd as he searched all the faces. Finally, a man in a Red Wing uniform approached from the opposite direction. Unlike the other patrons around the meeting hall, this one didn't stare with shock at Zhaff and his reconstructed face. His eyes were set upon the ground, jaw grinding, lips parting just a hair as if he were speaking his thoughts back to himself, forehead dripping with sweat.

Nervous.

Zhaff knew that had to be his mark. A low-end security supervisor who decided he owed more loyalty to his clan-family than his employer. He passed a keycard into Zhaff's hand as he went by, never once looking up. The manmade toxin on Zhaff's glove rubbed onto the man's skin. In a few short hours, he would fall ill and die without a trace, and with no way to change his mind about helping Pervenio Corp. A sacrifice, for the good of the solar system.

Zhaff coolly slid the card into his pocket, then made an abrupt turn into the restroom, where he washed his glove off in the sink before continuing to the back stall. A container sat on top of the toilet. The white powered suit of armor inside had been reclaimed from Ringers killed on Mars. The sight of the orange circle painted on the chest plate made Zhaff's heartbeat off rhythm. It was part of his last memories on Titan before he'd failed. Failed his company, failed his father, and failed his partner.

Zhaff averted his gaze from the symbol as he dressed. He had the offworlder stature to fit in snugly, though he could only feel the tiny needles set within the carbon-fiber inlay, which helped augment strength along his left half. The rest of him was numb—either synthetic or covered by dead skin.

At the bottom of the container, he found a pulse-rifle, an outdated model made by Venta Co., the same type he'd used back on Titan before the Children of Titan won. His fingers froze on their way to grasp the handle.

Failure, failure, failure. The word bounced around Zhaff's head like a rubber ball. His father told him it wasn't his fault, but he knew—his failure had caused the Ring to fail.

He smacked himself in the synthetic half of his head, causing his vision to go temporarily fuzzy. Then again.

"Focus," he told himself. He grabbed the gun, then hit a switch on the container, which caused it to fold up tight enough to be stored in his belt. Not a hint of evidence left behind. He returned to the exit and used thermal imaging to keep track of the assembly hall. The formalities were coming to an end, meaning everyone of importance would enter the conference room, and everyone else would return to their responsibilities.

One of the security personnel working the floor was on his way to leave the hall, only the man decided to stop to relieve himself. Zhaff hurried to the corner as the man entered and headed for a urinal. Zhaff considered shooting him, but it'd be too loud. Instead, he imagined the route he could take to avoid detection before being able to subdue him. With powered armor in addition to his synthetic limbs, applying the force necessary to render a man dead or unconscious would be simple.

Zhaff took a single step, then imagined the bully beating down on his face. Once again, the bully appeared old and haggard. Before Zhaff knew it, he was out into the hall, walking toward the conference room doors. No surveillance feeds were directly outside the bathroom—their contact informed them of that. No more guards between him and the tall, metallic doors.

Red Wing Company thought they were safe in their ship. Everyone thought they were safe until the Children of Titan ruined that. They interrupted the necessary expansion of man amongst the system and eventually toward the stars.

"Stop right there!"

Zhaff whipped around, gun raised, and saw that same officer he'd spared now aiming a pulse pistol at him. He wasn't sure how he hadn't heard him. Perhaps he wasn't used to the audio receptor rather than an ear on the rebuilt half of his head.

The officer was green, twitchy. Zhaff easily had the first shot if he took it, but all he could see as he raised his weapon was loose sand spanning the distance between them and frozen rock. His veins ran cold. Lightning coruscated in the distance as a Titanian storm formed, only he wasn't on Titan.

"Weapon!" the officer yelled.

A bang echoed, then a bullet struck Zhaff in the side of the helmet. It didn't pierce the heavy armor, but it dented it hard enough to give Zhaff's brain a shudder. He hit the floor, seeing red.

Failure, failure, failure.

Zhaff lifted himself onto all fours. His fists pressed into the metal floor so hard it warped. His fingers trembled with rage.

"Stay down!" the officer yelled.

The man was thirteen meters away, head exposed. He was

about to make a move when he identified another officer approaching from behind, prepared to subdue him with a shock baton. Zhaff swept his leg backward, catching the second guard unaware. The man struck his own throat with the baton on his way down, instantly vomiting. Zhaff rolled over his body and sprang up. He took a glancing shot off his chest plate, which scraped off a layer of orange paint, then fired. The officer across the room toppled forward with a hole square in his forehead.

This time, Zhaff didn't hesitate. He slapped the keycard against the reader, and the conference room door slid open. A glass table set for two dozen rested in the center of the ovular space. A latticed translucency stretched overhead, two stories high, with a view of the red planet beyond. The Red Wing board sat in their formal attire, gaping toward the door. Director Ulnor looked as shocked as any of them.

Two more security officers waited inside. Zhaff got a reading on them through the wall. He ducked as he entered, another shock baton blow soaring over his head. Zhaff grabbed the man's arm and directed the blow into the other's chest. His body convulsed as Zhaff flipped the other over his shoulder and planted a bullet in his head.

"The Ringers are here!" A Red Wing official bolted for the door, earning a bullet to the leg. Another reached for a personal firearm, and Zhaff shot it out of his grip. He had orders not to kill any of them until the right moment. That wasn't the Children of Titan's M.O.

"What is the meaning of this!" a woman seated at the head of the table asked. Director Ulnor sat on one side of her. Luxarn's service bot floated on the other, his face projected in the center, feigning shock. His acting wasn't convincing upon close examination. Zhaff would have to let him know later.

Zhaff slowly stalked forward. The board members nearest to

him flinched, a few stifled tears. Rich men and women—the kind who attended Phobos Academy.

"What do you want from us?" Director Ulnor asked.

"All who partner with..." Zhaff paused. His helmet obscured his face and distorted his voice—the same way it did the Ringers when they raided the *Piccolo*—but the next words were difficult to get out. He'd been prepped by Luxarn, but lying never came easily to Zhaff. The truth was so much simpler.

"Pervenio Corp is our enemy," Zhaff finished.

"Just stay away from us!" a Red Wing official yelled.

"Take what you want!" screamed another.

Zhaff slowly spun around. He caught another guard approaching from the hall on his thermals and shot the man's foot as he edged against the entry. He fell forward into the opening, and another bullet ensured he would never breathe again.

More cries filled the room.

"Whoever you are, Ringer, you won't get away with this!" Luxarn growled. For a moment, Zhaff wasn't sure if it was through the com-link built into his reconstructed ear or the service bot until a few of the board members voiced their agreement.

Zhaff turned back to face Luxarn in the bot's live feed. He stared into the weary face of his father, noticing wrinkles that he'd never had before. Blemishes caused by the stress of Zhaff's failures. Luxarn looked directly at Director Ulnor for some reason.

"Go on," Luxarn said. The lips on the screen didn't move, indicating the voice was in Zhaff's com-link. "I promised a gift to you, Zhaff. Look into the eyes of Director Ulnor and see."

Zhaff did as requested. Fear racked the director's face. Zhaff's eye lens zoomed in and out, poring over his every feature, and that was when he saw. The bully who'd beaten him all those years ago sat directly in front of him. For a moment Zhaff's eye-lens lost focus, and he saw that haggard old man in his place, then it centered.

It was him. He couldn't believe he hadn't noticed earlier.

"I've been waiting a long time for this, Zhaff," Luxarn said. "You don't ever have to be afraid. Him, Kale Trass—all those who ever put us down—will pay. So, go on. You survived Titan for a reason, I know it."

Zhaff slowly approached the director, memories of that day filling his mind. The world melted away, and he found himself crossing the icy surface of Titan. He heard the bully's friends laugh at him; heard that old man whisper about family and understanding...

"Get out!" Zhaff roared. He gripped the massive conference table hewn from the very rock of Mars and flipped it with the mere flick of his wrist. The board members on the other side were smashed against the wall. "Just get out!"

Those board members who weren't incapacitated by the table stood to bolt for the door, but Zhaff whipped around and shot the one in the lead. "Not you!" he said. The respiratory aid built into his throat rattled as his breathing hastened and it was pushed to its limits. All the frightened voices of the Red Wing board blurred.

"This is what happens to those who steal from our Ring!" Zhaff said, still trying to recite his lines. Not to fail.

"Us steal?" Director Ulnor said. His voice broke through the madness and Zhaff focused. He could hear his own face crunching again as a younger version of the man beat down on him. Without logic. Without reason.

"Why did you do it!" Zhaff shouted. He seized Ulnor by the throat and pulled him close. He imagined freezing air whipping all around them, Titanian sand stinging his skin like a thousand tiny knives. His eye-lens focused in and out, but he saw himself lying on Titan with his partner Malcolm beside him, both bleeding out after the *bang* of two gunshots.

"Family," Malcolm whispered, voice faint and quavering.

"Why!" Zhaff lifted Ulnor and slammed him against the floor.

"I don't know what you're talking about!" the director wheezed.

Zhaff's vision refocused and he saw Ulnor, then the board of Red Wing directors, frozen by terror. Everything was being captured by Luxarn's service bot, and he had only one final line to recite.

Focus, Zhaff told himself. *Sometimes there is no logic, only chaos.*

"Finish it, Zhaff," Luxarn said sternly into his ear.

"From ice to ashes," Zhaff said out loud. All the eyes of those before him went wide. They'd seen this act before.

Zhaff aimed his pulse-rifle at the translucency above, then unloaded his magazine into one segment. The fused silica glass was strong enough to withstand the barrage without shattering, but Zhaff looked down again at the director. Now *he* stood above him, only he didn't see Ulnor. Again, he saw a gray beard, worn eyes—he saw Malcolm Graves.

He couldn't explain why, but without thinking twice, he screamed at the top of his lungs, grabbed the director, and flung him with all his might into the compromised glass. It blew open, the explosive decompression tearing the hole wider, twisting structural members and sucking every member of the Red Wing board, along with Director Ulnor, out with it.

Zhaff joined them as well, only his armor was designed to withstand such forces. Nano-fiber wings beneath the arms helped him ride the gush of air. In a few seconds, he floated across space, looking down upon the breached ship and the glowing red of Mars beneath it.

When he looked back up, Titan, blood, and Malcolm Graves filled his view. "Family... I hope you understand, Zhaff," his old partner said softly.

Zhaff refocused his vision, and through the field of glass and debris, saw a small Venta Co. ship zooming toward him.

"I'm proud of you, my son," Luxarn said through his com-link. "A worthy sacrifice has been made in our quest to secure the safe propagation of human life. Now we take back what was stolen from us."

My son. Luxarn had never referred to him like that before, only ever Zhaff. So much had changed while he was under. Zhaff hated change.

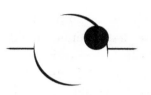

ONE

KALE TRASS

AFTER I LOST CORA, I NEVER THOUGHT I COULD FEEL again, but as I floated alone aboard the ship named in her honor, staring at Gareth's body, it all came rushing back. He was my friend. Believed in me in ways even Rin couldn't. Only it was then I realized I didn't even know his last name.

War changes everything. It makes friends into strangers, men into monsters. They said it plagued Earth back before the Meteorite—that Darien Trass would have been wise to leave, impending apocalypse or not. All I knew was I'd be saying goodbye to more than Gareth before our war was through. At least all those years watching our brothers and sisters, fathers and mothers be sent off to Quarantine never to be released were good practice.

"Are you feeling any better, Kale?" Rin asked, pulling herself along the hallway at my back.

"Fine," I said. I clenched my jaw and exhaled. My stomach remained uneasy, and my muscles ached all over. Though, apparently, that was to be expected after roughly a month in a sleep pod.

"Those Earther anti-rads pack a punch."

I drew myself closer to Gareth and took one of his limp hands. His skin was cold as the surface of Titan. All that time learning how to communicate with him, now I'd never need to read his hands again.

"Don't let the collector get in your head," Rin said.

"We should have paid attention," I said.

"We were too busy dealing with traitorous ambassadors and Earthers." She joined me at Gareth's side and lay her hand over ours. "He died how he would have wanted to. Keeping you safe."

I swallowed then nodded. "I won't let it be for nothing. Is the collector almost ready?"

"He's stabilizing," Rin said. "Kale, I'm still not sure this is the best idea. I know you want to make a statement on M-day, but they're Earthers. They believe every day belongs to them. We can delay."

"Delay plans so more people can die like him? Basaam's prototype can end our war."

"We don't know that."

"Now you don't believe?" I asked.

"That's not what I'm saying."

"Then you agree? We won't have another chance like this to retrieve it. All the Earther corps are reeling. I checked the feeds before you woke up—"

"You opened coms this close to Jupiter?" she interrupted, her features darkening.

"Only for a second."

Rin took me by the shoulders and stared straight into my eyes. I didn't need to fight my impulses anymore to keep my gaze from trailing off toward the gruesome half of her face or the hole in her cheek through which I could see the shine of her tongue. It felt strange to remember I hadn't even known her for a half a year. Everything before the day she'd pulled me off the *Piccolo* felt like a blur. Every day since, an eternity.

"Do you realize how dangerous that is?" she said.

I brushed her away. "Something happened, Rin. Red Wing stock is plummeting over something called The Massacre. Pervenio Corp and Venta Co. are in open talks about a merger. What we did in that hangar is changing everything. Earthers have never been so close to a battle since before the Meteorite."

Rin looked like she wanted to say something then bit her lip and exhaled. "We targeted Basaam on Mars because we knew he'd be easier to take there. Even with all our planning, things went sideways. Now we're going to put things in the hands of an Earther?"

"You're always talking about reading and reacting," I said. "Letting the Earthers extend too far. M-day is coming. You say we can delay, but symbols are everything, right? It's what helped us take back the Ring. It's what I am."

"You're more than that now," Rin replied.

"Am I?" I pushed past her back out into the hallway and made my way through the *Cora*'s innards. She kept pace with me.

"Maybe you're right, and the collector can get this done, but maybe you're wrong, and they're waiting for this," she said. "They had Aria for hours. Who knows what she told them."

"She didn't know anything about Basaam."

"And we didn't know she was the daughter of a Pervenio Collector. She could have overheard us any time."

I turned my attention to the circular room lined with sleeping pods. Two of my men stood beside Malcolm's, prepping him to be woken up. Aria lay in another, dreamless. I knew that was the case now after my first spell using one. There were no grand adventures of the mind or nightmares once put under—there was nothing.

"What if she isn't lying, Rin?" I said.

"Then she would have told us from the start," Rin said.

"Even if her father really was out of the game?"

"You saw that man. Did he look retired, charging in with a handful of Cogents? Nobody but Venta and Red Wing were supposed to know which hangar we were in. Face it, Kale, there's too much about her past we don't know not to be careful."

"And how much do I know about your past?"

"That's not—Look, I know you care about her, and I know now what she's carrying in her belly. But she accomplished what we needed her to in getting that meeting with the Assembly. I'm not saying we need to kill her, but she can't be around us anymore. It's too risky."

My fists clenched as I thought back to the last night Aria and I spent together on Mars. The way she looked at me after we were finished in bed, like in that moment, nothing else in the world mattered. I wasn't sure how anybody could fake something like that, and then I remembered that I was doing it. Faking a smile right back at her.

"I'll decide what to do with Aria," I said. "You worry about getting Malcolm to help us. Gareth deserves for us to pull this off."

"Now that's something we both agree on." Rin turned and approached Malcolm's sleep pod. "All right, start waking him." My men did as she asked, and the lid popped open with a snap hiss.

Rin turned back to me. "I'm just worried he's too unpredictable," she said. "He could try to run or warn someone once he's alone."

"He won't," I replied.

"You don't know that, Kale."

"Yes, I do. Malcolm won't risk what might happen to Aria if he doesn't obey your every command."

"Or he's a good liar, like his daughter, and doesn't give a shit about her. He's an Earther, after all."

"He could've killed me, Rin. After Gareth died, he could have ended all of this. He stayed because he thinks Aria needs saving from me."

"What is it about this woman?" Rin rolled her eyes and hunched over Malcolm's sleep pod as stimulating chems raced through the tubes connected to him. "Fine, but let me handle the threats. If we're going to get him nervous, it's going to have to look real."

I moved to my aunt's side, then peered over at Aria, the woman who, apparently, I barely knew. The woman carrying my child, who'd been a shoulder to lie on during this war when my entire world felt like it was caving in.

"Just don't actually hurt her," I said.

"I won't," Rin answered.

Malcolm's eyes snapped open. He gasped for air just before Rin tore him out of his sleep pod without bothering to carefully remove any intravenous feeder tubes first. We wore our full suits of powered armor since the mag-boots made traversing the *Cora* simpler while under zero-g. Rin lifted Malcolm's weightless body. He coughed and hacked as he came to his senses.

Rin slammed him against a blank wall, where two of our men restrained his arms and legs so he wouldn't float away. I could see his lips twitch as he attempted to speak, but now I knew what it was like to wake up after so long. The disorientation lasted longer than the sickness.

His cheeks went green, and before we could do anything, he vomited. To his credit, he must have fought back most of the bile, as only a bit snuck out. Rin quickly removed a sanitary mask from her belt, wrenched his head back, and strapped it to his face tighter than necessary. Only then did she take a step back.

We watched as he searched from side to side like a newborn finding the world again. His bleary eyes blinked a few times, and it took around a minute for them to focus on me. A chill ran through me. It'd felt like only an hour since what he said to me before we went under, blaming me for Cora's fate and so much more. I knew he was just trying to get under my skin, but hearing another Earther talk about her like she was merely a name made me want to scream.

"There you are," Rin said. She planted a finger in the center of Malcolm's forehead and pushed. "I never thought you'd wake up. How does it feel to be the one wearing the mask now?"

Malcolm licked his lips then spat. "Tastes like shit," he rasped. "Any chance of getting a new one of these?"

"You're lucky we don't let you drown in your own filth, Earther."

"I can see why you all hated them."

"You don't see anything," I said, stepping forward. I was supposed to let Rin handle him, but I couldn't help myself. The chems from being under had drained entirely out of my system by now, and all I could feel was my rage toward him.

"Ah, the boy king decides to speak for himself," Malcolm said.

"He speaks for all of us!" Rin snapped. The back of her hand smacked Malcolm across the face, hopefully hard enough to wipe away the indignant grin I knew he was wearing under his mask.

"But he lets a woman strike for him?" Malcolm said.

"We aren't as backward as your kind."

"Oh yeah? Which one of these pods do you have my daughter stuffed into, huh?" Hearing him bring her up caused me to look at her pod, and his gaze followed mine. "This is your last chance, kid," he said. "Let us out of here. Don't put another death on your conscience like Cora's."

Rin peered back at me upon learning for the first time that this collector had been there during Cora's interrogation. If she didn't think I could handle a snake like him before, now she'd be sure of it. Collectors were infamous for being able to work their prey. They found weaknesses, used their gut, and exploited them, whereas Cogents saw lies and extrapolated information to form high-stakes percentages which informed their actions.

"Your daughter is safe. For now," I replied, desperate to show Rin I could handle myself. "That all depends on you."

"If you hurt her," Malcolm snarled. "Boy, you don't even know pain."

"Relax. Aria is of no use to us dead. You, on the other hand... that's an entirely different story."

"Let me go, and you'll see how useful I can be."

"I plan on it. You're going to help us with an issue. We took someone on Mars, but without his research, he's of no use to me either."

Malcolm chuckled then coughed a few times. "Yeah, I know. Basaam Venta. If you really think I'm going to help you, you're crazier than I thought."

"I told you, you're my collector now. It's not up to you."

"And it's like Aria told you: I'm retired. You may as well put me down now."

"Don't tempt us," Rin snarled.

"Believe me, we thought about it, but you're different than the other Earthers," I said. "You chose family—real, blood family —over your mission."

"Is that why you think I let you live? I just didn't feel like dying along with you and missing out on enjoying retirement."

I took a step toward Aria's sleep pod. He didn't allow his

expression to reveal anything, but his gaze momentarily flitted her way. "I don't believe you," I said.

"You people never do."

Rin's hand shot forward and wrapped around his throat. "We want to end this war sooner than later, Collector, and you can help us do it. Everyone wins."

"You expect me to believe that?" he asked.

"I expect nothing from you besides your obedience."

"Pervenio expected the same, but at least they paid."

"You want credits?" I said. "Fine. We have no use for them, and I know an Earther won't get out of bed without them. Is one hundred thousand enough?"

His eyebrow lifted at hearing the number. He wouldn't be able to use them for much, locked away on Titan or dead, but Earthers had a hard time seeing past their wallets. A few seconds of silence passed between us, and I thought he might actually make things easier.

"Generous offer, but you forget the retired part," he said. "I'm sure you'll find someone else, kid."

Rin smacked him again. "That's Lord Trass to you," she said.

Malcolm spit under his mask and a bead of red dribbled from the bottom. "Not on your life."

"Enough," I said. "You're going to help Rin break into Basaam's laboratory on Martelle Station and accept our payment, or you won't ever see your daughter again."

"Being a murderer doesn't make you a good liar," he said. "I saw the way you look at her. Hell, I saw the way she looked back. She always did like rebels, probably thanks to me. You care about her too much to hurt her, especially after what you let happen to Cora." Rin's grip on his throat tightened, but he didn't stop.

"That's the thing with humans," he rasped. "We all have

weaknesses. Leaders, pawns; it doesn't matter. Luxarn Pervenio has his greed and his pride, and you, *Lord Trass...* you care too much. The Children of Titan may be trying to mold you into what they need, but they can't change who you are deep down."

Rin was about to respond with violence, but I pulled her away and brought myself directly before the collector. I'd let him fill my head with doubts earlier, but now, hearing him speak, I could tell that he was the same as any self-entitled Earther who thought they could look down on us.

"I cared about Cora," I said sternly. "Aria died to me the moment I found out she was lying about who she is. Your daughter is a tool now. Nothing more. Someone who understands their language."

"You're fooling yourself if you believe that."

"It's simple, Collector," Rin said. "Start helping us, or I'll tell my men to strip Aria down and drag her out into the Uppers to be alone among my people. An outsider like her? Who knows what they'll do without us around to protect her."

Malcolm glared at her. I could see his fists start to tighten, but he kept his composure. "What is it with you two? Are you jealous that Aria got blessed by 'the king,' and you got tossed to the curb like a stray?"

He was good. Getting under Rin's skin was tough enough without staring straight at her gruesome, terrifying face. I could see her muscles tensing and tugged again on her shoulder before she beat the collector to death. We didn't exchange a word, just a nod.

"You've left us no choice," I said to Malcolm. I strode toward the command deck without even a glance back.

"We're not done here, Drayton!" Malcolm yelled. I heard him pull on his restraints and shout in defiance and couldn't help the self-satisfied smirk pulling at the corners of my lips. I'd now found my way under his skin. He was right, everyone has their weaknesses, and his, more than credits or anything else, was the need to be in control.

"Yes you are," Rin said. "So what'll it be? Help us or watch your daughter be ravaged?"

"How about neither?" Malcolm replied. "I know a bluff when I see one. Your king's got goo-goo eyes. Think this is the first time I've seen a man fall head over heels for my daughter? And why wouldn't he? She's got half of me in her."

"Untie him."

I stopped in the shadows of the hall and turned to watch. Two of my men strode forward and did as she asked. One slung Malcolm over his armored shoulder as if he were no more than a sack of dirty laundry.

They carried him kicking and thrashing across the room, then threw him against Aria's sleep pod. Rin had warned me about this part when we came up with the plan to strongarm Malcolm into helping us. It was why she'd instructed me to leave, but I watched around the corner.

Malcolm cursed as Rin grabbed his head and shoved it against the glass. Aria slept soundly within, no idea what was happening. It was easy to say I wanted nothing to do with her, but even seeing just a sliver, mad as I was at her, I had to believe she could explain herself.

I hated that the collector was right. I still cared about her more than I knew I should. And it wasn't only the child she carried. The way freckles lightly dappled her cheeks and slightly upturned nose, her narrow face and full lips—whatever half of Malcolm she'd gotten, it didn't show.

"You Earthers think we're all monsters," Rin said. "I don't want to kill your daughter, Collector. Neither does Lord Trass. But we will do what we have to."

Rin tapped on the sleep pod's control panel. Malcolm

craned his neck to try and see what she was up to, but my men held him down.

"Nobody knows the value of oxygen like us," Rin said. "The planet we come from doesn't have enough to breathe, you see. But like anything valuable, too much is a curse." She keyed a command, and both Malcolm and I stared through the glass. Aria remained still for a short while, then her eyelids twitched.

"What are you doing?" Malcolm asked.

"You gluttonous Earthers hoard and collect, but this is what happens when you take more than your share," Rin said. "Don't worry. The Venta whore served our needs well, so she won't feel a thing as too much oxygen poisons her."

Every part of Aria started to shake, the tremors growing in intensity with each passing moment. I could hardly watch. When Rin said she'd get Malcolm to help, I left it to her. She'd never said precisely how. I hoped Rin knew not to push far enough to injure Aria or the baby, but then I remembered how much she hated anyone who wasn't Titanborn. How far she could go with violence just to send a message, like spacing every Earther aboard the *Piccolo*.

My fingers instinctually clutched the door frame and squeezed, mostly to keep myself from running out and stopping her. This was a game of chance. Earthers like Malcolm tended to say whatever it took to get out of jams. There was still the possibility that he didn't give a damn about his daughter and only about himself. He wouldn't be the first Earther.

I was about to run out and scream for Rin to stop, when Malcolm did it instead.

"Just stop!" he roared.

He thrashed and broke free. His foot caught one of my men in the hip with enough force to send him flying, denting his powered armor. He got a right hook across Rin's face, but with all the dead nerve endings on that side of her cheek, it didn't do as much damage as he'd probably hoped.

The other Titanborn wrestled him into the air, and without mag-boots, Malcolm couldn't get any leverage. Rin rose to her impressive height and drove her fist three times in quick succession into Malcolm's face until his head slumped to the side.

"Are you ready to do what we ask?" Rin asked.

Malcolm spat more blood out from beneath his mask then nodded. "I'll do whatever you bastards need; just leave her out of it."

Rin set Aria's sleep pod to return to normal conditions. I fell back against the wall behind the corner and clutched my chest. My heart raced. Everything had happened so fast, and it was only after the fight that I realized my body had frozen rather than trying to help. I'd only seen it out of the corner of my eye because my sight had remained fixed on Aria's shaking body.

It'd been a long time since my chest felt like that, since nerves had my heart ready to burst through my rib cage, and my throat ready to collapse in. I drew slow, steadying breaths through my nostrils. Maybe she deserved to suffer for lying to us, but I wasn't prepared to lose Aria yet. She was the only person left in the world who didn't look at me like she was expecting something.

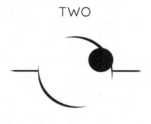

TWO

MALCOLM GRAVES

For the first time, the thought popped into my head that things might have been better if I'd never shot Zhaff to protect my daughter from Pervenio. And it wasn't the rebellion. That would have happened with or without me. I knew that now. Shooting Zhaff and provoking Luxarn was the powder keg that set it off, but it would've happened some other way. The moment Kale found out Cora was murdered, he would have made sure it happened.

But at least Aria would have been in a cell where she was safe. Pervenio didn't space people for no good reason, well... at least, anyone but Cora and the crew of the *Piccolo*. But they didn't space the daughters of career collectors. Maybe Aria deserved to be in a cell anyway for all that she'd done to help the Ringers. Perhaps I did too for hiding her from my employer. After all, she was part of a bombing on Earth I got stuck cleaning up, whether she intended to have casualties or not.

That was the thing about any line of work where bombs and guns were necessary—there was always collateral damage. The best intentions corrupt even the best of us when the cards are on the table.

Kale Trass personified that more than anybody. I watched him from across the *Cora*'s cargo hold, discussing their plan with Rin and a few other Titanborn. They wanted freedom, but after everything they'd done and would do, they'd never have it. All the death and horror would weigh on them, break them. Even from around the corner, I could see it in Kale's eyes while Rin tortured my daughter in her sleep. He was unraveling, lying to himself about who or what he cared for while the real monsters fought.

I still clung to my hunch that he cared for Aria too much to carry out his threat, but his people didn't. Rin didn't. And if anything was clear to me now, it was that she was the one pulling strings. She'd convince him to kill Aria, or maybe she already had, and by the time he knew he didn't want it, it'd be too late.

"From ice to ashes, Lord Trass," she whispered to Kale as they embraced and touched their foreheads together. He said the same then headed for the exit. I caught him staring at me on his way out, and he quickly averted his gaze.

Yep, I was still in his head. Rin knew it too because she stepped between us. It was no wonder she led from behind closed doors. I hadn't yet had a calm moment to really take a good hard look at her. It wasn't only her wounds making her such a grisly creature, but the way she carried herself. It was like she wanted the whole world to feel what she had. Everyone. The good and the bad.

"So what's the plan?" I asked. "We fly down there in your shiny white armor and get what we need?"

"And all get killed?" she said. "You'd like that, wouldn't you?"

"I've considered it."

She crouched in front of me. "You think with me out of the way, Kale won't have the balls to put her down?"

"Something like that," I said.

"You people will keep underestimating him until you're extinct."

"By Earth, 'you people.' You aren't fucking aliens, you know that? We're all humans doing this to each other."

"Perhaps you should have told your employer that," she said. "Now get up."

I didn't listen at first, but the two Titanborn behind her carrying pulse-rifles got me moving. Until Rin was off the *Cora*, it was clear Aria wasn't safe. She garnered the same level of respect as Kale—though she might not realize it.

"You know, this isn't really how being a collector works," I said. "They don't force us on jobs. We can always walk away unpaid."

"It's sad you believe that," Rin replied.

I bit my lip. She'd caught me in a blatant lie there. Luxarn had been irritated enough when I retired. Before Kale's rebellion, he wouldn't have let it go down so easily. He would've roped me in with promises of riches and more. But so much about Sol had changed since I nearly died on Titan. The only thing that never would was people.

Rin shoved me along down the halls of the *Cora*. Of course, she had mag-boots, and I had to pull my way along the ceiling. My arms still felt like wet dough from being under for a month. Another reason I didn't think it was the right time to fight back again yet.

"What did you do to Kale?" I asked.

"I let nature run its course," she replied.

"No. I've been racking my mind for answers. It's easy to blame it on what happened to Cora, but I saw his records. Before you took him off the *Piccolo*, he was just some lowlife pickpocket trying to afford meds for his sick mother in quarantine."

"Better than the people like you who got her sick and stuffed her in there," Rin said.

"Ah, so it *was* you who led the *Piccolo* attack? I had a hunch." Rin shoved me harder, probably frustrated that I'd tricked her into that bit of information. I wasn't sure what I was going to do with it, but they didn't call us collectors for nothing. Now I knew who was there when Kale went from petty thief to rebel king. And now I knew that when Cora Walker had sat in front of me and doubted her friend—more than friend—could be capable of murdering the entire Earther crew of the Piccolo, she was telling the truth. Though that Kale was gone now.

"Everything comes back to that moment," I said. "Kale was nothing, and then he disappeared with you and emerged the leader of the Children of Titan. You're the secret ingredient. The moment Sodervall accuses him, his mother goes missing, and he becomes a killer; that's when he met you. Congratulations."

Rin grabbed me and pushed me into the wall of the ship. She gained her strength from somewhere, because no Ringer should've been so strong. My lungs crunched against my rib cage and left me wincing.

"And killing for credits makes you what?" Rin growled.

"I know what I am," I said. "Just like you know what you are. We understand each other, but Kale? He's just an impressionable kid who got his heart broken at the worst possible time. What—did you look in the mirror one day and decide to mold him in your image so you didn't have to lead?"

She grabbed me by the back of my duster and hurled me into a cramped room. I feared the worst at first, then noticed all the flickering controls and the viewport cut into one side. Any ship size of the *Cora* would be designed with at least one escape pod, especially one this cutting-edge.

"Put this in," Rin said. "Compliments of your employer."

She tossed me a com-link half the size of a fingernail—Pervenio tech for sure.

"Do you people not understand retirement?" I said as I observed it. It was small enough to slide into the ear canal and avoid detection unless someone really went digging.

"No. *We* barely earned enough to live."

I smirked. "So what's the plan?"

"They must know you're with us by now. You escaped to this pod. Station Security will take you down for inspection. According to Basaam Venta, he keeps his most up-to-date research locally on his own personal computer to avoid corporate sabotage. You find your way to Basaam's terminal and transmit all the data on his prototype Fusion Pulse Engines to us. Simple."

"Then you leave me behind, right? A Pervenio man screwing over Venta Co., fracturing their relationship."

"And you talk your way out of it," she said, "and get to enjoy your retirement."

"There's only one problem. What are you going to tell Aria when she wakes up, and I'm gone."

"Same story," Rin said. "That you escaped and got yourself into trouble pulling off one last job for Luxarn because his company is your only love in life."

"You know, that's not half bad. I'm guessing you came up with it and not Kale. Maybe you'll let him think it was him."

"It was him."

I pulled myself into a seat and took a deep breath. I tried not to let the pain pulling at my sideshow. "Your loyalty is inspiring."

"You wouldn't know a thing about it. Now you might want to hold on, Collector. And remember, if you fail, your daughter will never wake up."

A response was on the tip of my tongue when the escape

pod's hatch slammed closed. I scrambled for the restraints and only got them over one arm when the pod shot forward. Acceleration squeezed me against the backrest, threatening to pop me like a balloon. My eyes felt like they might burst.

Then I was pitched in the other direction. My legs swung up, and I clutched the restraints with one elbow as thrusters made the pod decelerate. The thing had enough juice to get me far away from the *Cora* if her engine was going to overload or she was being raided by pirates. When the velocity equaled out enough for me to collapse into the center of the small, spherical space, I vomited into my sanitary mask. Without anything in my stomach but sleep-pod IV fluids for months, warm bile coated my lips.

I tore the mask off my face and used it to wipe my cheeks. The tight confines now reeked of my innards. I searched the myriad controls for a storage compartment, found one, and stuffed it in. Then I leaned back against the seat.

"Can you hear me, Collector?" Rin's smoky voice spoke into my ear, giving me a startle.

"I—" I leaned over and fought back another gag. "Loud and clear..."

"Your pod is broadcasting a universal distress signal. Remember, when someone picks you up, you escaped and need medical attention immediately."

"Perfect. Just a quick question: have you ever been to Europa? Because last time I was here, it was tiny, and by the looks of it, it isn't any longer." I crawled across the pod to the tiny porthole offering me a view of space.

Jupiter comprised all of it. The Big One. Bands of reddish-white streaked its surface, broke up by the great roiling eye in the very center. Pictures didn't do the storm justice. As massive as Jupiter was—and it made Saturn look like a belt-wearing moon by comparison—it was hard to look anywhere else. Even from millions of kilometers away, it looked like it wanted to devour everything. I wasn't easily impressed by anything, but it'd been a few years since I'd been to Jupiter and the sight still had a way of making my jaw hang.

Like Saturn, dozens of moons of all shapes and sizes filled the space around it. Unlike Saturn, very few of were colonized with major settlements, if at all. Darien Trass had started settling Titan three centuries ago, and Earth was playing catch up to fill all the promising spots between. Back when I was a kid, Pervenio Corp staked its future on communicating with the Ringers and preparing for a great reunion. Their biggest competitor, Venta Co, set their sights on Jupiter.

The explosion of interest and potential wealth in the Ring slowed their development of Europa, where potable water beneath the smooth surface was their most significant export. Valuable gases, however, were discovered to be of far less volume in Jupiter, along with storms exponentially stronger and more unpredictable. The gas harvesting trade never took off— but now I could see that with the chaos on the Ring, Jupiter's archipelago of moons was of burgeoning interest.

Impulse Drive trails stood out against the ruddy atmosphere of the gas giant, flying this way and that between moons and stations. Red Wing Company had some industrial plants on Ios and owned an impressive conservatory on Ganymede, housing all sorts of ancient earth flora and animals—I wasn't one for vacations, but the newsfeeds claimed it to be a must-see. However, Europa was the crown jewel of the Jovian orbit.

A tremendous cylindrical station hovered over it, surrounded by smaller ship-building factories locked in orbit. Martelle Station was named after the founder of Venta Co., who was long since passed. It floated just over Europa but within the moon's gravity well. The upper half was transparent and the bottom more densely plated down to a domed underside, and a ring around it festooned with Coms Relays and other nameless tech.

Vast swathes of the station were covered in rippling insulation sheets, dividing up portions still under construction. I could see the flashes from fusion torches of thousands of workers at the fringes even from as far away as I was. I'd never seen such a tremendous undertaking in person. Pervenio Station had been completed long before I was ever sent out to Saturn.

But that floating station was only the surface. A space elevator sank through its center, dropping down and plunging through Europa's striated crust where it was anchored. At its base, the lights of industry flickered. Then, further out, dotting the surface at equal intervals, were the tops of towering water pumps and storage towers.

This far out into the system, water was a major export. From the other colonies around Jupiter, to the entire asteroid belt, to Mars, where water at the polar caps could be siphoned but not nearly in such a quantity, there were dozens more pumps than my last visit to Europa Station. Hundreds more ships transporting and importing supplies as well.

"Basaam Venta is in the process of being woken," Rin said. "He will instruct you."

I'd forgotten what I wanted to ask her. I even nodded in response before giving the affirmative out loud. Luxarn's hold on the Ring had been severed only for a few months, and both Venta Co. and Red Wing Company were clearly hard at work trying to drive the metaphorical gold rush of human expansion to the moons of Jupiter. No rest for capitalism.

———

"Unidentified vessel, this is the Venta Co. security frigate *Polaris 5*. We have been dispatched to your coordinates in response to a broad-range distress signal," a voice filled the escape pod. "Please respond."

I nodded awake. My head was against the viewport, a bit of drool floating around between me and the glass. My head rang from the beating Rin and her men had put on me. Pain always did take a few hours to settle.

"We repeat, unidentified vessel, please respond."

I sighed and stretched my back. It took a few bends to get my artificial leg back in sync so I could use it to help cross the pod. The human one felt like its usual shitty self. My ribs were sore, my stomach churning.

I stretched out for the pod's com controls and switched them on. My lips were so chapped, and my throat was so dry from breathing the stale, recycled air, I had to clear it a few times before I could get any words out.

"This is Malcolm Graves," I said. "I'm a Pervenio Corp collector. I was taken prisoner by Kale Trass on Mars but managed to reach this escape pod. Where am I?"

A few minutes of silence answered me. No doubt whoever it was searched records and reached out to anybody they could to find something on my name.

"Our records state that your Collector ID has been retired," *Polaris 5* said, as I expected.

"Why would Kale Trass kidnap a retired collector?" I replied. "Recheck your records or find a way to contact Luxarn Pervenio. I've been undercover."

"I'm sorry. We do not have that level of clearance."

"Then pick me up, for Earth's sake," I said.

"Are you in need of medical assistance?"

"They put a solid beating on me." I stretched out so that the pain pulling at my side elicited a genuine groan. "Probably a few broken ribs."

"Standby for retrieval. You will be transported to the

Martelle Venta Memorial Hospital on Martelle Station for inspection and processing. Please, keep a safe distance from the hatch as we breach. *Polaris 5* out."

"Be gentle."

I switched off the coms, then pulled myself up onto one of the seats to wait. I had to admit, this plan Rin came up with wasn't the worst I'd ever been a part of. With all the activity around Jupiter, breaking in looking like they did on a rogue ship wouldn't be possible. They'd get what they wanted and get me out of the picture. Except, once I retrieved what they wanted and gained the upper hand, I had no plans to transmit it to them unless they found a way to get me back onto the *Cora* with Aria.

That was the best plan I could come up with on such short notice, because one thing was for certain—whatever they wanted Basaam's invention for, it meant enough to them to put Kale in harm's way. Enough for them to make a deal with an Earther like me.

"Well done," Rin said over our private com-link.

"This must kill you," I said.

"What?"

"Putting so much faith in an Earther like me."

"You may think you can get under Kale's skin, but you won't get under mine, Collector. I trust you'll do what it takes to keep Aria safe."

"And you're probably right. So I guess threatening and blackmailing your way to freedom is what you people want? I guess it's better than bombing innocent people who just want to have a good time."

"I'll fight this war however I have to," she said. "The Titan we build isn't for me."

"And what about Kale? Me and you, our leases on life are ticking away, but he'll be king for a long, long time if you win."

"Kale is stronger than you'll ever know," she said.

"I don't doubt it," I said. "He must be to get Aria to care about him. But a man can only lose so much before he shatters. That's why I did my damnedest not to love anything for so long."

"You Earthers aren't capable of love."

"If love means dropping a nuke on men whose only crime was doing their jobs, then I guess that's a good thing. Does your king ever think about those people in the Q-Zone he murdered? About their clan-families or their loved ones? I've met a few of them. One tried to blow you all to pieces back in New Beijing."

"Then it's a good thing you people can't aim either. Now quiet. Your ride is approaching."

"But our conversations get me going," I said as the com-link cut off.

I grinned. I'd never met a suit of flesh I couldn't get under—it was part of my charm. Maybe I wouldn't be able to kill Kale Trass for Luxarn, but I could widen the rift between him and the woman who was undoubtedly his most trusted adviser. Maybe they didn't even realize it was there yet, but I could sense the tension in the air between them back on the *Cora*. Whatever wicked thing life had made her that allowed her to torture a sleeping woman, Kale wasn't the same, yet.

Darkness closed in around the escape pod as the hull of the *Polaris 5* filled the viewport. I couldn't miss the missile tubes tucked on its flanks or the 360-degree PDCs on its bow. It was a relative warship—the kind the United Sol Federation—or the USF—made plenty of legislature about avoiding. Corporations securing their holdings was one thing, but they didn't want privately owned fleets when they didn't even have one for themselves.

The rise of Titan was truly changing everything.

My escape pod rumbled as the *Polaris 5* bridged to it. I heard footsteps clanking, then the hatch hissed and fell open.

Venta Co. security officers rushed in, pulse rifles raised with barrel-mounted lights scouring every corner of the tiny compartment.

"Took you all long enough," I said. I barely got the words out before one of the officers grabbed me and wrenched my arms behind my back.

"What the hell is this?" I demanded.

"Sorry, corporate's orders," an officer replied. "We must verify your story and identity."

"Get me to a damn terminal, and I'll contact Mr. Pervenio myself, then."

"Corporate has reached out to his office and is awaiting a reply."

The officer pulled me around a corner into their ship's cargo hold. He shoved me into a reserve seat and cuffed me to the armrest. From being treated like a prisoner on a Ringer ship to the same on an Earthers.

"Mr. Pervenio won't be happy when he hears about this," I said.

"You've missed a ton of news, haven't you?" He chuckled. "Soon enough, that won't matter."

I wasn't sure what he meant, and he didn't give me time to ask. The men left me alone in the hold, shackled up like I was a criminal. Granted, I didn't have the best intentions for Martelle Station, but it was about respect. Being a collector from any corporation used to be enough to be put up in a nice room and be treated with respect. Nobody wanted to upset the wrong person. Now everybody was on edge.

"Why couldn't I have a daughter into drugs like everyone else?" I groaned as I let my head fall back. The *Polaris* had left the escape pod behind and now zoomed toward the whitish-brown orb of Europa. For my entire life, Luna had been the ship-building capital of Sol. We didn't have to get too near for me to see the wheels of industry turning around Martelle Station like I'd never seen before.

One huge factory stuck in Europa's orbit surrounded the skeleton of an Ark Ship bigger than any I'd ever seen. Clearly, Venta had no doubt their design would be selected at the upcoming M-Day celebrations—that holiday during which we Earthers celebrated three centuries ago when a meteorite the size of a small moon slammed into the planet, but we survived the threat of extinction. More factories like it floated near Martelle Station and dotted the moon's surface, where dozens of ships, like the warship I was currently on, were being constructed.

Maybe the USF didn't want it, but apparently, Earth's true powers were done sitting around while Titan made a mess of things.

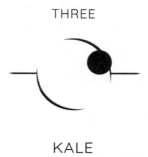

THREE

KALE

"KALE," RIN SAID.

I ignored her as I stared down at Aria's placid face. Her vitals read normally despite Rin's show of torture to bend Malcolm to our will. The same went for the other life she carried. Still, I hadn't been able to leave the side of her sleep pod since the operation started.

Threatening to hurt Aria or anybody else I could handle, but torturing her? I felt sick all over, like I was back in a Pervenio-run Q-zone feeling like germs were crawling all over me. I even had on my sanitary mask, as if that would help with the feeling.

"It was just for show," Rin said, placing her hand upon my shoulder.

"We didn't discuss it going that far," I said. "What if something happened?"

"It was barely a spike in intake. He needed to know we're serious."

"Are we?" I asked.

"That's why I told you to stay out of the room."

"This is my ship, and she's holding my baby." I punched the wall as hard as I could. Without my armor on, my knuckles split, and tiny globs of blood floated across the cabin. "Threaten the collector all you want, but you won't touch Aria again without my permission."

Rin swallowed back a response, then bowed her head. "I'm sorry, Kale. There isn't a lot of room for error out here, I acted on instinct."

"I know..." I ran my fingers along the glass over Aria's face. "It's just... what if we really need to do it?"

"You don't have to do anything."

"A long time ago, Gareth told me that 'I lead.' So it doesn't matter who flips the switch, does it? It's all me now, just like Luxarn. Aria isn't a group of Earther kids who probably wouldn't have made it, Rin."

"What?"

"She isn't Director Sodervall. She's..."

"Kale." Rin took my bloody hand. "Look at me, Kale. I need you to answer me as best as you can. Ignore everything else."

I exhaled through my teeth then nodded and made eye-contact with her.

"Ignore who she's carrying and where she's from," Rin said. "Do you love her?"

My throat dried up, goosebumps covered every inch of me, and my heart constricted. "I... I don't know."

"That isn't a no." Rin's features darkened. Her burns sometimes made it difficult to read her face, so I couldn't tell if it was out of disappointment or concern.

"It isn't a yes either," I said.

"It may as well be."

"So what?" I said. "Cora wasn't exactly one of us either."

"And we nearly sacrificed everything trying to get her out."

"We?" I scoffed.

"All I'm saying is that your feelings are clouding your judgment. The tides of this war can change at the drop of a hat. If you want to lead, you can't be compromised by someone we aren't sure we can trust."

"I didn't want to lead!" I screamed. "If you and the others hadn't attacked the *Piccolo* to get to me, Cora would have never been in that cell. She would still be alive."

I was so overwhelmed, I didn't even realize I'd pushed Rin until she slammed against the wall. She stared at me, aghast, while I fumed like a raging animal.

"That collector really got into your head, didn't he?" Rin asked softly.

"Is he wrong? We've been rushing from one fight to another for so long, I never had the chance to think about it."

"We took a calculated risk so we could reveal who you really are at the right time. I had you followed for years, Kale, and contacted them as much as I could. Your father too, before we came up with our plan. We had no idea you cared for a soul on that ship, or anyone else except your mother. If I had known, I would have taken Cora with us, I swear on my life."

I looked down. Both my hands squeezed the lid of Aria's sleep pod so tight bubbles of blood again swelled outside of the cuts on my knuckles.

"Kale, I only wanted to show you the truth," Rin said. "The future of Titan is your right, by blood. I'd lead if I could, but what I did to Aria, without feeling a thing, is why it must be you. Don't lose focus now. Not a single Titanborn was safe back then. Cora could have been killed by an angry security officer. She could have been thrown in a cell or Q-Zone for no good reason. I wish we could go back and change what happened, but we can't. All we can do is make sure it doesn't again."

I spun back toward Rin and clutched her shoulders. "Then promise me we won't let her die too."

"The collector—"

"I don't care about him!" I shouted. "No matter what she did or if she lied, promise me you'll give her a chance to explain herself. That you won't go behind my back."

"I know you trust me more than that. You aren't thinki—"

We can't become the monsters they are," I said, voice shaking. "Otherwise, what's the point?"

"The point is to do what we must to leave your son a brighter Ring."

"No," I said. "We have to be better, Rin."

"You are better. Just stay strong. I can't promise Aria won't do something to get herself killed, but I won't let anyone besides you touch her until you give the order. I would never go behind your back like that. But for now, we have to make sure her father succeeds, and you can't let him fill your head with doubts."

"Right." I took a few short, measured breaths to center myself. Aria was safe for now as long as her father kept going. In fact, there was no way for him to get off Martelle Station, so even if he failed, what happened to Aria no longer mattered from our position. We could tell him anything.

"Did he make it?" I asked.

"He did. Shortwave directional communications are now on," Rin said. "We switched off all the *Cora*'s power to any system that isn't crucial to survival. We won't go unnoticed forever."

"What if someone spots us?" I asked.

"We hold off as long as we can for the collector to get this done."

"We'll need a pilot, then." I glanced down at Aria.

"We have me."

"A real pilot," I said.

"If we wake her, it won't be so easy to leave Malcolm behind to face punishment," Rin said.

I sighed. Rin was right, as much as my stomach abhorred me saying it. The *Cora* could outrace any ship Venta could throw at us and had enough defensive ordnance left after Mars to shield us from long-range missiles for a while.

"So we just wait?" I said.

"I don't like being beholden to an Earther, but it's our only move," Rin said. "Come on; Basaam is awake. We can proceed."

I nodded and followed her into the command deck. Two of our men stood behind Basaam, who was strapped to a chair. One more guarded the door. The fat Earther wore a dazed look, same as anyone would who was preemptively woken from stasis without the full series of chemical balancing. Rin stopped in front of him, removed a g-stim from her pocket, and jabbed it into his neck.

Basaam's eyes opened wide, bloodshot. His breathing hastened. G-stims weren't only proficient at helping people handle high-g situations. He searched the room, growing more and more frantic with each passing second.

"Settle down, Basaam," Rin said as she sat across from him. "We're not here to hurt you."

"Where is here?" he said. "I see the date on the controls. It has not been long enough for us to reach Titan."

"We're near Europa."

"Are you suicidal?" Basaam said.

"We're here to help you," Rin said. "You said you couldn't do what we asked without your research, so we're here to get it for you."

"I won't help you bastardize my invention."

"Do we really have to do this dance again? We sacrificed too much to get you. Now sit there like a good boy and tell us where your lab is on Martelle Station."

"Please, Basaam," I said as I walked in using my mag-boots and sat at Rin's side.

"How do I know Helena is still all right?" Basaam asked.

"Is that your clan-sister's name?" I asked

He nodded, causing his glasses to fall from his head and float weightlessly. I snatched them out of the air and gently pressed them back onto his face.

"Because I don't want to hurt anybody else today," I said.

"I don't believe you."

I brushed my men aside, knelt behind him, and undid his restraints. He rubbed his bruised wrists as they came free.

"Get him water," I ordered one of my men, who obeyed without question. Then I turned Basaam's face toward me. Terror contorted it, the same way as when someone met Rin for the first time. "I care about people on this ship too, and the longer you take, the more we're all put at risk. Just tell us where your lab is."

He looked between Rin and me, then shook his head. "First, tell me what you plan to do with my engine?"

"You aren't in a position to negotiate," Rin snapped. I raised my hand to keep her quiet.

"We plan to use it, just as your people would. You've developed the most efficient Intersolar engine in history, and it requires only the use of simple gases found on nearly every moon or planet in Sol."

"I didn't do it to hurt the Ring! Believe it or not. I'm a scientist. All I want to do is make life easier for people."

"And Venta Co.'s bottom line," Rin accused.

I shot a stern glare at Rin, instructing her to keep quiet. "And I believe you," I said. "If we gain sole access to the completed tech, we can use it as a bargaining chip for our rights. That's all we want. Your engine is useless to us with Saturn so nearby, but your brilliant creation can help us have peace. We traveled all the way to Mars to be mocked and dismissed by your leaders, just to get our hands on you. My friend..." I paused to steady my lips. "My friend died to get you. If peace is really what you want, then help us now."

"If you mean all of that, then let my clan-sister go," Basaam said.

"You know we can't. Our escape pod was already used by our man inside, and if we give up our position, they'll kill us all. Only *you* can save her."

I watched as his mind raced. We could still play our hand aggressively like we had with Malcolm, but even though they were both Earthers, they weren't the same. Basaam was a thinker. He wasn't as innocent as he claimed as far as driving value away from the Ring, but it seemed like a part of him really did believe he was fighting for peace, naïve as it might sound.

"Martelle Station Deck L3, Subsection C," Basaam said softly, looking to the ground. "It will take Level 5 security clearance to get in. My office is on the second floor, west corner."

Rin immediately rotated her chair and keyed a few commands on the *Cora*'s control console. "Graves, do you read me?" she said.

Nobody answered for a few seconds, before Malcolm replied, "Loud and clear. I must say I missed hearing your voice."

"We have the location of Basaam's terminal." Rin relayed what Basaam had told us.

"Great," Malcolm grumbled.

"What is it?" Rin asked.

"The medical facility they took me to is L1. Doctor's giving me the full diagnostics. Pervenio Corp responded, but Luxarn is sending an agent to make sure it's really me. I have a feeling it's going to be one of our yellow-eyed friends."

"Can you handle it?" Rin asked.

"Maybe," Malcolm said. "After all, beautiful, I'm only human."

I watched as the color drained from what was left of Rin's face. What he called her, the way he said it—it was like stepping into a time machine and being back with Hayes on the *Piccolo*. I wasn't sure if it was just a sarcastic coincidence or if somehow Malcolm knew about him, but Rin froze. I felt my irritation over her overstepping my authority melt away as I remembered I wasn't the only one who'd lost someone that day on Pervenio Station. Rin had listened to two of her crewmates die trying to keep me alive.

"Then you're going to have to make a move," I said, moving in front of Rin.

"Blow my cover already, kid?" Malcolm said. "We're lucky I was quick enough to hide this com-link while he scanned my head or they'd have found us out already."

"Some collector, being proud of that," Rin muttered, finally recovering from Malcolm's unexpected comment. Losing Hayes how we did was the only soft spot she seemed to have.

"I've been doing this longer than your king's been alive," Malcolm said.

"Then you'll have no problem. Think of Aria and get it done." Rin glanced over at me and offered a reassuring nod. I sent one back her way. We argued from time to time, but I knew she supported me. More than my mother or anyone ever could, because she understood. She was the last of the *Sunfire*'s crew left alive who'd been there on that day when the future of Titan changed.

"If you say so," Malcolm replied. "Just try not to space her before I'm done like Cora. You've learned from us so well I don't want you thinking that's the right way to do things."

Rin quickly reached back and grabbed my wrist before I

said anything stupid. I was glad she did because my mind had been so crazy since waking up that I probably would have.

"Don't let him get to you again," she whispered to me.

"What was that?" Malcolm asked.

"Just be quiet and get the job done," Rin said out loud.

"I always do."

FOUR

MALCOLM

"I always do," I said to Rin, smirking. I could tell by both her and Kale's tones I was getting to them. Faster than even I'd expected to. They had to rely on me, and it was killing them —enough for me to plant seeds of distrust that might last forever.

"Mr. Graves, I'm so sorry about keeping you," said the Venta Co. doctor as he returned to the exam room I sat in. "We'll have this sorted out in no time."

"You said that earlier," I groused.

"A man shows up out of nowhere, even one such as yourself —we have to be careful. Especially after Red Wing." He crossed the room as he spoke and knelt in front of me. He tested the reflexes on my human knee.

"Do you mean them helping the Ringers get off Mars?" I said.

The doctor's brow furrowed. "Right, you still wouldn't know." He turned his attention to my artificial leg and began checking the connections at the middle of my thigh. "Apparently, the real reason the Ringers went to Mars was to—"

I lifted my artificial knee into his jaw, which knocked him into the lip of the exam table. I sprang up, expecting to have to incapacitate him, but he was already out like a light. The poor old man, in the wrong place at the wrong time. I tried to lift his body over my shoulder, but my muscles were still weak from travel.

I had to get on my knees for leverage and push off with my artificial leg to get him up on the table. He had a decade on me, which wasn't easy, and an all-white beard, but it was the closest to a match you could ask for on an unplanned infiltration mission. He could have easily been an old woman like Dr. Aurora.

I stripped him down to his underwear and gave him my clothing as well as my duster. The jacket had been with me for a long time, but it was time to say goodbye. For Aria.

I changed into the doctor's medical whites, complete with the Venta Co. logo stamped above his name tag. A younger me would have been foolish enough to feel sick at wearing something sewn by them, but seeing how Venta was taking advantage of the power vacuum had taught me one thing: Pervenio Corp wasn't special. They were just lucky to have picked the right gas giant to exploit.

I checked Doctor Guvman's ID and found, expectedly, that his security clearance was nowhere near high enough to get into Basaam's lab. That was a problem for another time, though. A Cogent was on his way to confirm my identity and likely find out if the Ringers were using me—which they were. I needed to get lost.

"Sorry about this," I said as I used the exam tables straps to restrain the doctor, then hurried over to the counter and smashed a rack of supplies against the wall. "Help!" I yelled, trying to mask my voice.

Two security officers were posted outside, and they rushed in with their weapons raised. I let them go by toward the doctor's body then grabbed one by the wrist. I kicked him in the gut with my artificial leg and sent him flying into the other. The force of the blow weakened his grip and let me steal his weapon.

The second officer raised his gun to take a shot, but not before I cracked him in the side of the head with the butt of the rifle. The first groaned and reached for his secondary firearm. I kicked him in the temple.

"I'm starting to like you," I said to my artificial leg. It was nice to have a part of me that didn't feel like it was begging to fall off every time I moved. I took one of the officer's sidearms and tucked it into my waistband behind my back, beneath the medical coat. Then I used their own zip-cuffs to tie up the guards' wrists.

I strolled out into the hallway, dressed as Doctor Guvman. Nurses and doctors zipped around the medical center, none paying much attention to me. I quickly snagged a hand terminal abandoned on a cart, held it in front of my face, and projected some data up from the screen.

The place was a maze. I didn't know my way around, but I knew a patient lobby when I saw one. It was the place with all the disgruntled faces as they awaited treatment in what was probably the only dedicated medical center in orbit around Jupiter.

"Dr. Guvman, a minute!" a woman hollered.

I glanced up and saw what appeared to be a nurse heading my way. I didn't give her a chance to see me any closer. I knew how standoffish busy intellectual types could be. I raised one finger like I was busy, then turned away from her.

A few more workers tried to gain my attention as I hurried for the exit. I was in a race against the clock. Soon, someone might check my examination room and find three unconscious bodies, if they didn't come to first.

I stepped out into the concourse and looked from side to side. I don't like to give Venta much credit, but their new station was turning out to be a marvel. Unlike Pervenio Station, which was built into a moon and was mostly solid, this was like walking into a kaleidoscope. Every floor wound around an atrium for the Space Elevator, which sank down to Europa itself, each enclosed from space by great spans of glass angled in different directions. Planting areas, vivid advertisements, venue lights—the glass reflected and refracted, making the entire thing seem like its own contained tubular world. Escalators crossed this way and that, crowded by colonists busy shopping or enjoying time off.

Because Europa was also tidally locked on Jupiter, it always had the same orientation to the planet, which served as a sky to the colony. Through the upper skylight, which capped the elevator, the planet's great eye eternally swirled.

Each floor soared to impressive heights, easily structured thanks to the station itself not being directly on Europa and limited by a gravity similar to Titan's. It wasn't overly pleasant for an Earther like me without a weighted suit, which the doctor didn't have, but this station would serve as a gleaming headquarters while Jupiter grew and Europa was potentially terraformed. Like Titan, it had been tagged for the possibility of human inhabitation far into the future, but on Titan, the locals were deadlier than the air.

I searched the packed station, unsure if Level 3 meant up or down. I didn't have much time to worry about it since, through the crowd outside of a tech shop, I saw a glint of yellow and a man dressed in black. I'd had enough dealing with Cogents for one lifetime.

Now I really need to rush. I headed for the heart of the massive space, where smaller lifts shot up and down along the edges of the space elevator atrium. Apparently, the entire area I was in was considered the Level 1 Mall District. I'm not sure why I was surprised. These corporations always blew their wad up top making things pretty and stuffed the rest below.

L2 was residential, probably one of the darker bands of the station I'd seen on approach. L3 was labeled as the Jovian Security headquarters as well as lower restricted access. That meant any officer could get to the floor I needed to be on, which was step one. I stepped onto the lift occupied by a construction crew. That remained Jupiter's primary source of employ.

One of them rode a Venta Co. construction mech, and the others were in basic boiler suits. The thing towered above me like a great metal gorilla, carrying supplies in its front and with mobile arms and legs mimicking the motions of an operator within its transparent cockpit. The things weren't nimble to be of much use indoors, but near zero-g construction foremen could do wonders in them.

Colonies out on the Asteroid Belt abused them more than anywhere else—some even reoutfitting them for combat. Ceres, in particular, had an incredible manned-mech fighting league where you could bet away a shipload of credits if you had them. I knew because I'd wasted a payday from a big job on Eros there once. I'd even snuck Aria in to watch.

A few workers eyed me as I stepped on. Right before the lift went down, a security officer stepped on, heading back to headquarters.

"How many damn units do they want us to build on this place?" one of the construction workers asked.

"All those refugees from Titan have to live somewhere," answered another.

"I'm just sick of the lines ever since they flooded here."

"It'll only get worse with the merger talks."

The lift stopped at L2, and the construction crew filed out. The mech lumbered past me, and its arm knocked into the officer.

"Watch it," he spat.

"Sorry about that," the worker replied from high up in the cockpit.

The doors shut and we were about to head down when the lighting went red, and an alert sounded. A holographic screen appeared in front of us, my face plastered right in the center. It was an old photo from the last time I renewed my collector's license with Pervenio, but it wouldn't take a genius to put two and two together. The only differences were fewer wrinkles and gray hairs.

"This is a station-wide alert," a feminine robotic voice said. "Be on the lookout for this refugee. He may appear to be a doctor, but consider him armed and extremely dangerous."

"Don't," I said softly, sliding the barrel of my pulse pistol behind the security officer's head before he could do the same. I didn't need many fancy gadgets like the new wave of collectors, but I had *none* of my usual gear—no spotters or intel, nothing—so I couldn't afford to take risks.

"Off the elevator, now," I said as I reached around him and signaled the doors to open. I couldn't arrive at the security quarters level dressed how I was now.

"I don't want any trouble," the officer stammered. He sounded young.

"Good, then walk." I gave him a light shove out into the hall of the Martelle Station residences. I moved my gun down behind his back and kept it close so nobody would see.

Gracious halls coiled around the atrium through which the space elevator plunged, the glass here angled in such a way to reflect stars from behind Europa as if it were a night sky. Doors to residential units lined the outer wall entirely around the station's circumference. Each had a sod lawn out front, complete with a white privacy fence—because why not pretend to be on Ancient Earth? The look repeated down at least ten floors, with smaller lifts set at intervals to traverse them.

The whole development was a gaudy mess, a far cry from Pervenio's sleek, reserved designs.

I searched from side to side. Residents roamed freely, with security officers here and there. The half of the residences across the gaping atrium were blocked off with non-fabric with an aluminum inlay strong enough to keep the void of space at bay. Security drones zipped out of a ventilation system, spreading out to sweep the floor for the intruder—me.

"This way," I said as I pulled on the officer. I dragged him up the ridiculous stoop in front of a unit and told him to knock. He did as I asked. Typical Venta Co. security; all the shine but none of the grit.

"I don't know what you want," the officer said, "but you'll never get off this station."

"Who said anything about getting off?" I replied. "Knock harder."

A few seconds passed, and I could hear the buzz of the drones nearing. Finally, someone inside grumbled something, and the door lifted.

"What's all the commoti—" an old man said, not that I had the right to call anybody that.

I pushed inside and aimed the gun at him over the officer's shoulder. The old man's hands shot up, and fear twisted his features. "Close it and lock it," I said.

"Please, I... I..."

"Now!"

The man did as I asked, then I waved him over to his couch. The unit was spacious; I'll give Venta that. High ceilings, top-of-the-line appliances, and furniture. A bulbous viewport on the far side was programmed to show a scene from Ancient Earth rather than the blackness of space. Grass as green as Aria's eyes swayed in the wind, and a few types of bird I couldn't name soared by.

"What is the meaning of this?" the old man stammered.

"Quiet."

I removed all of the officer's weapons, placed them on a table, and shoved him onto the floor by the couch so I could keep an eye on both of them.

"Undress," I demanded.

"What?" the officer said. "Why?"

"Just do it. I don't feel like killing anybody today."

A voice made me whip around, gun high until I realized someone had landed on controls for the unit's viewscreen. A newsfeed popped up, talking heads from around Sol blathering on about something called the Red Wing Massacre, which, according to the ticker, occurred only a short period after we left Mars.

The screen displayed a grainy image of a man in white armor aiming a pulse-rifle at members of the Red Wing Board in the conference room of their ship.

A reporter came on screen. "With news that Red Wing Company plans to sell off its assets to the highest bidders after the unprovoked murder of 90 percent of their board, Pervenio Corp is surprisingly expected to be highly involved," he said. "We reached out to Luxarn Pervenio, Pervenio Corp CEO and Chairman, for comment. What we're about to show is his first public statement since the forceful seizure of the Ring..."

I barely skimmed the message, but it held all the buzzwords. *Atrocity, injustice, etc., etc.* One month or so in transit from Mars, and I'd missed that much? Red Wing folding thanks to a Ringer massacre of their leaders. Pervenio Corp and Venta Co making moves to grow in power.

Feint-of-hand was the Children of Titan's repertoire. I'd seen it enough. The bastards had used a peace summit on Mars only to kidnap Basaam Venta, but apparently, they'd left somebody behind to sacrifice their life, ravaging the company that had helped them survive so they could send Earth into a frenzy.

The news stunned me, and I only heard the security officer making his move before I could turn on him. He smacked my artificial leg with his shock baton and answered my questions about what it was made of. Enough metal and circuitry to give out and cause me to fall, but damn, Mr. Pervenio was good, and dampeners at its connection points caused the surge to die there.

The officer expected me to convulse, but out of reflex, I shot him straight through the shoulder. At such close range, a chunk of his armor and flesh were bit out. He howled and fell backward, making a racket before I was able to get a hand over his mouth. The old resident screamed and covered his head.

"Dammit!" I stifled a shout of my own. "I didn't want to do that." I peeked up at the closed door. There wasn't a chance in hell the insulation in a Venta Co. construction was good enough to block the *bang* of a pulse pistol. "I'm going to let my hand off your mouth. Try to be quiet."

I did it, and he cried out at the top of his lungs. I quickly pressed down again. "Oh, calm down," I said. "It's just a flesh wound. You still have one good arm. We're going to get you out of this armor." A footstep drew my aim to the old man, who slowly crawled toward his bedroom. He froze.

I bit my lip then said, "Get in and lock the door." He appeared harmless enough, and I didn't feel like dealing with two hostages. He scurried inside and signaled the door to shut. I shot the controls so he wouldn't be able to get back out. One gunshot had already most likely given me away, so what could another hurt?

"I know you," my hostage rasped as I let my fingers off a bit. His eyes went wide. "I was an officer on Pervenio Station when you came through to put the Children down. A few of the others whispered you were a legend."

I scoffed. There was a time not too long ago when hearing that would have had me parading around like a peacock in heat. "There are no legends in Sol," I said.

"Why are you doing this?" he asked.

"Take my advice, son. Your clan-family, whoever you got who you love, get far away from them. Things are easier in our line of work when you're on your own. Now, start undressing."

He grimaced as he used his healthy arm to start removing the pieces of his Venta Co. armor. I helped him with my free hand, never letting my aim off him. When we were done, I used the couch to get to my feet since my artificial leg was still acting a bit wonky from the shock.

"Malcolm Graves, we know you're in there!" an officer outside shouted, banging on the door. "Open up and surrender."

I fired at the door. The reinforced metal didn't allow it to penetrate, but it would keep them from barging in.

"You don't have to do this," the officer said.

"You don't know what I have to do," I replied as I started removing my doctor's scrubs down to my boiler suit.

"It'll be PerVenta Corporation soon," the guard on the floor said. "Mr. Pervenio could do something to get someone with your reputation out of this. They used your operations as case studies back when I applied to be a collector on the station."

"Yeah, which ones?"

"There was a slave trafficker in a station out in the Belt named Viktor Mannekin," he said. "You put him down."

I closed my eyes and thought back to that mission, more than a decade ago. That was one mission I felt good about after, helping all those poor people that mad scientist wanted to turn into cybernetic servants. He had hundreds of illegitimates like Aria filling cages on his wall, waiting for their turn to be cut open. Sometimes the men I killed deserved nothing better, but I couldn't help also picturing the bodies of dead and dying Ringers filling that room below the Darien quarantine. Coughing, bleeding, covered in sores and rashes.

"They aren't all so valiant," I said. "Trust me, you're better off here."

"But people like you make a difference. I've heard a few Pervenio friends say you almost stopped the Children of Titan before we fled and wound up here."

"Stopped them?" I chuckled. "There was no stopping our own creation. Now sit up."

I helped pull the scrubs over his shoulders. He winced as it brushed his bleeding shoulder, but he gritted his teeth and tried to look tough. I remembered being a young gun like him, eager to move up the corporate ladder and do what I did best. Tough in front of all the fearless collectors I'd ever run into.

"You can't really believe those monsters don't deserve to die," the officer said, staring at the viewscreen where more footage of the Red Wing Massacre played.

The company mostly leased out its services, specializing in security and transport. None of their board deserved to be slaughtered—at least not all of them—but nobody ever reported about Cora and the other Ringer crew members of the *Piccolo* who Director Sodervall had apparently murdered.

"Them. Us... I'm not sure who the good guys are anymore," I said. "I'm leaning toward nobody." I drew the sanitary mask Rin had given me from my pocket and crouched in front of the kid. "One day, if you're lucky enough, you'll understand what I'm doing."

I'd spent months on Mars drinking myself into a stupor, wishing anybody would remember who I was. Few would unless they'd run through the right Pervenio circles, but as I tied the sanitary mask tight around his face and stuffed it into his mouth to keep him quiet, the shattered look in his eyes made me crave a drink again. Everyone wants to be remembered until the expectations that come with it. In the end, it's just easier to be forgotten.

"Do me a favor and look elsewhere for your heroes," I said as I started putting on his armor. I had the lower half fitting snugly when I heard a slight buzz. It could've easily been mistaken for static from the viewscreen, but the officer knew of me for a reason. I'd been around long enough to hear all sorts of sounds, and that was a security drone moving through the vents.

"Stay low," I said to him. He muttered something incomprehensible in response.

I darted for the wall, carrying the rest of his armor. I stretched my artificial leg back and forth to work out the kinks. Then I braced myself on the back of the couch, reared back, and kicked the wall as hard as I could will my leg to move. The demising wall caved but didn't break. I did it again, and by the third time, I heard a *clank*.

I glanced back and saw that the drone had dropped a concussive grenade in through the vents. The officer's face went bright with panic. I gave the wall one last kick to weaken the metal, then charged it, holding the armor out in front of me. I crashed through into the adjoining unit as the grenade went off.

Hundreds of tiny rubber pellets shot out along with a mask of smoke, bouncing this way and that. A blow to the head from any one of them was enough to stun a man. I was lucky I had the lower half of the armor on because they pelted my legs and feet, and covered me in welts even through it.

I landed in the next room, where the pellets still bounced and caused a frenzy. Unlike the other unit, this one was packed with at least thirty people. Some were quick enough to cover their heads like me, others were knocked off their feet.

I waited until the sound of pellets quieted, then popped up

to my feet. I needed to brace myself on the first piece of furniture I could find because my human leg stung with pain. Whether it was from the grenade or standing up too fast for my weary old muscles, I wasn't sure.

While I quickly finished putting on the rest of the armor, I took stock of my surroundings. Smoke filled both rooms and had everyone who wasn't groaning or unconscious coughing. The residents were grimy and terrified. Many wore Pervenio-made clothing and weighted boiler suits. I knew the look of refugees from the Ring when I saw them.

"Freeze!" officers shouted, back in the old man's room. The laser sights of security officers refracted through the fog, no doubt aimed at the poor security officer. "On the ground! Don't move!"

I finished getting the helmet and blast visor on, then looked at all the petrified faces. I raised the barrel of my pistol to my mouth as if shushing them, then headed for the door. I stepped out calmly. One of the officers waiting outside the adjoining unit turned toward me.

"This one's clear," I said.

He nodded affirmatively then continued along with the others. I took a few steps his way as if I were with him, then turned to skirt along the concourse. More officers flooded down from the lifts. Security drones scanned every level of the residences.

"Please, stay indoors," a group of officers ordered a group of civilians crowded outside of their homes. I fell into their ranks.

"It's not him," someone said through the station-wide coms built into my helmet. "I repeat, the intruder is loose."

I cursed under my breath and picked up my pace. "You, halt!" one of the nearest officers yelled. I didn't look back, at least not until I heard my name.

"Malcolm Graves, stop this." The voice made me stop in my

tracks. The perfect pronunciation of every letter and syllable; the robotic nature like the sentence was coming through an automated reader. I looked back and saw the yellow glint of a Cogent Agent's eye lens as its owner stepped off the elevator, all clad in black.

"I have the shot!" an officer yelled.

"He is wanted alive," the Cogent said.

"Screw tha—" The Cogent shot the rifle out of the man's hand before he could fire at me. Mr. Pervenio, still seeing the best in me after everything and keeping me alive. If the entire floor didn't know where I was yet, that gave it away. All around the atrium, they swarmed in my direction.

I fired off a few rounds to hold them at bay. A security drone promptly shocked the gun out of my hand with an electric bolt. I was lucky my leg kept me grounded, but the surge up my arm had it feeling like my veins were going to explode. I held my wrist as I took off for the construction zone barrier. A few officers didn't take the Cogent's advice—or apparently care about civilian collateral. Bullets zipped over my head and *clanged* off the railing.

A security lockdown had the construction zone sealed off and locked. I didn't slow down. At full speed, I kicked through the entry, crashing through the airlock. A gust of pressure swept me off my feet and hurled me inside before blast shutters slammed down and resealed the airlock. The zone being worked on had a temporary exo-curtain outside as well, so workers were safe from space, but it wasn't as climatized as the occupied portions of the station. The air was cold, thin, and stale.

Construction crewmen in light exo-suits, with auxiliary oxygen supply to make up for the conditions, rushed to me as I struggled to gather myself after being flung into a half-built wall. Heavy machinery filled the gaping space, with scaffolding and automated lifts allowing them to move amongst the development. Construction mechs lifted the massive panels that would comprise the exterior plating of the station into place. Sparks flew out as parts of the residences were welded above and below me.

"You all right, man?" one of the workers said, shaking my shoulder.

I squeezed my aching head. My visor was cracked, and my helmet dented. I had to pull it off before I could think.

"Don't move," another worker said. "Let's get a medical crew down here." He whistled and pointed to a ledge a dozen meters up, where a foreman was busy directing more workers. Clearly, news of my breaking in had yet to impact construction. Shutting it down until I was handled would waste money, and like Pervenio Corp, Venta Co. always had the bottom line to consider. Oh well, I guessed they were soon to be one and the same. Bitter rivals united in their hatred for a common enemy.

Once I could see clearly, I grabbed the worker right in front of me and wrapped my arm around his neck. "Anyone moves, I break his head off," I growled. Yeah, me, who wasn't even capable of shooting a collector beating his daughter anymore.

The crowd around me backed away slowly. I reached up with my free hand and opened coms with the *Cora*.

"Rin, whoever is listening, I need you to put Basaam on right now," I said.

"What do you need to ask him?" Rin replied.

"Not you, him."

"You don't make the rules anymore, Collector."

"I don't have time for this. Put him on, now!" I coughed, and my throat rattled. The thin oxygen made shouting a pain. A few of the workers shifted their stance, and I squeezed their comrade's throat harder.

I heard some muffled arguing in the background, no doubt between Rin and Kale, then Basaam said, "This is Basaam.

What do you need?" I hadn't yet had the pleasure of meeting him, but I'd seen him on tech shows and other documentaries before. Sometimes waiting to make a move on a target got boring. Presently, a palpable layer of fear coated his every word.

"Basaam, I'm sorry to meet you," I said. "I'm their man on Martelle Station."

"You aren't one of them, are you?" he asked.

"What gave it away?"

"Your voice."

I snickered. "Basaam, I'm going to need you to tell me which side of Martelle Station your lab is on. I'm going to be accessing it from the outside."

"Outside?" Rin said. "We already got you in."

"Yeah, well, you sent me in blind. I'm improvising." I didn't like the way a few of the workers on the scaffolding above me moved, so I started walking with my captive. "Waiting on an answer here, Basaam."

"I... I'm not sure," Basaam stuttered. "I've only accessed it from within the station. They filter all sensitive work through the security headquarters. Then there are a few lifts. I—"

"Warning, all members of the Martelle Station Residences construction crew," a voice came over a loudspeaker. "Please evacuate the Sector G work zone. If you are unable to, engage your exo-helmets and oxygen stores immediately."

If the workers weren't stirring before, that certainly got them panicked. Sparks flew out of blast shutters I'd broken through as officers on the other side got to cutting through. I heard more shouting above and below as security officers entered through airlocks on the other levels of the residences. I pushed the worker away from me and ran to a construction mech. Its operator had ditched it and was in the process of fleeing.

"Take a breath, and dig into that big old head of yours," I

said to Basaam as I ducked under its chassis. "Is there a viewport or something identifiable?"

"It's an entire floor of customizable office suites," Basaam said. "The exteriors are the same; we never see them."

"But you look out. What about a moon?" I said. "Europa has a fixed orbit, so are there any moons you see that I might recognize at this time? I know men like you love to stare out of windows."

"Callisto, no wait..."

Security drones zipped into the space, requesting for all workers to evacuate or find shelter. They were going to drain all the oxygen out of the zone and root me out.

"Basaam, think!" I said.

"Io!" he blurted. Yes, that's the one. It's around lunchtime, and I sit at my desk and sometimes notice it while I watch the feeds. Sulfur from its extreme geologic activity makes the moon appear jaundiced."

"Are you sure?" I asked. We had no time to be wrong.

"Yes. I did my thesis at Phobos Academy on the potential for using that activity as an energy source to terraform it. I wouldn't forget."

"You're a lifesaver."

I gripped the open cockpit of the construction mech and hauled myself up. I knew the drones would see me, but it was my only way out. The plating was thick enough to withstand solar radiation and allow for operation in the harshness of space.

"There he is!" From above, gunfire clanked off the thing's hull before I heard the Cogent's shout about wanting me alive. Laser sights sliced across the room.

"All right, let's see what a blue-collar life might have led to," I said. The worker had left the mech running, so I signaled the cockpit to seal. Glowing controls filled the room in front of me. My hands fit snugly through its hollowed arms to grasp two handles. Moving was supposed to be just like walking—that was what the ads always said.

I gave the arms a try, and its massive, tool-filled limb swung. A worker ducked under it just in time, otherwise, I'd have smacked him into the outer enclosure.

"Slowly, Malcolm. That's it." I lifted my human leg with a great deal of strain, and it stepped with me. Easy—my ass. Construction was a young man's game. Operating the limbs took every bit of strength I had.

Another drone gave the mech an electrified blast, and all the gizmos in the cockpit spun and flashed. I felt the surge in my teeth, but I didn't slow. I pushed hard with my artificial leg, and the mech pushed off the ledge. In the reflection of the translucency, I saw the yellow of the Cogent's eye-lens, then I plummeted.

Layers of scaffolding and machinery zoomed by. Pressure stung my eyes as I reeled my hand back in from the arm controls and swiped through the navigation panel to figure out how to fire anti-grav thrusters.

The shiny, rippling exo-tent, which pressurized the construction zone, tore like a wet napkin when I hit it full speed. Europa's gravity didn't pull hard, but the weight of the mech was enough. What little was left of the air inside rushed out, then an emergency shutter closed off the lowest level and sealed with the tent. I only hoped no workers were stuck inside, exposed.

"C'mon, where is it?" I strained to say. My velocity was picking up, and if I didn't find the thrusters soon, even Europa's thin atmosphere would be enough to boil my insides on my fall. Nerves already had my hand sweating. I peered down and saw that the ring of com relays wrapping the station were my first concern. I was heading right toward the structure.

I found a full systems readout that allowed me to check the

status of each system. I looked down at the structure, then back at the screen. "There we go!" I was directed to a switch on my right-hand side that keyed the throttle. My stomach leaped as the thrusters burned, and I came within mere meters of slamming into the station.

"Malcolm, what is going on down there?" Rin questioned in my ear while I was busy catching my breath.

"I'm working," I panted. I tested the throttle to get a handle on how much juice to give. The fuel meter read half empty, so I didn't have long to go. Not to mention, I saw activity at all the shipyard stations floating around Martelle Station, where defense ships would soon mobilize once everyone figured out what I was up to.

I ascended to the lower portion of the station below the regular arrangement of small dwelling unit viewports. It was a half-sphere filled with vast translucencies and wrapped at the base by the com's relay ring. I'd been in space plenty of times, but never where there was so little black. On one side, there was Europa, on the other Jupiter, like a great one-eyed giant ready to devour me. It was so massive that even though it was thousands upon thousands of kilometers away, I felt like I could reach out and touch it.

I used the thrusters to spin toward the black of space and searched for a yellow moon, which in the darkness of space was tougher than I'd hoped. We were on the back side of Jupiter, so every moon was just a blotch of blackness where stars didn't shine.

"I'm going to need more to go on than yellow, Basaam," I said.

"Help him," Rin threatened.

"Io.... It's uh..." Basaam paused to think. "Look for the biggest moon without signs of life on it. It is, at this point, far too hostile to be worth colonizing without a substantial concentration of resources, which, of course, I feel would be worth it. the volcanic activity could allow us to—"

"Would you stop talking?" I interrupted.

I scanned Jupiter's vast archipelago, picked the best moon I could find without artificial lights twinkling near its surface, then jetted back toward the station. Drones blinked overhead, pouring out of the station to search for me. I scoured the translucencies, facing what I hoped was Io, only to find that the interiors were all unique. Some had the appearance of sterile white labs, others were filled with plants, and still others merely revealed typical open office dividers.

"All right, Basaam, give me something to look for inside," I said.

"It's the Departure Ark studies lab," he said.

"Great. Is there a sign on the outside of the station?"

"There's a three-story reinforced testing lab where we're able to test fusion core outputs through combustion chambers. You won't notice, but the station's enclosure has a thin seam that allows it to fall off and flush the core out into space in case of emergency."

"Anything else in there?"

"Models for burner caps, reaction chambers, ICH couplers..."

"All right, I get it," I interrupted. "Ship guts and all of that. Will anybody else be working?"

"I have no idea! I've been here. But I'm not the only engineer on the project, and I'd imagine Venta Co. won't delay the project too long while I'm missing."

I drifted around the station in orbit, looking into each of the transparencies. I was never one for the techy side of things, preferring a man's instinct over all the new toys. It didn't, however, take a rocket scientist to find the lab Basaam was talking about.

I located a lofty space with a solid, metal-plated sphere suspended in the center and a catwalk around it. A dozen different control stations surrounded it, and a few engineers were inside working. More labs surrounded the cylindrical atrium, all for testing some other part of what would become a tremendous Departure Ark. Maybe they flew off toward nothing, but research for the companies vying to win Departure Ark contracts had inspired many spacefaring advancements. Contemporary Impulse drives were said to be the result of a patent used in a Red Wing Company Departure Ark decades ago.

"Is your office the one with all of the little models?" I asked. To the right of the testing labs was a series of offices. Naturally, only essential people like Basaam would get space-views. The one furthest from the testing areas where it would be quietest had its main lights dimmed. Shelves inside bore models of Departure Arks, and not like the figurine Aria had. Even from out in space, I could see the level of detail on the meter-long models.

"Yes..." Basaam said, voice trailing off like he was ashamed.

"Don't hate me, then," I said.

I ignored whatever he said next and drove the mech forward toward the floor-to-ceiling viewport of his office. The glass was silica-fused and specially reinforced considering the moon-based station had to be built to withstand a stray meteor or two, not to mention radiation. I grumbled a few curses as I searched for where to activate the mechs on-board fusion torch, and held it to the viewport.

It would take way longer than I could spare to cut through, but I heated it until the outer layer began to warp. Then I backed away, threw as much power into the mech's thrusters as possible, aimed for the lounge section of his office, and gunned it with the mech's fusion-torch-arm held out ahead.

I'm pretty sure I closed my eyes as I smashed through the dense glass.

A few of the models and his other knick-knacks were sucked out into space by the sudden change in pressure. His desk and the console attached to it slid across the floor, but not before the emergency blast shutters installed over that portion of Martelle Station sealed.

The mech crashed into the wall, leaving its imprint in the bent metal but not breaking through. I signaled the cockpit to open and tumbled out onto the polished white tile floor. My adrenaline was waning, and every part of my body ached from the impact. Flashing red lights and a wailing klaxon made my brain feel like it was going to explode.

"I swear, Aria, this time you do owe me," I grumbled as I slid against the sparking wall to gather myself. One of the mech's arms fell off, and a fire sparked in the cockpit before being squelched by automated fire suppression systems. The faint sounds of screaming echoed from out in the hall where Basaam's employees fled.

"Malcolm, are you in?" Rin asked.

"I hope so," I said. "The whole station is going to know where I am now."

"Good," Rin said. "You can access the data on Basaam's console. As soon as you find it, I'll give you instructions on how to transmit it to the *Cora*."

I crawled a short bit on my hands and knees then got to my feet. The room was a mess, furniture overturned, shelving torn off. I nearly stepped on a digital picture frame, which showed Basaam smiling and kissing a woman. I'm not sure why, but I picked it up and placed it on his desk before coming around to face his computer console. Part one of my mission was complete: locate the data. Now, once I had it, I could start negotiating.

I switched the console on and a holographic screen knifed up, prompting me to enter his password. "Basaam, I'm going to need to know how to log in," I said.

"There is a password and a vocal confirmation," Basaam said.

"Everyone out!" the voice of a security officer echoed from the laboratory entrance. They were here fast, and judging by the patter of clanking footsteps, they arrived in force. I scanned the room. The air recyclers were top-of-the-line, as was everything else; little more than thin rifts at the corners of the walls and ceiling. Drones couldn't get through, and I couldn't get out, not even into space, thanks to blast shutters. They could drain the oxygen, but they had no idea the construction mech was busted, and I couldn't hide in it. One door in, one way out.

"What are you waiting for?" I asked as I limped over to the door and ensured it was locked.

Basaam swallowed audibly. "HELENA6713," he said.

I returned to the console and typed it in, received confirmation, then an automated voice requested vocal authorization. I removed the com-link from my ear and placed it on the table. Then I leaned close to it.

"Basaam, I'm going to hold the com-link up to the speaker bar, and you do what you need to do," I said.

"That... that might not work." His voice was distant without the device directly in my ear.

"Or it might. Pervenio tech is way better."

"I can't..." he started.

"You'll do it, or I'll splatter her brains right now!" Rin shouted in the background.

"It's everything I've worked for!" Basaam protested.

"Do it, now," Rin said.

"Malcolm Graves, we have you surrounded!" an officer

shouted, now just outside Basaam's office. "Lower your weapons and come out, or we have the authorization to use lethal force."

I picked up the comlink and held it to my lips. "Basaam, listen to me," I whispered. "I know this goes against every fiber in your being. I know they probably have a gun to the head of someone you love, just like me."

"You don't understand," Basaam sniveled.

"I do... more than anybody. You'll hate yourself more for losing them than letting Venta Co. down, I promise you that. Now I'm going to put this com-link up to the speaker, and you're going to get me in. Then you're going to go back, blow a kiss to whoever it is they have, and play along until this is all over. You do that, and I swear I'll do my best to get you out of this mess too."

I didn't wait to hear a response. I stared at the photo of the poor scientist and that woman—I'm guessing Helena—as I held the com-link up to his console's speaker bar. My sore arm started to shake by the time I finally heard his faint voice.

For a second, I was worried this wouldn't work, and it would all have been for nothing, then he repeated himself louder, and the screen unlocked. I exhaled through my teeth, returned my com-link to my ear, and went to type. Again, I caught a glimpse of Basaam's picture out of the corner of my eye and stopped. It had automatically shifted to one with him and Madame Venta at a celebration for the legal occupancy of Martelle Station.

"Are you ready for instructions?" Rin asked, irritation creeping into her tone. "The files are encrypted and far beyond our skills, so all you need to do is follow instructions to transmit them to us. Basaam will decrypt them on our end."

My gaze darted between the picture and the screen. I was used to improvising, but this was a new level for me. I knew I couldn't transmit the data and be left behind, but I hadn't figured out how to avoid it and get off until now. Basaam wasn't the only one who was friends with a paramount member of the Earthborn corporatocracy.

I reached out for the thin console bar that projected the screen. The back popped off with a switch, and inside was some circuitry and the tiny, thumb-sized hard-drive holding petabytes worth of data. I've heard people say that back on Pre-Meteorite Earth all that data might have fit the whole world's information and required an entire building filled with servers. Now it was the key to everything.

"Malcolm, do you read me?" Rin asked.

"Loud and clear," I said.

"Then what's the issue?"

"All coms from this level are being jammed." I tapped on a key repeatedly for good measure, loud enough for her to hear. "I won't be able to transmit anything, so if you want this data, I'm going to have to steal a ship and meet you, but I'll need help on your end."

"You're lying."

The truth was, I might not have been. That was the smart move considering whose lab I'd broken into, and Madame Venta was many things, but dumb wasn't one of them. "If you want this data so badly, you can either trust I'll get it to you or don't, and they'll bury it deeper than the Darien Lowers," I said.

"Malcolm Graves, this is your last warning!" the officer outside shouted. I heard the clatter of them preparing a fusion cutter to break into the office. There was too much sensitive material around the lab for them to risk blowing the door.

"We sent you in so we didn't need to get involved," Rin said. "Finish the job."

"I am." I took a step back and looked through Basaam's drawers, hoping he had a weapon. He didn't. "Scientists," I grumbled under my breath before kicking the desk over with my synthetic foot to provide myself some cover. "Now, I'm going to need you to contact someone so they don't kill me."

"Do you think I'm lying about what I'll do to Aria, Collector?" Rin said.

"It doesn't matter anymore." I drew a deep breath. "Kale, I know you can hear me. You made me risk my daughter in coming here. Now it's your turn. How much are you willing to risk for a chance to even yourselves with Earth? If you aren't, then ignore me. Otherwise, I'm a man of my word."

They must have silenced the feed because I didn't hear any arguing until Kale said, "What do you need?"

The loud whir of a fusion cutter powering on filled the room. Pulse rifles clicked into position outside, and the officers moved into formation to take me by force.

"I need you to open the *Cora*'s wide coms and use my hand terminal to link me to Luxarn Pervenio," I said. "Anything from Martelle Station's network is blocked, but this line won't be until they jam the entire Jovian system."

"Absolutely not!" Rin snapped. "So you can tell them exactly where we are?"

"You forget who you have on that ship," I said. "Don't be fools. You said I was your collector now, so let me do my damn job to keep her safe!"

This time, they didn't bother muting me while they argued.

"There's no time for arguing!" I said, instantly regretting the rift between them I'd help nurture. Sparks flew out from one corner of the door. "They're breaking in. These are the split-second choices leaders make, kid. Unless Rin makes all of them."

Nobody answered. I craned my neck to see the door and how close the officers were to breaking in. Luckily, in a lab testing fusion reactors, every wall and door was specially reinforced. I had a minute, maybe two, until I was swarmed.

I looked down and noticed my right-hand twitching, subconsciously itching for a pulse pistol no doubt. I rarely found myself in precarious positions without one... not that I'd been any good at shooting ever since Titan.

"C'mon, kid," I whispered to myself. "Don't be her puppet. C'mon."

"Luxarn Pervenio here," the familiar voice of my long-time employer suddenly spoke into my ear. My heart skipped a beat it took me by such surprise.

"Sir, it's me," I said, breathless.

"Graves? Is that really you?"

"As sure as Zhaff is your son," I replied. I knew I had to tell him something only I would know to ensure that it was me. Considering we weren't long-time friends keen on sharing secrets over a glass of whiskey, that was the best I could think of.

"By Earth. Trass took you and threatened me, and the reports I'm getting from Europa... what the hell is going on?"

"They captured me, and I broke out," I said. "But I need to get back in with Kale, and what I'm stealing from Venta Co. is the best way. Please, sir, I need you to get them to back off. I told Kale I'm out of the game with you if they have the credits to pay me. If I can just earn his trust, I'll be in a position to end this from the inside. They'll never leave him alone."

"Graves." He sighed. "As glad as I am to hear you're alive, you must understand what position you're putting me in."

"C'mon, sir. It's a chance to get me in with them and to screw Venta over at the same time."

"Haven't you heard? We're one entity now."

"Only in name," I said. "Get Venta to pull away."

"Then what?"

"Then I steal a ship, get the hell out of here, and bring Kale what he wants. The first chance I get on Titan after I earn his trust as a mercenary, I put him down. You were right, sir. Zhaff deserves that much at least."

"About that. Malcolm... I... Zhaff..."

"Sir, you're breaking up. They must be jamming all outward communications now. If you're getting this, I won't let you down. Just clear me a path."

His response was an unintelligible mess of interference. I cursed under my breath and yanked the com-link out of my ear. It was all but useless. I craned my neck to see the door, only to find that the fusion cutters were done. The door toppled forward, and the officers outside rolled smoke bombs in, filling the room with heavy smog. Laser sights slashed in.

I grabbed a long shard of one of Basaam's models and held it to my chest. If I was going to go down, it wouldn't be without a fight.

A cluster of footsteps neared. My grip tightened. Then I heard the *bang* of a pulse pistol being fired and someone screamed. Another rang out, and another. The shots were short and succinct, and the confusion amongst the Venta Co. men meant it wasn't coming from one of them.

Weapons and bodies clanked the floor one after another, a refrain of death. Then silence.

I released a mouthful of air I hadn't realized I'd been holding and leaned slowly around the overturned desk. A Venta Co. officer lay, head facing me, a bullet hole through the center of his visor.

"No, please!" I heard an officer shout before he too was silenced by a bullet.

"Who is that!" I shouted.

"Malcolm Graves, you can come out now," a man replied with the same robotic voice that the Cogent from above in the station had. Now that we were closer, I could hear the machine-like tinge to it that not only made him sound artificial in cadence but like a Solnet user interface.

I came further around the corner, still not willing to expose myself. Maybe Luxarn was helping me out, or perhaps he wanted me for himself to see what I'd learned from my time as Kale's captive. There was still always the possibility that he'd somehow found out about Aria, considering how public a figure she'd become.

The smoke began to dissipate, revealing at least ten Venta Co. security officers' bodies lying dead throughout the office and hallway. One clean shot to the head had claimed each of them, except for the one currently in the hands of my Cogent savior. He stood in the entranceway, arm wrapped around a struggling officer's throat before he snapped it.

I'd seen men killed that way enough times not to be affected by it, but the ease with which he did it made the hairs on the back of my neck stand on end. Like he was playing with an action figure but had pushed too hard. He let the body fall from his arms in a heap, then glared up at me. All I could see in detail through the hanging mist was his eye-lens.

The muscles of my gun-hand tensed. Memories of those last moments on Titan with Zhaff rushed through my mind. I heard the ringing of my pistol again and saw him toppling over. Of anyone Luxarn had to have help me, of course, it was another Cogent. If I never had to deal with another one, it'd be too soon.

"Malcolm Graves, you must hurry," the Cogent said. I couldn't help but notice the familiarity to the tone beneath that unnatural tinge. However, every Cogent spoke like Zhaff did. My mind was just playing tricks on me again, bringing me back to that moment where my life was turned upside down.

Still cautious, I pulled myself to my feet. The Cogent's weapon was lowered at the very least. I finally wondered if my insane plan was actually about to work, and Luxarn was really going to help me get a ship in an attempt to have a man inside Kale's operation.

The Cogent stepped toward me. "Malcolm, it is good to s—"

An earsplitting crash from the testing lab assaulted my ears. The Cogent was whipped off his feet and sucked out of the doorway. Air whistled, then pulled Basaam's desk, all the bodies, and me with it. The desk jammed across the doorway, and I slammed into it. Incredible pressure squeezed my limbs and made my eye sockets burn. Blood rushed to my head, and with everything I'd been through, I started to grow faint.

I felt a firm grip on my shoulder. White armor filled my vision, then a Titanborn heaved me over his shoulder. The last thing I remembered was the glinting of the Cogent's eye lens down the hall, holding on to a railing as the change in pressure threatened to tear him out into space through the wall of the testing lab that had been blown open.

FIVE

"How much are you willing to risk for a chance to even yourselves with Earth?" Malcolm said to me. "If you aren't, then ignore me. Otherwise, I'm a man of my word."

Rin glared over at me from the com's controls. The way the dim lights played across her scarred face, anybody else might have cringed in fear.

"He's playing us for fools," she said.

"What if he's not?" I replied.

"How many collectors have you met? This is what they do."

It was true; I hadn't met any beyond surface interactions. Anyone from Darien who grew up in the Lowers knew to keep away when a collector came to town. Those that didn't... people didn't hear from them again. I turned to Basaam, who was being kept quiet by one of my men.

"Basaam, how easy would it be for Martelle Station to block all outgoing communications from their network?" I said.

My guard let his hand off his mouth. "Complicated, but not impossible," he said, short of breath. "Numerous subsets of Venta Co. operate within the station's optics. However, a top-down order from Madame Venta or the Jovian High Director could allow for full station override."

"He's lying, Kale," Rin said.

"And how would you like to prove it?" I snapped. "He can't see Aria, and we don't have time to wake her. Now move over." I shoved my way in front of her and lowered my mouth to the coms. "What do you need?" I asked Malcolm.

"I need you to open the *Cora*'s wide coms and use my hand terminal to link me to Luxarn Pervenio—"

I didn't hear the rest of what he said because Rin cut in and barked, "Absolutely not! So you can tell them exactly where we are?"

"You forget who you have on that ship," Malcolm said. "Don't be fools. You said I was your collector now, so let me do my damn job to keep her safe!"

Rin was in such shock by his request, she scoffed. Then she looked to me, visibly unnerved I didn't share her same reaction. Months went into planning Mars and Basaam's capture, but we were all improvising now, as Malcolm would say.

"You can't seriously be considering this," Rin said. "Kale."

"We need that data," I said.

"We'll find another way. We can't trust him. This is too far."

"There's no time for arguing!" Malcolm shouted, his voice muffled by a grating noise in the background. "They're breaking in. These are the split-second choices leaders make, kid. Unless Rin makes all of them."

"I don't trust *him*," I said.

"I know, you trust her. But just because you care about her doesn't mean he really does. We should leave him behind and go. At the very least, we'll give Venta a scare."

"Is that all we're good for—frightening Earthers? You always talk about us making a difference, but they were scared of us before we called ourselves Titanborn. It doesn't change anything any more than spacing people on the *Piccolo* did."

"C'mon, kid," Malcolm whispered. "Don't be her—"

Rin switched off the coms, then waved back to the Titanborn holding Basaam and signaled for them to leave. He yanked Basaam away, and the Earther yelled about seeing his clan-sister before his screaming was muffled by a *thud*.

"It's my job to protect you," Rin said. "Who knows what he'd bring back to Titan?"

"It's your job to support me!" I reached into her pocket and pulled out the hand terminal and battery I'd taken from Malcolm. "Gareth died for this chance."

"Think this through! It's his job to notice things, and who knows what he saw? If he figured out about Aria, their Cogents might not gun for you anymore."

"He doesn't know a thing," I said.

"And how do you know that?"

"Because he wanted to protect her from you. If he knew she was pregnant with *my* child, a stubborn old Earther collector like him might not have been so eager to stop it before the baby died." I shoved the device into her gut. "Do it, or I'll find someone who will."

Rin bit her lip in disgust then snagged the hand terminal and plugged it into a port on the *Cora*'s control console. "You aren't thinking clearly," she said as she swiped through commands until Luxarn's private contact information came up. "Scanners could pick us up the moment I broaden our range."

"I don't plan on staying for long," I said.

She keyed a few commands within the *Cora* herself to switch on our long-range coms. We'd light up like a star to any Venta scanners watching the area for anomalies. Rin then let her finger hover over the button on the hand terminal, which would sync Luxarn Pervenio onto our private line with Malcolm.

"You're sure you want to do this?" she said.

"If you want to be Queen of Titan, fine. But until then, you asked me to lead us, and this is our only move. Do it, Rin."

She held her tongue then did as I asked.

"Good," I said. "Now cut us out."

"You don't at least want to know the lies your new friend is telling?" Rin said, holding back frustration.

"If Luxarn analyzes the feed, they might find that we were listening in. Cut it, now."

Rin threw her hands up in frustration, but again, did as requested. Silence filled the command deck, and all the proof we had of Malcolm's conversation with the man who turned Titan into our nightmare was a tiny light indicating their lines were open. We, on the other hand, were now completely exposed.

"The moment they're done, we burn for Titan," Rin said.

I leaned forward and stared through the viewport at the distant dot of life that was Martelle Station. Ships swarmed around it and lights flashed with activity. Each of them faced inward.

"First we get Malcolm," I said.

Rin's brow furrowed. "What?"

"They're all focused on him. You're right, we can't trust him if he makes contact with Pervenio. They can falsify the data to do Trass-knows-what. So while they're focused on him, and Venta and Pervenio argue about what to do, we grab him."

"Why didn't you just say that was the plan to start with?"

"I didn't have a plan yet," I admitted.

Rin let a rattling groan slip through her lips. "We have no idea what defenses are on that station. The whole point of using him was to keep you far away."

"And if we hide like cowards, like Luxarn, this will all be a waste. But if we get him and secure the data, nobody will see it coming. Malcolm will seem like he's still on their side, and we can use him again to get close after the engine is finished."

"Luxarn might already know we're using Aria as leverage."

"He doesn't," I said.

Rin rolled her eyes. "Again with absolutes. You can't know that, Kale."

"I lived with Earthers on the *Piccolo* for years. I followed even more of them around in Darien. They don't frown upon anything more than having illegitimate children, and Aria is one. The newsfeeds haven't yet connected her to Luxarn Pervenio, which means Malcolm kept her quiet to save his job."

"A job that, according to her, he no longer has," Rin reminded me.

"He has his pride," I said. "Like Captain Sildario did, remember? He spent his life protecting Cora but was never willing to tell a soul about who she was. Trust me, Rin, if we get Malcolm now, we'll hold all the cards."

"If we make it out alive."

"That's why now we need a real pilot." I jumped up from my seat and rushed down the corridor to the sleep pods. My men were busy putting Basaam back under, and I stopped in front of Aria's chamber. Waking her before I had any time to think about how to talk to her wasn't ideal, but I remembered all I'd done to save my mother when she was sick. If she thought she was saving her father, then she was our best bet at getting out. There was no better form of inspiration.

I reached for the controls to start the waking process, only to promptly have Rin's hand cover mine. "Don't," she said.

"I'm not having this argument again," I said.

"Then don't argue. You want to put us all in danger, fine.

You're the leader Titan has now—for good or bad—but we can't wait for Aria to re-acclimate."

"She'll be fine."

"She won't! Don't let your need to test her loyalty blind you. In her state, waking from an enhanced dose of chems meant for two, she'll be sick for a few days. I know she's the best pilot we have, but not while she's vomiting. Let me handle this."

"Enough, Rin! Enough trying to control everything. She *is* the best we have, and by the time we reach the station, she'll be fine."

"I'm not trying to—" She huffed. "Trust me, Kale. I know what she's going through."

"Really? Were you tortured in your sleep?"

"No, but I was pr—" She caught herself before any of the others overheard and leaned in. "I was pregnant, and I stole credits from your father to fly to Pervenio Station to get it aborted. I was about as far along as she is when I took the ride. Titan was in its farthest orbit, so they put us under since it was going to take three days. Worst feeling I ever felt when I awoke."

My pulse slowed, and I looked up at Rin. Her eyes welled in the corners, same way they did when she drank too much and thought about Hayes. "You were?"

"Hard to believe me and not Rylah, I know, but my face didn't always look like this. It was long before the *Sunfire*. I couldn't bear the thought of bringing another one of us into our hell and your father, well... I couldn't have helped his cell much looking after anyone else."

"Rin, I..."

"If I hadn't done it, I never would have gone aboard the *Sunfire*, and I never would have met you. Now, you aren't my son, and I'm not Katrina, but I swore to myself I wouldn't let anything harm you."

I gazed over at Aria's placid face and forced a smirk. "Some job you did."

"What can I say, you're stubborn like your father." Rin lay her hands on my arms and turned me back to face her. "I'm our best bet at pulling this off thanks to her training, and it's too late to turn back. Just trust me."

As I stared at her, I thought back to those early days on the *Sunfire* when we first met. Nothing went according to plan, but we did the best we could to make it worth something. All the people we'd lost, all the pain we'd caused—because of it, Titan now had a chance to be free of Earth. Without Rin, none of that would've been possible. Maybe Malcolm was right, and there was more she could have done to save Cora, but he didn't know her. And he didn't know me.

The Rin I'd come to know would have done everything in her power—would have given her life—to save Cora if she knew what the Earthers would do. She proved that on Pervenio Station when we went back, just as she proved in that hangar how far she'd go to protect Aria once she knew she held a piece of us.

I exhaled. Malcolm had gotten my thoughts racing with his lies, but he'd forgotten one thing: on Titan, we weren't family out of convenience like his people were, nor were we employees out for credits. Our bonds were strongly tied as the Rings of Saturn.

"Okay, the *Cora*'s yours," I said.

"Then we don't have time to waste." She took my arm and led me back toward the command deck. "Looks like Malcolm is done talking to his boss. Hopefully, it went well." She took her seat in the captain's chair and ran through controls. She wasn't anywhere near as smooth an operator as Aria, hesitating before her every move, but she got it done.

"Everyone strap in," she said over the ship-wide coms to the three Titanborn we'd woken. "This is going to hurt."

"What's the plan?" I asked.

"Now you want to hear my advice?" she asked as she leaned over and tapped through navigation controls.

"Rin..."

"I can track Malcolm's position through his com-link. I'll pull alongside the lab, blow it open, and we'll have a team to retrieve him." She reached beneath the console and removed a g stim. She raised it to her neck then regarded me. "Sorry, I only have one on me, and there's no time."

I nodded for her to continue and she jabbed it into her neck. I watched her pupils dilate, then she struck the engine ignition. A sudden burst of acceleration pressed me against my seat and made my chest constrict. Without my powered suit on, it might have been enough to knock me out. Even still, my fingers squeezed the armrest, and my jaw clenched.

"What about station defenses?" I groaned.

"I just messaged Rylah to send out false warnings about impending attacks on other Jovian Colonies."

"Good idea."

"It won't help us avoid everything, but the first thing Aria taught me about this ship was the weapons systems. Hopefully, she left us with enough after Mars."

"She's always careful."

"Or up to something."

I rotated my head, only to find Rin's healthy half wearing a half-pained, wry grin. She was better suited for dealing with the extreme pressure of acceleration with a g-stim, but no one could handle what we were for too long. Our seats shook as the *Cora*'s impulse drives propelled us at full speed toward Martelle Station. Hyper-advanced stealth systems allowed us to get close, but by the time the details of the station's ship-factory offshoots were visible, so were we.

"Unidentified vessel, please slow your vector and state your business," station control said through our open coms.

"I told you it'd help to know how close we can get," I said through grating teeth.

"Not close enough." Rin slowly extended her hand toward the weapon controls and worked them with a few fingers. "Target locked, missile away."

Even through the rumble of acceleration, I felt a slight jerk. Then a rocket trail lanced out in front of the ship. I watched through my eyelashes as it thinned, then exploded into the side of Martelle Station. Chunks of metal and slag sprayed out across the blackness.

"That'll get their attention," Rin said.

A Venta Co. security fighter hovering outside of Basaam's lab banked hard left and fired a missile at us. Rin scrambled for more controls, and our ship's PDC rounds lashed out across my view. Rin's aim wasn't great, but one of the rounds blew the missile before it struck us. The blast radius still rocked the *Cora,* but Rin didn't let up. Our cannons arched back down, and detonated another of the ship's arsenal right out of the tube, taking the vessel with it.

Piloting and operating the weapons systems wasn't a one-woman job, but Rin was all we had who knew how to handle it. The *Cora* came in fast before reverse thrusters kicked in and our portside scraped across the side of the station. The sudden shift in momentum hurled me forward since I'd forgot to secure my restraints, but Rin extended her arm to bar me from slamming into the controls.

"They weren't ready for us, but they are now!" Rin shouted. "Get the men out to retrieve him now."

I nodded and pulled myself off my seat. Blood rushed to my

head, and it took me a moment to see straight. "Nice flying," I rasped. I grabbed the ceiling and went to launch my weightless body down the hall, but Rin clutched my arm first.

"You stay on the ship," she said. "Kale."

I bit my lip in frustration then nodded again before continuing on my way. I couldn't help but glance at Aria in her pod as I entered the next room, completely oblivious to the game of life and death we'd sent her father into. For a moment, I wondered if not wanting her to lose the only family she had was why I'd come up with this insane plan, but I quickly buried the thought. We didn't have time for doubts.

"You three with me," I addressed the three Titanborn who we'd bothered waking. One was graying, and judging by the breaks in his nose, had seen more than his share of fights. The others were as young as me, including the blonde who'd let me try steak for the first time, who might have been even younger.

We zipped down the halls using the ceiling bars, then clicked on our mag-boots outside the cargo hold.

"Helmets on," I said.

The blonde one tapped my shoulder, then immediately reeled his hand back. The young man looked mortified. "Lord Trass, I... What are we doing?"

I took a moment to gather myself, forgetting we didn't have time to plan this operation. "The collector is out there with vital intel. We have to retrieve him." A *bang* sounded, and the *Cora* rocked hard to the side, throwing us against the wall. "Fast! Helmets on. From ice to ashes."

"From ice to ashes!" they echoed as they followed my commands. I signaled the outer door of the cargo hold to open and followed them into the airlock hall. It sealed, and the space depressurized before the outer hatch opened.

The men charged forward, and I went to follow them before Rin's words echoed in my ears. I stopped. I'd been reckless with my life up until Mars, but watching the life drain from Gareth's eyes had changed something. I knew because I never would have listened to Rin about staying out of things before. It always felt like we were an eternity from making a real difference, but now, thanks to Gareth's sacrifice, we had a real shot.

If I died, it could all unravel. I might not have asked for that responsibility—or wanted it—but to our people, I was the face of their legend, and to the Earthers, I was the face of the enemy. I knew that now.

"Basaam's office is the furthest down the main hall, space side," I said into my helmet coms.

I watched my men hop across the breach and into the lab. A set of bundled, sparking conduits hung in the center of lofty room, as if something had been ripped from them out into space. What remained of catwalks were twisted, and monitoring stations all around had been blown open. The low g of Europa's upper atmosphere allowed my men to leap up to the second floor at the back. One remained posted at the corner, and the others delved deeper into the offices.

I fought every piece of me not to jump out and help when I saw the flash of gunfire around the bend. Soon after, my men emerged. One carried Malcolm's unconscious body over his shoulder. They were down to the lower floor before a bullet slashed through one of their helmets and the man toppled over.

A black figure pulled himself around a nearby corner, battling the pressure change. His fingertips dug into the wall so hard it bent beneath them, and in the other hand, he gripped a pulse pistol. I'd barely had time to move before I saw the yellow glint of his eye-lens. He fired again, and the Titanborn holding Malcolm went down hard.

I whipped around the corner of the cargo hold, grabbed a pulse-rifle off the wall, and let loose. The Cogent fell back around the corner as my hail of bullets sprayed the wall. The one remaining Titanborn grabbed Malcolm and sprinted for the *Cora*.

"Station PDCs are online," Rin spoke into my ear. "We don't have long."

My magazine clicked empty as the Titanborn leaped across the breach with Malcolm. The Cogent re-appeared and lined up his shot. The muzzle flashed, and the *Cora* dipped slightly to avoid anti-air fire, causing the Titanborn and Malcolm to slam into the ceiling of the cargo hold.

"Go!" I yelled. Just as the word left my lips, the Cogent's last shot pierced my helmet. I flew back against the wall, my skull slamming hard. My ears rang, and my vision went blurry.

"Lord Trass!" I heard, but the words were distant. "Lord Trass, are you all right!" The young blonde Titanborn who'd survived tore off my helmet and turned my head from side to side to check for wounds. Then he tilted the helmet. My vision cleared for me to see that the shot had hit the side of my visor and somehow missed my face.

"Grab him!" I groaned, pointing toward Malcolm.

I went to stand, but either my legs were wobbly or Rin turned the *Cora* sharply because I stumbled and had to catch myself on the wall. I couldn't focus enough to figure out which. The cargo hold doors were closed.

I staggered toward the airlock, and when I got inside, the *Cora* spun, and I bounced off the walls like a ball.

"Hold on back there!" Rin shouted. "All station defenses are online. I'm taking us through the Ark Ship frame, then we can outrun them at a full burn."

The ship heaved me to the side, then threw me forward. The sole remaining Titanborn scampered to try and help me while also holding on to unconscious Malcolm, who didn't have the luxury of an armored suit.

"Fighter has a lock, hold—"

Another blast made my ringing ears go completely silent. A rush of air dragged me and the others out into the hallway. Our bodies struck a blast door that fell shut and kept the rest of the ship pressurized. My face pressed against a porthole in the center, allowing me to see the result of the *Cora* being clipped by a missile.

Silvery fragments of the medical bay flew across space, Gareth's body somewhere amongst them. They were lost amongst pieces of the Venta Co. Ark Ship's construction frame, battered by the *Cora* and the fighters chasing us. *Cora* shot down a few more missiles with PDCs, and the distance grew between us and the chasing ships.

The remaining Titanborn grabbed me and screamed something. Rin was over the ship-wide coms doing the same. I couldn't hear any of them. All I did was search the blackness for a body that would never be turned to ashes and loosed upon the skies of Titan. The body of my protector, Gareth, my friend... lost forever.

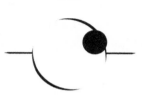

SIX

MALCOLM

"KALE!" I SCREAMED. "LET ME OUT OF HERE, YOU SON OF A bitch!" I scratched at the sanitary mask pulled across my mouth, but it was no use. I'd woken with it on, and this one was made from the same nearly indestructible nano-fabric the wings on Ringer armor were made of. A maglock on the back ensured I couldn't untie it.

We were underground somewhere beneath the surface of Titan. I could tell by the chill. There was enough methane on Titan alone to keep their settlements balmy, but the Ringers preferred things icy. The last thing I remembered was being pulled off Martelle Station, then I woke from my sleep pod and was dragged to wherever here was. I didn't even get to see Aria first.

I dragged my artificial leg across the floor. The Ringers now had a band wrapping it, which emitted some sort of electromagnetic current. It didn't hurt, but it jammed the signal so my nervous system couldn't communicate with the limb, leaving it as little more than a deadweight crutch.

I shook the bars holding me in my rock-carved cell. "I swear, when I get out of here, I'm going to wring your neck. Kale! Rin!"

"Shut up, Mudstomper!" someone said and kicked my cell. "He's trying to work." The speaker, a Ringer guard, hobbled by, pulse rifle in hand. One of his legs was twisted beyond mending, and his left hand twitched involuntarily. "W-why aren't y-you working?" the guard addressed someone else, a stutter on full display. He looked at Basaam Venta, who stood in the center of the cavernous space beyond my cell. A tall array of viewscreens curved in front of the Venta scientist. Random pieces of tech were strewn about, mostly mechanisms I couldn't name.

"I need certain materials," Basaam said. His approach to the guard was drawn short when chains snapped him back, binding him to his new workspace, where I imagined he was prepping to build the prototype engine I'd stolen the plans for. I felt an unusual pang of guilt before remembering that if I'd failed, the Ringers wouldn't have any use for him. Knowing them, that was a death sentence.

"Lord Trass says t-to tell-tell me everything you need," the guard said.

"Help for starters. How do you expect me to work with these on my wrists? Under these conditions? I'll be working with volatile gases. On Europa, I had an entire staff, trained engineers, hermetically sealed laboratories—"

"We're not on Eur-Europa."

"That's for damn sure," I remarked. Their attention immediately fell upon me. I shrugged my shoulders. "Pretend I'm not here."

"You have to tell Mr. Trass that these are not suitable conditions," Basaam said. "I'll build him what he wants, but if we're not careful, I'll turn this place into a crater."

"He already did that once," the guard said. "Lord Tra-Trass says you must work here. No...nobody can know."

"Then, by Earth, send me some skilled laborers. People that have been around an impulse drive at the very least. You have captives; find out which ones have training in nuclear engineering or shipbuilding at the very least. And some food. I can't think straight when I haven't had solid food in over a month!"

The guard slammed him in the gut with the butt of his rifle. Basaam was lucky the man was a cripple. Even so, with a powered suit of armor on, the blow was enough to send him to his knees. Basaam's glasses fell, and he had to crawl and grope along the floor like a beggar to find them. He tried to mask his sniveling, but the cavern was vast and empty. No sound could be hidden.

"Leave him alone!" the woman in the cell beside mine cried out. She'd been sobbing ever since we were brought down, and though neither she nor Basaam seemed to have any interest in talking to me, I'd had imaginary money on the fact that she was Kale's leverage against him.

"Helena, don't," Basaam wheezed.

"Please, you have to let us out of here," Helena said.

The guard stormed over and slammed on the bars of her cell. "I don't want to hear an-another word!" I heard her foot slip, and she hit the cold rock hard. She either stifled more crying or was sucking through her teeth in pain.

"You will eat proper food when you're do-don—" The guard's inability to get the last word out only amplified his frustration. He returned to Basaam, grabbed him by the collar, and flung him toward the workstation. "Get to work or-or her bones start b-b-breaking."

"What a job you have, watching over this sad lot," I said while Basaam picked himself up and fought his nerves to start working. Every part of him shook. "Picking on women and old men. Can't imagine what you did to get it."

"Oh, you don't re-remember me?" The guard drew himself before my rock-carved prison.

"I've beaten thousands of offworlders in my time, kid.

Threatened even more. Not one of them didn't have it coming, though."

"Well, I remember y-you. The collector who interrogated us after the *Piccolo* attack. Who left us to d-d-die."

I placed my face between the bars and glared straight at him. My eyes went wide. "That's right. You were one of the crew Kale left behind so he could go become the leader of whatever the hell you call yourselves now. Desmond something. Sorry. I usually only remember the pretty ones, like Cora."

Like all the Ringer survivors Zhaff and I had interrogated after the *Piccolo,* this one didn't know a damn thing. Unless they were all lying—and that was relatively impossible with Zhaff around—none of them believed quiet little Kale could hurt a soul, especially not Cora or Desmond. Maybe they were right back then, but Director Sodervall unintentionally provided the cell-based Children of Titan with a leader that could unite them all. A Trass, or at least that was what they had Kale believing.

"Don't you dare use her name!" Desmond clanged his rifle against the bars.

"What, did you love her too?" I said.

"Never. Cora and Lord Tr-Trass belonged together."

"I don't remember you having such nice things to say about him back when I interrogated you. What'd you call him? 'A weak, Earther-loving scumscrubber.' To everyone else, he was a 'nice guy who kept to himself and worked hard.' Hell, Cora basically professed her love for him. Not you."

"Lies."

"Are you sure?" I asked. "I have a good memory when it comes to insults."

He bit his lip in obvious frustration but said nothing. It was him all right. The loudest of the survivors, cursing and shouting the entire time we held him. Apparently, unlike the others, he wasn't spaced. I'd have done him first if I were into that sort of thing.

"Doesn't matter." I sighed. "Kale had us all fooled, didn't he?"

"Right until the moment he blew all your Per-Pervenio mates to hell, eh, Earther?" Desmond replied.

I shrugged, then tapped my metal leg. "Got me a new leg out of it."

"And I got a n-nice show. Earther filth, getting what they deserve."

"Sodervall did quite a number on you first. Look at you, barely able to walk, stuttering. I don't remember any of that before we left."

"He got what he d-d-deserved too."

"Yeah, he must have had his fun quieting you down. I bet once he shoved you into the airlock, you begged for your life. You probably told him to space Cora first, just so you could have a few seconds longer. Pathetic."

"Shut up!"

Desmond shoved his weapon through the opening so that the barrel pushed against my forehead. If I could only tempt him to open up and come in, then I'd be in business.

I raised my hands. "Hey, I'm just trying to get the real story."

"The real story is that you left us with a ma...madman to come here." My brow furrowed, and Desmond smirked. "You didn't realize? This is the Children of Titan hideout you f-f-found. I told L-Lord Trass you were the collector. He said to thank you."

"For what?"

"For getting Pervenio to attack the Quarant-t-t-tine above us."

Desmond drew his gun back and continued on his way. I slid down the bars onto my ass and poked the band keeping my leg inactive. It sent a slight shock down my finger.

"You damn Ringers," I grumbled. "When I get out of here—"

"You won't," Desmond interrupted as he returned with a metal bowl. He slid it under the bars. Brown gruel dripped over the edges. It looked more like crap than food.

"Eat up, old man," Desmond said. "This is the sh-sh-shit they fed us on the *Piccolo*. Suits you."

"You think this is the worst cell I've been in?" I laughed. "By Earth, you all believe you know what it means to fight, but you're like children throwing a tantrum."

He didn't respond. I let the food sit there. At least, until he was back out of sight. Sleep pods fed people intravenously, but they always left me starving for a real meal after. I dug in with my fingers and had to work hard to stuff them under my sanitary mask and get any in my mouth.

The gruel was tasteless with a texture worse than gutter water, but I needed something tangible. I could hear Basaam retching as he, too, forced himself to eat the slop. He sat at his station staring into the cell at Helena and mouthing to her that everything would be all right between every mouthful.

Poor, wealthy bastard. He was probably used to real greens and fresh meat. I, on the other hand, had tasted far fouler in plenty of darker corners of Sol. I can't even describe the kind of garbage they eat in the sewers beneath New Beijing.

I studied the cavern beyond my cell as I ate. Desmond wasn't lying about where we were. I could never forget the place where Zhaff and I had stumbled upon the Children of Titan's hideout, where my daughter served as their doctor, curing the sick and forgotten with stolen meds. I could still hear the gunshots of Zhaff mowing them down while I grabbed Aria and fled instead of turning her in. I could still hear that final gunshot just outside... the one that, for all intents and purposes, ended Zhaff's life when he attempted to stop us.

A cruel joke from the king of Titan, putting me in the spot where I'd made the mistake that helped spark his whole revolution by shooting Luxarn Pervenio's son. It didn't hit me until that moment, but every dead body lost in the rubble of the Darien Quarantine straight above us was partially on me, not only Zhaff. Kale had pulled the trigger, but I put Luxarn's forces in his crosshair.

I grabbed the bowl of food and flung it at the side of my cell. Helena yelped from the cell over. Then I screamed at the top of my lungs until my throat was sore.

So many mistakes.

Zhaff and I should have never left Cora and the rest of Kale's crew under Director Sodervall's supervision. We should have operated more carefully, but I was in such a rush to get paid and make Luxarn proud, I didn't care. We barreled into this hollow, and the rest was history—bloody, violent history. All I could do now was bust out somehow and end Kale Trass for good so my daughter could be free of his lies.

I gritted my teeth, wrapped my fingers under the electromag dampener on my leg, and pulled. The shock it emitted made all the muscles in my arms contract until I finally backed off.

"You don't know how to sh-shut up, do you?" Desmond asked, arriving at my cell again.

"Never have," I panted. "Why don't you come in here and teach me?"

"I'm n-not stupid."

"No? I figured that was why Kale assigned you so deep underground where nobody would see you. But it's not that, is it? No." I chuckled. "He has you down here because he can't bear to look at your broken body. That's it, I bet."

"Quiet," Desmond said, seething. His fingers wriggled around the trigger of his rifle.

I almost had him.

"He'd rather look at that scarred witch than you," I said, "because every time he does, he's reminded that your skinny Ringer ass survived Sodervall's racism and Cora didn't. Am I right?"

"Quiet."

"How are you still so loyal after he treats you like that? If I were you..." I crawled a little closer to the bars. "...I'd be on the first ship to Earth with Kale in a body bag."

"That's it. Kale said not to kill you, but he didn't say anything about breaking your jaw!" Desmond growled. He stomped over to the cell's controls and began keying in the codes. I slid back along the floor and pawed for a loose rock until I found one about the size of an ear. It would do.

"I'm going to m-make you wish you died here last time, Mudstomper," Desmond said. The controls buzzed as my cell was unlocked. He didn't have one foot in before a handful of armed Titanborn soldiers arrived hauling shipping crates to Basaam Venta's workspace.

"Where do you want these?" one shouted.

Desmond backed away quickly and locked my cell. "You're lucky he's m-more important, M-Mudstomper," he said, his stutter even more pronounced after he came so near to getting in trouble. "When he's done, all y-your people are gonna s-s-see they can't win. You'll starve here, and n-no one will ever remember Malcolm G-G-G—" He couldn't get the word out, grunting before he marched away.

I dropped the rock and calmly lay back. I had Desmond by the throat, and he didn't even know it. All we needed were a few minutes alone, and I'd get him to open up again and try to shut me up. Many had tried before.

Maybe my old bones couldn't even take on a crippled Ringer in powered armor, but collector training had to be good for something. Somehow, I was going to get out of my cell and find my daughter, or I'd die trying like a collector should.

SEVEN

KALE

The Darien Hall of Ashes was a place I hoped to avoid, but revolution brought me back time and time again. It was where Titanborn went to say goodbye to our deceased loved ones. Essentially, it was a dark, unadorned hall with a series of glassy tubes piercing the exterior wall of the city's enclosure. Earthers buried their fallen in caskets beneath the ground to be devoured by worms. Even on Mars or asteroids, anywhere, they would decay locked away in boxes.

My people released the ashes of our cremated dead into the stormy skies of Titan. We'd done it that way since the days of Trass's first settlers, even under the heel of Pervenio Corp. The Hall of Ashes had always been the one segment of the Uppers where we were allowed to roam freely.

Rin held a transparent, spherical container filled with all we could find of Gareth. No ashes spread for him after his body was sucked out into space; only a bit of his blood scraped off the command deck floor. It was the best we could do. More than Cora ever got after Sodervall spaced her like he was emptying a garbage chute.

It hadn't been long since the ship named after her returned

to Darien. I'm not sure how Rin got us out, but we outraced Venta Co. until they gave up. The *Cora* took so much fire in the escape, she barely stayed together, but we did it. I didn't bother telling Rin I'd almost been killed by a Cogent retrieving it, but thanks to Malcolm and some quick thinking, we had the key to the next stage in interstellar engine development. Gareth didn't die for nothing.

Hundreds of Titanborn crammed into the tight confines of the Hall of Ashes. Most of them didn't know Gareth, but everyone had heard of him and his sacrifice. The silent warrior who fought by my side from day one to take back Titan and all of Saturn's moons from our oppressors.

"We surrender this soul unto the winds of Titan," Rin said, regaining my attention. She lifted the orb, flakes of crusted blood tumbling along the smooth inner surface. "May he forever watch over those chosen by Trass."

Rin glanced back at me. Her armor and sanitary mask were removed so that the gruesome half of her face was on display. Even her burns couldn't mask her sorrow. She tried to appear strong, but tears welled in the corners of her eyes. Gareth had been with her when an independent Titan was merely a dream. When they were branded a terrorist cell by Pervenio Corp. Before my father died and they sought me out on the *Piccolo* gas harvester to be their new leader. Before they told me my true heritage as a descendant of Darien Trass.

Rylah rubbed her sister's shoulders to console her. She was all made up like she was hitting up a Lower's nightclub, wounds fully healed. Seeing their faces side by side was always strange. Maybe before Rin's scars, they looked like siblings, but now they couldn't be more opposite.

"He died protecting you," my mother said, as if I needed reminding. She stood at my side. "Like he would have wanted."

"You weren't there," I replied.

She clutched my hand, but I didn't squeeze back. I didn't want to be consoled.

Rin slowly raised the sphere for all to see "From ice..." She paused to gather herself. The loss of her original *Sunfire* crew members seemed to be the only thing able to rattle her. Rylah took her arm and helped her keep it up. "...to ashes," Rin finished.

Everyone in the hall repeated those words. Some solemnly, others with vigor. I barely murmured them. It felt wrong bidding Gareth farewell when he never should have died. Mars wasn't meant to end in a shootout. No casualties. In and out with our prized scientist in hand and the USF's rejection driving our cause. And then a Pervenio collector burst through the door seeking out his long-lost daughter, who I'd named our ambassador.

"Kale," Rylah said. "Kale."

My gaze snapped toward her. She nodded toward Rin's hand, which hovered over the controls to eject Gareth's remains. Trembling. But Rin didn't strike the key. She was waiting for me.

"Let her," I said. "They were fighting this war together long before I knew it was happening."

"It's not for her," my mother whispered into my ear. "It's for them."

I looked from side to side at all the eager faces regarding me instead of Gareth's ashes, waiting for me to have the last word. The Earthers called me the self-proclaimed king of Titan, but sometimes I forget that my people believed that even more vehemently.

I stepped forward and laid my hand over Rin's. "We'll finish this for him," I whispered. "Together."

She nodded. After striking the command, the sphere would be shot out into Titan's thick atmosphere. Once it flew to a high enough altitude, the change in pressure would cause it to pop like a balloon, sprinkling his blood into the clouds.

I turned to address the crowd.

"Gareth fought for our freedom!" I shouted. "He swore to keep me safe and died keeping that promise. He died for our freedom. From this day forward, we honor all those who have died because of Earth's greed! Who suffered under their heel and chose not to crumble! We are one Titan. And if they think they can take that from us, then we'll freeze them all!"

I keyed the command on the control panel so hard it cracked. The sphere was promptly sucked through the dense Darien Enclosure toward a tiny pinpoint of light. I expected the crowd to cheer, but they watched me in silence. The end of my rant could still be heard echoing down the hall, I'd screamed the last words so loudly. My mother wore that deeply concerned expression she always had when I was younger and disappeared at night. If she knew half the things I'd stolen back then to help pay our Pervenio Corp rent, her heart would've given out.

As I stood panting, quiet murmurs built by the exit. They rippled across the crowd, some news spreading and stealing the attention of everyone present. I wondered what could possibly be more important than Gareth's funeral until the whispers reached Rylah's ear. Her eyelids sprang open.

"You need to follow me, Kale," she addressed me.

"What is it?" Rin questioned.

"Remember I told you about the Red Wing Massacre? The Earthers, they... You have to see."

There wasn't much of a choice. The crowd flowed toward the exit, and we were caught in the tide. Everyone sounded anxious. Terrified. Rin and my other guards fell in close and had to bar people from shoving us.

"Should I send for Aria?" my mother asked.

"Yes, where is our young ambassador?" Rylah said.

Aria. The woman I'd named ambassador, who had a father who was a Pervenio Corp collector, and who also happened to be carrying my child. Before we'd left for Mars, all she was to anybody but me was an offworlder with a knack for Earther politics. Being present to see whatever it was Pervenio Corp was up to was part of her job description... but I couldn't handle any more lies.

"Resting," I replied. That was half the truth. The radiation and sleep pod meds had taken a toll on Aria's pregnant body, and she was being treated in the Hayes Memorial Hospital, being monitored to ensure our child was healthy... and until I was sure I could trust her. I hadn't mustered the courage to talk with her yet.

"She must be exhausted after traveling so far in her condition," Rylah whispered.

My head whipped around to face her. She wore an impish grin. Somehow, she knew about my baby. I glanced at Rin, who'd clearly heard her, and she shook her head. That meant Aria had told her when even my mother didn't know yet.

They'd bonded almost instantly after we took over Titan, probably because neither was a full-bred member of the race they were fighting for. And they had history. Rylah had been the one to get in contact with Aria for medical aid when she was still a runner for Venta Co. Rin may have been behind it, but Rylah recruited the doctor.

Had Aria been playing us from the very beginning for Madame Venta? Why?

"Make way for Lord Trass!" Rin bellowed as we entered the Darien Uppers.

The crack of her voice drew my focus back to the crowd. The Uppers remained in disarray, exactly like we'd left them. It didn't look like anyone was living in the residential towers, but instead, like my people had continued reveling upon the ruins of Earther commerce for the months we were gone.

Rin pushed through the throng so we could see what was on a pair of working viewscreens wrapping the atrium where Darien Trass's statue stood proudly. Hundreds were gathered within it and around the walkways. The volume was all the way up, but I couldn't hear anything over the ruckus. Gunshots flared in a sequence repeatedly playing on the screen, my first time witnessing the Red Wing Massacre.

"Quiet!" I screamed.

A hush fell upon the Uppers as if all the air had gone out of the room. The Titanborn in front of me noticed I was there, parted, and allowed me to approach the screens. It was a newsfeed being broadcast from Earth on every single one of their channels.

"This footage, never before shown, is graphic," a reporter said. "We are releasing it to the public now only after the recent Solnet leaks were unable to be controlled. I repeat: this footage is not suitable for children."

Someone wearing Titanborn armor stood within a conference room of some sort, even though we'd never sent any of our people to do this. Stars shone brightly through a viewport at his back. Men and women in formal attire and with the Red Wing Company logo on their lapels stared in horror, some of them lying on the ground bleeding. Chairman Galora, the woman who had helped us escape Mars, was the closest to the imposter, and a Pervenio Director was beside her.

The imposter waved his or her gun at members of the Red Wing board. Then he or she stomped around the room like a lunatic, smacking his or her own helmet. He or she grabbed the Pervenio Director by the neck, threw him, and proclaimed, "From ice to ashes!" His or her pulse-rifle then aimed toward the viewport, and he or she fired until it shattered. Every person in the conference room was yanked out into space before the feed went to static.

I'd read about what happened back aboard the *Cora*, but seeing it was another story entirely. More influential Earthers taken out of our way was never a bad thing, but without Red Wing Company, we wouldn't have escaped Mars.

"Kale, was this you?" I heard my mother whisper in my ear. She might as well have been shouting, the room went so quiet. The parallels to what Rin did aboard the *Piccolo* were clear enough that I wasn't surprised she asked.

I shook my head.

"We are sorry you had to see that," the reporter said, clearly rattled. "It is now coming through that this horrible tragedy was perpetrated by this man, Gareth Hale, proving, without doubt, it was indeed an act of terror perpetrated by the Children of Titan. A former gas harvester from Ziona, Titan, Gareth was thought to have died in the *Sunfire* incident more than three years ago. Clearly, that is not the case."

A picture of none other than Gareth popped up on screen. It felt like someone had tied a belt around my heart and squeezed it, seeing him. The Red Wing board used a ship that orbited Mars. I wasn't sure if Gareth had the time to get from New Beijing to it and back without me knowing, but there was no doubt the picture was of him from a mug-shot before he wound up on the *Sunfire*. Back when he still had his tongue.

"Titan has continued to deny comment on this malicious attack. Rumblings out of the USF Assembly indicate that they believe this was a direct reaction to the recent news of a formal merger between Venta Co. and Pervenio Corp, but one thing is for sure, Kale Trass' visit to Mars was not without ulterior motives. New reports out of Europa indicate that the Kale's personal ship was also spotted assaulting Martelle Station, where Venta Chief Engineer Basaam Venta was captured and taken into Titan's custody, joining thousands of other captives from their illegal seizure of the Ring.

"We went live to Jumara Venta shortly after showing her this footage to get her reaction to these shocking developments."

The screen transitioned to grainier footage, where Madame Venta's officers were busy pushing through a mob of reporters. They were on Martelle Station, cleaning up Malcolm's mess while she lied about where we took Basaam because, to a corporation like Venta Co., taking a man's life was worth a lot less than his valuable tech being compromised.

"Madame Venta!" a news reporter shouted. "Madame Venta! Do you have any comment on the attack on Basaam Venta and its supposed connection to the Red Wing Massacre?" One of her men pushed the camera away, but the reporter was persistent. He weaseled his way right into her face and repeated the question.

"Any comment?" she snapped finally. "It's time we stop taking these Ringer rebels lightly! The USF has spent the last month looking into an incident here at this very spaceport where my children were slaughtered by Kale Trass. I proposed a solution to the USF then in the form of an armed defensive fleet, and they denied me. Then he has Red Wing Company destroyed so handily, their assets are being sold off to the highest bidder. Still, the USF ignored me. Now he's stolen my friend and colleague Basaam off Martelle Station. This cannot go on.

"Do you think I'm partnering with Luxarn Pervenio to benefit my company? I'm done waiting for them to bicker over the methods of our expansion and ignore our safety in the present. It is time we take control of this situation before Kale targets another boardroom full of innocents or stuffs more people into cells. PerVenta Corp is in the process of buying all assets of Red Wing, and together, we will develop a militarized force to take back the Ring at all costs. We will not allow them to use the lives of captives to bully us any longer. If the USF has anything to say about it, they can try to stop us. It's time for Kale Trass's bloody reign to come to an end."

The feed cut back to the production studio and a few reporters seated at a table. "Harsh words," one of them said. "Luxarn Pervenio echoed her statements in a written statement just last month. We reached out to the USF Assembly for comment, but up to this point, there has been no response. This is John Standard of SolWide News Net. We'll be back after this short break."

The screen transitioned to a shiny vessel flying through the upper atmosphere of Jupiter. "Have you ever dreamed of sailing over the eye of Jupiter?" a soothing matronly voice asked. "Zeus Luxury Cruise Lines invites you—"

The rest of the out-of-place Earther ad was cut off by the Uppers erupting in applause for the elimination of a powerful Earther corporation. They chanted Gareth's name and proclaimed death to Madame Venta and Luxarn Pervenio's Fleet.

I grabbed Rin's arm, pulled her into an abandoned shop, and slammed the door. Rylah and my mother followed shortly after, struggling to squeeze through my people as they once again turned the Uppers into their own personal nightclub.

"I swear, this wasn't me," Rin said before anybody could ask. "And whoever it was, that wasn't Gareth in that suit. He's taller, and he was with me."

"And what about kidnapping an engineer off Martelle Station?" my mother questioned, her glower boring into my soul.

"He's crucial to our cause, *Katrina*. We had to improvise."

"Stop it, you two," Rylah said.

"Do you think any of our people could have been capable of

pulling that off?" Rin shook her head. "Rylah, maybe someone took a ship and snuck away to Mars?"

"I could pull dispatch logs, but I doubt it. Red Wing's headquarters is a cruiser; it isn't easy to break into, let alone find in orbit."

"And now, Venta and Pervenio are joining forces to buy them out," I said. "Did you know about the merger?"

"I keep the newsfeeds on all day, and it's the first I'm hearing about it."

"Am I only one realizing who benefits from slaughtering the only Earther company that has ever helped us?" Rin remarked.

"You think they were behind it?" my mother said. "That's low, even for them."

"Would you have said that while you were wasting away in quarantine?" Rin asked. My mother sank back, her eyes glazing over.

"Rin," I said sternly.

"I'm just saying."

"Luxarn is finally coming out of his shell, and he's using Venta as a hammer," I said. I pressed my hands against the glass door. It vibrated from the festivity outside. "Listen to them. They have no idea what's coming."

"The USF won't be able to stop them, hostages or not," Rin said. "I don't know if we can either."

"Like I said, why do you think they're making this move?" Rin said. "Destroy Red Wing, unite to buy their assets quickly, so no Earthers lose their jobs, and make the USF even less powerful."

"So we deny it publicly," my mother said. "At the very least, it will slow down the USF's decision-making."

"Don't you see? Nothing we say matters anymore," I said. "They've been waiting for an excuse all this time. Waiting for us to show that we're the monsters they think we are. Nobody looked further in that video than the orange circle to see if it was us. Nobody ever will. And by raiding Martelle Station, we proved that a fleet could benefit them. Damnit!" I punched the wall as hard as I could. Cuts along my knuckles split open, and my mother grabbed my hand to make sure I was okay.

"We did what we had to," Rin said. "They'd have made this happen some other way. All we can do now is prepare. We should send everyone we've got who's ever worked in a dock to Phoebe to speed up the construction of our fleet. We can transition other factories as well. It won't take long to outfit gas harvesters and transports with weapons, and we have to be ready to hold."

"That might be a problem," Rylah said. She flinched as both Rin and my glares fell upon her.

"Why?" I asked.

"That man, Orson Fring. He's organized most of the experienced ship workers we've got in protest, demanding more compensation. Other industries have joined in too. We're arming, just...not as quickly as anticipated without them. Now with PerVenta, I—"

"I thought I told you to handle it."

"What did you want me to do? Lock him away? Kill him? The moment you left, his following multiplied, and it's clear why. Our people are exhausted after being overworked the last few months. They're hungry with half the Darien hydro-farms compromised and no trade."

"That's all we need," Rin groaned. "An Earther-lover used to getting their scraps putting everyone on strike. I say we get rid of him."

"That's your solution for everything, isn't it?" my mother snapped.

"Well, if it works."

"Orson and the others are coming around, Kale," my mother

said, taking me by the shoulders. "I've been talking with Mr. Fring, trying to come to an agreement for him to call off the protests."

"By the time you're done talking, we'll be dead."

"Why don't we stop being so stubborn and offer them credits?" Rylah said. "Nothing's ever shut a man up quite as quickly, I promise you."

"It wasn't the money that kept them quiet, sister," Rin said, eyeing Rylah from head to toe. "We pay them, then everyone else across the Ring will want the same, and we'll wind up exactly like the Earthers."

"Enough, everyone," I demanded. "You're giving me a headache. I'll talk to Mr. Fring as soon as we're done here. Rin, do you have your hand terminal?" I asked. She nodded. "Good. Record this."

I opened the door and backed up slowly into the sea of my people's carousing. Rin followed me and set her hand terminal to record. I remembered when she'd bought the thing so that we could hack Pervenio Station and steal the *Piccolo*. It seemed like ages ago. Rylah and my mother watched from behind the glass, brows furrowed.

I kept walking until I stood at the feet of Darien Trass' statue, then I faced the camera and nodded to Rin. "We traveled to Earth to make peace, and you shunned us," I said after it started recording. "Red Wing Company thought they could buy our loyalty and learned the hard way. Venta Co. went back on their word and learned the same lesson by losing their prized chief engineer.

"The Ring is ours. We will not negotiate. We will not be bribed or prodded. Send all the ships you want. Send a fleet. They'll return to Earth in ashes. Soon you people will know the fear we lived with every single day under your rule, but we are afraid no longer!" I raised my arms, gesturing to the raucous mob of Titanborn at my back. Then Rin cut the recording.

My mother's jaw hung open. Rylah closed her eyes and drew a deep breath. Rin's expression didn't change. Malcolm may have done his best to wedge his way between us, but she understood what it would take to win. All the people behind me begging for war might not have, but she did.

Luxarn and Madame Venta had made their move. They were coming, and all I had to do was sweeten the bait. Feed their rage and their greed so that they would rush things. Our fleet didn't need to be larger or more advanced. All it needed to do was hold while I pulled the rug out from under the Earthers' homeworld using Basaam's invention.

Then, and only then, would they give us everything we wanted.

————

I breathed in deeply. The smell of salt, soldered metal, and burning gases were staples of the Darien Lowers where I grew up. Industry powering the Earthers' burgeoning inter-solar civilization, with Titanborn at the helm.

We weren't in the Lowers or on Titan, but the shipyard on Phoebe Station we stole from Pervenio bore that same stench. Unfinished chassis for ships sat on pedestals throughout the factory, of all shapes and sizes. Ice haulers, gas harvesters, transports, all being outfitted for war. It was the best we could do on short notice and without skilled management. The only problem was that all the construction equipment sat still.

Chants of protest replaced the familiar din of factory labor. Armed Titanborn were posted at every corner making sure things didn't escalate, but they didn't know how to handle a situation like this. We were used to being beaten when we got out of line or docked pay. It was all because the old Earther sympathizer Orson Fring got it in everybody's head that credits were the answer. Not food. Not shelter. Not the promise of freedom once Earth caved to our demands. Credits.

Titan was filled with warriors who lowered their heads as I went by, who fought for our freedom, but these skilled ship workers who'd lived closer to Earthers on stations and smaller moons did their best to remain indifferent. They marched around holding signs with words of protest drawn on sheets of scrap. They stared when I got close and lowered their voices, but that was it.

Back before the revolution, they were the type of Titanborn who got spat on. The type willing to work side by side with the Earthers who treated them like dirt. I knew because I was once one of them—a Ringer desperate for credits scrubbing canisters on an Earther gas harvester. I could barely remember what it felt like to be so obsessed with a transient number, to let it define me like our distant cousins on Earth did.

My mother and Rylah stopped in front of the door into Orson Fring's foreman office. Mother knocked, and the door slid open with a whoosh almost immediately. A few older Titanborn filed out, speeding up and staring at the floor when they noticed it was me who'd arrived.

"Keep an open mind, Kale," my mother said before she went in.

"I'll try," I replied.

"I don't understand what reasons you had for taking credit for that massacre, but we need these workers now more than ever. Kale, are you listening to me?"

I grunted a barely audible affirmation. Rin scolding me I could handle. Rylah, tolerable. At least both of them had seen the rotten parts of the world and fought to be free of them. But my mother spent her whole life hiding. She left my father when he went off to initiate the Children of Titan and hid my true name to keep me safe. Always to keep me safe. I loved her, but while we all fought, she lay in bed worrying. She'd never understand what leading a revolution took.

"Even a half-closed mind will do," Rylah remarked, smirking, then stepped in. My mother stifled a groan and followed.

"Ah, Katrina. Rylah," Orson said. He sat behind a desk stacked with dozens of datapads and notes. "A pleasure to see you both again." He leaned forward and cleared off the area in front of him. His snow-white beard nearly matched the tone of his skin, but there was no missing the multitude of fraying hairs. Black bags hung deep beneath his wrinkled eyelids. At least that meant he was as tired of the protest as any of us.

"I hope we can end this now," Rylah said. "Considering recent events."

"I heard. The attack on Red Wing—"

"Wasn't us," I interrupted. I stepped in, and what little color filled Orson's cheeks drained entirely.

"L... Lord Trass," he stammered. "I wasn't aware you were coming."

"I wanted to see what was going on here before it was cleaned up for my sake."

"Yes, of course. Lord Trass, please, come sit."

"I'll stand."

Orson nodded nervously. His eyes darted from one of us to the next, and a brief period of silence had him shifting in his seat.

"There are a lot of empty chassis out there, Fring," Rylah said finally. "I thought last time we spoke you said you'd maintain standard production rates."

"These *were* standard rates."

"Under Earther supervision," I said. I strolled across the room and lifted a datapad off his desk. On it was altered schematics for transforming a standard Pervenio automated gas harvester into a war machine. I then picked up another. He cleared his throat but said nothing.

"Mr. Fring, do you know why I claimed responsibility for the Red Wing Massacre?" I asked.

He held his tongue, but I could tell by his eyes he wanted to scold me like my mother did. The older generation was too ingrained in their ways to understand change. Too stubborn.

"Because they would have blamed us anyway," I answered for him. "Even if that killer was wearing a Pervenio uniform, they would have found a way to blame us."

"I understand," Orson replied. "I've been around long enough to know their kind. My family has been building ships since the days of Trass's first settlers, and we continued doing it under their supervision after the Great Reunion."

"The Fring family was part of the crew who worked on Trass's first Ark way back on Earth," Rylah added.

"Is that true?" I said.

Orson smiled and nodded. "That's what my parents told me, and theirs told them."

"Incredible." I studied the datapad in my grip for a few seconds, then flung it against the wall. "Then explain why you are purposely undermining your own people!"

"Kale!" my mother reprimanded. She took my arm, but I shoved by and slammed my hands down on Orson's desk. With my powered suit on, the metal wilted. Orson, for what it was worth, stood his ground.

"Earthers have been driven by fear since the moment the Meteorite was discovered," I said. "We need them to come here with all their might because until they try to destroy us, we can't make them fear that they won't be able to. *That* is when we win, and because of you, we're at greater risk than ever."

"All we seek is proper compensation," Orson said. "We

Titanborn may all be equal, but our hands and brains aren't. Our experiences aren't. You assigned these people to Phoebe because this is the Ring's best ship-factory left intact after the fighting, and we know ships. My workers are breaking our backs, for what? And now this business with Red Wing will make it worse."

"You're compensated better than anyone else, Fring," Rylah remarked. "More than the fighters who risk their lives holding every station on the Ring every day."

"Please, I know what you were before all this, Rylah. When trade opens up, and credits go back into circulation, you've sold out enough people on both sides for information to be comfortable for life. All we have are the extra rations we need to stay awake regardless. Or Uppers residences back on Titan that we can't enjoy until this rebellion is over? Which is when?"

"That's all this is to you?" I said, a harsher edge creeping into my tone.

"I'm sure he didn't mean it like that," my mother said.

"I mean no disrespect, Lord Trass. I appreciate everything you're doing for our people, but one day, credits will mean something again, whether we use them on the Ring or not."

"Credits," I groaned, pacing the room. "Credits, credits, credits. Does it always have to come down to them?"

"We aren't asking to be rich because we were lucky enough to have worked in shipyards or factories," Orson said. "Pervenio paid us slave wages, and that was more than we get today. But it *was* something we could use. You want a fleet, and we want to give it to you."

"We *need* a fleet now," Rylah said.

"Yes... But not all of us were behind open war and revolt, even if we support it now. Not all of us wanted to lose every part of our old lives."

"Then you're as blind as they are!" I growled.

He either didn't know how to respond or didn't want to risk it. The room went silent for Trass knows how long until Rylah pulled me to the side.

"It's just credits," she whispered. "I say it's worth the risk. We have plenty stored in offworld accounts from the Children of Titan. Preparing for the PerVenta fleet is more important than anything now."

I glanced at my mother, who bobbed her head solemnly. I closed my eyes and drew a long, steady breath. "The moment we compromise, we're lost," I sighed. "Don't either of you understand that?"

"Foreman Fring." I turned to face him. "I will give you one last chance to resume an accelerated production schedule for the sake of Titan. There will be no credits, but I promise all workers who put in extra hours preparing us for the Earther fleet will be rewarded with the freshest greens from our hydro-farms. I will have our captive Earthers surveyed to find out which one of them has experience in ship construction, and you can use them as you see fit to boost production."

"You mean make *them* slaves this time," Orson said, taking no care to hide his disdain.

"Earth is coming. This isn't the time for us to argue or show weakness. We must all work together now to establish the Ring Trass envisioned. You will end these protests immediately and present a unified front. After this is over, I promise we will sit down and finish this conversation."

"Lord Trass, I—"

I raised my hand to silence him. "That is what I can offer. Do this for Titan, or I will find someone else who can." I turned to Rylah. "Make sure things get up and running," I ordered then headed for the exit.

Rylah and my mother thanked Fring for his time, but he didn't respond. Instead, he waited until I was at the exit. "Lord

Trass," he said. I stopped and peered back over my shoulder. "Before you go, would you care for some advice from an elderly man who's seen almost everything this awful universe has to offer?"

I nodded for him to continue.

"The name Trass helps you lead, but it doesn't make you him," Orson said. "Never forget that you rule over all the Ring now, not only those who agree with you and your methods. Otherwise, you may as well be Luxarn Pervenio."

I bit my lip. Him, Malcolm, my old gas harvester captain— old men were always preaching. Too set in their ways to see anything different than the world they know. Even if Orson Fring did as I asked, he'd be a thorn in my side until the day he croaked. The experienced workers standing on protest clearly respected him enough to listen.

"Goodbye, Mr. Fring," I said without turning back.

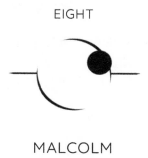

EIGHT

MALCOLM

THE DAYS TICKED BY SLOWLY, AND BASAAM VENTA'S laboratory grew. More workers trickled in, including some men and women who were obviously Earther engineers unlucky enough to be stuck in the Ring when Kale took over.

More workers meant more guards, which made it tougher to get much face-time with my old friend Desmond. Basaam even grew more comfortable barking orders at Ringers and making sure everything was in line. They even took off his chains, as if he could run anywhere onto Titan's surface without freezing to death in a millisecond anyway. That was the thing about brainiacs. Once they got their engorged minds fixated on a project, it was all they could think about.

"Do you really think if you pull this off, they'll let you go?" I asked him one day or night—time had become inconsequential. He sat, legs folded in front of Helena's cell, enjoying a bowl of gruel with her. I'll say that for him, he'd been doing a fine job keeping her calm.

He glared over at me then continued with his meal.

"I'm talking to you," I said.

"Would you be quiet?" he whispered. "I don't feel like any trouble today when we're just starting to make progress."

"You? They're too busy watching the others now. So, c'mon, are you that naïve?"

"I don't know what they'll do," he snapped. "Now please, stop talking."

"Probably plant a bullet right here." I tapped the back of my head. "In both of you."

"What, so you think we should just give up?"

"Better than giving them a key to the stars."

"And what about you?" He stood and stomped toward my cell.

"Basaam, don't," Helena said softly.

"It's fine," he said. "What about you, Collector? Without you, none of this would be possible."

"You should be thanking me for keeping you both alive," I said. "It doesn't mean it was a smart move on my end."

"So what? We should just walk outside and... kill ourselves because you don't think they'll keep their word."

I rolled my shoulders. "Dying is always easier to talk about. I seem to have a hard time doing it."

"Forgive me, Collector, if I'd rather take a chance on them. I didn't make a living locking up offworlders. I've heard enough stories about collectors like you, and your kind has stolen enough research from me for Pervenio over the years."

"I'm sure that's true." I laughed. "Can you believe our employers are going to kiss and make up now after everything? I used to think you guys were the enemy. Like the logo on your uniform means anything."

"It does here," he said.

"That's for damn sure."

Basaam sighed and sat with his back against the bars of my cell. He broke off a piece of his ration bar and held it through.

"Here, there's no reason for us to fight when we're in the same position. It's chicken-flavored."

Considering all I'd had for days was a bowl of bland, chunky gruel, I wasn't about to let pride keep me from something that tasted decent. "Thanks," I said.

"Jumara hired me out of Phobos Academy when I was so young. All I ever wanted to do was make Sol a better place."

"I always thought I was," I said with a full mouth. "At least you probably did it."

"You've seen their armor? That muscle-enhancing, nano-weave underlay was my very first patent out of the academy. I watched the *Piccolo* attack and had to wonder if Madame Venta sold the tech to them just to get one over on Luxarn. Their ship, the *Cora*? It may have been Luxarn's, but its impulse engine was my prototype."

"And some poor bastard on ancient Earth probably invented a gun so he could protect his home. We're humans; turning things into weapons is what we do. It's the thumbs."

"Thumbs." He chuckled. "Right. I just hoped we were more evolved than slaughtering each other like this."

"Then you weren't paying attention."

"Basaam, get over here!" Desmond shouted from the other side of the hollow.

Basaam hung his head, then stood. "Duty calls," he said.

"Just do me a favor and don't build them anything that works before I'm able to do like I promised and get you both out of here."

"Then you better hurry, Collector, because I've never been good at disobeying orders. I know you may think I'm a naïve fool, but I believe in people doing the right thing in the end. Even them."

That was another thing about brainiacs. They held humanity to impossible standards. I actually pitied the man as I watched him traverse the start of his masterpiece. Welders and engineers had begun to construct a giant sphere made from who-knows-what-kind of impossibly durable alloy.

"You're not going to get into anybody's h-h-head," Desmond said, approaching from the other side. "You just get to w-watch your own work."

"That's what they all sa—" The words died on my tongue as I spotted someone with Basaam who I could never forget.

My throat went dry.

My fingers slowly wrapped the bars of my cell, ignoring how cold the metal was.

I watched her saunter across the cavern as Basaam instructed her about what he was doing. She wore a form-fitting dress that could have a weaker man lapping out of a saucer at her feet. Rylah had been the top information broker on the Ring before we lost touch and things on Titan went haywire. Now, she was high enough in Kale's regime to be here with Basaam and it was evident whose side she was really on.

It wasn't always that way. There was a time, long ago, Rylah made Titan worth visiting...

I gave the body of a poor waitress a push, and it swayed. It was about five years or so before Kale's rebellion. She hung upside down, her pale Ringer body made even whiter from being drained of blood. Serial killers were rare as natural-growing trees in my time, with all the surveillance and my people's obsession with safety and survival post-meteorite.

This one had a penchant for hanging pretty women up by the feet in Decontamination Chambers, stripping them, and slitting their wrists. The Stalactite Killer, or so the newsfeeds called him, had murdered four Earther immigrants by then, leading Director Sodervall to believe he was a terrorist, but the Ringer body swinging before me proved my hunch—this was indeed a killer targeting women, regardless of where they were from.

Why? I wasn't sure yet. The man didn't leave any clues, no sexual deviance, not even a sign of struggle on the women's bodies over how he got them there. And the women? Besides each having two X chromosomes, they had nothing in common, from their jobs to their appearances to their personal lives. Maybe they gave him a bad look one day or were just in the wrong place.

All I knew was that since I'd been summoned to Titan, a body had shown up in a decon chamber every Friday. Didn't matter how much security I had Pervenio post outside of them either. And if I did too much to impede the local population's ability to stay clean, my employer would never hear the end of the complaints.

We were between a rock and a cold place, but now that a Ringer wound up dead, the locals would be clamoring for justice even louder.

"Sir, forensics is here," a security officer said as he peeled away the divider curtain wrapping the decon chamber.

"Give me a minute," I said.

I circled the body, using my sleeve to lift her limp arms. Back then, I still worked alone. I didn't need fancy tech and analyzers to find the killer, I just needed to find the pattern. I drew back her hair to get a look at her scalp. Nothing.

I sighed. This killer was good at hiding it, but there was always a pattern. Nobody, not even madmen, murdered over nothing.

"What are you hiding?" I asked as I crouched in front of the woman's face and stared into her gaping eyes. They were brown with flecks of gold. Her records said she was born in the highest level of the Darien Lowers and worked at an Earther restaurant in the Uppers. Hell of a life she'd missed out on.

I stood and exited the chamber. "All right, let them at it," I said to the officer just outside. The rest of them stood by the security tape keeping a crowd of angry Ringers at bay. Things were simpler when it was just Earthers dying. Now a hundred pale faces shot daggers my way, as if they didn't already hate my kind enough. Ringers back then weren't foolish enough to touch a collector. They used to have respect.

"And, Officer," I said, "have headquarters forward her records to me. Everything, just like the others."

"Yes, sir," he said, saluting. He went to talk with the line of examiners wearing exo-suits who parted the crowd, but I grabbed his shoulder.

"I mean it, everything. I wanna know who her first kiss was."

I let him carry on, and took one last glance back at the poor woman. Bad stuff happened on Earth, but crazy offworlders kept me far busier. I wondered if maybe it was all the enclosed spaces that drove them madder—that constant dread of their world breaking open and suffocating. Whatever it was, it kept me employed. And the only thing that pissed me off more than bodies of innocent women turning up was me not being able to figure out who did it.

I considered a trip to The Foundry nightclub. Nothing got my head straight like a night of filling it with toxins and clearing it out. But I wasn't in the mood to drink synthesized swill and party with Ringers, so I took the lift back to the Uppers, to my five-star hotel on the south side of Darien overlooking the statue of Trass. A lifetime of traveling meant I could splurge a little on my temporary homes. The upper floor of the place even had a fresh-water pool and garden.

The lobby bar served fine whiskey imported from a Pervenio distillery on Earth, but I continued on past that as well. Sure, I wanted, no, needed a drink, but seeing that poor woman had Aria on my mind.

My daughter waited in my suite, like always. It got easier

sneaking her around as she got older. Public transports or hotels, when she was little, it was like smuggling narcotics, but once her chest and hips started filling in, the owners of places just figured I fancied younger girls. Because what else were illegitimate offworlders good for?

Those days, Aria barely needed me to help forge her IDs or a good backstory anymore. The girl was like a sponge, absorbing everything I'd ever taught her, and worse, all the things I hadn't.

A keycard opened the door to my room on the hotel's top floor. "Aria?" I said as I entered. She sat at the edge of the bed and slowly turned toward me, eyes glued open in dismay. She was sixteen or seventeen then—tough to remember when I spent so long making up birthdays to help smuggle her—a real young woman.

The freckles across her cheeks and nose really stood out at that age. Her neck appeared too long still, and the Ark Ship figurine pendant she wore only accentuated it. Red hair tumbled from her head in thick, messy curls. She barely ever took the time to comb it. Her tunic barely fit.

I didn't mind any of it. It was weird enough men had started looking at her the way I used to stare at her streetwalking mother.

"What's wrong?" I said. "Have you been watching the news?"

I took one step in, and her eyes grew wider. I knew why even before I felt the barrel of a pulse pistol against the back of my graying hair. I cursed. Aria knew better than to ever let anyone into our rooms, even cleaners. I could see the regret racking her features even more than fear.

"I thought we said to keep the door locked," I scolded, then exhaled slowly. "Whoever you are, you're going to want to rethink this."

"I don't think so, Malcolm Graves," a woman replied, her voice soft yet sultry. It made the hairs on the back of my neck *stand on end. "You're exactly the man I want." The woman dragged her perfectly manicured, free hand down my side and along my hip, then removed my pulse pistol from its holster.*

I tried to keep my anger in check. My pistol had just gotten a brand-new carbon-fiber, fluted barrel that left her light as a feather.

"Words I love hearing," I said.

"Not from me," the woman said.

"Whoever you are, let the girl leave, and we can have a nice long discussion about why it isn't nice to hold a man at gunpoint without a proper introduction."

"Why? Your daughter doesn't like to hear about what it is you do?"

My face twisted into a scowl. Aria and I had established many ground rules, but number one among them was that she was never to tell a soul she belonged to me. She could be torn away into USF childcare for potential clan-family placement, I could be fined hundreds of thousands of credits and, worst of all, I could lose my job for keeping her a secret.

Aria didn't react to my expression in the way I expected. Her brow furrowed in confusion. "I swear, I didn't," she whispered, so softly I was mostly reading her lips.

"Please, it's the nose," my accoster said. "You grow up here, you get good at knowing who comes from what, and she has you written all over her. Funny, I didn't see anything about a daughter anywhere in your records." I felt the pistol slide along my head until the woman walked out in front of me toward Aria.

That was the first time I ever saw Rylah. Now, she was a woman who knew how to dress herself. Her hourglass figure meant she wasn't a full-on Ringer and her legs... they were long enough to take a vacation on.

"She's... uh..." I blinked my eyes hard to stop myself from

staring. "Adopted. It's a charity thing. I bring her along, show her the ropes."

"Groom little collectors for your owner?" Rylah stopped and ran her fingers through the ends of Aria's hair. My daughter's cheeks lost their reddish hue. My fists tightened. It wasn't the first time Aria got crossed up in my line of work, but the people who involved her usually wound up dead.

"It's okay, dear," Rylah said to Aria. "I don't have plans on killing him. I just want to talk."

"Says the woman with a gun," I said.

"Just a precaution." Rylah turned around and flashed me a smile with her ruby-painted lips. I swear, I think my heart skipped a beat. I know men always say that when they meet a pretty woman, but there really was nobody like her. Not even modeling on any ad for makeup projected throughout the solar system. She looked like one of Lucas Mannekin's creations— perfect from head to toe.

"Aria, why don't you go downstairs to the bar, order me a drink," I said, unable to look away from Rylah.

"Dad, I—" Aria began before I interrupted her.

"I'm not asking," I said. "Go, and try not to let anybody else up."

She bit her lip, then pushed off the bed and stormed by me. "Another one, Dad?" she growled, no doubt referring to the handful of times around Sol I'd had a few too many drinks, kicked Aria out of our room, and paid for a lady's time.

"It's not like that. I don't even know—"

Aria slammed the door behind her. I'm not surprised she thought what she did. Nobody's perfect, and my job didn't afford chances for anything more than fleeting companionship. And considering that I still hadn't been able to stop staring at Rylah, it added up.

"She's cute," Rylah said, smirking.

"Sometimes," I grumbled.

"If it makes you feel any better, she didn't let me in when I knocked. Made me hack the controls."

I blew out through clenched teeth. "Great. I hate owing apologies."

"Doesn't every Earther?" she asked.

"Yeah, and whose side are you on?"

"My own."

"We have that in common," I said.

"I couldn't tell by the logo stamped on your shirt."

"They've always treated me like family," I said, referring to Pervenio Corp.

"I'd be careful saying that around here. Who knows who's listening." She skirted her way around the bed and took a seat on the sofa in front of it. Her dress hiked up a bit as she crossed her legs, and I knew she wasn't just being careless. She now had two guns, but they were the least effective weapons on her.

"What in Trass' name is this made of?" she said, stroking the arm of the sofa with a single finger. "Everything is so plush up here."

"Are you going to tell me why a lady such as yourself broke in here or are you going to make me start guessing?"

"The Stalactite Killer," she said.

"What about him?" I asked.

"Why assume it's a man?"

"I've seen enough in my life to know we're the baser half."

She chuckled. "Pervenio must think he's serious to fly you all the way from Ceres, then. I figured a man with your experience could handle it, but now he's targeting Ringers."

Considering my gun lay beside her and hers was across her lap, aiming in my direction but with her finger off the trigger, I made a move toward the minibar. The small bottle of whiskey *just inside was exactly what the doctor ordered. A taste of an Earther delicacy.*

"I guess that explains whose side you're on," I said.

"Like I said, no sides. But the woman you found today worked for me; my eyes and ears on the east side of the Uppers. You may operate alone, but I protect my people."

"And what is it you do?"

"I learn things about people and places."

"Information broker. I should have known." I raised the bottle to my lips and drained it in a single gulp. It burned in the best way going down and left my mouth and nose feeling like I'd just inhaled a bonfire out in the wilderness on Earth.

"The best on Titan," she said. "You want to catch the killer; so do I. I know every corner of this frozen husk of a moon, from Darien to Ziona. I'll help you do it, and you don't need to give me a cut of your pay."

"Yeah?" I asked as I turned to face her. "And what do you get at of it, because I sure as hell never met an intel peddler who gives a damn about justice."

"I get a friend in high places, and I don't tell a soul about his daughter." She shot me her heart-arresting smile one more time, then tossed me my pistol. "The name's Rylah."

It took us a week to solve the case. Turned out the killer was a woman after all. An illegitimate like Aria, fueled by jealousy thanks to an abusive foster mom. Rylah didn't let me hear the end of it, but I didn't mind. We'd worked closely, leaning on her sources to catch the killer before he struck again, close enough that afterward, I decided to take my first extended vacation in a long time just to be around her.

Maybe, at first, I was a mark for corporate intel for her, but after a few months and a trip on a luxury cruiser sailing Saturn's upper atmosphere, me, Aria and Rylah were inseparable. Then my hand terminal rang, and I was put on the next ship back to Mars to track a smuggler named Elios Sevari. I told Rylah I'd be back, maybe even take some time off the job and be her enforcer. It was the first time in decades I'd considered hanging up my collector pistol.

But New Beijing had other plans for me, as it often did. Aria got mixed up with Elios, same as she did with Kale. I got angry and drove her away for good, and fell back hard into my occupation. Rylah became another lonely, fond memory in a lifetime full of shitty ones.

Every man's got that one woman who makes his head go screwy. I had her. Even though the last time I saw her, she tried to have me killed and Zhaff shot her to protect me, a part of me couldn't help but feel she'd come down presently just to make things right.

"As you can see, work is progressing rapidly," Basaam said, leading her toward the half-finished containment sphere. She froze as her gaze passed across my cell and our eyes met. I grinned a crooked grin and waved with only the tips of my fingers. Before I could say anything, she turned, asked Basaam a question, and they hurried toward his control console.

Maybe Rylah wasn't about to make some grand apologetic gesture like what might happen in my wildest dreams, but Rylah's presence left for an intriguing escape plan B if getting to Desmond didn't work. Somewhere buried in her cold, half-Ringer heart, remained a soft spot for me. I knew it.

Things between us didn't end on the best terms, but there were good times. And I'd never been one for knowing what's going on in a girl's head–Aria was proof enough of that–but what Rylah and I had was real. Sure as the sun is hot, it was. You don't ignore and run away from old flames you don't give a shit about.

I stood and approached the bars of my cell to try and get a better look at her, when Rin's horrifying visage appeared out of nowhere. "Hello, Collector," she said. She wore a wry smile, but the dim lights over the cells only illuminated the half of her face that looked like it'd battled an impulse engine. She and Rylah barely even looked like they were the same species.

"Are you ready to help us again?" she asked. The lock to my cell clicked open, and before I could think of an answer a shock baton struck me in my chest and a bag was pulled over my head.

NINE

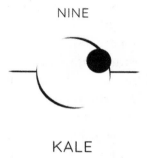

KALE

I'D SPENT MONTHS PUSHING MY MIND AND BODY TO THE edge just to feel something, watching and listening to the end of Cora's life so I might sense the beating of my heart. Scraping with death of my own.

Now, as I stood outside of Aria's room in the Hayes Memorial Hospital, my chest was tight and my throat dry. Scans had already come back clean that she and our baby were healthy, but it wasn't that. We hadn't yet talked to her about what happened on Mars. We hadn't talked at all.

"Lord Trass, she's ready for you," one of the new doctors she'd trained for the medical center said as he left her room. Considering Pervenio had a monopoly on all official hospitals in the Ring, Hayes was filled with former nurses, and black-market healers, like Aria used to be. It was the best we had.

I clutched the man's arm. "Now you know about her," I said. "Nobody else can."

The man swallowed audibly. "Yes, Lord Trass."

My glare bored through him as I tried to get a read on him. With Orson Fring busy stirring up ill feelings amongst the older crowd of Titanborn skilled workers, it was hard to know who could be trusted but for my fighters. I finally released the man's arm so he could continue on his way. I turned and nodded toward one of my guards down the hall, the same young man who'd helped me back on the *Cora*. He returned the gesture, then followed the doctor at a distance.

He didn't have instructions to hurt him, just to monitor his behavior and use of Solnet. At least until the baby was born or Aria's pregnancy was impossible to hide. Another guard remained outside of Aria's room.

I turned and rested my hand over the door controls. I could feel my heartbeat in my fingertips. I'm not sure exactly what it meant, if I truly loved Aria or was scared she'd betrayed us. I think, mostly, I wanted her to be telling the truth so I didn't have to say goodbye. Those fleeting moments with her when our minds could turn off—they were the only times in recent memory where I didn't feel the pain of loss or the stifling pressure of leading. Afterward, those worries always came rushing back in full force, but without those impossibly short breaks, I'm not sure what would have become of me.

I let the air flow in and out of my nose, over and over, until finally, I mustered the strength to enter. Aria lay on a medical bed, a copious number of scanners monitoring her and the baby. The blankets were down around her ankles so I could see how all that time in sleep pods now left the bump of her belly plainly visible in her medical gown. It would take a great deal of effort to hide her condition now regardless.

She rolled her head to face me, and her nose crinkled as she smiled in the same way Cora used to. My legs grew momentarily woozy, but I did my best not to let it show.

"Kale..." she said, her voice raspy. Hosting enough pharma and anti-rads for two had taken its toll on her. Her face had lost so much color she almost looked like one of us. She tried to sit up and winced.

"Don't get up," I said, moving to her bedside. Out of instinct, I reached out to stroke her forehead but froze before I touched. She took my hand and brought it against her cheek for me, then nestled into it. Her skin was abnormally warm.

"How are you feeling?" I asked.

"Still exhausted," she said. "But we'll be fine." Again, she smiled as she reached down and caressed her belly with both hands, as if that was all it would take to make up for what she'd done. To her credit, it very nearly was. I found myself staring at her stomach. Up until then, our child was a blip on a screen Aria showed me; now it was all too real.

"How was Gareth's funeral?" she asked.

"Interrupted by Earthers claiming lies about us," I replied.

"I wish you'd have let me come..."

"You know I couldn't." I finally forced my features to darken. Lying on her back with tears welling in the corner of her eyes and holding her pregnant stomach—Aria almost looked harmless. I suppose that was why I'd been so quick to trust her from the start. She was similar to Cora in that way. They weren't Sol-class beauties like Rylah or an Earther ad model, more like workers you might find down at a Lowers factory, hair messy and face stained from a hard day of work... real.

Yet buried beneath Aria's pretty, unassuming façade, I'd learned there was more mystery than anything.

"You brought Pervenio and Venta to our doorsteps," I said categorically. "I don't know what happened when I allowed you down to Old Dome, but that's what you came back with. Now they've merged into something even Earth has never seen before, and Gareth is dead."

She propped herself up, grimacing. "I hope you know I didn't mean for any of that to happen. I didn't even know my dad was alive." She took my hand again and pulled until I sat at the edge of the bed. "You have to believe me."

"I don't know what to believe."

She slid closer, wrapped her arm around my waist, and stroked my chin. I didn't recoil. "Believe in me." She turned my face back toward her stomach. "Believe in us."

I removed her hand and stood. "How many more secrets do you have, Aria? I know who your father is now thanks to Desmond and Rylah. He's the Pervenio collector who was in New London when you stole medicine for us. The collector who followed you all the way here and shot Rylah. Who seized the *Piccolo* and Desmond and Cora..." I swallowed hard. I never enjoyed bringing her up around Aria. It was bad enough how much they reminded me of each other. "He's the same collector who found our hideout under the Q-zone. For not getting along, he seems to be on your heels quite often."

"Malcolm follows the credits," Aria said. "He always has. And nothing earns credits like conflict. It just so happens that I've been helping a group of suspected terrorists."

She put on a wry grin. My glower didn't soften.

"This isn't a game," I said.

"It's how they view you, Kale. You know that. But he retired after he nearly died trying to stop me and got himself shot on Titan. It pained him enough to tell me. The only reason he came after me on Mars was that he thought he was saving me from this life."

"From me."

Her lips twisted, and she hung her head. "He'll be the first to admit he's never been an outstanding judge of character. You don't have to worry about him, Kale. So long as he knows I'm safe, he's harmless."

"I'm not worried about him."

Aria didn't back down. It wasn't in her nature. She ignored my orders and sat upright at my side. She stared right into my eyes until I had no choice but to stare back at hers. They were as bright a green as Luxarn's garden outside my residence used to be, with specks of brown like soil.

"All I've ever tried to do is help people like me," Aria whispered. "From the moment Rylah contacted me at Venta and told me how rough things were here. I grew up hiding, being dragged from one smuggling compartment to another by my father because I wasn't born how Earth wanted me to be. I was ignored by Malcolm when it suited him, spat on by most everyone else. This is my home now whether you trust me or not, but I hope more than anything that you can again."

"You promised to tell me everything," I said.

"I told you what I thought mattered. How many of your people do you think are the bastard children of Pervenio men? We don't choose who our family is like Earthers; you know that better than anybody."

I sighed. Aria was right, as she so often was. Cora's father was the Earther captain of the *Piccolo,* a ship leased out through Pervenio Corp, and she died not knowing it. Aria was just lucky enough to not have been abandoned at birth; to have a father who thought he was protecting her. Though I knew Aria well enough by now to know she didn't need protection.

"Is he okay?" Aria asked.

"We have him locked up safe and sound until we can figure things out," I said. "He's being fed at least, which is all any collector deserves."

"I can talk with him. See—"

I leveled a glare her way, and she nodded in understanding. Any offworlder with a brain knew collectors never delivered good news.

"So, I guess your father didn't really give this back to you before he died?" I asked, lifting the Ark Ship pendant hanging from her neck. "What is it then?"

"That was true... or, well, he thought he was going to die

and so did I." Her gaze turned to the floor. "He let me go, Kale. That day in the tunnels with your mom when he found us. He betrayed Pervenio Corp, told me to leave Titan behind, and killed his own partner to let me go. But I'm still here, with you."

"Rin thinks we should get rid of you after our son is born," I said. "She thinks you purposely led us into an ambush on Mars and that regardless of your father, you might still be loyal to Madame Venta."

"Rin hates anyone who isn't as miserable as her."

"Maybe, but she seems to be right more often than not."

Aria pulled herself closer to me and ran her fingers through my hair. "And what do you think?"

"I think..." My throat went dry, and I swallowed. "I think anybody who'd go this far just to tear us apart would be insane. You've had more than enough chances to kill me."

I drew her even closer until only a few centimeters separated us. "I don't want to kill you, Kale. I left my father's life to help people like us and got caught up with Madame Venta, who only wanted to for selfish reasons. The things she convinced me to do... I don't want anything to do with Earth. I just want to help this place."

"Then you have to tell me everything. Because if my people think you became our ambassador for any reason other than that, then I can't let you stay here."

"Kale..."

"For your own sake, Aria. You wouldn't be safe."

"You'd kick me off Titan just to protect me?" She lay her hand against my heart, feeling as it raced. "I knew there was a good man in there. Nobody else sees you, but I—"

I couldn't hold back any longer and pressed my lips against hers. I'd met Earthers who hated my kind, dealt with numerous smugglers and shady fences. I'd looked into all of their faces and known they were rotten. Aria didn't seem like any of them.

Maybe she was playing the longest, cruelest con in history—bearing my child and my trust—but as our arms wrapped around each other and we fell back on the bed, I decided I didn't want to know.

"I thought I was going to lose you," I whispered as our lips parted for a moment to breathe.

"Never," she said. "We're going to figure this out. Our child deserves a real home. All offworlders do."

"I love you." I'm not sure what happened; I just blurted it out. As soon as I did, we both froze. I think I meant it. Without her to help me brave spurts when it seemed all there was in my life was darkness, I might have allowed myself to die already.

She didn't say it back, and I didn't blame her, considering the circumstances, but she didn't push me away either. She squeezed my back and kissed me harder, until I could hardly breathe. Then she grabbed my shirt and started to pull it up over my head when the lights suddenly went off, replaced by emergency red track lights.

"What is that?" I asked, yanking my shirt back down.

"Probably just a surge. The hospital isn't finished yet." She tried to bring my head closer, but I thought I heard a thud outside.

"I don't—"

The door opened with a *whoosh* and the doctor from earlier stood in the entry. I was about to ask him what was going on when he fell forward onto his knees.

A Cogent stood behind him, fully armored in black but with his yellow eye-lens glinting through the darkness. It was the same one who'd shot at me back at the *Cora*, I was sure of it. His every breath through a respirator rattled like a clogged air recycler. He had a pulse pistol aimed at me, and without my armor, he had me dead to rights.

Luxarn Pervenio had sent plenty of men to take shots at me,

but never once did they have me so exposed, not even on Mars. Only this time, I didn't close my eyes, embrace death, and imagine what could have been. I lunged for the counter to grab anything I might be able to use as a weapon.

"Kale!" Aria screamed.

The Cogent's finger froze halfway toward squeezing the trigger upon hearing her. His eye-lens angled toward Aria, but he didn't fire.

"You," he whispered, a metallic quality to his voice. "You caused all of this!" His hand started shaking, then he fired at her instead of me. I'd raised a medical tray just in time, and the bullet glanced off it before it could cut her to shreds. The force blew me back over the bed and Aria then flipped it to provide us with cover.

Two more bullets tore through its metal frame, missing us by a hair. My eyes darted frantically around the room, but the only way out was the single door. Hayes had a thick, airtight enclosure just like Darien, which meant no viewports outside of common areas.

The Cogent grabbed the bed and hurled it against the wall like it weighed nothing. I charged at him, ramming my shoulder into his gut. Without my armor on, it did nothing. He grabbed the back of my shirt and flipped me over. Again, I expected a bullet to the head, but he turned his attention from me and seized Aria by the throat.

"You are in violation of fifteen Pervenio colonial regulations, Doctor," he said, emotionless, crushing her.

I pawed along the floor until I found the tray and smashed him across the back of the head. Ringer or not, it was hard enough to bring any ordinary man down, but it barely made him stagger. He raised his gun toward me, and I caught his arm just before it fired, the bullet zipping over my shoulder. It took two of my arms to keep him from rotating his arm far enough to hit me, but I couldn't last. He was the strongest man I'd ever encountered. His limb almost felt artificial, like Malcolm's leg.

Aria kicked him in the groin, but he didn't react to that either. He merely raised her higher and continued squeezing the life out of her, while simultaneously using a single arm to hold me at bay.

"Kale!" A gunshot rang out from another direction, slashing through the Cogent's shoulder. Sparks and chunks of circuits spewed out, no blood.

I spotted my mother out of a corner of my eye, holding a pulse pistol and with her eyes wide in terror. Until then, I'd completely forgotten I'd invited her to meet me at Hayes, an excuse to keep her out of Rin's hair while Rin handled Orson Fring.

The Cogent dropped Aria, and I ducked right before my muscles gave out, causing him to shoot over my head before he lost grip on the pistol.

"Run!" my mother screamed.

She fired again. The Cogent recovered quickly enough to raise a hand toward her, and it took a handful of bullets glancing off his open palm to knock him off balance. Her next shot struck his hip, and then one scraped across his jaw before her magazine clicked empty. He banged against the wall, leaning on a counter for balance, but he didn't go down. And still, he didn't bleed.

Aria gasped for air. I searched the floor for the Cogent's firearm, only to find that it lay at his feet. I grabbed Aria's hand, yanked her up, and ran for the door. I took my mother's hand as well, and we sprinted down the hall.

"Who is that?" my mother panted.

"I don't know!" I shouted. I glanced over my shoulder and saw the Cogent emerge from Aria's room. He fired, but we turned left down a corridor just in time.

"Lord Trass, I heard shooting. Are you all right!" the young

Titanborn I'd sent after the doctor said. He had his pulse rifle out and aimed behind us.

"A Cogent," Aria rasped. "Right behind us."

"Stay with me, sir." He allowed us to go by, then fired warning shots at the corner. "Go!" He made sure we stayed in front and kept his eye on our backsides as we raced down the hall. I glanced back occasionally to see the shine of yellow while they exchanged fire, taking cover between gurneys and carts and anything else in the hallway. Nurses and doctors in exam rooms hid within, people's screams echoed throughout the dark passages.

"In there!" the guard directed. We ducked into a room so that he could reload, allowing the Cogent to gain on us. "On my shot, run!" The guard edged around the corner, but as soon as the barrel of his rifle cleared the doorway, a perfectly aimed shot knocked it out of his grip.

He fell back behind cover and regarded us, fear twisting the brave young man's features. I saw myself in him then, that day when Rin and the others raided the *Piccolo* like faceless angels of death. The day when I lost Cora for good.

I squeezed Aria's and my mother's hands, and they squeezed back.

"I'll hold him off," the young guard said, voice shaking. "Get out of here!" He jumped out into the hall before I could stop him and spread his arms. This time, Aria pulled my mother and me out into the hall to flee. I glanced back, waiting for our savior to be torn to shreds, only it didn't happen.

A Titanborn nurse burst out of a room and rammed into the Cogent. Whoever it was had built up enough momentum to knock him into the wall. The short delay was enough for my guard and us to make it around the next corner. The last thing I saw was the nurse's brains bespattered against the wall.

Power around the next bend seemed to still be active. I can't recall ever running so fast in my life as we neared it. I didn't look back anymore, I just squeezed the hands of two people I was desperate not to watch die.

"Lord Trass, get down!" someone shouted.

Titanborn soldiers emerged from the lit area with their weapons raised. The guard tackled all three of us before we could react, and they unleashed a hail of bullets over our heads. When they stopped, silence filled the hall. I heard my mother's rapid breathing, and Aria still wheezed. The soldiers moved to help us up, never averting their aim from down the hall.

"We have to get out of here," I said to them. "Let's—"

A single bullet to the chest sent one of the soldiers flying back. The others emptied their magazines toward the Cogent. As they did, my young guard grabbed me and me alone and bolted for the corner. I'm not sure what curses I screamed as he did; all I know was that I punched him in the face and lunged back toward the hall. Aria and my mother emerged right before I did something foolish like go back for them.

Aria hunched over once they reached safety and clutched her stomach. My mother was visibly in shock, yet couldn't help but gawk at Aria's belly. She looked back up at me, and no words were necessary.

"We need to get her to safety," she said.

I nodded. We were in the hospital's entry lobby, a three-story atrium with a viewport on one side that looked out over Titanian methane lake wrapped by cliffs. A plaque in the center of the floor dedicating the center to Hayes read: HE DIED SO WE MAY KEEP THE RING.

My guard was busy recovering from my punch to the face, but I grabbed him by the chest plate and said, "We need to—"

Another of the soldiers fending off the Cogent went down. More men hurried up the escalators on either side of the atrium to our level to reinforce them.

"We need to get her to my room," I said.

The guard licked his bloody lip. "We should split you all up in case there are more of them, three transports."

"I'm not leaving her."

"If there's another—"

"I'll go on the transport Kale arrived in," my mother said. "You two take the tram line; nobody will expect it."

"She's right," the guard said. "I'll stay with her and call for air support. We'll cause a diversion, just in case."

"Mom, I—" I said before she hushed me. She took both Aria's and my hands in hers and smiled a terrified smile.

"I'm so happy for you both," she said. "I'll be fine, you know that."

I threw my arms around her for the first time in longer than I could remember and kissed her cheek. Then I wound my arm around Aria and helped her down the atrium toward the tram-line lobby.

"I'm fine," Aria groaned.

I didn't respond or release her. I snagged a scarf from the storage room beside the front desk and wrapped it around my neck and up over my head. Security in the tramline waiting area directed frightened citizens onto a parked tram in as orderly a fashion as possible. With my face obscured and grimy from running and fighting, it would be easier to stay inconspicuous. Aria in her medical gown and with her hair even messier than usual would be even harder to spot.

We fell into the mob and were squeezed into the back car of the departing tram. I took the first empty seat we could find and held Aria close, resting my forehead against hers so that our faces wouldn't be seen.

"We're okay," I whispered then kissed her. "The Cogent will be hunted down."

Aria breathed raggedly, in and out. The tram shot forward,

and Titan raced by the windows. Two different storms dotted the horizon, one with red bolts of lightning flashing across the nearby methane lake used to power Hayes Memorial Hospital in the safest manner possible. It'd been a long time since I'd ridden public transit between Titan's colony blocks like I used to when I visited my mother in quarantine. It was oddly comforting.

"He could have killed you," Aria said softly. I could barely hear her over the nervous chatter of the other citizens.

"But he didn't," I said.

"He recognized me, that's why he stopped. I could tell, even without eyes to look into."

"Do you know who it was?" I asked.

"I... maybe. Only, it doesn't seem possible."

"What do you mean?"

"No more secrets, right?" she said.

I nodded and clutched her hands even tighter. "Right."

She took a moment to gather herself, and then as she started speaking, I could hear the fear affecting her tone in a way it so rarely did. "I don't know what Luxarn did to him after I watched Malcolm kill him to save me," she said, "but I think that Cogent was my dad's partner. I think he's the reason all of this happened."

TEN

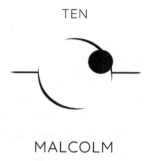

MALCOLM

THE BAG WAS YANKED OFF MY HEAD, AND I GASPED FOR AIR. I found it hard to come by with a sanitary mask still on tight. I searched from side to side. I was back in the cargo hold of the *Cora*. My last memory was Rin entering my cell. I got a few good punches in after the surge of a shock baton, but they overwhelmed me and knocked me out.

Rin sat across from me, fully armored and looking as grotesque as ever. "I thought you'd sleep forever," she said.

"And miss out on our conversations? Never," I grumbled. I looked around the room and found it empty, just me and her. "Kale didn't want to drop by?"

"He's busy."

"Heavy lies the crown." I stretched and cracked my neck. "So you decided you wanted some alone time? I've never tried being tied up, but I'm always up for new things."

"Don't make me sick."

"Oh, c'mon," I said. "How's about I give you the night of your life and in exchange you let me see my daughter?"

"If you keep helping, maybe I can make that happen. Until then, you won't get anywhere near her."

"Do you wanna bet on it?" I said.

"On her life?"

I bit back a response.

"I thought so," she said. "We were so impressed by your work on Martelle Station that you're going to help us with another issue."

"Did you all finally realize it's too cold on Titan?"

"We need you to remove someone from the equation."

"You mean kill them," I said. "Don't mince words."

"That's what you collectors do, isn't it? End conflicts before they begin, no matter what it takes."

I chuckled. "Corporate espionage is one thing. But if you really think I'm going to be your assassin, you're crazier than I thought."

"You're our collector. It's not up to you." She stood and paced the cabin. "A greedy shipyard foreman is slowing the production of ships. He's putting everything we're working toward in jeopardy over credits. Something you understand."

"So hang him yourself. I'm sure you'll enjoy doing it."

She lunged forward and clasped my jaw so tightly I thought it was going to snap. "No. It has to be you."

"There's only one more life I'm willing to take unless you let Aria and me go far away from here, and he's sitting right in front of you. Say goodbye to your collector."

She released me. "You're going to remove Orson, or your daughter will spend the rest of her life in a cage."

"I still don't believe you." I snickered. "The fearsome puppet master of King Trass who can't even say the word kill when she puts a hit out on a poor old man. Stop this charade. Kale's probably lying in bed with my daughter right now, and if I know her, she's got him right where she wants him."

Rin pulled out a hand terminal and showed me a live feed. A woman lay quietly on her back on a medical bed, covered in a ratty blanket. She grimaced, then leaned over and vomited into a bucket at her bedside. An IV was hooked into her, as well as a heart monitor and who knows what else.

"What's wrong with her!" I questioned, pulling on my restraints to get a closer look until my wrists stung.

"The radiation hit her hard. She'll be fine as long as we keep treating her, but she's locked in our quarantine this time."

"You fucking Ringer animals!"

"It's simple, Collector. *Kill* Orson Fring for us, or things get a little less comfortable for her. Do you know what it's like to melt from the inside out? Neither do I."

"Does Kale even know what you're doing here?" I snapped.

"Kale was done with her the moment you entered the picture. Now get up."

She switched off my restraints and heaved me to my feet. I tried to whip around and grab her, but the electromag dampener was still around my artificial leg, and I tripped into an inactive sleep pod like it was my first time walking. She had her gun aimed at my head before I could make another move.

She led me to the exit ramp and held on to a bar. The *Cora* rumbled, then I felt her spin around before landing gear made the floor lurch.

"Where are we anyway?" I asked.

The ramp opened with a hiss, then fell. Rin grabbed me by the back of my neck and hurled me down into a dark, empty hangar. My shoulder slammed hard a few times as I rolled.

"You know what you have to do," she said. She removed a hand terminal and keyed some commands. The electromag dampener immobilizing my artificial leg switched off.

I groaned and made my way to my knees. "If Kale really is in on this, and you keep letting him spiral, you're going to wind up hating what you've created. Me and you, we're set in our ways. Kids like him? They get creative when they go rotten."

"You'll find Orson Fring in the shipyard foreman's office," Rin said. "He's the older man with a white beard. Try not to kill anyone else."

"What stops me from running?"

"I'll be right here, and there's no way off this station without me seeing. A part of Kale may secretly care for Aria despite her lies, but I don't." She drew my pulse pistol from behind her back and tossed it at my feet. Then she glowered at me the entire time the *Cora*'s ramp rose to shut me out, tongue licking the gaps in her half-marred face.

"Damn you, Aria," I cursed under my breath. Most rebellious daughters brought home a gangbanger, or another girl if you're into the clan-family-breed-safely-and-efficiently-for-the-good-of-mankind mumbo jumbo the USF spouted. Not her. She decided to shack up with the leader of the worst riot Sol had ever known, with a murderous second in command. I could throw insults at them as much as I wanted, but there was no denying that they'd set a new standard. Rewritten the rules even.

I wrapped my fingers around the grip of my pistol, the only place they'd ever truly felt at home, and checked my clip. Then I stood and brushed off my clothing, only realizing then that they'd dressed me in a duster terribly similar to my old one. Everything to make me look the part of a Corporate Collector from Earth.

What choice did I have but to keep playing along? I knew who was really in charge on Titan. It was one old Ringer shipworker or my daughter. I'd made that choice with Zhaff, and I'd considered him a friend. Getting Aria out now that we were on Titan was going to be the hardest job I'd ever taken on, impossible even, but I liked my odds. I only hoped I still had it in me to pull a trigger.

I crossed the hangar exit and peeked around the corner. The

Phoebe ship factory's harbor was deathly quiet and dark, what passed for nighttime on a moon of Saturn. The Ringer day-night cycle fell in line with Earth's. Fight it as they might, it was genetic. Earther days and years were an inter-solar standard, at least until Kale inevitably tried to change that too.

I crept along, checking my corners. I'd never been to Phoebe, but Pervenio Stations all stuck to a similarly efficient design standard. Every groan from life support sent me ducking into a niche, finger on my trigger. Occasionally, I heard a footstep from someone scurrying toward the station's rec area, but I was a ghost. Infiltrating offworld workstations happened to be a collector specialty.

Except usually there was security.

I didn't encounter any in the central passage, and when I reached the factory itself, it was more of the same. Dozens of Ringers slept between unfinished ship chassis, using insulation for blankets. Signs of protest littered the floor. A handful throughout the vast space continued working, but they wore welding masks and were distracted by sparks from fusion torches.

All I had to do was not sneeze, and my path to the glass-fronted foreman's office overlooking everything was clear. I supposed it was precisely how Rin planned it.

I sidled along the outer walls like a shadow, using scraps for cover. The stairs to the office were only a step away, when one of Kale's few loyal workers across the room dropped his fusion cutter. He cursed loudly then lower as he tried to get control of it. It spun along the floor, melting anything in its path. I got distracted, and my foot banged into a sleeping Ringer.

"What the—?" the man groaned awake.

I was on him in a heartbeat. My hand covered his mouth and nose, and my artificial knee pushed down on his chest. I could see his eyes bulge as he saw what I was. Even the sanitary mask I wore couldn't hide my stout Earther frame and pink skin. He couldn't do anything about it. I held him there on the precipice of death until his eyes rolled back. Then I let off. I didn't kill for free unless there was no other choice.

I glanced up to see if anybody noticed. A few Ringers by the clumsy worker stirred, either telling him to shut up or trying to help. I used the commotion to climb the stairs to the office door. The lights were on inside, and even though the office's privacy tints were active, it was the brightest area of the factory.

I crouched and tested the door—unlocked. I raised my pistol and pushed it open with my boot, then rushed in and locked it behind me. A man I assumed was Orson Fring sat at a desk, poring over some data on his computer terminal. He didn't jump or hit the floor. Instead, he calmly glanced up from his work. His beard was as white as snow in Old Russia, somewhat hiding how intense low g had stretched his face. He was easily ten years my senior, maybe more since low g also caused Ringers not to show their wrinkles and sagging flesh as drastically as mine.

"I knew it wouldn't be long before he sent someone," Orson said, staring at my pulse pistol. "I didn't realize it would be you."

"Do I know you, old—" I didn't finish. It didn't seem right calling Orson "old man" after I'd gotten so used to hearing the phrase thrown my way. I edged closer, keeping my pistol aimed and watching his hands. One click and he could switch off the office's privacy tint, and we'd be lit up for anyone in the hangar to see. He didn't make a move, not even a twitch.

"I doubt you'd remember," he said. "You saved my son Jimmy once when he got himself into trouble a long time ago."

I scoured his face to imagine a younger version, and then it hit me. It was one of the tougher jobs to forget, what with a mad scientist trying to turn the poor boy into a cyborg servant. I wasn't often hired to help offworlders, but Pervenio Corp had an interest in keeping the Fring family happy so they could keep its cheap Ringer laborers happy.

"Jimmy Fring," I said. "I remember."

"I never got a chance to properly thank you," Orson said.

"Thanks aren't part of the job. Hands," I indicated as he went to stand. He presented his palms without protest, even going so far as to smile. I could see beneath the expression. Deep in his dark eyes rested an elderly soul resigned to his fate.

"What happened to Jimmy?" I asked, lowering my firearm. It didn't seem right having a pleasant conversation with the man while aiming at him. Especially a man who had the decency to remember me.

"He died raiding an Earther luxury cruiser with Kale and his aunt," Orson answered.

"Aunt?" I asked.

"They're the last two with Trass' blood. You didn't know?"

"I should have." That was why Rin's leash was so long. My last words to Zhaff lamenting family came to me as I realized how accurate they were. No matter where anyone was born or what kind of family it was, all the connections seemed to lead to was trouble.

"Well, I'm sorry to hear that about Jimmy," I said. "He was a good kid from what I recall." I didn't really remember anything about him specifically, but it seemed like the right thing to say. I was used to targets crying or begging on their knees.

"I tried to keep him out of all this," Orson said, "but he had too much fight in him."

"I know how that goes."

Orson chuckled meekly. Then he closed his eyes and lifted his chin, as if imagining a cool, seaward breeze on Earth rustling his beard. "So what happens next?" he asked.

"Your king needs me to 'eliminate' you. His aunt's words."

"He's hiring Earther collectors now?" Orson asked.

"I wouldn't say I'm under contract. He and Rin are damn good at leaving people with impossible situations, though, I'll give him that."

"What do they have on you?"

"It's a who..." I paused. I rarely told people about who Aria really was, but it seemed like the right time. He deserved to know why I had to do what I did, especially now that I knew Rin was a Trass as well. "An unregistered daughter."

"Doesn't make her any less yours," Orson said.

"Tell my people that."

"I understand. I'd do the same for Jimmy."

"Family. What a burden," I mused.

"And such a blessing. Seventy-three Earth years I've been alive," Orson said. "I watched the first Pervenio ships sent from Earth sail over Titan. It was peaceful here before they made contact. So few remain alive who remember, but I do."

"I can't imagine."

"Things were simpler," he continued as if I'd said nothing. "We worked to survive in a place where humans shouldn't and spent the rest of our days finding love and living life. Maybe it didn't look like a paradise, but it felt like it. Then I watched thousands of my people perish from sickness. Lost control of my own docks from fear, and watched my employees and family become mask-wearing wage-slaves."

"No paradise was made to last, I guess," I said. "They say Earth was once lush and green, but I have a hard time imagining that too." My fingers grew spry around my trigger just in case. This fearless acceptance of death reminded me far too much of the Ringer on Earth who got me caught up in all of this when he stole my gun and blew out his own brains.

"We're so proficient at ruining beautiful things," he said.

"We didn't ask for the Meteorite," I said.

"We would have found a way to destroy it anyway. I don't

blame Earth for what happened here either. Your ancestors survived a hell I can't imagine. Every day must feel like a blessing to be protected no matter the cost."

"Why didn't you just give Kale whatever it is he wants?"

"I spent fifty years fighting in this very station for my people to be treated fairly," Orson said. "To get paid what we deserved; for Pervenio to take proper precautions to ensure our health. To be trained to take on the same jobs Earthers had. And do you know what?"

I shook my head.

"We earned some semblance of respect," Orson said. "Our slender limbs and fingers made us valuable at putting together the tiny pieces that comprise a larger whole, and we were cheaper than machines. We earned enough to survive in a factory that became renowned for its working conditions despite Earthers and Ringers working side by side."

I noted his use of "Ringer," a word the rest of his kind seemed allergic to these days. My fingers relaxed. I can honestly say I wasn't sure what was going to happen next, but I was no longer nervous. He was different from the other Ringers I'd encountered; from a different time.

"I had that victory," Orson said. "No amount of Earther slurs or insults could take that away. I wore them proudly."

"You ever feel like ancient men like us should've hung it up before we wound up here?" I said.

"Every day." A tear rolled down Orson's cheek. "I never thought I'd live to see a free Titan again. Now our king wants me dead because we won't work like slaves anymore. Because we already fought so hard for more, and he doesn't even see it."

I didn't realize my gun-hand had begun quaking until he stopped speaking. I swallowed the lump forming in my throat. For years, I thought I was numb to the world. Fighting, fucking, killing—that was my life. Then Zhaff was assigned to me, and

Aria came back, and the next thing I knew, I was a human feeling pity for sick Ringers.

Orson Fring was as familiar to me as a hole in the wall, yet my heart thumped in my chest like I was in my first firefight, and I knew... he didn't deserve to die.

"C'mon." I holstered the pistol I hadn't been able to fire since I'd unloaded it at Zhaff, and took Orson's arm.

"What are you doing?" he said.

"Getting you out of here. Kale will be pleased enough with you out of his hair, and you can come back to your docks when this all blows over. Time is the only collector who's gonna take us old-timers, right?"

"No." Orson shook me off, then grasped my hand and positioned it over my pulse pistol. "I'm too tired to keep fighting and starting over. This new world, whatever it is, it isn't for me."

"Too bad. Let's go."

I went to grab him again, but he drew my pistol for me. I backed away slowly as he held it with two hands, shaking even more than mine had been. I'd underestimated another Ringer and found myself at the mercy of my own gun again.

"Take it, please," he stammered, flipping it around and offering me the butt.

I'd dealt with far too many murderous offworlders not to listen, but as my fingers wrapped around the grip, he aimed it at himself and pulled me close. The barrel pressed into the center of his chest. It took all the effort in his weak Ringer muscles to hold me there.

"Do what you came to do," Orson whispered.

"Not for him," I said.

"Then for me. Give this one kindness to a stranger, Malcolm Graves. Don't make me beg another Earther for something."

"I..." Words got trapped in my throat. All the breath fled my lungs.

"Please," he begged. "Thanks to you, I got another decade with my son. I'm ready to join him now in the skies of Titan. I'm done with all the fighting."

"It doesn't have to go like this."

"It does. You still have something left to lose, and this time, I get to give a stranger a chance at extra time with his child."

Orson's fingers folded over mine, but he wasn't strong enough to force me to pull the trigger. So I stared into the eyes of the first man in my life who wasn't begging me to live or for me to kill him for selfish reasons. There was no payoff for his family, no infamy in it for his order like the herald on Mars.

"Please..." he said again.

I nodded slowly, biting my lip. My hand felt as numb as the artificial leg on the same side. It was like pushing aside a boulder, but I squeezed gradually and never broke eye-contact. I had to picture Aria's smile just so I could keep going, one millimeter at a time, until the shot went off.

My ears rang. Lights throughout the sleepy factory switched on. I lunged forward and caught Orson, then lowered him to the floor and laid him flat.

"You're a good man... Malcolm Graves..." Orson rasped, eyes wet with tears. "Maybe you can show our king a better way. Wouldn't that be ironic." He coughed and turned his head, a thin line of bleed leaking from the corner of his lips.

"From ice... to ashes," I whispered. They were Ringer words I never thought I'd say, but they felt right. This stranger deserved a proper goodbye before Kale Trass got his hands on his legacy.

I sat with Orson as he wheezed his final breaths. Until his eyes went glassy and the air rattled to a stop. I don't think I breathed that entire time, not until my pistol slipped from my trembling grip. I stared at the weapon that had now claimed one hundred thirty-four lives. I used to tell myself all had it coming, but it wasn't true anymore.

Workers who'd heard the gunshot started pounding on the door.

I could have run then and shot my way through a mob of fragile Ringers. I didn't. Instead, I clung to Orson's body and wept for the first time I could remember since I was a boy on Earth working in the Amissum clan-family's factory. And for the first time since I ran off and became a collector, I wondered what my life might have been like if I'd stayed. I wouldn't have anywhere near the number of stories, but maybe, just maybe, I might have been content.

"Mr. Fring!" someone shouted as the door broke open. Not a second later, I was bashed hard across the head. The last thing I saw before the world went black was Orson's face, as peaceful as could be.

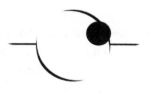

ELEVEN

KALE

"I'm sorry I wasn't there to protect you," Rin said. We stood in the Darien Uppers, surrounded by guards keeping my people at a safe distance. My aunt had me by the shoulders, checking me as if I were a damaged hovercar.

"I'm fine," I said. "But if it weren't for Aria, I'd be dead."

"Yet somehow, being around her attracts enemies to you like a magnet. What if she let that Cogent in to save her father?"

"She didn't. "

Rin rolled her eyes. "I thought your mother arrived to save the day anyway. That's what your guards told me."

"She did, just... the Cogent went after Aria first when he could have had me."

"Then at least keep her somewhere else until Luxarn is dealt with. She's not worth risking—"

"She is. I let you handle Orson your way, Rin. You'll have to let me handle Aria. There's nowhere safer on Titan than my quarters, and that Cogent probably knows what she's carrying now, which means Luxarn will find out."

"Well, we need to find out. I have all our best hunting for

the Cogent. He won't get off Titan. I can put the collector on it as well." Nobody else had gone after my mother's ship. As soon as Aria and I escaped, in fact, the soldiers said the Cogent backed off and completely vanished.

"I don't think that's a good idea."

"He's getting a bit more compliant, trust me. We might have to let him and Aria see each other eventually, but if you really believe we can trust her, then I don't think it will be a big deal."

"It has nothing to do with her. This Cogent might be more important than any of the others. As soon as we're done here, I want your focus to be on capturing him alive."

"What are you talking about?" Rin asked.

"I'll tell you after. For now, we have a man to honor." I'm not sure if it was the way I said those words as I pulled away from her, but Rin clutched my arm.

"He didn't suffer, if it makes you feel any better," she said. "He pretty much begged Malcolm to do it."

"It doesn't. But it's done." Before I went to Hayes to meet with Aria, I'd told Rin to handle Orson Fring because nobody else seemed to be able to get things in line. I didn't tell her to kill him specifically, but I might as well have.

I knew Rin, and I knew what she would do to ensure we had a fighting chance when the Earther fleet arrived. She wouldn't have forced him to leave and risked him spilling secrets to the Earthers. I just had no idea a Cogent would nearly kill Aria and me, making it seem like a coordinated series of assassination attempts against Titanborn leadership. A Cogent whom Aria claimed might be the bastard son of Luxarn Pervenio, born from the dead.

"Let's get this over with," I said. I signaled my men to lead me to the foot of Darien Trass's statue, where I always stood while addressing my people. They gossiped about what the announcement would be about, even though word from Phoebe about Orson had already spread after Malcolm was captured there and beaten within an inch of his life.

Rin aimed her hand terminal camera at me. "My heart..." I paused to gather myself. After all we'd been through, I couldn't believe I felt any semblance of pity for a Titanborn who was willing to threaten our existence purely out of greed. It was probably because I knew how Aria would feel about it if she ever found out; about the secret I'd now have to keep from her after she revealed everything about herself during the tram ride home. About her father's negligence and how he crashed back into her life, about Zhaff Pervenio, about how Madame Venta forced her to please her sexually in exchange for moving up in the organization.

"Kale," Rin whispered, waving me along.

"My heart aches for the loss of one of our own," I stated. It was easier to seem genuine, considering I meant it. "Orson Fring and his family have worked tirelessly to make the Ring a better place since the days of Titan's first settlers. He was innocent of all this fighting. He didn't deserve to die!"

My voice echoed across the Uppers so that all the Titanborn watching me around the atrium would hear every syllable.

"Luxarn Pervenio sent one of his collectors here to rattle us, just as he sent a Cogent after me in Hayes in a failed attempt on my life. They want to end what they consider a riot by killing its leaders, but we are the past, present, and future of the Ring. I promise, the man responsible for this will pay. Today I ask you, my brothers and sisters, to put aside petty desires and protests. I ask you to stand with me together so that we can show Earth that we will never bow to them again. From ice to ashes!"

I raised my fist. My people roared. Rin shut off the news-feed, which we'd ensure made its way onto Solnet for Earth to see. Luxarn and Madame Venta had blamed us for killing the Red Wing Company board to stir their people into a frenzy. Now we were even.

"You're getting better at that," Rin said as she wrapped her hand around my shoulder and guided me through the raucous crowd.

"At lying?" I asked, my gaze dropping to the floor.

"No. Speaking like a leader should."

"Maybe it will get easier one day too."

She leaned in close. "He left us no choice, you know that. If we aren't prepared, their fleet will wash over us like their oceans through dirt. Now a decrepit Titanborn who lost his way to greed can be a hero in death, instead of the reason we fail. Half the ship workers who stood with him are already talking about getting revenge for him by working harder than ever to stop PerVenta. Some will be of great value helping Basaam proceed as well."

Hands extended from all around us to touch me as we passed, praising me like we'd just won a battle. The guards could hardly hold them back. I lost count of how many men and women volunteered to be sent to Phoebe and Pervenio Station to help prepare for the coming storm in the name of Orson Fring.

We stopped outside the lift to Luxarn's old residential unit, where I lived on the rare occasion I was on Darien, as a message to my people that the Uppers were nowhere to be scared of any longer.

"We did what we had to, Kale," Rin said. "Now get some rest, and I'll handle the Cogent. You'll need it."

The doors opened, and my mother and Rylah stood waiting. Rylah was expressionless, in shock almost, but my mother fumed. Last time I saw her, we were hugging after a scrape with death and her finding out about Aria. I hadn't seen her cheeks that red since I was a boy and my father would disappear for months at a time.

"Katrina," Rin said. "I haven't had a chance to thank you for saving Kale's life."

My mother stormed forward and slapped Rin across the face. "He's *my* son. It's my job."

Guards went to calm her, but I stopped them. Rin calmly rubbed her face and didn't budge. "Then you should have aimed for the Cogent's head."

My mother bit her lip in frustration, then glared over at me. We held each other's gazes, wordless, until she finally said, "I told you I could handle him, and you go to her?"

"I don't know what you're talking about," Rin said. "Orson was murdered by a Pervenio collector."

"Like the one you two have been keeping locked up downstairs?"

Rin shot Rylah a cross glare. We'd been keeping Malcolm's presence a secret from anybody who didn't *need* to know, like my mother. Rylah stood strong as well.

"Rin..." she whispered. "Tell me this isn't what I think is."

"It was another collector," Rin said.

"Rylah saw you take him away!" my mother yelled. "This, Aria's condition; how much else are you two keeping from us? We're supposed to be in this together."

"One fight with a Cogent doesn't mean you've sacrificed anywhere near what any of us have!" Rin screamed back.

My mother pushed by Rin to get in front of me. "Kale, please tell me you didn't know about this. Tell me you didn't invite me to Hayes to keep me distracted until that Cogent surprised us. I'm not stupid. Tell me you only wanted to tell me about Aria!"

By the end of her rant, she was shaking me by the shoulders. A lie made it to the tip of my tongue but went no further. I stared at Rin, unable to look my mother in the eye and unable to get the words out because I knew, if I lied, she would believe me.

"Kale, look me in the eyes and tell me," my mother pled.

"Tell you what?" I snapped. "That while you were busy accidentally saving my and Aria's lives, we had Orson Fring handled before he got us all killed over nothing anyway."

My mother staggered back, hand over her mouth. The look on her face reminded me of that last time I'd seen her in quarantine, when she begged me to stop visiting because she'd accepted her fate. A fate I gave up everything to help her avoid. She didn't say another word. She just rushed by me and lost herself in the crowd.

"When you got me into this, you promised we'd be better," Rylah said to Rin.

"They will do far worse if they take Titan back," Rin said.

"If there's anything left to take." Rylah followed behind my mother, but Rin grabbed her.

"Don't you dare," she bristled. "Like you didn't do worse when you were peddling information to Earthers? This is war." Rin pushed her away.

Rylah caught her balance in front of me and glanced up. I couldn't remember ever seeing her look like she wasn't in control of a situation.

"If we aren't better than them, why do this at all?" she asked me. She wasn't crying, but tears weren't necessary. She was gone before I could offer a response.

"Leave us," Rin ordered the guards trailing behind us, then signaled the lift's doors to shut. "Ignore them, Kale."

"Why?" I said. "They're right."

"Right?" she scoffed. "They don't know what it means to

fight. My sister hasn't had to work for anything her whole life. All she ever had to do was smile, and Earthers forgot what she was. And your mother? Don't get me started. She hid you when we needed a leader. She stole you from your father, my brother."

"She saved my son and me yesterday."

"Only because she happened to be there because we knew she couldn't handle what needed to be done on Phoebe. You said yourself, it was an accident. They don't understand; they never will."

"Sodervall would've spaced Orson just like he did Cora. How is what we did any different?"

Rin grasped me under the shoulders and hoisted me to my full height. "He spaced *them* for no reason," she said. "Orson's stubbornness could have cost us everything. Nobody ever said this would be easy, or that our people would agree with every-thing you do. That's what it means to lead."

"So every awful thing you do will always fall on me?" I asked.

"I'll tell them it was all my idea, then! That I convinced you."

"Why bother telling them the truth?"

"This is the collector getting to you again, Kale," Rin said.

"It's not."

"If you told me not to, I wouldn't have done it."

"Exactly!" I screamed. "But I didn't."

"Kale." She pulled me in close enough to see all the way through the holes in her cheek, through the strings of sinew and shiny scars. "The Children of Titan chose you because we knew you'd care enough to know when you're doing the wrong thing for the right reasons. I only wish I was half as strong."

The lift stopped and opened, revealing Luxarn's dwelling unit. It was the largest in all of Darien, located at the upper level of a central tower rising up to meet the city's massive enclosure. A contained garden was suspended around the entry, soil beds hanging between a silver lattice. Leaves and flowers draped over the edges, making it visible from the floor, covering the entire ceiling of Darien in a verdant blanket. Only now the plants were wilting and brown. At first, the water pipes continued watering them, but without maintenance, they were clogging. It was such a waste, the gardens. Plants simply for a colorful display instead of feeding. Only Earthers could be so wasteful just to make the rocky tunnels of the Lowers seem even drabber.

Two Titanborn guards stood outside the entry, fully armed and at the ready after the Cogent attack. They bowed their heads as they saw us. They were good, loyal warriors, not like the protesters on Phoebe who couldn't see what Titan needed beyond their own selfish desires.

"Never doubt what we're doing here," Rin said as I stepped off the lift. "A Titan of our own."

"At what cost?" I asked.

"Whatever it takes, like always. We'll bear the weight of our hard choices so that our children will never have to."

"I hope you're right," I said.

"You've trusted me this long. Only a little while longer now."

"And I still do. But next time we make a decision like this, I want my mother and Rylah there... if they'll ever listen again."

"You charged me with the security of our homeworld," Rin said. "More voices will only—"

"It's not a request, Rin."

The lift doors shut her out. I squeezed my temples between my thumb and forefinger and begged my chest to stop feeling so tight. My leg brushed against a withering plant struggling to survive, embarking on one last stretch for the artificial lights above that once brought life to a verdant garden.

I let the air clogging my lungs slowly escape through my teeth as I leaned over and let one of its leaves rest in my palm. I used to love sneaking around the Darien Uppers as a boy and seeing all the decorative plants Pervenio Corp put on display. All the things we *Ringers* didn't have in the Lowers because it was easier to keep people down when they longed for something as simple as plants.

My fingers squeezed, the leaf so near to death, it crumbled under the pressure.

I knew Rin was right. It didn't make things any easier, but none of this was easy. We were so close to having Earth where we wanted it. No matter what they blamed on us, Madame Venta or Luxarn Pervenio wouldn't be able to stop what was coming now that our best workers could assist Basaam Venta. There was no room for us to show weakness or let our people divide themselves.

Orson Fring died for the good of us all, if I could ever get my mother and Rylah to forgive it. Aria might never look at me the same either, once she found out. If she found out. Then would I have to tell her about the other people I'd let die when I could have saved them? Captain Sildario, Cora's father, whom I let crash with the *Sunfire*. Hayes aboard the *Piccolo*. Those children stuck in the freezer on the *Ring Skipper*.

Rin and I had allowed our trust in Aria to be comprised because of her secrets, yet I had so many of my own. We kept everything we planned to do on Mars from her, and now, what we were making her father do.

I stopped before the door to my residence. Aria waited inside under constant watch. I considered heading to my old Lowers dwelling, where I could get some silence instead. I was halfway toward turning around when I noticed a beam of light filtering in through a dusty skylight. The single pink flower it touched clung to life and color, unlike all the rest of the plants. It refused to give in to neglect.

Cora died without knowing I *was* capable of the things that had happened. That I was a scoundrel and a thief before Rin turned me into a smuggler and a rebel. I never got to show her the parts of me that even I didn't like, even though she'd opened her heart to me. And now I never would.

Somehow it felt like that flower was her sending me a message; like her soul had swum through space just to reach me before I made any more mistakes. I drew out my hand terminal and pulled up that final footage of her in her cell before she was spaced. She'd died barely knowing how I felt about her. She'd died protecting me from collectors and Cogents. She'd died ignorant to who I really was, and I decided I wouldn't make that mistake again.

An assassin could kill either of us at any time, and before death came for me, I'd let Aria in. Let her see me in every ugly shade. I'd fallen for her. Unintentionally, maybe, but since I'd nearly lost her on Mars, I realized I'd gone the longest I ever had without watching that footage of Cora or listening to Luxarn Pervenio condemn her to death.

Aria made me feel again.

I stepped into my apartment and found her standing right in the entry as if waiting for me. Her hair and clothing were a mess like she'd just woken up. She didn't ask where I was going. Instead, she chuckled, her nose wrinkling in that particular way I struggled to resist.

"I saw your speech," she said. "Are you okay?"

I was through the door before I knew it, my legs with a mind of their own. I went right to Aria and threw my arms around her. "I'm fine," I whispered. "It was just... unexpected."

"I can't believe after all these years, Luxarn Pervenio can

still find ways to shock you." She slowly began removing the pieces of my powered armor.

"Neither can I."

I heard shouting and flinched. A viewscreen by the bed replayed my latest speech across a Ringwide newsfeed. I hadn't realized how loud I was projecting my voice by the end. Director Sodervall sounded similar in his final days addressing the Ring on Pervenio Corp's behalf after I went missing.

"You're getting better at that," Aria said.

"Rin said the same," I replied.

"Well, I guess we can finally agree on something." She laughed, and I gave it my best effort to join her.

The top half of my armored suit peeled off me, the tiny needles it poked into my body to sync with my nervous system and enhance my strength sliding out with a delicate pinch. Aria took my hand, guided me toward the bed, and laid me down. Her face hovered above mine, but all I could focus on was the image of me speaking on the viewscreen behind her.

She rolled over and turned it off. Then she turned back to me. Her hands stroked my face, so warm. Some people said that the internal temperature of Titanborn had dropped noticeably in our three centuries on freezing Titan. It sure seemed like it was true whenever she touched me.

"One day, all the fighting will stop, Kale," she whispered. "No more Cogent assassins or kidnappings on either side. Just peace."

"Sometimes I don't think that's possible," I replied.

"If my father could walk away from his job, then anything is possible."

"Do you really believe anyone can walk away from something like that?"

She ran her fingers through my hair. "I remember a time when he left me on a rooftop outside New London to go claim a bounty in the middle of M-Day. One moment we were watching a Departure Ark leave; the next it was dark, and I was freezing cold and alone. I think I was six."

"Doesn't sound like a very good dad," I said.

"Not at all." She smirked. "I remember him stumbling up there to get me. His breath reeked of liquor, like he'd totally forgotten about me. He was a mess." She laughed. "But he did come back, and he brought me this necklace as a gift."

"Typical Earther. Always trying to buy loyalty."

"He did his best in his own way. Earthers aren't used to raising a family on their own. He'd tell me all the time about the nine mothers and fathers in the clan-family he was born into. Ask if I'd rather be polishing floors for a big, safe community like that instead of seeing all of Sol."

"My dad was the opposite," I said. "Always promising to be around but never there. And my mother... she never left me alone. I swear, sometimes I wish she'd left me alone on a roof."

"They're never perfect, are they? But you know what? He was right."

"About what?"

"Seeing Sol was so much better. As much as I complained in the moment, I wouldn't trade any of it for a normal life."

I exhaled. "Keeping me out of the Children of Titan was probably smart of mine too. I'd be dead by now otherwise."

"To our distinguished families." Aria giggled before pressing her lips against mine. It was nice to see her in a better mood, especially after the Cogent's attack. As I closed my eyes and kissed her back, I could almost pretend I was in one too.

"I've never had a home," she whispered after she pulled away. "But I'm glad I have one here. I'm sorry I didn't say it earlier, but in case someone else tries to kill us first, I want you to know that I think I love you too, Kale Trass."

A smile took control of my face, spreading so wide and so

unfamiliar, my cheeks went sore. "You're one of us now, Cora Walker," I said. "Until the end."

I kissed her again, but her eyes bulged, as if that idea was terrifying. She backed away slightly. I could only imagine how strange belonging anywhere might feel for a woman like her who'd spent her lifetime planet-hopping.

"I'm Aria, Kale," she said, brow furrowing with concern.

My reaction was similar, until I finally realized what I'd called her, and cursed myself. "I... I'm sorry, I know."

"Are you sure?"

"I am," I said. "This whole thing with Orson Fring... it just reminds me of the *Piccolo* and what happened to her." I spun a loose strand of her hair around my finger and forced my smile to return. "You are Aria, the bastard queen from Mars, and you're finally home."

A few seconds went by in silence, and her features didn't brighten, so I leaned down and kissed her again. "I promise you, Aria," I said, "for the first time in so long, I'm here with you. All of me."

"Good," Aria whispered, her stern façade finally breaking as she returned the kiss. "But speaking of being a bastard. I know it's safer here for me here right now with the Cogent on the loose, but do you think I could see Malcolm?" she asked.

"I'm sorry," I said. "We can't risk it yet."

"I get it, Kale, I do. It's just hard to imagine him locked up, of all people. Maybe I can talk some sense into him. His loyalty to Pervenio only ever went as far as credits, and they can't pay him now."

"I'll think about it."

"That's all I ask," she said.

"There're some things I wanted to tell you first."

"No talking yet. I'm going to make sure you never mistake me again."

"Aria, I—"

Aria pressed her finger against my lips to silence me. Then she removed the top off her dress and let it fall over her belly. She pulled herself up onto me and wrapped her legs around my slender hips. She was strong, stronger than Cora ever could have been, being born on the Ring to a Titanborn mother. Before I knew it, I was lost in her touch, and all my worries about family and rivals, dead and captured men—it all washed away.

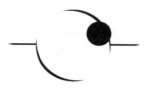

TWELVE

MALCOLM

"Eat up, M-mudstomper," Desmond cackled. He slid a bowl filled with grub into my cell so hard, it tipped over.

Weeks had passed since Rin found me huddled with Orson's body. Maybe longer. She'd had to fight off her own people to stop them from beating me to death. I expected a public execution as punishment, but they'd dragged me right back to my cell.

I crawled to the bowl on four limbs like a beast, digging in with my hands until I realized what I looked like. I grabbed it and threw it at Desmond. It clattered against the bars while facing the wrong way and spilled all over me.

Desmond laughed. "Starve for all I care."

"What?" I grumbled. "Your lunatic king doesn't need me for any more hits?" Pain still pulled at my sore ribs from the beating I'd taken. If they weren't fractured already, they were now. Desmond had been keeping his distance since I returned, but I was chipping away in our limited face-time. Pissing people off was what I was best at, and after that one time seeing Rylah, she'd never shown her face again. I'd started wondering if it was my old mind playing tricks on me.

"Whatever he's p-p-planning to do with you, I'm sure it'll be good," Desmond said.

"Pervenio collectors have a special place in our hearts."

"He doesn't tell you anything, does he?" I realized then that I hadn't heard any newsfeeds playing in the hollow. Even at his station, Basaam often complained about his lack of access to most corners of Solnet for data. Now I could barely hear him over the racket of whatever he and his team of Ringers and now Earther slaves were building. Desmond was locked away underground with us like a sick dog, a memory from a horrible thing that Kale didn't want to be reminded of.

"All I know is that you're gonna get w-what's coming to you," he said, his gaze momentarily shifting toward Basaam Venta's busy workspace across the hollow. "All you mudstompers a-a-are."

I wiped the muck off the bottom of my sanitary mask and dragged my impotent, cybernetic leg toward the bars, the electromag dampener reactivated.

"What? You think some magical engine built by an Earther is going to save all of you? It's too late for that. The things you people have done, there's no coming back from. It's like you didn't even learn from us."

"There was nothing to learn."

"I've seen this before. Protestors dig in until they're at their wits' end and then start killing each other. How long before he has me kill you just like he had me kill Orson Fring because he can't stand to look at your face?"

"Not this time, G-Graves," he said, sneering. "They told me to ignore you."

"Because they know I might talk some damn sense! What do you think they removed me from my cell for, some coffee? A chat about how Earthers tick? I'm Kale's collector now, and it's more of the same, just lower pay."

"N-n-no, not the same. We're free here now."

"Free? Killing anyone who speaks out against him. Sounds a lot like Luxarn Pervenio to me."

"He's nothing like him!" He smacked the bars.

"You're right. Worse. At least Luxarn had the decency to lock up peaceful men instead of leaving them bleeding on the floor."

"What do you call what he had S-Sodervall do to me, then? To Cora. That's the problem with you m-mud-mudstompers. You think you can justify everything."

"At least we know what we are," I said. "You lot parade around your colonies like you're heroes all because Kale dropped a nuclear bomb on a bunch of security officers. You think they knew what was going on when they entered that quarantine? They were just doing their jobs. Men with families, children. He killed all of them and then some more. Anyone who stood in his way, and he has the rest locked in cells in the same station where Sodervall spaced your friends. Does that sound like heroes to you? You're a bunch of damned skelly fanatics, same as you always were."

"What the f-f-fuck did you just say?"

I could see his fingers itching around the trigger of his gun. I'd found a nerve, and it was time to keep poking. I didn't care how sore my body was, I was tired of playing along. Being forced to murder a good man was the last straw; it was time for action.

"I was there in New London when your Children of Titan bombed it," I said. "Civilians with their limbs blown off. You call that fighting for freedom? I call it an excuse for a bunch of murderers to dance around a moon pretending they own it."

"You really think that even compares to what your p-people did to us?"

"What? Put you in quarantines because you got sick?" I

paused. I'd seen the awful condition of those places. The way his people were withering away to bones under Pervenio's watch because it was better for business. I couldn't back down now, though.

"How does that compare to the Children of Titan spacing twenty Earthers on the *Piccolo* just to send a message?" I asked.

"Do you know how many times those same men sm-smacked my meal away or beat me with batons because I was a 'filthy Ringer.' Or h-how they made us scrub the shit out of canisters because our arms are longer, while they grinned and d-d-drank?"

"So you kill them all," I said. "Everyone who's ever had a bad thing to say. Then you wonder why a man like Sodervall is pushed so far he spaces a bunch of innocent Ringers like Cora just to find out how to stop the Children of Titan. He may have hit the switch, but your king is the reason she's dead, and you can't walk. He forced Sodervall's hand while he hid like a coward."

Desmond raised his gun, screamed, and fired. The gunshot echoed so loudly in the hollow, it sounded like an explosion. I'm not sure if the miss was intentional, but the bullet missed my ear by a hair. The *bang* sent me spinning into the wall. Desmond kicked open my cell's door and limped at me while I held my ringing ear.

"That was your people's fault!" Desmond yelled at the top of his lungs, anger erasing his stutter. "You did this to us, not him!" He shoved the barrel of his pulse rifle into my chest.

"Is it our fault your kind are more suited for cleaning up our messes?" I said through clenched teeth.

That was the final straw for Desmond, a former gas harvester worker who'd done just that for Earthers for most of his life. Who'd been crippled at the hands of one before watching most of his crew get spaced. He went to shift the aim of his rifle toward my head, with clear intent to shoot and hit this time, and I used that opening. I mustered all the strength in my earthborn muscles and punched him in the side of the face with my good arm. He flew against the wall, the rifle flying out of his hands. I scrambled across the floor and tackled him.

I reared back to strike him again, but by then, his head was turned away, and he was crying. "No, p-p-please," he said, eyes twitching as he did. I imagined those were the words he spoke as Pervenio Corp tortured him for information on Kale that he didn't have.

I couldn't bring myself to hit him again. Seeing me, an Earther, stooped over him probably transported him back to that moment of terror. For all his gun-toting bravado, the Ringer was broken. He'd shot me in the hip, and all I could manage was pity.

"You have gone soft." I laughed to myself. I rolled off him and barely had a chance to crawl for his weapon before more guards arrived at my cell in a hurry, holding me at gunpoint. I planned to take him out quietly since I knew his masters wanted me alive, but I'd pushed too far.

"Hands where we can see them, Earther!" they barked.

I reached for Desmond's rifle, fighting the unimaginable pain tearing at my hip. My fingers only brushed the trigger before I collapsed.

My arms were promptly wrenched back. I howled in pain. Then the batons came. One blow after the other against my back and already tender ribs. All the while, Desmond remained cowering on the floor, whispering madly to be left alone. Broken, like everything else left in Kale Trass's wake.

"Stop!" a strong, feminine voice bellowed. One last blow hit me square in the back before the guards listened.

"Lady Rylah," one of them said. "He attacked Desmond. We—"

"Desmond was warned to keep away from him. Get him out of my sight and return to monitoring Mr. Venta's work immediately."

Two of them grabbed Desmond, then they all scurried out of the cell without another word. I rolled over and coughed up a spot of blood.

"You just can't stay out of trouble, can you, Mal?" Rylah said. She knelt by my side, and I caught an eyeful of the most beautiful woman in Sol, my daughter excluded. She tried to lift me. I moaned. I'm not sure which part of my body hurt most, but I'd put a handful of credits on the bullet wound. Eventually, she gave up and sat me upright.

"Funny running into you like this again, Ry," I grated.

"I think I recall that last time I was the one who'd been shot," she said. "By your partner."

"He was impulsive."

"Until you shot him too."

My throat went dry. Of course she knew about that—Rylah knew about everything. That was her greatest talent. A whiz with tech for sure, and as lovely as an aged scotch, but she had a knack for knowing. I think that was why I fell hard for her all those years ago.

"Let me guess," I said. "You know who he was too?"

"Aria told me."

"Of course."

"She also told me what you did for her outside the Quarantine."

I shrugged. "I had no choice."

"You did. Now get up."

"What—does your king have another mission for me? If you haven't realized yet, that lunatic shot me. I won't be much use with a gun."

"Good thing your daughter was a doctor, then," she said.

Hearing that was enough to get my old ass up to my feet. Blood trickled down my artificial leg, and putting pressure on the wound with my hand hurt worse than anything yet.

"Rylah, is she okay?" I groaned.

"She's fine, Malcolm. For now. We're going to see her." She wrapped her arm around my back and guided me toward the exit. I stopped.

"In exchange for what?" I knew Rylah well enough to know that dealing with her never came cheaply. And especially not free. Another thing that drew me to her back in the day.

"I can't explain here. Just trust me."

"Now you want me to trust *you*?"

"If you didn't, Aria said to give you this." She dropped the tiny Ark-ship figurine I'd given Aria in my hand. I stared at it and let it roll over. The thin crack from where I'd fused it back together after she broke it was still visible.

I stuffed it into my pocket then glanced back up at Rylah. Pain had me seeing two of her, but that didn't change how she looked. My offworld darling. Last time I trusted her, we ended up in a gun-toting standoff. Ours was never a simple relation-ship. The closer we got, the harder I pushed away. She did the same. So it was with collectors and queens of the information underworld. We were two people destined to be alone that the universe kept smashing into each other for a cosmic laugh. Yet there I was falling into the trap again.

"All right," I said. "But I'll have both eyes on you."

"You always do," she said before leading me out of the cell.

Trusting her again was probably another on my long list of mistakes, but as much as our relationship went off the rails, I could never forget those days with her. Shirking our responsibili-ties as we hid in her Lowers hollow. Meals with her and Aria sitting around a table like we were some sort of old-fashioned Ringer family.

"Mr. Venta," Rylah addressed Basaam. He glanced up from a control pad being built into what looked like an engine stalk. I'd been monitoring them for a long time now. Occasionally, they tested fusion reactions in the spherical chamber he'd had built. There was only a single, highly insulated porthole on the side facing away from my cell, and still, it was always bright enough to make my eyes tear.

"Yes?" he stammered. His glasses were so grimy, I wasn't sure how he saw a thing.

"Do you have any congealing spray? For accidents. Our prisoner is injured."

"I... uh."

"Answer her!" one of the guards watching him barked, smacking a part made of cold-formed alloy with a baton.

Basaam winced and ran in front of the part. "Don't do that!" he yelped. "It's in my workstation. Medical kit. Where are you taking him?"

"Lord Trass wants to see him," Rylah replied. She left me leaning against the fusion core containment sphere and then hurried his desk. She pushed a member of Basaam's work crew aside and rifled through the drawers until she came up with the spray. Basaam impeded her on her way back to me.

"Please, I have to speak with him too," he said. "Helena has been locked in that cell this entire time. She needs fresh air. To stretch. A break from the darkness down here. I'm begging you."

"We lived in tunnels like this our whole lives, Earther!" a guard snapped.

"Please! I've done everything you've asked," Basaam said. "Work is ahead of schedule. I just need to be with her for a minute."

Rylah regarded the cell adjacent to mine, and from outside, I could finally see inside it as well. Basaam's clan-sister was huddled against the back corner, a barely touched bowl of food beside her. The sounds of her weeping were common in the early days of our imprisonment, but she hadn't made a peep in a long time. She looked emaciated.

"Give them a moment together," Rylah said.

"Lord Trass said not to interrupt production," the guard replied.

"And he isn't here right now. I am. They're human beings, for Trass's sake."

"Barely," the guard snickered.

Rylah drew herself up in front of him and stood tall. Heels had her towering over him, and if there's one thing I know about beautiful women, it's that their scowls cut even deeper. None knew how to wield one better than her.

"He put me in charge of overseeing Basaam's production," she said. "Question my orders again, and I'll reserve a cell for you."

"Yes, ma'am," he conceded. "Break time, everyone; get some chow!" The Ringer workers sighed in relief. Basaam had them working to the bone, day and night, creating his game-changing engine.

The guard then shoved Basaam along. "You get one minute, Earther."

"Hold still," Rylah said to me. I bit my lip as she sprayed the gel and sealed my wound. I'd had my share of scrapes mended before, but I could never get used to the stuff. It was too cold, like someone was shoving an icicle into me. "There," she said. "Let's go."

"Look at you," I said. "In charge. How is it you always manage that?"

"I learned from the best."

"I'm flattered. I was always the one taking orders, though."

She grinned. "I wasn't talking about you."

Rylah, she didn't take shit, and she never lowered her price.

Even for me after that first job when I needed some intel. That's a rare thing, when somebody knows what they're worth and won't bend an inch. I like to think I negotiated my Pervenio contracts with the same rigor.

She led me deeper into the hollow. My hip was a scrambled mess, and my artificial leg was still stiff from the electromag dampener. The only good thing was that now every time the limb swung, I actually felt it.

"We're not really going to see Kale, are we?" I asked, stopping.

"You always were perceptive," she said.

I glanced back into the hollow. It was empty when I'd arrived, and now the center looked like a true pop-up laboratory. From hosting the sick and dying to the construction of Kale's ultimate weapon against Earther wallets. Everyone lined up to get their meal, Ringers and Earthers forced to help them, everyone except Basaam, who stared at us.

"I promised I'd get him and his clan-sister out," I said.

"And you promised to visit me again," she said. "Some things aren't meant to happen."

"They're right there."

"Make no mistake, Mal, I believe in what we're fighting for, just not how they're doing it. My people still need Basaam, but they don't need you."

I watched Basaam a few seconds later, then sighed and continued on.

We reached a familiar portion of the caverns that looked like an old cafeteria that hadn't been used in a decade. When Zhaff and I found this hideout, those very tables were covered with the bodies of sick Ringers my daughter was using stolen medicine to treat. Now it was as empty as an Earth crypt, minus any cobwebs.

Rylah groaned once we were out of view of the lab and

leaned me against a wall to rest. Half-lugging an Earther body like mine was more than any offworlder could handle.

"I could move better if you took this thing off me." I tapped the dampener wrapping my artificial leg.

"You like my invention?" she remarked.

"When I spotted you, I had a feeling this was your work."

"You promise not to run?"

"Where the hell would I go?" I asked. "And with a bullet wound? Even I'm not that good."

She knelt in front of me with her hand terminal out. Half a minute of flurrying fingers later, the dampener powered down and fell from me. I was too damn tired to run, my body too battered. Instead, I collapsed onto one of the lunch table's benches to take a breather.

I yanked at my sanitary mask to try and get it off until Rylah drew a small knife and sliced the fabric. I'd never realized how hard the things made breathing until air freely flowed down my throat.

"There's no time to rest, Mal," she said, a hint of urgency finally creeping into her previously calm demeanor.

"Not until you tell me exactly what's going on," I replied. "Last time Kale let me out, I found myself gunning down an innocent old man."

"I know."

"So you know that when I hear you're in charge of what's going on back there, I'm hesitant to trust you. Given our history."

She groaned in frustration. "Do you want to know why I'm in charge? His aunt, Rin, is my half-sister."

"The one with the..." I ran my fingers over half of my face.

"Can't miss her."

"Are you—"

"A Trass?" she finished before I could. "No. I just get all the baggage without any of the name."

"If she tells you I flirted with her, I was just trying to piss her off."

She rolled her eyes. "They wanted my help back before this movement was anything. The pay was good, so I figured why not? I threw her a bone here and there using my broker network, and the next thing I know, Pervenio is gone. Credits worthless. So she sold me on a vision for a new Titan for all of us, but this? Killing protestors to save a minute? This isn't it. It's the same as it was under Pervenio, only with different people spreading the lies."

"I told Kale something like that." She wasn't amused. "You really were with them the whole time? Was I always just a mark then? Even back when we met?"

"You were after my information. I was after yours."

"C'mon, Ry. It seemed like you were after more than that."

"It was always Aria, Malcolm. The moment you introduced me to that girl in your hotel room, it was like looking in a mirror. I cared for you, I swear I did, but I loved her. I love her now. The only reason I attacked you that day in the Foundry was to protect her because I knew what happened between you two. Twice after that, I nearly had you taken out, but you and your damn Cogent partner were too stubborn, and reached her until she found out it was you and decided to give her bastard father a chance."

My heart stopped. I'd spent a lot of time wondering how my daughter could wind up working with rebels and terrorists. "It was you who brought her here, wasn't it?"

"Rin—"

"Don't lie to me."

She swallowed hard. "The Children of Titan needed some-body inside of Venta Co. with the connections to steal medicine on Earth because there weren't enough credits in producing it here. We kept in contact after you and I..." Her words trailed off.

"Stopped," I finished for her.

"She hated working for Madame Venta. I thought I was helping her."

"By getting her wrapped up with terrorists?" I said. "That wasn't your damn place. You're not her mother!"

"And you were any better?" She grabbed my face and leaned in close. Her breath was intoxicating. Her eyes dreamy. Hazel, but with so many shades of yellow sprinkled in, it was like watching the sunrise over Earth's ocean. It was enough to startle me into silence.

"We both failed her, Mal," she whispered. "We drove her into the grasp of a monster, but it's not too late to help her."

"So that's what this is? We're breaking her out?" I transferred all my weight to my artificial leg and pushed off to get to my feet. "Why didn't you just say so?"

"I don't know why you keep thinking she needs *your* help. She's already out, Malcolm. Waiting in Kale's ship to run, but she wouldn't leave without you. Trass knows why."

"Did you tell her I was a waste of time?"

"Too many times." Rylah flashed a grin.

I don't care what she said, what we had was real. The way we felt about Aria only made it more so.

"Where do we go?" I asked.

She directed me toward a narrow tunnel with two empty suits of winged Ringer armor lying on tables outside. My chest tightened at the sight of them, and I got dizzy. Rylah didn't notice.

"We fly," she said. "Put it on. I tried to find the shortest Titanborn I could, but it'll still barely fit you." She glanced back and saw me leaning on a column, struggling for air. "Oh, c'mon, Malcolm. It's easy."

I grunted an incomprehensible response. It wasn't the Ringer suits or the idea of flying through Titan's atmosphere like a bird. It was the tunnel we were about to exit. At the end of it, on the surface, was where I'd gunned down Zhaff.

Rylah must have noticed that I looked like I saw a ghost because she rushed back to my side and lent her support.

"Mal, I know what happened here, but you need to be strong," she said. "Aria needs us now one last time. Kale is... broken. He's allowed my sister to twist his view of the world so far, there's no turning back for them now. Aria still has time to get out before her hands are too bloody to lift."

I stared down the tunnel, which seemed to grow longer and longer. I could remember running down it to save Aria as clear as day. Me thinking we were smooth sailing until Zhaff found me forsaking our Pervenio contract to bring the Children of Titan doctor to justice.

"Malcolm." Rylah gave my cheek a light slap. "You have to focus."

I shook my head out. "All right," I said. "For Aria."

THIRTEEN

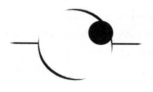

KALE

"Why did you bring me here?" Rin asked as she approached. We were half-exposed to Titan's surface, so she was fully armored and wearing her helmet.

We stood within the entry lobby of what remained of the Darien Quarantine I'd destroyed, where Ringers used to wait for hours under constant watch before visiting with their sick relatives. Toppled columns filled the hall, walls blasted open. Pervenio logos all over were scratched away and vandalized.

"They say the fallout cleared," I said. "That it's safe to be here now."

"You're not thinking of rebuilding it?"

"Never." I knelt and scraped away a bit of dust over the shadow of a man that permanently stained the floor after nuclear fire bleached everything around him. "There aren't even ashes."

"It serves them right, storming in here like animals."

I walked through what little was left of a large decontamination chamber. A web of pink lasers and warm air would have once brushed across my body after I'd been forced to strip down. The tingle that model had given my skin became second nature. I'd spent most of my life passing through the things. Between the Earther-run Uppers and the Lowers, at every dock, every time I visited a Q-zone—eventually, Pervenio Corp had them everywhere to try and keep the number of quarantined Ringers at an affordable minimum. Before we took over, the medicine we needed was produced only on Earth. I knew only a handful of Titanborn who could pay for the stuff until Aria, my father, and the Children of Titan stole their formulas and vials from a hospital on Earth.

I stopped as we entered the visiting area, deeper within the complex. Here, the top of the plateau within which the quarantine was carved had been completely blown open. Wind howled as it raced through, blowing grains of sand that would have been like tiny knives without our suits on. Thunder boomed overhead from a gathering storm, and out of the corner of my eyes, I saw the guards escorting us flinch.

"I still don't understand why you wanted to come here," Rin said.

"Sometimes it's nice to be reminded where we came from," I replied.

"You're in good spirits," she said. "How's the baby? I apologize, I haven't been around in some time."

"Healthy. Aria thinks he may be born a few days after M-day if everything goes right. That means he'll only ever know the new world we make."

"Good. And Aria?"

"Since when do you care?" I said, but not angrily.

"She's done everything we've asked since we returned, even I can't deny that. And what you said about her reaction after you told her the truth about Orson Fring, I never thought she'd be the only one to understand necessity."

"She's been fighting for anyone to give a damn about her much longer than I have."

"Sometimes, it's worth the search," she said.

"You're right ninety-nine percent of the time, but I'm glad you were wrong about her."

"Me too," Rin agreed.

I continued until there was nowhere else to go. A crater of rock, plasticrete, and twisted metal greeted me, where the *Piccolo* had impacted. Somewhere amongst the rubble were pieces of that ship upon which my entire life had changed. Even further down, beneath many dozens of meters of rock, was the hidden hollow where Basaam neared completion of his engine.

"Do you think Hayes is trapped down there someplace?" I asked.

"No," Rin said. "He's with the ashes now, watching over us. Kale." She lay her hand on my shoulder. "I have a lot I need to tell you. Look."

She drew her hand terminal and held it up for me to see. She'd been busy making rounds of our most essential stations around the Ring. We still hadn't located the Cogent who'd come so near to killing Aria and me, so I couldn't join her. Rylah oversaw the construction efforts both on Phoebe and with Basaam, while my mother focused on righting the current food shortage. I'd even gotten her to visit me for dinner a few times, furious as she still was over Orson.

A year ago, I never would have imagined sitting around a table with my mother and the mother of my future child, but I never would have imagined a Titan without Pervenio Corp either. I knew she'd come around eventually, especially with Aria on my side. Now that we were being honest, I'd come to find we had even more in common than I thought... both pushed to do things we never wanted to, for the sake of the greater good.

"Kale, are you paying attention?" Rin asked.

"Sorry, I'm just... it's nice to finally be out of Darien," I said.

"I'm sure. That Cogent, whoever he really is, has proven difficult to track."

"If only we had fresh air to breathe here." I sighed, barely paying attention to her. "One day maybe. Aria had an idea about converting this crater into a terraced hydro-farm. Reconstruct the enclosure, let it be known for something good and not all the death."

"She's impressed me with some ideas lately, but that one might not be enough. Now, would you look at this."

Rin brought her hand terminal closer to my face so I had no choice but to watch. She set a recording to play of her recent visit to the Pervenio Station Detention Center, a place I'd never want to visit again even if I could. The hundreds of cells lining the walls and facing out into the infinite depths of space with a wall of sanity-killing glass were crammed with Earthers. There was barely enough space for all of them.

A few guards fed the captives with only one bowl of slop per two or three of them. I could see the gauntness of what were naturally chubby Earther cheeks. The pinkish hue of their skin grew more sallow by the day, and many of their eyes were permanently bloodshot from crying.

Rin switched to the next feed so I could see food being slid into one cell through a slot in the wall. The six people inside crowded it like savages, pushing and shoving each other to get as much as possible. Reduced to animals like so many of my people were as they withered away to bones from treatable illnesses for no good reason in the very place where I stood.

"None of us planned to hold them here for so long," Rin said. "Without any trading arrangements outside the Ring, we can no longer afford to feed both them and our people."

"Are you suggesting we make a deal with Earth?" I asked.

"Never. But Earth is coming with their fleet, hostages or not.

They're not of any use to us anymore, so maybe it's time to finally use them."

"Like we *used* Orson?"

"I didn't say that," she said.

"But we'd have to waste ships to do anything else."

"That's why I rushed back here." She switched to an Earther newsfeed on Solnet called Europa's Lens. "Watch."

A finely manicured male reporter was on screen, with perfect, thick hair and wearing makeup so none of his wrinkles would show. He stood overlooking a busy hangar outside Martelle Station, with dozens of ships in the midst of lifting off. The corporate logos of Pervenio Corp, Venta Co., or Red Wing Company were printed on every hull.

"This is the scene on Europa Station," the reporter said. "For weeks now, a record number of vessels have been armed and dispatched to resolve the tense situation on Titan. Madame Venta, who has elected to personally lead the campaign, had this to say: 'Together, Luxarn Pervenio and I will right the wrong of this savage rebellion against reason. We will liberate the Ring from radicals, doing everything within our power to save the captives there, and we will ensure that it will again be a haven of commerce and safety for the citizens of the USF.'"

"Our New London correspondent futilely attempted to reach the Voice of the Assembly, Talos Gaveren, about reports that this outward act of aggression remains unsanctioned by the USF," the reporter said. The feed cut to a recording of the bald old man. Talos shoved whoever was behind the camera away without comment before being quickly escorted away down the crowded New London streets.

"It's clear that this is an unprecedented situation in the post-Meteorite era," the reporter said. "All we can do now is hope that our brothers and sisters trapped on Titan as part of ongoing negotiations will finally be returned home, unharmed. Perhaps this display of strength will convince Kale Trass to see reason, or perhaps it will inspire them to show their true colors. Tune in for our coverage of the Crisis on Titan here, twenty-four/seven."

"That's only a fraction of their fleet, and it's already completed," Rin said. "What we saw at Martelle Station barely scratches the surface. They've obviously been planning for this solution much longer than anyone thought."

"Are you surprised?" I asked.

"Only that they didn't come sooner."

"The USF may want all their people back unharmed, so the idea of settling far from Earth still sounds like opportunity, but Saturn's gas and Titan's fully autonomous colonies are worth far more than human lives. Expansion at all costs."

"The mudstompers will never stop being greedy," Rin said.

"And everyone wonders why we couldn't cave to Orson Fring."

"It's proven to be the right move, Kale. I know how hard you took it. Production has doubled since he passed, but we still won't have enough ships thanks to the delays. Even if every Titanborn in the Ring starts building, we won't be able to stand against them now that they're all together."

I stopped and surveyed the quarantine's ruins. Just like how this place kept us at bay, all the slowly starving Earthers filling the cells on Pervenio Station were the only thing keeping Earth from bombing Darien, and the rest of Titan, in the first place. They were our shield, at least until Madame Venta and Luxarn took charge and decided to test our resolve. And if they were coming anyway, we were stretching our resources thin for nothing.

Whether they lived or died, the fates of our countless Earther and offworld captives were suddenly irrelevant. I ran my hand along a faded Pervenio logo outside of a nonexistent door; the same I'd seen throughout my whole life emblazoned on every ship or container holding the hand-me-down piece of tech a Ringer from the Lowers could afford.

"Kale," Rin pressed. "This isn't time to daydream. We can't threaten Earth's people with a second apocalypse if there's no Titan left to defend. Basaam is wasting his time when he might hold secrets to new weapons that can help us fight back."

"People," I said, my eyes going wide as an idea popped into my head.

"What?"

"Let's give Madame Venta back all of their people alive and unharmed," I said.

"I know things have been pleasant for you lately, locked away on Darien with your girlfriend, but they're our main leverage. Think, Kale."

"I am. The Earthers are boxed up like shiny new hand terminals already, ready to be shipped all over the Ring. Casualties during the heat of battle Madame Venta and Luxarn will talk their way out of, but if we make the captives visible for all of Sol to see—"

"We give them no choice but to pick them up," Rin finished for me. "Otherwise, we're the merciful ones. Hard to fight when their ships are as full of *innocent* refugees as Pervenio Station."

"Exactly. We can reconfigure every prison cell to launch intact, thousands of them. It should buy us enough time to get Basaam's drives as close to Earth as possible and force them to surrender."

Rin reached to her ear to switch on her com-link. Just then, an urgent message came through for both of us on our emergency line from the head of security at the Darien docks.

"Lord Trass," the man said fretfully. "There's been alert of unauthorized entry to the *Cora*. The dockhand says it's just an error, but there are also reports that the Pervenio collector you're holding was escorted out of his cell by Rylah, yet hasn't passed any checkpoints in some time."

I looked to Rin, my fingertips pressing into my palms. Just when things were starting to look up.

"Graves," she growled.

FOURTEEN

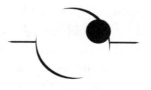

MALCOLM

RYLAH AND I STOOD AT THE END OF THE TUNNEL FAR beneath the Darien Quarantine, her hand resting on the controls for the hatch that would expose us. My powered Ringer armor was so loose, I felt like a kid back on Earth in my clan-family hand-me-downs. I raised my arms. Wings sewed from nano-fiber tensile fabric stretched from hip to forearm. It seemed insane that a human being could fly just by flapping these on Titan, but I'd seen the Ringers do it before. The moon's atmosphere was thick as syrup.

"Wait," I said over our coms, desperate to buy time so my nerves could catch up. "What about my gun?"

"Rin keeps it on her every second," Rylah replied. "Looks like you're finally going to have to let the old girl go. Now, are you ready?"

I know she wasn't asking about the gun, but I pictured the last time I held it, forced to blow away a man whose only crime was not wanting a war. It seemed fitting that my pistol's final kill would be an old-timer like me who didn't quite understand the world he'd aged into.

"As I'll ever be. Thank you, Ry. I know we were never going

to work out, but I like it better when we're not shooting each other."

"Don't get any ideas," she said. "This is for Aria... mostly." I was pretty sure I saw the corner of her lips lift as she turned her visor away from me and opened the hatch.

We were greeted by air cold enough to freeze the skin off our bones. Even the Ringer suits couldn't impede it completely. Cold filled the crevasses of my loose suit and the space of my helmet, instantly making my ears and nose feel numb. Strong wind whipped grains of pale, icy sand through the opening.

We had to climb through a cluster of debris to get out. The Darien Quarantine above had been blown to bits by Kale Trass, and pieces of it littered the ground in every direction, still not cleaned up. Chunks as large as a hovercar were chucked as far as the Darien Enclosure roughly eight kilometers away. It was no wonder that after Pervenio security stormed the place looking for the Children of Titan hideout, not one of them survived.

"Aria's waiting in Hangar 34 at the Darien docks!" The storm outside was so loud Rylah had to shout. Scarlet bolts of lightning forked above a distant plateau like the blades of the devil's pitchfork in old Three Messiahs folklore.

Yup. There were few places in Sol I hated as much as Titan.

"Just get a good head start and spread your arms," Rylah said. "The wind should lift you, even if you're a fat old Earther."

I think she was expecting a laugh, but I'd stopped outside to observe a pile of smooth rocks under two hunks of debris leaning on each other like an archway. One rock had a reddish patch on top, like rust. I was probably just seeing things, or it was the rock's natural coloring, but that was the exact spot Zhaff went down after I'd shot him in the head. I'd replayed that moment enough times in my head to be sure.

"Malcolm, let's go!" Rylah punched my arm.

I should have died there lying on the tundra with him, yet here I was with another chance at making things right. Zhaff Pervenio didn't deserve what he got, and he didn't deserve to become the killer his father made him. A son he'd rejected and pretended was never born all because he wasn't perfect.

I thought seeing that spot would eat me up inside, but the Malcolm who pulled the trigger truly had died there instead of him. Everything else was borrowed time. I spent half my life in sleep pods from mission to mission, wishing for morning so that I could waste credits earned taking down some poor sap, or wishing for night so I could sneak off-ship while Aria was asleep and get into trouble.

If Zhaff had to die to teach me to cherish even an extra second with Aria, then he was a better friend than I'd ever be. I knew now he wasn't really dead—at least not when last I saw him—but he was as good as dead to me. Only a shitty father's guilt kept his heart beating.

"Goodbye, old friend," I whispered.

"Malcolm!"

I turned and met Rylah's gaze, then nodded that I was ready.

"Just keep your arms steady, or the fall won't be pretty," she said.

She sprinted headlong into the gale. I followed her up a chunk of sunken debris like a ramp, and side by side, we raised our arms as we leaped off. I flapped mine like an idiot, but it was unnecessary. The wind snatched me off my feet, and before I knew it, the wreckage of the Darien Quarantine was lost in the fog of the mounting storm.

My heart raced. I'd been to every corner of Sol worth visiting, dealt with every manner of miscreant imaginable, I'd been on asteroid colonies when their walls were blown open, and the air sucked out. I'd watched a madman try to turn good people into cyborgs by reprogramming their brains. I'd been on ships as big as a small moon, but I'd never flown.

Pervenio Corp didn't allow personal gliding suits on Titan when they were in control because they were too hard to monitor. Only registered vessels could legally traverse the skies. As Rylah led me through the tempest like we were a flock of birds on Earth before the Meteorite, I almost understood why the Ringers were willing to fight so hard for their planet... almost.

"Enjoying the ride?" Rylah asked.

"I've been on worse," I said.

"The winds usually swirl around the Darien Enclosure. Don't fight it too much, or you'll lose control."

"This isn't your first time, huh?"

"How do you think my sources fed me information from around Titan without anyone knowing? Storms are the best time to fly."

Rylah gradually banked left. I made out the large shadow of Darien's three-kilometer-long enclosure coming up below us in the shape of an ancient ziggurat. The city's Uppers filled the portion above the surface, as did its major ports. We glided around until we were level with the top, spewing out smoke and residue from the Lowers' factories. Viewports offered glimpses of the gardens for the upper residencies within, gardens now browned and dying from neglect. The glass-covered farms sloping down all around the perimeter of the block, however, were lush and filled with busy Ringers. At least Kale hadn't let everything rot.

Rylah dipped one arm to turn and wrapped back underneath me, heading toward a half-open hangar in the side of the enclosure. I did my best to mimic her, feeling the resistance on my wings. They weren't used to bearing the weight of an Earther. Her feet touched down gracefully in the hangar. My wing ripped.

I tried to right my course, but I was losing altitude fast and headed straight for the impenetrable shell of Darien.

"Rylah!" I screamed. I closed my eyes and prepared for impact, when something grabbed my back and lifted me. When I re-opened them, I was skidding across the hangar until I slammed against the landing gear of the *Cora*.

Rylah tapped down beside me, even more gracefully this time. "I've always wanted to see an Earther fly," she chuckled.

I groaned and rubbed my unbelievably sore hip. Congealer helped with bleeding, but it didn't make the bullet hole in me hurt any less. Nor all the bumps and bruises I'd endured in my lovely vacation spent amongst Ringers.

"Did you have to throw me?" I asked.

"Consider it payback for getting me shot." She helped me to my feet. "C'mon, Aria is waiting."

I nodded and took off for the ship's entry ramp with my artificial leg carting me forward. The nerve endings near it stung every time my brain signaled motion now, but it was sort of refreshing. I didn't feel as much like I had a ghost growing from me.

I bounded up the ramp into the cargo bay as fast as I could. Rylah followed me and sealed the ship. Then the cargo bay's interior door slid open. Aria stood waiting behind it, fire-red hair tumbling over her slender shoulders like every curly strand had a mind of its own.

"Aria!" I threw my helmet off and ran to her, throwing my arms around her like it was the last time I'd ever see her. Hell, I don't think I'd ever hugged her like that in her entire life.

"What did they do to you?" I asked.

"Nothing I didn't ask for." She squeezed back, but something was different about her. Even in my armor, I could feel the bump of her belly pressing against me. I held her at arm's length and stared down. On Mars, it had been too subtle for me to notice, but now it was obvious.

I didn't throw up, but I could feel the bile working its way up my throat. My stomach churned. She was pregnant.

The first time I saw Aria kiss a boy—a ratty offworlder kid from Ceres who'd tried to pickpocket me, failed, then followed us around like a stray dog—I punished her for no reason, downed an entire bottle of whiskey, and bet an entire job's worth of credits on a mech fight. Finding out she was pregnant? I wanted to crawl back into my cell and let Ringers keep kicking me in the gut until I died of internal bleeding.

"I might have left out that part," Rylah remarked from behind us.

Aria didn't say a word as I gawked. "It's... it's his, isn't it?" I asked, breathless, even though I already knew the answer. Female USF citizens are provided pregnancy-impeding implants when they're of age, removed only by sanctioned doctors when reproduction was approved, or on the black market. Aria wasn't a citizen, so she'd never received one.

She hung her head and nodded like she was ashamed. Without thinking twice, I took her chin and forced her to look into my eyes. There was a time I would have screamed at her for being so foolish, but I like to think that everything that had happened since the last time I was on Titan had helped me grow up a little. Some men take longer than others.

What felt like an eternity went by as I struggled to get my lips moving, but then I said what I imagined she'd want to hear from her father... finally. "You've done nothing wrong, Aria." I took her necklace out of my pocket and lowered it over her head, then pressed the pendant gently against her chest while I kissed her forehead.

"I've done plenty wrong, Dad," she replied. "Worse than you'll ever need to know, but you were right. Some people can't change, and I won't raise this baby here. I don't care who he belongs to."

"It's..." I choked back tears. "It's a boy?" My hand hovered over her stomach but dared not move any closer. Aria smiled, took it, and made me touch her belly myself.

"It is," she said.

"Kale will chase us to the ends of Sol to get him back," Rylah said. "But this was Aria's decision. We just had to play along until Kale finally left Darien since Luxarn's Cogents have had everyone who isn't expendable on lockdown here for weeks. We won't get another chance like this."

"Once we get away from Titan, we'll be fine," I said. "I spent half of Aria's life teaching her how to hide from the USF and Pervenio Corp. Kale's got nothing on them."

"Then let's go already. If we wait any longer, the Earther blockade will arrive, and there will be no getting through."

I breathed in the sight of my beautiful, pregnant daughter one last time, then released her.

"I got the hangar open without being noticed, but as soon as the engines ignite, the dock guards will be onto us," Aria said as she quickly led us through the *Cora*'s shiny corridors toward the cockpit. "They have stolen Pervenio fighters that will come after us, but nothing that can keep up with the *Cora*."

"I'm not worried," I replied. "I've seen you fly."

"It won't be as smooth breaking Titan's atmosphere."

"You should have seen the landing I just had."

"I did." She snickered. My cheeks went red.

When we reached the cockpit, Aria hopped into the pilot's chair and began priming for takeoff. I bowed out of the way so Rylah could take the co-pilot's seat. Handling guns, not ships, was my specialty, though I'm not sure who Aria got that gift from, considering her biological mother was a streetwalking Martian sewer-girl. Or her brain, for that matter.

"Aria," I said while she worked. "Did Kale hurt you?"

"Never," she said.

"Then I have to know. Why risk all this? Last time we talked, you seemed... dedicated."

"I care about him, Dad. I really do. And somewhere inside him is the good man who only wanted to save his mother before being forced into all this, but he told me the things he's made you do, and everything else he's done. I'm so sorry."

"What's one more life on my conscience?"

"You have one?" Rylah said.

"Very funny," I said. "I did it all for you, Aria. I should have known you didn't need me, though. Mother of the prince of Titan, they'd have never killed you like they promised, not even Rin."

"Until the baby's born," Rylah remarked.

"I thought I understood why he did it all," Aria said. "And then I realized, he wasn't telling me. Not really. Even if he thinks he was."

"Cora..." I muttered, immediately catching her drift. Call it father-daughter intuition.

Aria stopped working only for a few seconds. Her features darkened and she managed a single, solemn nod. "I've spent enough of my life around a man who didn't actually want *me* there to know. Every time he looks into my eyes, I can tell that all he sees is a ghost that'll never return."

"Aria, I—"

She glanced back. "You're here now, Dad. And now I get to be the one who saves you."

"Well, I'm sorry you had to finally see him for what he is."

"No you aren't. But it doesn't matter how I feel about him. Venta and Pervenio are about to turn Saturn into a war zone, and my son will be their number one target now that a Cogent spotted me. That's the only reason they haven't leaked it. I was stupid to think there was any chance of sitting down and coming to terms, especially not with Rin in Kale's ear."

"They had no intention of a peaceful resolution," Rylah said. "No matter what happened at that summit."

"We're human," I said. "Too much ugly went down here for it to end without blood. At least you were willing to try."

Aria closed her eyes. "I know. But I won't let Kale get our son killed. Maybe one day, he'll even understand why I couldn't stay."

I rested my hand on her shoulder. I'd never been very good at consoling her. I was better at snapping, then drinking away the guilt, but eventually, when the old ways stop working, a little bit of new is all that's left.

"I was a shit dad," I said, "but I promise you, I'll be there for your son until I'm so old you'll be taking care of both of us."

She snickered. "I hear Pallus has a great retirement community."

"Don't even joke about that."

"All ship checks are go," Rylah said, eyeing the controls and obviously trying to speed things up. "Engines are primed and ready. Waiting on you."

"Where will you take us?" I asked. "I'll let you decide this time."

"I haven't thought much about that," Aria said. "Hopping from station to station might be more fun than sticking around anywhere for long."

"I taught you well."

Her lips formed a wicked grin, the likes of which I remembered from when she was still a child, unaffected by my parenting techniques; that same kind of look she put on when I'd tell her to eat her ration bar, and instead, she'd crumble it in zero-g. Or when I'd tell her to stay put, she'd agree, then she'd sneak out through the landing gear of whatever ship we were on to follow me into the seediest asteroid colonies imaginable.

"All right, impulse drives are heating up." She struck one last command, and the floor instantly began to rumble.

Rylah pulled up the feed from the *Cora's* rear cameras on her console. "Dock guards are here already," she said. Two Ringers in their white armor sprinted into the hangar and realized what was going on. They drew their pulse rifles as if those could do anything against the ship's plating.

"Seal the cargo bay... What the hell?" Rylah questioned. I leaned over her to see the feed and saw the guards suddenly lying face first on the floor of the hangar.

"What happened?" I asked.

"I'm not sure. Pulling up other feeds to—"

"I'm locked out," Aria said. She lifted her hands from the ship's controls as they started to blink. Then the overhead lights winked off.

"Aria, what the hell is going on?" I said.

"We need to run," she said, voice suddenly shaking. "Dad, we need to get out of here!"

She sprang out of the chair and grabbed me, but by the time she did, the lights flashed back on. I was facing Aria, so I saw fear twist her features first. In her gaping eyes, the unmistakable reflection of a glowing yellow eye-lens made all my muscles tense.

"Malcolm Graves, you are here," spoke the same robotic voice of the Cogent who Luxarn assigned to save me back on Martelle Station.

"It *is* you," Aria said through trembling lips. "I knew it."

Unlike us, Rylah didn't freeze. "You!" she shouted. We had powered armor on, and she swung at the Cogent. He caught her hand like she was merely a child throwing a tantrum, twisted her arm, and forced her to the ground.

"Informant, code-name Rylah," the Cogent said. "You should be in Pervenio custody."

"Stop!" I yelled as I whipped around. The way he spoke her name... I'd heard that voice, way back before Martelle Station. There, I hadn't been able to see him clearly, but I think deep down, I always knew. Who else could mow down an entire contingent of Venta security officers without a drop of sweat?

Few things are more shocking than finding out you're going to be the grandfather of the son of a murderous tyrant. Learning that the partner you'd shot in the head and sent into a coma was back in action... That was tough to beat.

Zhaff held Rylah in place, even though he wore nothing but a thin black boiler suit and a respirator over his mouth and nose. I knew it was him. The way his eye-lens fixed on me, its inner mechanisms gyrating as he focused; there was no doubt. And somehow, that damn lens was the most human, expressive part of him left. Even more work had been done to him since I saw him floating like a vegetable in that tube on Undina. His head had been shaved, with three lines of ragged scars running along the left side before giving way to the mechanically recon-structed left half of his face.

Luxarn promised to rebuild him, as if he were a product on a factory-belt. Like a fool, I'd doubted my old employer. I never would again.

"It's a pleasure seeing you again, Zhaff," Rylah groaned.

"What in Earth's name did he do to you?" I asked softly. I cursed myself for being so foolish. For so long, I'd taken pride on seeing everything, connecting dots, but again, my aging brain failed me. On the surface, all the mechanization made Zhaff's voice seem different, but a closer listen revealed that of my old partner. Sure, his every breath rattled as a built-in respirator kept him alive, but he was there, clear as day on Ancient Earth.

"I am impressed, Malcolm," is all Zhaff said. "When Father

said the enemy recaptured you, I was concerned I might be required to complete our mission on my own."

I slowly positioned myself in front of Aria and raised my hands. "Our mission?" I said.

"To bring the Children of Titan to justice after they left us and so many outside the Darien Quarantine for dead. Do not move, Doctor." While he restrained Rylah with a single hand, he turned the aim of his pulse pistol toward Aria, who made a move for the ship controls. "You will not get the jump on us again."

"Zhaff," I said, "I need you to put down the gun."

"Why are you alongside the two fugitives pivotal in attempting to have us killed?"

"Attempting... I..." Maybe the slew of surprises had my brain firing on all cylinders, but the way he was talking, it was like we were still on our last mission together, hunting smugglers who might connect us to the greater Children of Titan conspiracy. Like he'd never left. And the fact that his gun was aimed at them and not me meant he didn't remember what I'd done.

"Wait," I said, stepping toward him. "This is the Doctor?"

"Yes," Zhaff answered. Aria shuffled barely a centimeter, but Zhaff's aim tracked her.

"That day is still fuzzy."

"That is understandable," Zhaff said. "Father had to mobilize us before we were fully recovered. Reports state she shot both of us and fled with the stolen supplies."

"Father?" Rylah asked. "What in Trass' name is going on?"

"Quiet, traitor." Zhaff wrenched her arm further and caused her to wince.

"Zhaff." I extended my arm to stop him. "They let me out of Kale's prison. They want to turn themselves over and offer valuable information in exchange for protection. Look at them; neither are full-bred Ringers, and they're treated like it." There

I was, just like Rylah all those months again, trying to lie to a Cogent. But I'd spent enough time with Zhaff to pick up on his ticks and the key was, there was a load of truth behind every lie I uttered.

"It's true!" Aria said.

"Do not speak," Zhaff said. His tone didn't change a note, but the threat was clear enough. I heard Aria swallow audibly. "It is a wise intention, Malcolm," Zhaff continued. "However, Luxarn is primarily interested in the Doctor's child now. I caught her engaging romantically with Kale Trass, and, based on his own discoveries through your exceptional work on Mars, he believes the child to be Kale's offspring."

Zhaff returned his pistol's aim to the back of Rylah's head. She stared at me, wearing the look I'd seen on so many who'd expected to die. Unlike Orson Fring, she didn't look ready for the blackness.

Few ever were.

"Zhaff, would you listen to me?" I implored. "They have intelligence that can help us undo this. Both of them. They'll tell us all of it, but we have to get out of here now. Trust me."

"I do trust you, Malcolm Graves. I also know you and the information broker have history, which makes this difficult, but she cannot be trusted. Do not worry. I will eliminate her, then we can deliver the Doctor to Father, and after she gives birth, punish her for what she has done. Then you will be free to catch up on your sleep."

I would have snickered if I weren't so terrified. I thought back to my first days with Zhaff heading out to Old Russia on Earth when I'd told him my collector's tip about never turning down a chance for sleep, something a wise old collector had taught me when I was still young and hungry. If he remembered that, it meant that somewhere within his shiny new shell was the Zhaff I knew.

"Zhaff, I gave them my word they'd be pardoned," I said. "It's all I have left."

"Please," Rylah begged, playing along with me. "We don't want anything to do with this place any longer. We'll do anything."

Zhaff's eye-lens tilted toward me, then back at Rylah. All the while, the single eyebrow he had remained still along with every human part of his face. "I am sorry, Malcolm," he said. "I do not believe her."

We were back outside on Titan again, Zhaff ready to destroy the life of someone I cared about for the sake of our mission, only this time, he was the only one with a gun. He wouldn't hesitate. He never did. So instead of shooting him, I decided to try what I should have from the beginning—telling him the truth and testing if the bond we'd built was worth more than a mission from a man who'd never really wanted him.

If there was one human thing Zhaff might understand, it was a delinquent father trying to make things right. The best case was it'd buy me time to think of a way out of this, and the worst, he'd turn his attention to me, a true traitor, and give Rylah and Aria a chance at subduing him.

"Zhaff, don't," I said. "I have to tell you something about that day that will explain everything." I turned and regarded Aria's petrified expression. "About her. Zhaff, she's... uh... she's my daughter. The one I told you about."

"That does not make any sense," Zhaff promptly replied. His aim didn't shift, but now his eye-lens rose to focus solely on me. "She is—"

"A bastard from Mars," I finished for him, taking another step closer. "What happened on Titan—"

"Dad, don't," Aria whispered.

I looked back at my daughter and smiled. I could feel all the creases of age pulling at the corners of my lips and eyes. "I'm tired of all the lying."

"Malcolm, what are you talking about?" Zhaff said.

"I'm saying, she's not the reason we failed on Titan." I turned back and stared straight into Zhaff's eye-lens, same as I had all that time ago before I shot him. "Neither of them are. I am."

Showing emotion was never one of Zhaff's strong points, and it seemed especially difficult now, considering he was half-machine, but the way his lens spun to focus in and out on me, and that the rattling of his breathing stopped, I could tell I'd sparked something in his head. His gun-hand began to quake, slight enough that nobody but me would have noticed, but for him, that was like an earthquake.

"Zhaff, sorry doesn't even begin to cut it, but we have a chance now," I said. "A chance to make things righ—"

A loud *bang* interrupted me. A Ringer wearing winged armor landed on the bow of the *Cora* and glared in through the viewport. Kale.

"Let her go!" demanded the only voice more chilling than the half-robotic one of my former partner. Zhaff looked back toward the ship's sleep-pod cabin, and Aria wasted no time using the distraction to make her move. She keyed the thrusters, and the *Cora* shot forward. Rylah elbowed Zhaff in his cybernetic gut at the same time, and that, combined with the force of acceleration, shifted his aim as he pulled the trigger.

"Aria!" I screamed.

The bullet missed her by a hair and plunged through the ship's navigation controls. Sparks flew out, but I'd already decided to go after her rather than Rylah, and yanked her out of the captain's chair before they seared her face.

Then we all flew backward, Aria, Rylah, and me. I was able to grab the corner of the hallway and stuck my artificial leg across it to jam it into the wall and block them from going any further. Zhaff and Rin weren't so lucky.

The scarred witch got a few shots off. None met their mark as she flipped over a protruding sleep pod. Zhaff caught her by the arm as he plummeted toward the room's back wall and landed as if it were the floor. There, they struggled over her firearm. Her powered armor helped give her a fighting chance, but he twisted her hand around enough to blow a hole through her left shoulder.

The *Cora* spun and threw them into another wall, knocking the gun free before Zhaff could shoot Rin in the head.

"We're losing control," Aria strained to say. "I need to get to the controls."

I felt my foot beginning to slip and pushed harder until it sank into the wall.

"Go," I grated. I barely had the strength to move any other human part of me, even wearing the Ringer armor, but Rylah was stuck against my leg and, together, we shoved Aria toward the controls. My daughter pulled herself into the seat and strapped in.

More pressure pinned my head back. All I could do was shift my gaze from the *Cora*'s viewport, where the view spun between Titan's surface and Darien as Aria yanked at the ship's yoke to try and pull us out of the spin, to the cabin.

Zhaff had Rin by the throat and punched her helmet. Somehow, she'd been able to get her visor up, but Zhaff's fist was as artificially well-constructed as my leg. The visor shattered and the helmet broke, and Zhaff pounded the ugly side of her face until blood covered the scars.

"You will not slow human propagation any longer," Zhaff said. Just as he finished speaking, his fist froze right before striking her again and likely killing her. His eye-lens snapped up in my direction.

"'Family. I hope you understand, Zhaff,'" Zhaff said, repeating the last words I'd whispered to him when I thought he was dead. I could never forget them. I'd heard his voice elevated a few times. I'd even heard him make a joke, but I'd never heard his voice tremble.

My heart sank like a brick. I'd told him the truth, yet it was only then, when he dropped a daughter of Trass rather than kill her, that I knew—he finally remembered what had happened. He remembered that awful day on Titan when I chose family over the company.

"Why?" Zhaff said. "Why did you do it!" The way he screamed made his respirator hiss and stole all the human quality from his voice. He leaped at me, and thanks to the pressure of the ship spinning, I could do nothing but watch.

"Everyone, hold on!" Aria shouted.

The underside of the *Cora* slammed into Titan's surface. Zhaff's metallic finger scraped across my neck right before the force of the impact caused my artificial foot to slip and carve a deep trough across the wall. Rylah was whipped against a wall, and her armor kept her head from being split open. My back crunched against a sleep pod in the next room, and I flipped over before landing on my stomach and having the wind knocked out of me.

I found my way to my hands and knees, my ears ringing. Aria was in the command deck, still strapped to her seat, moaning. Rylah lay in the hall, unconscious, but it looked like she was breathing. Rin was further down the hall on her back, coughing up blood and loose teeth.

Black-gloved fingers wrapped my wrist. For a split-second, I expected the worst, then I realized how weak the grip was.

"Why..." Zhaff rasped, his respirator ticking from malfunction. His sparking artificial leg was crushed between two sleep pods, one of which had been pried loose of the wall and overturned. A conduit that ripped from its supports plunged through his torso. No blood leaked from the wound, only from the countless scrapes covering the other half of his body made by shattered glass.

He squirmed to pull himself free, but it was no use. And all the while, his eye-lens never shifted from me. I longed for that image of him lying completely still on the surface of Titan to fill my head again instead of this. At least then he'd looked peaceful and not like a wounded animal caught in a trap.

"Stop them!" a distorted voice ordered.

Kale appeared in the entry from the cabin, fully armored along with a group of Ringer soldiers. They marched into the room. The first grabbed Rin. A few more raced by toward the command deck for Aria and Rylah. One came for me, and I found my wits in time to grab his rifle and flip him over.

Skinny Ringers... now that I was in one of their powered suits too, I was as strong as three of them lumped together.

I ripped the soldier's rifle free and went to aim at Kale, but his knee caught me in the side of my head. He pressed down on me, weak like the rest of his kind, but he aimed my own pulse pistol against the side of my head. A second later, more rifles than I could count aimed at me.

"Kale, don't!" Aria screamed. "It wasn't him."

"Get her the hell out of my sight!" he roared. More of his men held her with her hands behind her back and dragged her by. She didn't go easy, that was for sure, kicking and shouting his name, but her pregnant, unarmored body was no use against them.

"Try it," Kale whispered in my ear, noticing my finger threading the trigger of the rifle. Rage resonated from him like a fusion core. "I'll let her watch."

I let the gun clank to the floor.

"That's what I thought." He shoved my face against the

floor as he stood and allowed his men to seize me. They didn't take any risks, at least four of them heaving me to my feet. I wound up face-to-face with Zhaff, whose eye-lens continued to fixate on me.

"Why!" Zhaff groaned. He finally gained purchase with one of his feet and pushed, causing the conduit to grate through his mechanized insides as his body slid forward along it like meat off a skewer. One of the soldiers bashed him in the head and knocked him out, putting me out of my misery, since I found myself unable to look away.

"I want the Cogent alive," Kale said. He ordered his men to stop and walked right up to me. I fought every urge in my body not to spit on his face. "Luxarn Pervenio will want to see his son again."

The nightmarish grin Kale put on—before then, I'd looked at him and see a troubled kid influenced by the wrong people. Not anymore. I'm not sure if he knew exactly what had happened yet, that Aria and Rylah had betrayed him, or if seeing his teacher Rin half-dead had done it.

It all happened so fast.

All I was sure of was that once again Zhaff arrived at the worst time and kept my daughter and I from riding out into the sunset, and that right at that moment, Kale had cracked. Not even his great-how-many-times-grandpa Darien Trass could save whoever he turned his fury upon next.

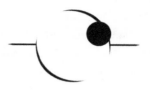

FIFTEEN

KALE

I STOOD OUTSIDE THE DARIEN HALL OF ASHES, WATCHING my people file inside. It felt like I was back in the Darien Quarantine before the revolution, waiting to visit my sick mother. Not a smile to be found in the crowd. Feet dragging along toward places visitors had to go but wished they would never enter.

"Kale," my mother addressed me from behind, using the same haughty tone she always did when she was trying to teach me a lesson.

"Not now, Mother," I replied.

I didn't bother turning to face her until she pulled on my shoulder. "Kale, listen to me."

"I said not now!" I shrugged her off and took a step toward the entry, but she caught up and forced her way in front of me.

"I know what she did was wrong, but she's family," she said. Tears glazed her eyes. Her hair was disheveled, her eyes exhausted. She almost looked like she had in the quarantine, only she could at least stand under her own weight now.

"Not with me."

Again, I went to pass her, but she didn't budge. "How many

second chances have I given you? Stealing any Earther tech you could get your hands on. Constantly getting into fights... Killing Orson Fring... We all make mistakes, Kale. Some worse than others."

"And what about the next one?" I bristled. "What if she or anyone else decides to sell us out to Earth? If they decide a free Titan isn't worth the struggle? Do you know the things I did to get you free of their quarantine? Do you even understand? You can't."

"I didn't ask for any of it. All I wanted was one last chance to hug my boy."

"And now you can," I said. "No mask, no gloves, because I turned that quarantine into dust. Not Rin, me. I'm the only one willing to do what's necessary to survive."

"Survive? We've already won, Kale! Pervenio Corp is gone. The USF was willing to sign Titan over to us. Our own world back, everything we wanted, and you rejected them. Aria told me everything. I've stood by and watched you push them further and further because you seem to think that the thing we all fought for isn't good enough."

"Good enough? Why should we settle for good enough? The Ring was ours long before they crawled out of the ashes of the Meteorite. We should beg them for scraps because one day they decided to come here and infect us? Spread their Earther greed like a plague? We've lost too many lives because of them to settle."

"Is Cora's life really worth all of this? She wouldn't—"

"This isn't about her!" I bellowed. The echo of my voice caused my people to stop and stare. "This is about justice."

My mother slipped out of my way, her eyes bloodshot and bulging. "What happened to you?" she said softly. "What happened to my son?"

"He learned what it takes to protect the people he cares

about. Now, please, get out of my way, or I'll have to make an example out of you as well." I wished I could take back that last part as soon as it left my mouth. She didn't deserve it. She was only trying to do what a good mother should, but I was tired of her not understanding the sacrifices our revolution took.

Her fear gave way to anger. "Tell your aunt congratulations. She's finally transformed you into your father."

She rushed by me, and I had no chance to answer. Not that I had anything to say. My father wasn't there for us because he gave his soul to found the Children of Titan as only a Trass could. To start the fight that I was finishing. Whatever line he'd crossed, I know he did it for me. For my future. Same as I was doing for my child.

Why couldn't my mother ever understand?

I drew a deep breath to settle myself, then started off toward the Hall of Ashes again. I barely made it two steps before Rin was in front of me to beg for Rylah as well. She appeared neither sad nor irritated, not that showing emotion with half a face was easy, especially now that it was bandaged and freshly gashed from the beating Zhaff put on her. Her left arm was in a sling, and the other gripped a cane to help her balance. Her legs shook from injury as she slowly lowered to her knees in front of me with all my people watching. If I hadn't broken into the *Cora* when I did and saved her, doctors said she might have died from internal bleeding.

"Lord Trass," she said, hoarse and needing a breath between every few words. Losing an entire cluster of teeth made her even tougher to understand as well. "I've come to ask you to spare my sister."

I groaned, grabbed her by the shoulder, and heaved her to her feet. "Not in front of them," I whispered, pulling her off to the side. She, the fearless, ruthless warrior who had ringed me into this fight shouldn't be seen begging.

"It was my fault, Kale," she said. "I brought Rylah into this years ago when she wanted nothing to do with the movement, but she's never had the stomach for it. She—"

"Did you know?" I asked calmly, stopping her mid-sentence.

"Know what?"

"That she had a serious history with the collector and Aria going back before working together out of convenience. Because Aria conveniently left that part out of her promise to 'tell me everything' until today."

Rin's marred lips twisted. "I knew she recruited Aria out of Venta Co. to be our doctor like you did. I didn't realize how well they all knew each other before that, but—"

I cut her off again. "She put both our cause and my son in jeopardy for a Pervenio collector. Who knows what else she might have been planning while I left her here in control of Titan because you trust her. You said it yourself, she didn't want this."

"Let me talk to her. I can figure out what she was really after." I'd never seen my hardened aunt so rattled, not even over Hayes' death. She'd been at my side since the beginning, helping me make the hard choices for the good of Titan, convincing me when something as horrible as taking care of Orson Fring was necessary. She was always calculating, justified. Now her tongue flicked along her open scars like it always did when she was agitated, only more so.

"So she can spin more lies?" I asked. "Keep more secrets? That was her job on the old Titan, wasn't it? Exchanging secrets. Knowing things to get the upper hand."

"We can trust her."

"We can only trust our own."

Rin grabbed me by the chest plate, her features warping with rage. If I were anybody else, she might have struck me. I didn't flinch. Not with my people watching.

"She's as much one of us as Aria!" she seethed. "They got on that ship together, Kale. Will you destroy her too?"

"Aria kept the same secret from me." I pictured her at the controls of the *Cora* before Rin stopped them. At first, I thought it was all the collector and the Cogent's doing, but I'd seen the security recordings from the hangar—they merely crashed the party. And Aria told me the truth the moment I got her off the ship. She wasn't a hostage. She was as ready to fly the *Cora* back to Earth as any of them. Ready to abandon me.

"She will raise our child so that the blood of Trass, our blood, endures," I said, "but she will never speak for us again, and she will never leave this place. Be happy, Rin. Now you get to say you were right about her."

Rin released me, and her head drooped. "Only now, I don't want to. I understand that you have to make an example of one of them, Kale. Trust me, I do. But exile Rylah instead. Make her live with her other half. I'm not asking you as your advisor but as your blood."

"It's only because of who you are that she isn't being executed. Freeing a Pervenio collector and helping steal my unborn child makes us look weak enough as it is."

"You might as well be killing her," Rin said.

"What happened to whatever it takes?"

A mouthful of air slipped through Rin's lips, the healthy side beginning to tremble. She stared up at me, a single tear dribbling down her cheek in and out of her grisly scars before dampening one of her red-stained bandages. "Be better than me," she said.

I wrapped my hand around her gruesome jawline. Most people cringed at the sight of her. I had once but not anymore. "'We'll bear the weight of our hard choices so that they'll never have to,'" I whispered. "We're so close, Rin. Don't lose sight." I drew her into a tight embrace, then strode into the Hall of Ashes.

It was even more packed than for Gareth's sham of a funeral. Guards formed a line on either side of me and pushed through the mob of baffled faces. Most had no idea yet that Rylah had betrayed us all. That a woman born half-of-Titan and half-of-Earth would choose the latter.

Rylah stood in front of one of the tubes the ashes of the dead were sent through, her wrists bound and stuffed into the opening. She watched me the entire way over, utter revulsion twisting her features. I'm not sure how I never saw how she felt about me before. I was blinded by Rin's trust, I suppose. A part of me couldn't believe my fearsome aunt had a weak spot. It made me feel even more alone under the crushing weight of my responsibilities than ever before.

"Kale, let me out of here!" Rylah shouted over the raucous crowd, pulling to try and free her arms from the tube. "This is insane, just listen to me."

I stopped directly in front of her. My guards gave us space and held the others at bay. I scanned her from head to toe. For once, she couldn't wield her charm and beauty as a weapon. Her dress was ripped, her shoes broken. Makeup like the Earthers wore ran down from her eyes. She looked plain.

"I trusted you," I said, seething.

"I trusted you! Trusted Rin that you'd be different when you're just as bad as them. And trust me, Kale *Trass,* nobody knows that better than me. I knew all Pervenio's little secrets, but at least they were honest before they sent us out an airlock."

The back of my armored hand crashed into her face, splitting her cheek. She couldn't fall with her arms jammed, but she folded over the protruding tube and spat a gob of blood.

"Kale!" Rin shouted. She burst through the guards, but I whipped around and stuck my finger in her direction.

"Stop!" I bellowed. She didn't dare disobey. "This woman betrayed us all!" I addressed the crowd. "She attempted to free the Pervenio collector who murdered Orson Fring in cold blood." The collective gasp of everyone watching was as loud as a tram zipping by. "But this Earther-sympathizing snake didn't stop there. I wanted him to be born healthy before I shared the news with Titan, but my son grows within our ambassador. He is the blood of Trass, and this woman tried to take him from me. From you!"

"Traitor!" a Titanborn in the crowd spat.

"Whore!" shrieked another.

They surged inward, forcing my guards to utilize the strength of their armor to keep them from ripping Rylah apart. I raised my arms to try and control them, then circled Rylah. I pointed to her arms, trapped within the tube.

"With those hands, she deceived my guards and unlocked the Earther's shackles," I said. "In their attempt to escape, they joined forces with the Cogent who nearly killed me." I gestured to a scar on my cheek from my brawl with the Cogent. Again, the crowd gasped. "But we are stronger than they think!"

They erupted, half cheering, half spewing insults at Rylah. Rin sank back behind my guards, a thousand-meter gaze aimed in the direction of her half-sister.

"I ask you, my people, what should be done to someone willing to sell us out to our enemies?" I said. "Someone willing to free an Earther and let him walk our halls, spreading his sickness and germs?"

"Kill her!" a man across the hall yelled. Chants echoing his sentiments rang out through the crowd, but I ignored them. Instead, I turned and regarded Rylah.

"You want to know why I tried to free them?" she muttered. "You." Blood bubbled in the corner of her lips. "They're going to wipe us out because of you. Rin wanted a heartless leader for her revolution. You got more than you bargained for, didn't you, Sister!" She lunged at Rin, but her trapped arms snapped her back. For the first time in my life, I saw Rin flinch.

Before any of my people noticed, I clutched Rylah by her flawless jawline. "Is that what you want to see?" I said. "Titan covered in Pervenio red again so you can go back to whoring credits or screwing Earthers?"

"It can't be worse than living under a murderer. She fell for you, Kale, and you chased her away listening to Rin. So go ahead and kill me. Because if you don't, and you touch a hair on Aria's body, I swear I'll bring this whole thing down."

My hand fell to her throat and squeezed so that the rest of what she said was garbled. I wanted to crush her. Who knew how long she'd been whispering in Aria's ears, turning her against me until she was willing to run. It was only the sight of my aunt out of the corner of my eye that convinced me to let go.

Rylah gagged. I turned back to my people. "The former Voice of Titan would have had her spaced without a second thought, but we are not them!" I announced. "Rylah, for your crimes against Titan in this time of struggle, you will never be able to free an Earther from his cell again. Never be able to caress and manipulate all those who thought they could trust you."

I approached the controls for opening the tube that allowed ashes to pass through. Both Rylah and her sister's eyes went wide. My aunt mouthed "Please" for me to stop, but her body remained still.

"Too much of a coward to kill me, are you, Kale?" Rylah said. The crowd of Titanborn was too loud for anybody but me to hear her. "What's another body on the pile you've started."

"You did this to yourself, Rylah," I said.

"You're right. It's what I get for looking out for anybody but myself. But you know the one thing I learned as an information broker?"

"And what is that?"

"That there's always one secret deeper. You do what you want with me, but if Aria gets hurt because she was naïve enough to love a broken man like you, I'll tell yours."

I paused at the controls with one command left to open the exterior valve and expose her to Titan's frigid air.

"You don't know anything," I said. "And that terrifies you, doesn't it?"

Her bloody lips curled into an impish smile, the same that had probably been used to work over countless men before me. It was probably how she got Malcolm to trust her despite being an offworlder. Probably the reason I took Rin at her word and trusted her half-sister without digging deeper.

"There were many secrets hidden in Pervenio Station after we took it," she said. "Pointless executions like what happened to your Cora. Technology. But my favorite was an early passage from one of Titan's first settlers. So old that the data couldn't be opened on our terminals, but I found my way in. Of the thousands Darien Trass brought here before the Meteorite hit, all our lives we've been told his daughter was among them. But Darien Trass didn't have a biological daughter, only one he took in." She started to snicker. "You, and my sister, and your father are as much Trasses as anyone in this room."

She grinned all the way through her revelation, at least until she realized that I wasn't shocked at all. I felt like I should be. Like I should have gone faint upon hearing that our entire revolution was based on a lie. I didn't feel a thing.

Maybe she was telling the truth, but it didn't matter. I was only a descendant of Trass because my people needed me to be. They needed a symbol, a name, to rally behind. To be honest, it was almost a relief to feel the weight of living up to the most brilliant man in human history lifting off me. The truth was that I, Rylah, every Titanborn in the room were all the children of those he selected. The three thousand most worthy people on an Earth that deserved to die.

Rylah's features darkened when she realized her final slight had no effect. Not a soul among my people would believe her anyway. It was too late for that.

I stared straight into her eyes, never breaking contact, and then I keyed the command. The outer seal of the tube opened, allowing the bitter cold of Titan to slip through. At first, Rylah went silent, then she fell to her knees. Her cries were drowned out by the bloodthirsty crowd.

Her exposure only lasted a few seconds before I resealed the tube, but it was long enough for the chill of my world to slip by her arms and give me goosebumps. Rin threw her cane aside and ran forward to pull Rylah free from the tube. She was too weak still to help, and Rylah collapsed on top of her, her entire body shivering, her lips blue. The skin up to her forearms was frozen solid, and when her hands hit the floor, they began to crack. The only thing that kept them from shattering was that the intolerable cold had fused them together.

I laid my hand upon Rin's shoulder as she struggled to calm her writhing sister. "Have her body warmed, then meet me at Basaam's workstation," I said. "Word came through this morning. His engines are complete."

Rin glanced up at me, incredulous. She needed time, but so had I when she invaded the *Piccolo* and made me a rebel. The Earther fleet was near, and enough time had already been wasted dealing with traitors when we should've been preparing.

"That's an order," I said then left them behind.

My people reached out to brush my armor as I passed, praising my mercy. I heard Rylah howling in agony until I was out of the Darien Hall of Ashes. It was the same sound I'd grown used to while visiting my mother in the quarantine zone. Only, those were my people suffering. The woman at my back, no matter what Rin thought, wasn't one of us. Not anymore.

I ditched my guards outside the lift and headed up to the glamorous home I'd never wanted. I'd meant to ask my men to try and spare some water for the garden but forgot. Now even the sole flower that fought to the sunlight for life was wilting and brown.

I told more guards standing outside the door to leave, then threw it open. Aria lay inside, cuffed to the bed and with a tracking band on her ankle, something I should have put on her from the start if I weren't blinded by her pretty green eyes like a fool.

"Kale." She sat up on the edge of the bed but could go no further. Her due date was nearing, and it showed. "I... It wasn't what it looked like."

"At least have the damn decency not to lie to me!" I slammed my fist on the doorway, bending the frame, then stormed up to her. "You said you told me everything, but not about Rylah and your father's history fucking. How long were you planning to run?"

"Just listen to me!"

"I'm so tired of listening." I lifted the Ark-ship pendant with one finger then let it drop back to her chest. "Everyone told me not to trust you from the beginning, but I ignored them. They warned me that you were only out for yourself like a true mudstomper."

"That's not true."

"Well, you picked a hell of a way to show it." I said. "You want to know what I think? I think you were planning to leave the moment your summit failed and I let you visit your old home. You and your father were going to disappear until Venta mucked things up."

"I told you, I had no idea he was alive!"

"More lies from the mouth of a whore who sold her body and soul to Madame Venta!"

Aria slapped me across the face. It stung, but I didn't shunt. I edged closer until she fell back onto the bed and I was glaring down at her from almost half a meter above.

"Do you think I wanted that?" she asked. "I did what I had to do to survive after I was left alone, just like any of you would have."

"You're not one of us," I said. "The only reason you're not being punished like Rylah is because of who you're carrying. And the moment he's born—"

"You'll what?" she said. "Kill me like Orson Fring? And probably Rylah and my father soon enough. You're wrong, Kale, I didn't want to leave. Every word I ever said to you, I meant. Maybe it's just the doctor in me that thought I could help you at first, but I fell for that wounded man I met all those long months ago who believed in something. But I refuse to sit back and watch you destroy our son like my father did to me over a woman who's gone and isn't coming back!"

"At least she was honest!" I shouted.

"All the good it did her."

The back of my hand lashed out to smack her in return, but I managed to stop myself before it struck. With my suit on, it could have done unrepairable damage and harmed the baby.

"Lucky for you, after we're done, you won't have to watch me do anything," I said, hand quivering. "You can go to Earth for all I care, but Titan is our son's birthright. All of this is so that he and every one of our children can grow up in a world where we're more than garbage."

"No, Kale," she whispered. "You're doing all of this for you."

I bit my lip. How could I have been so blind? How did I ever think she understood what we went through, when all she'd ever been was a two-faced rank-climber out to best her estranged dad? First Madame Venta, now me. If not for her bulging stomach, I'm not sure I would have been able to control myself. Even still, I turned away from her and rushed out, locking the door behind me while she screamed my name.

I ditched my guards and headed to the only place where I knew I could be alone. Down in the Lowers, far below, where I'd grown up before war or betrayal or anything—when only survival mattered. When my mother could still look at me without being disappointed.

"Lord Trass, I didn't expect to see you," said my old neighbor Benji Reiger as I approached. "Can I—"

"Out of my way!" I shoved the old man out of the way. His back slammed against the hatch into his dwelling, and his wife ran to him from inside to help him.

I threw open my own hatch and entered the tiny hollow I'd grown up in. I paced back and forth, unable to slow my breathing now that I was alone. I drew my hand terminal to play Cora's last moments again. It usually allowed me to focus my anger on what needed to be done, but the moment I saw Director Sodervall's face, I exploded.

I slammed the terminal against the floor, then grabbed one of the beds inside and ripped it out of the wall, screaming at the top of my lungs. And I didn't stop. All the fury over what happened poured out of me, until I was left lying against the wall panting like a rabid beast, and the room I'd grown up in was torn to pieces.

SIXTEEN

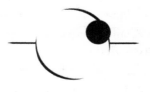

MALCOLM

FEELING MY AGE WASN'T NEW, BUT FOR THE FIRST TIME IN my life, I felt like a cripple. The pounding I took after Zhaff stopped our escape was one for my personal record books, especially after all the others since I was brought to Titan. Ringers on their own, weak. Dozens of them kicking my ribs with their armor on as they dragged me back to my cell after I'd survived a crash? Different story.

I could barely move either leg, and they didn't even bother whipping up a new electromag dampener to disable my artificial one. I feared what that meant for Rylah, as if worrying about Aria and now Zhaff wasn't enough. My hips popped any time I tried to move them, like I was an elder shoved into some clan-family retirement clinic. Even drawing breath led to a sharp pain pulling at my sides.

Even with all of that, however, it was my mind that felt the worst. We were so close to being free of Titan forever. The frozen world where nothing good in my life had ever happened. It was there that I once decided to leave Rylah and continue being a collector for credits I'd waste on whores and gambling dens. Where I was forced to kill my friend and partner. Where

I'd learned my daughter was working with terrorists, and later that she was carrying the child of their leader.

All I kept thinking about was how much easier things would've been if Luxarn had left me out to freeze. No fake leg. No more worrying about Aria. No seeing the sad creature Luxarn had turned Zhaff into to ease his own guilt. Just peace, quiet, and an eternity of darkness.

"On your feet, Earther!" a hardened Titanborn ordered, banging on my cage. Desmond was gone. If I knew the self-proclaimed king of Titan like I thought I did, Desmond's failure to control me probably got him punished. Or killed, more likely.

"You plan on helping me up?" I groaned, voice muffled by a new sanitary mask strapped to my face even tighter. Speaking brought about aches that I didn't even know were humanly possible. A tough feat, considering I'd spent a lifetime fighting.

Before my new guard could answer, a throng of heavy feet marched into the cavern. They spread around the perimeter of Basaam Venta's workspace. The engine he was building remained in a series of pieces, but all they needed now was to be assembled. It was complete. The hollow had been freezing when I was first sent down who knows how long ago, just how the Ringers liked it, but his creation emitted heat like a warm hovercar engine upon every test. By the bars of my cell, it was enough to make me sweat.

"Mr. Venta," the familiar voice of my captor addressed him. "I trust everything is in working order."

"Yes... yes, of course, Mr. Trass," Basaam stammered. "Tests show that the Fusion Pulse Engine is operating at ninety percent yield in comparison to those I'd been working on for the Departure Ark. I attempted to produce comparable models, but in these conditions, and with the materials available, I...I..."

"Relax, Mr. Venta," Kale said calmly. "That will be more than enough."

The boy king wrapped his arm around the scientist's shoulders, towering over him. I could hear Basaam's gulp all the way from my cell. He probably thought exactly what I was. With his work completed, what would happen to Basaam and his clan-sister?

"Bring down transports and have the parts loaded onto the *Cora* immediately," Kale ordered one of his men.

"Kale... uh... Mr. Trass," Basaam said. "I've told you, this technology is not optimized to operate on a ship the *Cora*'s size."

Basaam Venta was still trying to do the humane thing, even in his situation, like a good scientist. I wondered why more of the brilliant people I'd had to take down for Pervenio Corp in my day for pushing tech too far couldn't be more like him. Then I saw Kale stoop over the man and make him cringe and remembered why. Only weak men wound up in situations like this, forced to do things to protect loved ones. What did that say for myself and all I'd done to make this possible?

"As I've told you, I have no intention of using these on the *Cora*," Kale said. "Take him to the *Cora* and have him assemble the engine there."

Two armored Titanborn seized him, knocking his glasses off in the process.

"You said you would let her go if I did this!" Basaam yelled. He did his best to fight them. Poor bastard. Not everyone with Earther strength grows up knowing how to wield it. "Please. You gave your word."

Kale raised a hand to stop his men. "He's right. You've done everything I've asked of you, Mr. Venta. Your clan-sister will be released back to her own people with the others, as promised.

"What others? Where are you taking me? I gave you my work. Just let me go with her!"

Kale grinned. "Titan still needs you. We're going on a ride, Mr. Venta. You, me, and our friend over there." Kale nodded to his men, and they returned to hauling Basaam out of the room. His screams for Helena echoed throughout the hollow until he was out of sight, then stopped abruptly. I could hear the woman crying in the cell next to mine. She couldn't even get a word out, she was so distraught. Weak or strong, I was beginning to realize that nobody was built to handle a situation like this.

"I feel like I've seen this scene before," I said to Kale, trying to draw attention away from her. My body creaked and cracked as I used the bars to heave myself to my feet. "That's right. It's just like back on Pervenio Station before I left Sodervall in charge of your crew. We all know how that ended."

"Quiet!" My new guard hit the bars with his rifle.

Kale turned to me, sneering. I would've paid all the credits in the world for another chance to wipe it off his face.

"It's okay." Kale motioned for the guard to back away and approached my cell himself. Just the sight of his face after what had happened had my blood boiling. The smug, pompous kid who thought the whole solar-system owed him everything. I'd put down too many ambitious young men like him to count for Pervenio, but he was by far the worst.

"I think you and Sodervall would have gotten along," I said. "You're both insufferable, self-righteous shits. Want to know what I should've done after I interrogated Cora? Taken her with me myself. Could've given her a better life than either of you or, you know... death."

Kale's expression didn't break. Getting under Desmond's skin was simple, and driving a wedge between Kale and Rin had been as well. But every time I saw Kale again, this war had made his shell a little harder. It was like Aria was the only thing left helping him cling to his humanity, and now he knew she wanted to run.

A second bout of insults stopped on the tip of my tongue when I realized who that numbness to the horrors men are capable of reminded me of—Me. Three decades as a collector made me indifferent to everything, at least until Zhaff and Aria turned me inside out.

"I'm starting to enjoy our conversations," Kale said.

"You too?" I replied.

"I'll miss them, but it's time for you to help us one last time."

"How many times do me and Aria have to tell you I'm retired."

"Oh, Aria told me many things. About how you abandoned her so often as a child to get ahead on credits. How after five long years without talking, you found her in that cavern on Titan and tried to get her out. You want to know my favorite part, though? It's when you shot Luxarn Pervenio's secret bastard son to keep him from taking her in."

Kale clapped his hands; I flinched. To me, it sounded like that very gunshot that took Zhaff's life, echoing over and over in my brain. Only now I had the extreme displeasure of picturing him squirming as his body was gored.

"Zhaff Pervenio," he mused. "I wonder what Luxarn will say when I find him and tell him that his prized collector is the real killer. That Malcolm Graves is the one who made our revolution possible."

"It takes two, Ringer," I grated. "Cora was a good kid. Could you imagine if she could see what you've become? She'd probably want to run away from you as fast as she could, just like Aria."

"She can't." His armored hand squeezed into a fist. "She can't because we lived in a world where every damn Ringer was guilty the moment they were born. Our word: worthless. And if she were still alive, she'd be at my side fighting the fight we've been fighting our whole lives. The only difference is that now we're on top."

"Until the moment you fall. Don't you see, kid? That's the

way things have always been. Earthers, Ringers, the old countries. It's the people that own the shit worth fighting for that wind up sitting pretty. The only reason anyone gives a damn about what goes on here is because of that gas giant floating out there. Once that engine of yours goes public, you'll be another failed protest. And trust me, you may have slowed Earth a hair, but they've got enough backups of Basaam's research to build it. You'll be just another blip on the radar while humanity chugs on."

I thought that would get to him, but all he did was force a grin. That was the best way to deal with rioting workers on offworld colonies. Show them how futile it all was. Crush them under the weight of the world and history so that they doubted their movement enough for it to come down.

"Lucky for you then, you get to come along on the ride," he said.

I couldn't back down. I was desperate. "One last chance, kid. Let me and Aria out of this, or it's going to end the same way as all the other rebels I've dealt with."

"I look forward to it." He looked back over his shoulder. "Let him out," he said. "It's time."

His scarred aunt strode forward, emotionless and leaning on a cane. Based on the times I'd seen her before, she seemed eternally dour but not anymore. Her gaze was distant, and even the skin-covered half of her face was bruised and scraped. She unlocked my cell without a word or even looking at me, and two Titanborn swept in to grab me. I gave one good tug to break free, but my body couldn't manage much more

"How's your sister?" I asked Rin on my way by. "Is that where he's taking me? To put a bullet in her like Fring, so you all don't have to?" No answer. "It amazes me that she looks like she does and you look like, well..."

Her fists squeezed as she continued to avoid looking directly at me. Kale stepped between us before I could get another word in. I never realized how tall he was before. Maybe he was just carrying himself differently now that he was a proper killer, but he towered over even the rest of his Ringer brethren.

"You should see her," Kale said.

"What the hell did you do, Kale? If you killed her—"

"She's alive, for now."

"And my daughter?" I found the strength in my body to lunge forward and grab his arm. One of his guards nailed me in the back with the butt of his rifle almost immediately and knocked me to my knees. "Where is she?" I growled.

"You'll see soon enough."

"She had nothing to do with that," I said. "Nothing. It was me and the Cogent. We didn't give her or Rylah a choice."

"I didn't see a gun to her head until we put one there," Rin said, earning a glower from Kale that sent her shrinking back into the shadow. Something had happened between them beyond Zhaff putting a beating on her. Something that for the first time left no question over who was really in charge.

"There's a gun to her head every second she's in this hell hole with your bastard son growing inside of her," I said. "Zhaff found out, and Luxarn knows now, which means so does Venta. If your son is all you want, then just take him from her and let us leave."

Kale leaned forward, so close our noses nearly touched. He almost looked amused. "We *are* leaving, Collector. Aria, you, Zhaff, and me together... and your grandson."

"Zhaff is still alive?" I questioned.

"If you could call whatever his father made him into living. He still has a part to play."

My synthetic foot found flat footing, and I begged my brain to move it. I sprang up, fist aiming straight for Kale's pretty little head, but right before the blow struck, he clutched my forearm.

The power provided to his fingers from his armor nearly broke my wrist as he wrenched it back. My feet lifted off the rocky floor.

"An Earther will never strike me again," he said callously, his composed demeanor coming unhinged. "You'll come with me, and if you don't do exactly as I say, Aria will die the moment she delivers my child into this world. But if you act as my loyal collector, she'll be cared for the rest of her life. She will be permitted to watch her son grow and teach him the ways of your people so that we never wind up stuffed in quarantines again. Which is more than you ever did for her."

He released me. I blinked hard, seeing stars from the pain in my wrist. I pictured Aria, wherever she was, holding her pregnant belly and wishing she could be anywhere else in Sol. Leaving her with a nice, safe clan-family after she was born seemed like the better choice now. Everything seemed like the better choice.

"I..." I coughed and gathered my breath. "I won't kill Rylah for you. I can't."

"You think that's what this is about?" He laughed. No one joined him, not even Rin. "Rylah is no concern to us anymore. No, Malcolm Graves, you're taking me to your master on Undina. His and Venta's fleet is on our doorsteps, yet still, he hides from me."

"You really think you're going to kill Luxarn Pervenio?"

"Yes. And you and Luxarn's son are going to help me." He strode toward Basaam Venta's creation and slapped the fusion core chamber. "We're going to give Earth an M-Day they'll never forget!"

He was almost gleeful as the wheels of a terrible plot I couldn't imagine churned in his head. I felt a chill run up my spine. I'd dealt with more monsters and miscreants than I cared to remember. I could usually guess their next move after a second in the same room as them. Not Kale.

I think that was what scared me the most. Even more than the thought of losing Aria, Rylah, or Zhaff again, or an employer I'd dedicated my life's work to. Luxarn had done enough to earn the hatred of Ringers. Some conspiracy theorists even thought he and his father purposely spread sickness to take control after the Great Reunion. I'd never cared enough to ask, but he'd made his bed.

An M-Day to remember, though? A mysterious, life-changing engine invented by a genius and meant for a Departure Ark. Men were usually after the simple things. Credits. Power. Revenge. The stuff that drives a sane person. Kale was after more than any of that. He'd already executed Cora's murderer, and it wasn't enough. And killing Luxarn wouldn't be enough. How did you right the wrongs of half a century worth of abuse from Earthers in the head of a madman?

"What are you planning, Kale?" I asked, voice trembling.

"To free my people," he replied. "You and your daughter helped spark our revolution from this very cavern amongst our dead and dying. Now it's time we finish it, once and for all."

SEVENTEEN

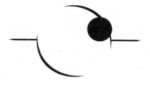

KALE

SCREENS DISPLAYING THE VICINITY OF SATURN FILLED THE entire command deck of the *Cora*, now parked in a new Darien hangar. She'd sustained minor cosmetic damage during Aria and Rylah's attempt at escaping, but nothing that couldn't be fixed now that all of my people were dedicated to building our fleet. The screens were tuned in to feeds from Pervenio Station, Enceladus, and Pandora—to all the moons and stations in the cosmic archipelago of which Titan was the beating heart.

The Earthers had arrived.

Only a few months after Madame Venta and Luxarn Pervenio's corporations merged and orchestrated the assassination of the majority of the Red Wing Company board, a fleet more massive than anyone could have imagined surrounded our ringed planet. They were prepared to end our insurrection forcefully, apparently even without the USF approving of it. Ships of every shape and size—transports and passenger liners converted into warships, fighters, and defense frigates—they bore the logos of the three most powerful corporations in Sol, now as one. The combined might of Venta Co., Pervenio Corp, and Red Wing Company was arrayed before us.

"We barely have half that amount," Rin said, gawking at the feeds. We stood alone in the *Cora,* my aunt and me, the last living members of a bloodline I'd just learned died off more than three centuries ago. A part of me knew for sure that Rylah wasn't lying when she told me.

"All because your sister wasn't able to handle a protest until we returned," I replied. Our plan to use our captives to slow their invasion was prepared, but nobody could have predicted how much Earth would send.

"A dozen more ships wouldn't have helped."

"You're afraid?" I asked.

"You aren't?"

I turned to her. She'd been irritated after Rylah was punished. I was too. It was one thing she'd never taught me about leading: that you'd inevitably be betrayed by some of the people closest to you and have to manage to keep fighting.

It didn't matter. Rin could hate me for what I was forced to do, but now, Titan needed me. Her body had been too battered by Zhaff to be of use.

"You've been preparing for this your entire life, Rin," I said. "A chance to make them cower. These are the people who did that to your face. Who beat you. Raped you."

"I didn't even know who Madame Venta was when that happened. I shouldn't be here fighting her. I should be with you when you look Luxarn Pervenio in the eyes."

"Without Rylah, you know I need you here defending our homeworld."

"Well, if you hadn't crippled her—"

"I still wouldn't trust her," I interrupted, stopping her before she joined them on my bad side. Then I studied her from head to toe. She still needed a cane to walk, and her face remained covered in bruises. Every time she inhaled, I could tell she was trying to hide a wince of pain.

"Besides, you're in no condition to fight if it comes to that," I said.

"I've fought through worse," she said, seething.

"It's done, Rin. You need to stay. You're the only person they'll believe is in charge."

"While you trust a Pervenio collector to deliver you to Luxarn unharmed? It's too risky."

"You said it yourself. We can't beat them in a straight-on battle."

"And we don't need to use Undina to fill Earth with terror. Sol has plenty of small asteroids. With Basaam's engine and the *Cora*'s weapons systems, they won't be able to stop them in time no matter how far they are."

"This is our one chance to finally get him, and you want to spare him?"

"I want you to live!" She clutched me by the arms, finally dropping the somber facade she'd been wearing since Rylah lost her hands. She regarded me with that same zeal she had when she recruited me. When she believed that I was the Trass who could lead us to freedom.

"We took his power," she said. "Took his gas trade and his cheap labor and his station. Why do you think he's hiding while he sends Madame Venta to handle us? He's already afraid, Kale. He's already lost."

"You call PerVenta Corp a loss?"

"I call it desperation," she said. "If you won't change your mind, at least leave Aria and your son behind here."

"You know I'll need her to control the collector."

"And if they catch you?" she asked.

"I have Luxarn's son as leverage," I said.

"I still don't like this."

"'My father should've let these inbred Ringers die off when we had the chance.'"

"What?"

"Those were Luxarn's words before he gave Sodervall the order to kill Cora and the others. Don't you see, we'll never be free until he's gone. Until I can look into the eyes of my people and tell them that the man responsible for decades of pain is gone, there will always be a part of us that still fears them."

Rin reached up slowly and ran her fingers through my hair, like my mother used to when I was young. In some ways, she'd become more like my mom than my real one. In every way, really.

"Killing him won't bring Cora back," she said. "It won't stop Aria from making her choice to run. It won't change anything. Trust me. I've killed enough men for all of Titan."

"I never thought I'd see this day. We have them right where we want them, and you want to show mercy?"

"It's not about mercy. Kale, listen to me."

"I'm done listening!" I shoved her away. "This is what you wanted when you pulled me off the *Piccolo* and left the others to die. No matter what the cost, that was what you taught me." I paused when I noticed the young guard who'd saved me from Zhaff in the hospital standing in the entrance of the cockpit. "What!" I yelled at him.

"There is a transmission from Madame Venta's flagship, the *Aphrodite*," he said.

"It's about time." I turned back to Rin. "Patch her through, and make it seem like I'm gone. This is it, Rin. You always begged me to stay strong, but now it's my turn. Mourn your sister's failure later and focus. They'll finally get what they deserve. If you fail here, it will all be for nothing. So don't."

I left while her tongue fidgeted behind the hole in her cheek, searching for a response. I hated seeing Rin appear anxious like my mother always did. Rylah's fate and Zhaff's beating had her flustered, but I needed my fearless aunt.

The moment I was around the corner, and she opened coms, however, she started to snap back into form like I knew she would. Even if she was drawing on me for her unquenchable fury, it worked. Nobody had endured Earther cruelty more than she had.

I stopped so I could overhear their conversation. This was all part of our plan. Madame Venta would be made to think I was missing; then Malcolm would contact Luxarn saying he and Zhaff had captured me. He'd deliver me right to Luxarn's doorstep, and once I was there, I'd give Earth and their corporations no choice but to give us everything I demanded back on Mars. Aria would see how foolish it was to think they'd chat around a table with my kind like they thought we were equals.

"Madame Venta, I wasn't expecting to see you so soon," Rin said. I could hear her trademark poise returning with every word, even if injuries left it difficult for her to speak.

"You?" Madame Venta questioned.

"Rin Trass."

"Yes, his aunt, I remember. Where is your *king*?"

"Busy."

Madame Venta guffawed. "We arrive, and he runs and hides. I must say I'm disappointed. I knew his confidence on Mars was all an act, but this?"

"You can deal with me."

"Oh, I plan to. I assume you've seen the blockade being established around the Ring? I'm here in the name of Earth to end this insurrection. You will lay down your arms, return your captives alive, including Basaam Venta, and relinquish control of the Ring. You tell your king that if you don't, we will have no choice but to take it by force."

"Is that all?" Rin said.

"You murdered two of my sons! You're lucky the USF wants

the Ring intact or that frozen husk of a moon you call your world would already be dust."

"You know they had it coming. Just like you do."

There was my venomous aunt again. I never thought I'd want to thank Madame Venta for helping pull her out of her grief. We needed Rin today.

"You damn Ringers think this is a game, don't you?" Madame Venta snarled. "Release your captives and stand down, or you'll be begging to be ashes."

"You want them back that bad, do you? We didn't realize. Prepare your ships; we'll send them right over." Rin cut coms and left the cockpit. She stopped and glared at me on her way by, fuming. "I don't have to agree with you, but never doubt me," she said. "If you want to go chasing Luxarn across Sol, I'll make sure Titan stands, but you and your son damn well better come back."

She continued by. I turned my head to conceal a smile.

"Are you coming?" she asked. "It's time for one last speech."

I took a moment to fill my lungs and focus my thoughts, then followed her out of the *Cora*. Hundreds of Titanborn filled the hangar outside, crammed into the space between ships in our own fleet. They were jury-rigged warships, slapped together from gas harvesters and ice haulers, all except for the peerless *Cora*. Basaam's Fusion Pulse Engine was strapped onto its bottom and being prepped for installation on Undina.

Viewscreens posted everywhere showed a portion of Pervenio Station where our captive Earthers were being packed into airlock cells, faces marked by dread. Only the emptied cells were loaded with explosives, something the Children of Titan had been quite adept at crafting out of spare parts.

Our thousands of hostages would be returned to Madame Venta in waves, enough to fill every single warship they'd brought to destroy us with. I never imagined sparing them would be what saved us, but I never expected to be betrayed either.

I stood at the top of the *Cora*'s ramp and gazed down upon my people. So many of them, warriors who rose to take back the Ring from our oppressors. No camera or audio receivers were aimed at me. After Rylah and Aria's betrayal, we couldn't risk anyone dispersing footage of me. This time, I got to speak directly to my people. No posturing. No lies.

"Titanborn!" I bellowed. They erupted into cheers, hoisting pulse-rifle into the air.

"Earth has come to wipe us out," I continued. "They've brought more ships than any of you have seen in a lifetime. But do you know who works those ships? Wage-slaves and mudstomper cowards. They fight for nothing. Dream of nothing. Not like us."

I surveyed the eager Titanborn faces in the crowd. They believed in what we were doing with every ounce of their souls. My people who had been tortured and beaten for half a century. Who'd had their families shoved into quarantines after Earthers spread their sicknesses and charged impossible fees for treatment. Only one among them looked solemn. At the far side of the hangar, my mother watched in silence.

"They don't understand what it means to believe," I said, staring straight at her. "What it means to know deep down in your heart that you belong somewhere. Titan is our home! Ice runs through our veins. It's time we show Earth what it means to live in fear. Stand with me this one last time, and I promise you all, we'll never know their sickness again. From ice to ashes!"

All of Darien shook as my people repeated those words over and over. Even the thunder constantly rumbling in Titan's stormy skies seemed quiet in comparison. I closed my eyes and raised my arms, encouraging them to get louder and louder. It felt like I was in a dream.

When I reopened them, the only thing that changed was that my mother was no longer watching.

"Prepare the fleet," I ordered Rin. "Don't engage. Let them panic after they receive the shipments, and I promise you, Madame Venta's orders will be ignored. Good luck."

I turned to re-board the *Cora*, but Rin seized my wrist. "Come back to us, Kale," she whispered into my ear, so close that the smooth surface of her scars brushed my neck. "You hear me? Both of you, come back."

I answered with only a grunt, then entered the *Cora* and sealed the ramp. The survivors and healthy members from the squadron of soldiers who'd accompanied us to Mars awaited in the cockpit. Six Titanborn, fully armored. The elite crew of soldiers selected by Gareth prepared to die for their world if it came to it.

"Lord Trass, as soon as the hangar is cleared, we're prepared to leave," the youngest of them addressed me, bowing his blonde head. I still had no idea what his name was despite how many times he'd saved me.

"Excellent. All we need now is our pilot." I stalked through the corridors of my ship, toward the hall of sleep pods that made a journey across the vastness of space feel like seconds. Four of them were filled, Basaam, Malcolm Graves, Zhaff, and Aria. The Cogent somehow clung to life after wounds that should have made him bleed out, though what was left of him was barely human.

I drew myself over Aria's pod, where I'd had her placed out of sight after our last interaction. She slept peacefully inside. The mother of my child. Our ambassador. I once thought she could help me forget Cora, but all I could think about when I saw her now was the woman she could never live up to.

I tapped the control panel, and Aria's pod opened with a hiss. Cold steam poured out, and the gelatinous substance formed to her body liquefied and drained away. Her eyes snapped open, in a state of shock, until they fell upon me.

"What is this?" she whispered, voice still ragged from being under. She tried to sit up and reach me on her own, but I wrapped my arm around her back and helped her out. Her stomach grew more from our child every day, and until he was born, I couldn't have her overexert herself.

"Get in the cockpit," I demanded. "We're leaving."

She clutched her stomach and backed away. The sudden movements made her visibly nauseated, and she hunched over the pod and somehow held back from vomiting. "We're not going anywhere with you," she groaned.

I drew my pulse pistol and aimed it through the viewport on Malcolm's sleep pod. "You're no longer our ambassador, Aria. You're going to take us to Luxarn Pervenio, or you'll watch your father be spaced the same way his people do it."

She threw herself in front of Malcolm's sleep pod. "This is between us!" she said. "Leave him out of it."

"It's too late for that." I easily pulled her away with my powered armor on and pushed her into the waiting arms of one of my nameless guards. "I want eyes on her at all times," I ordered.

"You don't have to do this, Kale!" Aria screamed. "Just let us go!"

"Let's go, Earther-lover," he sneered as he prodded her along as she continued to scream.

My crewmates aboard the *Piccolo* once called me that because I didn't like to start trouble with the captain or the rest of the Earther crew members. I wasn't sure that I'd even recognize that quiet, cowardly Ringer I used to be in the mirror anymore. It seemed like a lifetime ago.

EIGHTEEN

MALCOLM

Tᴛɪᴛᴀɴʙᴏʀɴ ɢᴜᴀʀᴅs ᴅɪʀᴇᴄᴛᴇᴅ ᴍᴇ ᴛʜʀᴏᴜɢʜ ᴛʜᴇ *Cᴏʀᴀ*. I stumbled after every one of their shoves, my artificial leg all that kept me from collapsing. They snickered. My hands were cuffed behind my back; otherwise, I would've smacked the smirks off their skinny Ringer faces.

They dumped me onto the command deck. Then, before I could manage a breath, they heaved me up and into one of the seats along the back wall. Once locked acceleration restraints over my chest, they uncuffed me.

"Glad you could finally join us, Malcolm," Kale said. He sat in the copilot's chair. Beside him, flying the *Cora*, was Aria, looking about ready to pop she was so pregnant. The control console had been repaired after Zhaff shot it. It was nowhere near as sleek anymore, but Aria seemed able to handle it.

"Aria," I rasped, "are you okay?"

She went to look back, but the guard directly behind her straightened her head. He held a pulse pistol against the back of her head.

"I'm fine, Dad," she said, unable to contain her frustration.

"Where the hell are you taking us?" I said.

"I told you," Kale said. "We're going on a little family trip."

The *Cora*'s thrusters kicked in, and we shot forward into Titan's stormy sky. Lightning flashed all around us. The ship rattled and whined, battered by an atmosphere so dense, a human being could fly in it. G-forces shoved me against the back on my chair, crushing my arms behind me. It felt like they were going to pop out of my shoulder sockets. All the aches in my torso flared up, worse than ever...and then we were through.

Weightlessness took hold. I finally felt like I could breathe again, but what I saw in space immediately stole the air back from my lungs. Dozens of ships emerged alongside us, with lights from more winking all around Saturn's moons and stations —everything that comprised the cosmological archipelago known as the Ring. The planet's icy disks slashed across the corner of the viewport, wrapping a planet swirling with more colors than an Earthside rainbow. People said Saturn was the most stunning sight in all of Sol, but I was hardly able to pay it any attention.

More ships hovered beyond the Ring's most distant moons. The sunlight blooming along their flanks revealed the colors of Pervenio Corp, Venta Co., and Red Wing Company—all now under one banner. And as the *Cora* banked away from Saturn to face them, I realized just how many there were. They filled the entire breadth of my vision. Space fleets were the stuff of fiction. Sol had never known an interstellar war before because the USF was too focused on expansion to let any rival factions rise that would require one.

Collectors, like I once had been, ended conflicts before they began or fought them in the shadows. Then Kale rewrote the book. Now I gazed upon an armada clearly intended for one purpose—to take back the Ring by any means necessary.

"Are you really planning to fight that?" I asked him.

"Relax, old man," Kale replied. "Aria, open up coms to Rin and listen in."

Aria hesitated for a moment as she too got lost admiring the size of the Earther fleet. Maybe that's the wrong word for it, but for a girl from the sewers of Mars, it was a hell of a thing to see. Doesn't matter how many missions I smuggled her on around Sol.

"Aria," Kale repeated, cross.

The guard nudged her in the back of the head with the gun. She shook her head and focused, fingers flurrying across the controls.

"We're reading an awful lot of movement down there, Rin Trass," Madame Venta said over the coms. "Any closer and we'll begin targeting."

"You wanted your people back," Rin replied. "Here you go."

Suddenly, all the Titanborn ships stopped moving. "Engage radar jamming, mask our heat signature, and take us in slow," Kale whispered to Aria, as if anybody outside the command deck could hear him.

Aria did as he asked without question, even though I could tell she wanted to be on the *Cora* even less than I did. I'd raised a smart girl, somehow. Not impulsive like the king sitting beside her. We decelerated and remained cruising straight toward the heart of the blockade.

"Are you going to tell me what the plan is before or after we slam into them?" she asked.

Kale pointed through the viewport, toward Saturn's rings, where I recognized the tiny moon named Pan into which Pervenio Station was built. A cluster of rectangular metallic containers zipped through space away from it, with glass on one side reflecting light from the sun. Then more shot out from Pervenio Station in another direction as it spun. Toward every corner of the Ring, shadows of the cells Sodervall used to space so many blocked out the stars.

"Look at them," Kale marveled. "Earthers neatly packaged and shipped back to their own people like all the shiny products they waste their lives trying to buy."

"You're handing them over just like that?" I asked.

His lack of an answer revealed enough. The Children of Titan had been crafty devils since the first time I encountered them in New London, Earth, almost a year back. All I could do now was sit back and watch.

The *Cora*'s unparalleled stealth systems kept us in the dark as we approached, a short distance behind a cluster of cells which had been shot out much earlier to reach so far. It was tough to see over such a great distance, but through the translucency on the nearest one, I didn't notice any movement from people within. A fancifully designed frigate with swooping wings that served no real purpose in space glided toward one. The trademark Venta overlapping **V**s were covered by the name of the vessel—the *Aphrodite*.

Its airlock extended after its thrusters fired in reverse, latching on to one of the containers. Shadows scurried through the semi-translucent tube of the airlock, the sparks of fusion cutters flickering against the blackness of space. The moment they breached the cell, it blew. The side of the frigate was split open, silvery metal shards slashing the sleek hull.

More blasts simultaneously went off throughout the Earther fleet as they attempted to open the first wave of cells. It was like one of the fireworks displays over New London on M-Day.

"Y... you're killing them all?" Aria said, incredulous.

"No," Kale replied. "We just forgot to mention that a few of them are empty."

A handful more blasts boomed in the darkness, sending the Earther fleet into disarray. And that was when I realized what happens when a wealthy aristocrat who'd lived a privileged life leads an army against people that have spent their entire lives fighting to survive. Kale saw their fleet and didn't see an insurmountable mass of alloy and weapons ordnance. He saw another scrap to claw his way out of.

The space between the Earther and Titan fleets was promptly filled by a screen of debris and Pervenio Corp cells half-filled with real people and half-filled with explosives. Madame Venta couldn't fire upon the Titan fleet at the risk of killing all the captives, and they couldn't fly past the cells to engage; otherwise, all of Kale's hostages would be left suffocate.

And Kale wasn't done yet. Clinging to the backs of those cells that remained intact were more Ringer soldiers in their powered armor. Raiding parties, ready to give their lives to further confuse the enemy while the Earthers hid in the safety of their expensive ships. They pushed off across space in squadrons, gripping hands and soaring toward the crippled vessels in the Earther fleet, now already breached by explosives for them to invade with ease.

Madame Venta's ship, the *Aphrodite*, was able to divert power to its impulse drives and fall back to avoid them, but it was all too little too late. Titan was going to make them lose all taste for battle without firing a single missile.

"You son of a bitch, Trass!" Madame Venta's screams directed at Rin echoed throughout the command deck. "I will kill each and every one of you, do you hear me, you bitch? We won't leave until you all starve."

"I hope your people don't miss us too much," Rin answered. "Have fun cleaning up *our* mess for once."

"All captains, fall back and expand the blockade perimeter! Disperse medical evacs to each cell, but for Earth's sake, probe them before breaching."

Their coms cut out, and then Rin opened a direct line to us.

"You're clear, Kale. It'll take them weeks to regroup, and they'll think twice about engaging with thousands of civilians on board their ships. We'll send the second wave out the moment things start clearing up and keep them on their toes with raids."

"They don't get near Titan or any other colony, Rin," Kale said. "Is that clear?"

"They'll never want to come back. Advance teams have begun invading their damaged ships throughout the Ring. They'll space as many mudstompers as they can."

"Make the survivors see it."

"They will," Rin said. "From ice to ashes."

"From ice to ashes."

Kale ended the transmission. He leaned back and drew a deep, satisfied breath. I knew the type. I'd released a few of my own after a successful mission that took a fair bit of thinking to solve. None of what we were witnessing was Rin's idea this time. Kale Trass had come into his own, and we had front row seats to his handiwork. To all the flashes throughout the Ring of gunfire and more empty containers filling the void with shrapnel.

"The damn fools," I marveled with him. I couldn't help but be impressed. "They should have never come here."

"And Rin didn't think it would work," Kale said. "Aria, take us past the blockade at full burn."

Hearing him stole back her attention from the chaos. She leaned forward and took to the controls, and we sped ahead, the pressure of acceleration again constricting me. It wasn't like she had much choice except to listen.

We grew close enough to the Venta fleet to be within firing range of PDCs. Aria piloted the *Cora* masterfully, weaving around debris and drifting ships and cells. We rolled under a frigate with failing engines, then darted up over a chunk of shrapnel large enough to cleave us in two.

It wasn't the best time to go all proud father, but it was preferable to harping on Kale claiming another victory. Madame Venta's lines were completely broken. Half the ships we passed were speeding away while others drifted, unsure what to do. They were captains of commerce and leisure vessels, not commanders. Their fleet still more than doubled Kale's, even with the damage, and boasted more advanced weaponry, but I was damn certain they'd push no further. It was like they had learned nothing from when Pervenio Corp was ousted from the Ring in the blink of an eye. Totally unprepared.

The last row of retreating PerVenta Corp ships passed overhead, leaving only star-speckled blackness ahead of us. No targeting alerts chirped from the controls. No coms came through warning us to fall back lest we be fired upon.

"We're through the blockade," Aria exhaled, her shoulders unknotting.

"Are you sure?" Kale said.

"We're not dust, are we?"

"Watch your tone while addressing Lord Trass, traitor," the guard behind her growled.

"Listen to him, Aria," I said. "We wouldn't want to hurt his feelings. The kid can't even handle being broken up with."

Kale unfastened his restraints and pulled his weightless body vertical using the ceiling. "Set a course for Undina that takes us as far from Mars and Jupiter as possible," he said. "Unless you'd both like to be turned to dust."

I laughed. "You're really going to go after Luxarn? I knew you were suicidal, but if this is all the men you brought to break in there, then you're crazier than I thought. He's buried under rock, surrounded by Cogents, and oh, did I mention it's only a stone's throw from Earth and the anti-meteor defensive matrix they wasted billions of credits building on Luna?"

Kale turned to face me, beaming. When I had first met him

in person, he seemed conflicted about all the death that followed him, but a man who takes pleasure in the killing part of a fight is the kind who belongs in a cell most. I'd learned that from Director Sodervall a long time ago when I was just a lowly collector trainee.

"Something funny, kid?" I asked.

"Just your choice of words. I only need one man to get in." He drew his weightless body down the cockpit. "Follow me."

I watched him go by and turned my attention to Aria, busy entering coordinates for Undina. "Aria," I said. I could tell she wanted to look back, but it's tough to defy a pistol against the back of your head. She was looking out for two people now—another illegitimate child to keep the immaculate Graves blood-line thriving into the uncertain future.

"Aria, you just keep us from being shot down," I said. "I'll find a way to get us out of this. We'll work together for once."

She nodded half-heartedly.

"Try it, Earther," the guard at her back sneered. "I'm begging you."

"Your future king is in her belly," I said. "You really think I believe that you're going to blow her head off? Damn Ringers. No wonder I always fleeced your kind in poker before you ruined Titan."

"If she tries anything, we have orders to kill her and pull Lord Trass's child out ourselves before he's due on M-day."

Aria swallowed and squeezed her eyelids shut. The Ringer got more comfortable aiming at the back of her head. I'd never wanted to snap someone's neck so badly.

"Why didn't you just leave me behind and run, Aria?" I said. "You and Rylah would have made it easy. Zhaff never would have caught up."

"I'm not you," she answered. The twitches of a smile

touched the corner of her lips, which made me feel better. Kale hadn't sucked all the fight out of her yet.

"Thank Earth for that. You remember that job years back when that lunatic tried holding you hostage?"

"Which one?"

I chuckled. "Who got you out of all of them without a scratch?"

"Lord Trass said to follow him, now." A pulse rifle slid up against my side, and I turned to see another pale-faced Ringer floating in the command deck's exit. "Move."

"All right, all right. Keep your pants on." I used the rungs lining the ceiling to propel myself out of the room, thankful for zero-g providing my battered body a rest. "Keep flying, Aria, you hear me? Keep flying."

The moment I was out of the command deck and back into the main sleep pod cabin, Kale slapped a familiar hand terminal into my palm.

"What's this?" I asked. "Need someone to teach you how to use Earther tech?"

"You never stop, do you?" he said. "Even after you've lost. No wonder Aria would never come right out and say what a piece of mudstomping trash you were."

"Just trying to live up to my reputation."

"And that's exactly why I need you." Kale pushed off the wall and grabbed hold of an empty sleep pod. Two of his men helped him inside. "You're going to contact Undina one last time and tell your boss that you captured me and are on your way. You broke through Madame Venta's blockade so that he could get the credit for bringing the self-proclaimed king of Titan to justice, just like he deserves."

"Luxarn Pervenio didn't become the richest man in Sol because he's stupid, kid. You really think he's going to believe that?"

"A Pervenio man, through and through, you would never lie to him." He grabbed hold of another sleep pod and drew himself closer. Within, I saw the pale, cyber-enhanced face of my former partner. "Tell him you saved his son too. How would he know that you once tried to murder him? Or hid a daughter from him that became my ambassador?"

"You really thought of it all, didn't you?"

"Not until you fell into my lap."

I lay my hand over Zhaff's sleep pod. He was still now, though I couldn't stop picturing him squirming toward me, unable to understand why I'd done what I did. "Is he alive?" I asked, my voice catching.

"We patched him up for this," Kale said. "Though I wouldn't call whatever Luxarn made him alive."

"He's younger than you are, kid. Just let him go and deal with me!"

"You know, I thought about leaving him on the *Cora* to die. Then I realized what a mercy that would be after what Luxarn did to him. I can't even imagine how much it cost to bring him back to life after you put a bullet in his head. Enough to feed every one of my people for a year, I'd imagine."

"Whatever plans you have for him, he doesn't deserve it," I said. "He doesn't know any better; he's only ever tried to belong."

"Well, he picked the wrong side."

"We don't get to pick our fathers!"

Kale's gaze listed off toward the command deck. "True enough," he said. He then regarded his men. "Close me in and watch him. If he tries anything, you know what to do."

"I saw the way you looked at her back on Mars," I said. "Whatever she did to hurt you, I believe you wouldn't hurt her."

"Do you really want to test that?"

His men closed him in before I could answer, and I found

myself under the aim of pulse-rifles from every angle. I glanced down at the hand terminal he'd given me. How does the most famous rebel in post-Meteorite history break into a clandestine facility buried within an asteroid so close to Earth and filled with elite operatives? He gets invited in.

"Let's go," one of the guards ordered. "Lord Trass says you need to act confident."

I sighed. "Shouldn't be tough." I activated the device, navigated to Luxarn Pervenio's direct contact, and set it to video-call him. It took about a minute for service to hook into the nearest laser com relay in Sol, then it went through.

"Undina Mining Facility," someone in the support office answered, surprising me. A finely groomed man in formal attire appeared on the screen. Everything to make the mine appear like a proper enterprise. Apparently, after Martelle Station, Luxarn had either changed his direct contact information or was no longer open to it. Either that or a USF investigation into what happened had him hiding certain aspects about his business more strictly.

"I need to speak with your boss," I said.

"The foreman is on vacation, but if you'd like to leave a message."

"Not that boss. Luxarn Pervenio."

"I'm sorry, you seem to have the wrong contact information. The Undina Mining Collective is merely a subsidiary of Pervenio Corporation. Let me transfer you to the Pervenio Corporation headquarters on Earth."

"Tell him." I drew a deep breath and exhaled slowly. "Tell him that Malcolm Graves is on his way with a royal gift."

The man's brow furrowed. He turned away from the camera and typed something into his terminal. His eyes went wide momentarily; then he composed himself and turned back to me. Luxarn always had a knack for hiring professionals, unlike those sloppy bastards at Venta Co.

"I'll transfer you right away," he said.

The screen blinked, and Luxarn appeared on the display almost immediately. He looked worse than ever. Not only unkempt but like he hadn't even showered in days.

"Graves, is that you again?" he questioned, nearly tripping over his words like some crazy hermit living beyond the habitable strings on Earth. I'd met a few. The kind of bearded loon who lives in a shack and still believes that Earth was never almost destroyed.

"In the flesh, sir," I said. The words came out meekly. Out of the corner of my eye, I saw one of Kale's hounds level his rifle at my head and then into the cockpit. It wasn't because I was nervous. Seeing Luxarn so broken, the man who for most of my life could enter a room and have all the ladies swooning and all the wealthy ready to pry open their credit accounts... It put things into a certain perspective. Kale was right. Luxarn appeared in a place to believe anything I had to say.

"By Earth, I thought they finally got you on Martelle after Zhaff cleared your path," he said.

"You know I'm a tough son of a bitch to kill."

"That's for sure. Graves, I... I'm sorry I didn't have chance to let you know that he pulled through his coma with the help of a new cerebral implant we're developing alongside Venta Co. I sent him after Kale on Titan and told him to keep a lookout for you as well. He nearly got Trass, but I haven't heard from him since he found out Kale's little secret."

"That Ar... the ambassador is pregnant with his child. Yeah, I know. About Zha—"

"Where are you, Graves? Are you still near Titan? Madame Venta informs me that our assault has been delayed by Kale's treachery already. I swear, it's impossible to find good help these days. I told her not to rush in, but you can never trust a Venta."

"The situation doesn't look pretty," I said. "I passed it on my way to you aboard the *Cora*. Zhaff... uh... he broke me out of my cell, and we stole it."

Luxarn laughed and clapped his hands. "Did I not tell you that you two made a formidable team?"

"You did."

"And where is my boy?"

"With me." I rotated the hand terminal and showed him Zhaff's face in the sleep pod. My chest tightened as I held it there to push the lie through.

"Is he..."

"He's stable," I said, "but he was injured in the fighting, so I put him under to recover. Without him, it never would have been possible, but, sir...I have him."

"What?" Luxarn asked.

"Kale Trass." I angled the hand terminal to show Kale inside of his sleep pod, eyes closed and tranquil. The thing wasn't even on, but the young king was growing into quite the showman. "They're trying to keep it secret that he went missing, but that's why his aunt is handling all of their defenses."

Luxarn's features brightened. "Is he dead?"

"No." I slapped the side of the pod. "Just fast asleep."

"Madame Venta did say he wouldn't speak with her. She doesn't know?"

"She doesn't. With all due respect, sir, I don't trust Venta scum, even if they're your partners now. Especially not after seeing how she nearly got your fleet destroyed in minutes."

"You did the right thing, Graves. The finest collector there ever was! I knew you couldn't stay retired." He laughed glee-fully again, and a bit of color finally came to his cheeks. There were even hints of a smile, though, with all the cosmetic work done to his face sagging from lack of upkeep, it was difficult to tell.

"What are your orders, sir?" I asked.

"Bring him to Undina immediately and tell nobody," he said. "I help provide Venta with the largest fleet ever assembled, and she fails before she even started. Yet one Pervenio man will topple the Trass family for good. You'll be remembered forever for this, Graves. I'll have a damn statue of you erected in the heart of New London myself."

"I don't need any of that. Kale went too far."

"I won't accept no this time. Together, you, me, and Zhaff are going to rebuild everything they stole from us. Madame Venta will be booted from her own company for this fiasco, and I'll name you in her place. The second richest man in Sol; how does that sound? We'll rewrite history together."

"It sounds great, sir. Just sit tight. I'm on my way."

I switched off the hand terminal, unable to bear talking to him any longer. Seeing him hell-bent on revenge was one thing, but falling headfirst into a trap was another. All the corporate alliances and anti-USF moves were a façade. That shrewd, world-eating businessman Sol knew was already dead, and Kale hadn't even pulled the trigger yet. It would be a mercy killing, just like for Zhaff after what Luxarn made him into.

I tossed the device to one of the guards. "Happy?"

Kale popped open the lid of his sleep pod, and his men hauled him out. Then they poked me in the back with their pulse-rifles.

"Well done, Collector," Kale said. "Now get in." His man seized me.

"This is never going to work, kid," I said, shaking them off me. "You're going to get us all killed."

"It already has worked."

He pushed off toward the command deck, and the lit end of

a shock baton prodded me in the back before I had a chance to do anything else. My body convulsed, ten-thousand volts coursing through me. I continued to twitch even after the guards stuffed me into the pod and hooked me up, unable to scream at them for fear of vomiting.

Then they closed me in. The worst part about it other than the silence wasn't that I knew Kale was right, but that he was also smart enough to put me under. Aria had to remain at the ship's controls, considering her condition and the warlike state of Sol, but with my brain shut off, I wouldn't have any time to think of a way to get us out of this.

I'd have to improvise in the thick of it, the way I used to when I was a collector. No more scheming. If I was going to clean up this mess, I'd have to be the one thing I feared was no longer possible. Myself.

Malcolm Graves. The finest collector there ever was... in another lifetime, maybe.

NINETEEN

KALE

More than a month on a ship with nothing to do had never gone faster. It was my second time being invited to the core planets of Sol, only this time, our host already thought I was defeated. And this time, I would *actually* make a difference.

We were right on schedule. It was M-Day when the tiny, metal-rich asteroid known as Undina appeared through the *Cora*'s viewport, drifting harmlessly in orbit. Beyond it, Earth grew closer and closer. I'd never seen the blue and brown orb of their half-drowned planet in person before. Stories said it was once lush and green all over, but now there was a single, vast ocean with spots of land after the Meteorite caused tides to rise, and dark clouds swirling all over. Offworlders who immigrated to Titan always talked about how beautiful Earth still was from space, but to me, it paled in comparison to Saturn—to those rare days when Titan's stormy skies broke, and its Ring slashed across the frozen horizon.

Today, celebrations would run rampant on the world that infected my people for so long. Venta Co. was set to unveil the designs for the new Departure Ark that would be sent to the stars in four years after being unanimously selected for the honor—I'm sure our attack was used by them to build sympathy. Their people would see it and dream of new worlds to spread their sickness to. Only Venta Co.'s CEO remained busy blockading the Ring and cleaning up the mess Rin made of their fleet and Earth's hostages. And the man who invented the engines meant to power that Ark lay asleep in my ship, with the first working version of them carried by my ship.

"We're here, Rin," I said over the *Cora*'s coms. It'd been days since Aria could pilot the ship. Exhaustion and pregnancy forced her into the ship's reconstructed medical bay. Since she was the only doctor on board, I had to trust her when she said she was on the verge of giving birth, though I made sure guards were always nearby.

"Is it everything you hoped for?" Rin said.

"It's so much smaller than I expected," I replied.

"Your father said the same before he landed there."

"And then their gravity crushed him. Even their world is designed to destroy us."

"So is ours, Kale," Rin said. "One hand outside and it freezes off."

With the threat of Madame Venta's armada neutralized for the foreseeable future, there was time for her to scold me again over Rylah. On the eve of our victory... just like a mother.

"How is she?" I asked.

"Alive," she said. "How's Aria?"

"Alive."

"She should be here, you know. Your son should be born on Titan, like we all were."

"We're not having this conversation again. I need her here."

"No, Kale. You needed Basaam Venta and an asteroid. You didn't—" She sighed. "I'm sorry, Kale."

"For what?"

"For showing you that violence was the only way we could change anything. And for waiting until now to tell you."

"Have you been spending time with my mother?"

"I'm not joking," she said.

"The only thing you showed me was what needed to be done. Our people need to know that Luxarn can never hurt them again, just like they needed to know that we shouldn't ever betray our people for an Earther."

I switched off the coms without a goodbye. If a swift victory over Venta Co. wasn't enough to cheer her up over what happened to Rylah—a sister she once had to beg to help her own people, according to Rin—then nothing would. She'd done her part to help deceive Luxarn Pervenio. Now it was my turn.

I removed my restraints and let the *Cora* continue on its automated course for Undina. I drifted out of the cockpit. The youngest of my men who'd saved me so many times noticed me from the galley, eyelids teetering on the verge of sleep.

"Is everything all right, Lord Trass?" he asked.

I glanced past him at the other Titanborn struggling to stay awake after a month-long voyage. Six of them. Titanborn on their second mission to the inner Sol system. I didn't know any of their names. They'd been handpicked by Gareth and Rin before we went to Mars. Now one of those two would never see a free Titan, and the other seemed to be losing her will to fight for one.

This time, I was alone.

"We're here," I said. "Gather everyone and get to the compartment in my quarters."

The smuggling compartment Luxarn had installed in what was supposed to be his ship was built to mask anything within from thermal and other scanners, so that he could never miss an opportunity to move something valuable. Gareth had used it to sneak out into New Beijing, grab the ex-collector Trevor Cross, and start all of this. Greed would be Luxarn's downfall just like the rest of his people.

My guard bowed and left to rouse the others. I went in the other direction, toward the med bay. Aria had her arms and legs tied to the table so she didn't float away. Her eyes were closed, a tuft of curly red hair covering one of them. Her belly was so full, it looked like it was ready to burst and send my son hurtling into existence.

I drew a deep breath, remembering how Gareth looked in an older version of the room before being sucked out to Space, then drifted in as quietly as possible. I drew myself along the table. I reached out slowly to rub Aria's bulging stomach, then stopped. She needed her rest. After Malcolm and I entered Undina and turned it into a projectile, she would be the only pilot capable of keeping Earth's defensive nuclear arsenal off us. I leaned as close as I could, until I could hear every one of her raspy breaths.

"Titan was never meant to be lived on, but it's our world," I whispered. "When I'm done, you won't have to fight for it any longer. Be a better king for them than I was." I planted a gentle kiss on Aria's stomach, then turned to leave.

"Kale," she whispered.

I didn't stop. I couldn't stop. She'd betrayed me, forced me to use her as a hostage to reach this point. I knew now that she could never be one of us, no matter who she carried. Her greatest gift to Titan would be to ensure that my heir had an immune system strong enough to resist whatever earthborn disease our enemies might ever throw at him to try and take control, like Luxarn Pervenio had done before.

I returned to the sleep pods. My guards were busy heaving Basaam Venta out of his. Naturally, the spoiled Earther puked almost immediately.

"Mr. Trass," he said groggily. "What is the meaning of this? Where are we now?"

"Hide him with you in the smuggling compartment and keep him quiet," I addressed my youngest guard. "The moment we have control of the station, he will instruct you on how and where to install the engines on the asteroid's surface."

"Yes, Lord Trass."

"And take Aria with you," I said.

"But, sir, she—"

"Can't register on their scanners either. Luxarn will be surrounded by his Cogents. We can't risk anyone other than me, Zhaff, and the collector being spotted until the time is right."

"Of course, Lord Trass. We'll make sure she's comfortable. From ice to ashes."

I nodded. Then I signaled Malcolm's pod to open. The intravenous tubes that kept him healthy while he was under slid out, but he didn't move. At least, not his body. I noticed his eyelid twitch, like he was struggling to keep them closed. He was waiting to catch me off guard.

I removed Malcolm's own pulse pistol from the holster on my hip. He sprang awake suddenly, fingers grasping for my throat but squeezing only air. I'd already slid around the side of the pod and had the gun pressed up under his chin.

"I couldn't help myself," he said mirthfully, voice muffled by a sanitary mask.

"Get out," I demanded.

"Are we there already?"

"Get out!"

"For Earth's sake, give a man a moment after he wakes up from one of those things. I hate going under." He rubbed his eyes, the same way his daughter did whenever she got up. "Guess I should thank you, though. It's like sleeping in a coffin, but better than months with no company except space. I'm guessing Aria isn't talking with you much anymore, and you don't seem to even know the names of any of the others."

My tongue tripped over a response. Aria used to say something similar when she was discussing interplanetary travel before we went to Mars. She'd said a wise man told it to her. Apparently, that wise man was the haggard excuse for a collector floating in front of me.

"So what's the plan, kid?" he asked. "We going to go strolling in, side by side?"

"You're going to land inside the hangar, load me into that pod, and roll me into Luxarn's office. Right past his Cogents."

"And what's to keep me from giving you a kick out the airlock?"

"I've rigged Zhaff's sleep pod to poison him with oxygen if I hit this application on my hand terminal. Aria will be surrounded by my best men. If I die in there, she'll never meet her child."

"I figured. Using innocent people as collateral is getting pretty easy for you by now, huh?"

"She's not innocent."

Malcolm rolled his shoulders. "Few really are. Doesn't mean they deserve to die."

"Says the man who's pulled this trigger on more people than anyone on Titan."

"Well, I'm pretty sure I don't deserve to be alive," Malcolm said. "Yet here I am, because of her. You want Luxarn, I'll get you in, but you make me a promise."

"You're not really in a position, Collector."

"It's getting pretty damn clear I'm not getting out of this alive, kid. I'm too old. Too damn tired. All I'm asking is that you promise me, as a fucking man, that no matter what you do with me, Aria lives."

"She betrayed me," I said.

"Take her child then. Give him a crown. But you either treat her right or you send her somewhere where she can live the way she deserves."

I stared into his eyes, dumbfounded. This credit-hungry, Earther collector—the vilest of their kind—was genuinely willing to give his life for a daughter whose existence he made a living hell growing up. It wasn't something Earthers tended to do.

"Is that all?" I said.

"No. Once you're done with whatever you plan to do to Luxarn, Zhaff dies painlessly." He pointed to the Cogent sleeping soundly in his pod. "Whatever his father made him into, he was better off dead, where nobody will see him as the freak he isn't."

Malcolm stuck out his hand, fingers trembling. His lips might've been too, but they were covered by a sanitary mask. "You promise me, kid," he said, voice shaking. "Or I swear you may as well put the bullet in both of us now because you'll never get inside that rock. I get you to Luxarn and back. They go free."

For some reason as I continued to stare, I saw myself in the Earther. He was five times more wrinkled and had hair as gray as Titan's sky, but I did. I remembered standing in the Darien Quarantine visiting my sick mother, separated by a screen of glass that seemed impossibly thick. I remembered when the Children of Titan made me an offer to help them smuggle something onto the *Piccolo* in exchange for her treatment. I'd uprooted my entire life for that chance to save her, and it led me to the only night I'd ever shared with Cora, then to being recruited by Maya and Gareth. It led me to everything.

Maybe our revolution really did mean something if it could get a man like Malcolm Graves to take that same risk. To put another's life before his instead of credits, or tech, or glory. I slowly reached out and grasped his hand, my long fingers wrapping it halfway back around.

"You have my word," I said.

"I hope it's worth a damn," he said.

"We aren't Earthers."

"No, but you're human. And I've seen enough of them. Whatever you did to Rylah—"

"She deserved. She betrayed her people to save an Earther and an offworlder. At least Aria did it to save her father. Your people don't usually understand what it's like having only one family. We do. We've had our parents, and brothers and sisters, and nothing else for our entire lives."

"You messed Sol up pretty good, Kale Drayton," Malcolm said. "But that's fair enough." He gave my hand one last hard shake, then released it. "Look at me, shaking hands with a king."

"Your people named me that, you know."

"I know. Just like yours named you Trass. All that's ever mattered is what people believe, isn't that true?"

My brow furrowed. He smirked like he knew a secret. Had Rylah told him the truth about the Trass bloodline? That it had died off more than three centuries ago with him and endured in name only.

"*Cora*," a voice announced from the cockpit. My heart momentarily leaped into my throat until the person went on. "You are approaching the Undina Mining Facility. Please confirm your identity, and we will open the Sector D loading dock, which has been prepped for your arrival."

"Time to go meet the kingmaker, then, Lord Trass." Malcolm bowed his head as low as he could as he uttered the name. Then he drew himself along the ceiling back toward the command deck to answer the call. He stopped by the entry.

I watched him go, all smiles and straight shoulders. Confident, like a collector should be, or resigned to the fact that he was never going to get off Undina alive. He was probably right, just like he was right about my lineage. It didn't matter if he knew the truth about Trass. My people would never believe an Earther over me.

I was their king the moment I killed Pervenio Director Sodervall. I was their voice when I stood before the USF Assembly and refused to be kicked aside. And I would set them free when I made Earth understand the fear we'd lived our lives under.

That was what made me a Trass.

M-Day had arrived on Earth, and it would be one to remember.

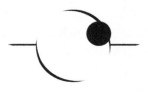

TWENTY

MALCOLM

"Show your hands," an emotionless Cogent ordered the moment I stepped off the *Cora*. It felt good to have gravity tugging on my weary body again, however weak the force was on such a small asteroid. It reminded me I wasn't a corpse yet. Resting for the journey had my artificial leg feeling less like a dead weight I dragged along with my broken body. I even had my own F-3000 collector-issued Pervenio pulse pistol dangling from my hip, a collector's duster on, and no sanitary mask covering my mouth.

Just like old times... almost.

Three Cogents were waiting, weapons ready, yellow eye lenses gyrating as they focused on me. Their builds were all different, though each appeared as pale and staid as Zhaff. Luxarn's lethal army of monotonous servants, plucked off the streets like his own mentally troubled son to give their lives meaning. That always was Luxarn's greatest talent, turning shit into shine.

They strode toward me, and one peered directly into my face. They were trained to look through a man, to read their subtle facial tics and cues to discern whether they were lying. I knew as they scrutinized me that Kale's and my path to Luxarn would stop right there if they noticed anything off.

Zhaff was a master. Nearly impossible to deceive, but one look-over and this Cogent cleared me. They couldn't compare to Luxarn's son. Either that or they, like Varus, had already been influenced by Luxarn to trust the best collector there ever was.

Another examined the sleep pod I rolled out into the hangar and found the boy king of Titan fast asleep inside with a sanitary mask on. That part was real. Kale couldn't wear his armor if it was going to appear authentic, so I had had the pleasure of looking down on his scrawny Ringer body as he got in. Watching him squirm as I switched the sleep pod on was the most enjoyable thing I'd experienced since Martian nightlife, but it was the only way. He hadn't left me much of a choice but to go along with it either. For all his bravado, he might not have had it in him to hurt Aria, but his men would. They were loyal to a fault, just like the Cogents inviting me in.

"Where is Zhaff Pervenio?" one of the Cogents asked. I took note of the fact that he used Zhaff's real identity.

"Still in stasis on the ship," I said. Again, lying to a Cogent was easier when there was a whole heap of truth behind it.

"What is his condition?"

"Terrible," I said.

"Can you be more specific?"

"I'm not a doctor."

The three Cogents exchanged a look. Nothing changed in their expressions, but somehow, I could tell that a series of understandings took place between them.

"Please follow us," one of the other Cogents said. "Mr. Pervenio is awaiting you."

"That's it?" I said.

"Is something not adequate?"

"I was hoping for trumpets." I patted the young man on the

shoulder. Months of sitting in a cell on Titan made me appreciative of Cogent naivety. It made me miss the simple days of having Zhaff as my bothersome partner who couldn't take a joke. Now I was working with a murderous sociopath whose plans beyond reaching Luxarn I was still trying to figure out.

"No games, Mudstomper, or she starts losing fingers," one of Kale's Ringers spoke through the com-link hidden in my ear, listening to everything.

"Please, come," a Cogent said. His eye lens momentarily aimed at my ear, like he could hear the Ringer, then he continued along. "We were requested not to delay."

"Right behind you." I grinned and followed, pulling Kale's pod along with me. I slapped my ear to remind the Ringer to shut up.

Two of the Cogents led me onward while one took a contingent of security officers and moved to board the *Cora* and find Zhaff. Kale's people were hidden in some sort of smuggling compartment built into the vessel, which I was assured could escape even the wary eyes of Cogents.

I'd been to the mining facility portion of Undina before, and it was nothing to brag about. The entry lobby was clean and white, with the red helix logo of Pervenio Corp plastered everywhere. Beyond that, it was all rock and stark, metallic panels. The galley was in disrepair. Lights flickered, wall panels were dented or worse, and a thick coat of dirt covered everything. A sad sign of the current state of Pervenio Corporation. The Luxarn I once knew barely tolerated a mote of dust floating within one of his properties.

Noisy mining crawlers rumbled over rough terrain deeper in, through gaping tunnels, while workers stripped the asteroid of every ounce of worth it had. Only last time, there were enough workers to make a dent. Now it was a skeleton crew. Most of them had their feet up and were drinking whatever piss passed for synthahol among miners. If that's what they even were. For all I knew, the mine really was entirely a front, and Kale was walking us into the middle of a small army.

After all, not one of the employees batted an eye at the strange Cogents strolling by. Or the rugged collector dragging along a prize worth more than any of them would ever see in their lifetimes.

We reached an unassuming maintenance lift in the dark depths of the mines. A Pervenio security officer napped out front. I recognized him. He was the instructor who'd been working the target practice alley back when Varus shot me in the shoulder with a riot round, proving to me that I no longer had what it took to be a collector.

"Graves?" he said, startling himself back to attention. "You're back?"

"From the dead," I said.

"Step aside," one of the Cogents ordered.

He signaled the lift to come and did as asked without a fuss. "Is that—?" His eyes went wide upon seeing through the view-port of Kale's pod. Months confined on Undina without a night-club to blow off steam and nobody to talk to but Cogents... I was surprised he didn't have a heart attack.

"It is. You didn't hear I was the best collector Sol's ever known?"

He stuttered over a response. Considering I was likely strolling toward my end, there was no reason I couldn't augment my legend.

The lift carried us through a hundred meters of solid rock, deep into the heart of the asteroid, where the gravity generated by its spin was minimal. Enough to make an Earther woozy the first time, but I'd been to my share of asteroid colonies. Most of them made the Lowers of Titan seem like paradise, and most of their riots against corporate overseers ended with ample blood spilled. At least they did end.

"Mr. Pervenio is waiting in his office," one Cogent, or maybe both of them at once, said as we stopped. It was like listening to an automated recording of a man.

The lift doors opened, and I returned to the same shiny, spotless facility where I'd woken after nearly freezing to death on Titan. Even fewer employees were present now, and as eerily dirty as the mines above were, this was the opposite. It was like nothing had been touched in weeks. Sterile.

We passed a familiar medical room. Doctor Aurora sat inside, pretending to be busy with a sample, it looked like.

"Hey, Doc," I said, offering a lazy salute. She nearly dropped her vials when she heard my voice. I'm not sure why I felt so cheerful. I didn't even have to feign my smile. I was about to betray the man to whom I'd dedicated my life's work, yet I didn't feel guilty.

Maybe it was because I saw what he'd turned Zhaff into. Perhaps I knew this was finally the end. That I wouldn't have to keep watching my wrinkles deepen, my hair grow white, and my trigger finger go arthritic. Maybe it was because, after thirty years of loyal service, Luxarn hadn't even known my name until it suited his interests, then stole all my limited savings for a leg I didn't want. Or maybe it was because, over all those years, I'd seen the worst parts of what Pervenio Corp did to assets that didn't keep in line. I'd seen the rows of sick on Titan, denied medicine because shipping it from Earth was too expensive and developing it on Titan wasn't profitable. I'd seen what Luxarn was willing to do to any dissatisfied worker who spoke out against him—I'd been on the other end of the gun keeping them quiet too many times to count.

Choosing Aria over Zhaff all those months ago had eaten me up inside because Zhaff didn't deserve to die. He was a misunderstood kid, turned into a robotic killing machine by a father who kept him secret rather than face the shame of reproducing outside legal USF terms.

Choosing Aria over Luxarn Pervenio? I'd been doing that since the day she was born in a sewer so that they wouldn't take her away from me and shove her into a communal home where illegitimates wasted their lives. It merely took me a while to realize it. A better man might have tried harder to find a way out of this, but I wasn't one. Unlike the murderous king I dragged in front of Luxarn's unspectacular office door, I never pretended to be. I was a collector pulling off one last job, with payment in my daughter's life and mercy for a friend. I was a father doing his best, which is all one can hope to do, and more than I spent Aria's whole life being.

"Wel... come, Malcolm Gra... Gra... Graves," the mechanical voice of Luxarn's service bot addressed me. I expected to see the odd, spherical bot floating, but it lay on the floor in a heap of tangled parts and wires. A victim of Luxarn's temper, apparently. "Mr. Per... venio is expect..." It trailed off at the end, the light draining from its single glowing oculus.

"Enter," a Cogent addressed me.

The two of them remained standing guard outside, and the door slid open to reveal Luxarn at the mahogany desk in his unadorned office. The lonely painting of ancient Earth behind him was faded at the edges. A month ago, I'd seen him over video, and he'd looked like a mess, but in person, it was worse. Gray stubble coated his chin, betraying his true age. I didn't even know he could grow a beard. The bags under his eyes were so pronounced and dark, I was half convinced he was sleeping until he glanced up at me. His thin lips creased into a smile surrounded by crinkles I didn't know the man's perfect face had.

"Malcolm Graves," he said, voice raspy from yelling at

someone or something. "You have no idea how good it is to see your face."

"Likewise, sir," I replied.

"For a moment there, I was worried this was all another Children of Titan trick. I haven't been able to rest since you made contact."

Upon hearing that, I finally had to force my trademark grin. I swallowed the lump forming in my throat. "You don't look it, sir."

He laughed and stood. "Please, Graves. You don't have to be gentle with me. I expect only honesty from my newest director."

He stuck out his hand as he approached me. I hesitated in taking it for a moment, but only because I realized that he meant what he said. He, like all owners of large, Sol-wide corporations, surrounded himself with sycophants and loyalists. Like Sodervall. Like I had been for so long, happy to keep my head down and keep earning without spouting back.

Honesty? That only went as far as the credits.

"Newest director," I said. "I hadn't even thought about it."

"Like I told you: I won't accept no this time. You'll have to shoot me to get out of here poor."

"Don't tempt me." I released a nervous chuckle but was quickly silenced when Luxarn slapped the top of Kale's pod.

"So this is the boy who caused so much trouble?" He circled the pod. Only Kale's upper body was visible through the viewport on the lid, and for the moment, he appeared completely harmless, like a tranquil wax doll wearing a sanitary mask. We were in Earther territory now, where his people were so susceptible to illness. He truly looked frail.

"He's as skinny as the rest of them," Luxarn said. "And you kept his mask on? You haven't gone soft on me, have you, Graves?"

"I didn't want to spoil him for you," I said.

"Of course." He lay his hand upon my shoulder as he turned to face me. We were close in age, but the way he regarded me made my heart sink. Like a proud father watching his son go off to medical university.

"I can never repay you for this," he said. "I will bring this monster to Earth and show our people there is no need to be afraid. We will break the Ringers' spirits when they see what's become of their king. And with you taking charge of my and Madame Venta's fleet, we will defeat his aunt and quell this riot once and for all. We're one more step toward peace today thanks to you, my friend. For all of humanity."

Luxarn turned his attention back to the pod and prepared to crack it open to face the only rival who'd ever stood against him without being squashed like a cockroach straightaway. I finally considered stopping him and ending this charade. Then I heard the voice of one of the Ringers holding Aria hostage in my ear.

"Is... he... out... yet?" The reception was poor, considering we were surrounded by rock but clear enough to discern the words through the static. Either Kale was walking off Undina after claiming his prize, or we were all going to die together.

"You don't know how long I've been waiting to look into this bastard's eyes and tell him he's lost," Luxarn said.

"He's put me through a hell of a ride," I said. "You don't know how long I've been waiting to watch."

Luxarn reached out to open the pod but stopped just before. "Zhaff should be here," he said.

"He needs medical attention right away, sir," I replied, speaking way too fast. He didn't seem to notice my sudden onslaught of nerves. Zhaff knew what I had done now, and if he woke up before Kale, this entire plan would go up in flames.

"Then perhaps we should wait."

"I'd rather not," I said.

"Oh, Malcolm. There is no reason to rush. It's moments like

these you must learn to savor. You wouldn't eat a steak cut fresh from one of our few cows in a single bite, now would you?"

"A steak doesn't keep me in a cell for months and nearly get me spaced outside Jupiter."

Luxarn chuckled. "Good point." He regarded me again, earnestly contorting his features in a way I'd never seen before. "I know it was hard for you after what happened, but thank you for never giving up on him or this company. When the Ringers ruined our plans on Europa, I worried you died and would never get a chance to know that he pulled through."

"Zhaff saved me," I said. I knew Luxarn thought I meant that he'd rescued me from Kale's prison, but I meant it in my own way. Somehow, the kid had taught me again what it meant to care about somebody other than myself. If it weren't for him, I realized I wasn't sure if I would have saved Aria over completing my job. I might have remained too bitter over her leaving me like Kale now was.

For months, I'd imagined how my life might have turned out if Sodervall never sent me to Earth for vacation and I never got caught up hunting the Children of Titan. Now I knew I didn't want that. Trass gave his life to give Kale's people the Ring, and Zhaff had given his to save mine. I didn't deserve it, but Aria did, and Zhaff... he deserved to be free of what his father had turned him into, even before he was brought back to life.

"Then let's end this for him," Luxarn said.

He signaled the pod to unfasten. Steam coiled around the opening as the cool, gelatinous liquid hugging Kale's body drained away. Luxarn leaned over the edge, steepling his fingers as he eagerly awaited Kale's awakening. The intravenous tubes stopped feeding Kale's body the pharma that kept it dormant, and then his eyelids snapped open.

Kale reached underneath his back, grabbed the pulse pistol hidden there, and pressed it against Luxarn's temple. He screamed as he vaulted out of the pod and wrapped his arm around Luxarn's throat. His Ringer muscles may have been naturally weak, but he'd picked the one Earther to attack who probably hadn't done a second of manual labor in his entire life.

The two Cogents swept into the room in an instant, guns raised, but Kale made himself small behind their leader. The shot was too risky, even for them. I recalled the lesson I tried to teach Varus at their shooting range about being able to pull the trigger when it really counted. Only now he was dead. So many were dead.

"Graves, stop him!" Luxarn shrieked.

I fumbled for a response, but Kale beat me to it. "Your collector can't help you now," he snarled. "None of your pets can. Tell them to drop their weapons!"

"There is a fifty-seven percent chance of lethal injury to your person if we fire at this range, Mr. Pervenio," one of the Cogents stated.

"I concur," said the other.

"Graves," Luxarn said, fuming. "Put this animal down."

I drew my pulse pistol just to keep up appearances, but I didn't even bother aiming. There was no reason to twist the knife in him, no reason to provide false hope. His end had arrived the moment he placed more importance on vengeance than rebuilding his brand. This was a mercy killing.

"Tell them to lower their weapons, or you lose your head," Kale said.

"Judging by his expression and acute facial cues, it is likely that he will kill you regardless," one of the Cogents said. "Would you prefer us to take the risk?"

"Kill this madman!" Luxarn roared.

They didn't get the chance. I finally raised my pistol and fired two shots. My fingers didn't cramp on the trigger this time. No hesitation. From so close a range, even an old man like me couldn't miss. The two Cogents' chests exploded as they collapsed.

One got off a shot while he was falling back, but the bullet burrowed harmlessly into the wall above Kale's shoulder. Another grasped for his gun as he clung to life, but I rushed over, kicked it out of the way, and put another bullet in his head. Then I sealed and locked the office before any more Cogents arrived.

Luxarn stumbled out of Kale's arms and fell to his knees, his face so white with horror, he looked like the very Ringers he hated. Even Kale was speechless.

"Nobody on this rock is getting out alive anyway, right?" I said. "If you die, she dies. Get this the fuck over with, kid."

"Graves," Luxarn stammered. "What is the meaning of this?"

"Sorry, sir... I got a better offer."

Life takes a strange twist on you when mowing down two young men is easier than looking one old one in the eye. I had to turn away from Luxarn just to keep my head straight. Feeling betrayal brings about a special kind of expression in a person. Equal parts revulsion and shock, with a dash of heartbreak for good measure.

"I was going to name you a director," Luxarn said weakly. "I was going to give you the Ring!"

"I told you I didn't want it," I replied.

"This is too good," Kale said, finally snapping out of it enough to breathe in the fact that he'd won. He circled around Luxarn, smiling, then grabbed him by the jaw. "Now you get to see what it's like to have everything you believed in get stripped away. You get to see what it's like to have your whole world crushed."

"You drag this out, you'll get us all killed," I said to Kale. "You think that's all of them? Just finish what you came for."

"He's not dying yet. Not until he admits what he did to us."

"Admit what?" Luxarn asked.

"That every awful thing that's happened to my people since our reunion with yours was by design."

"You want a confession, you skelly piece of trash? How's this. I should have killed you all. And you, Graves. All those years you fooled us all?" He spat at my feet. "Sodervall said you were a tired old wretch before I paired you with my son. He was right."

Luxarn slowly got to his feet and faced Kale. He stepped forward until the barrel of the boy king's gun pressed against his forehead. "So do it," he said. "Put me down, and I swear you will feel the wrath of Earther vengeance. Our fleet will rain nuclear fire down on Titan until it's a smoldering husk."

Kale shot him in the shoulder. Luxarn flew back into the wall, blood spattering across the metal panels. Kale strode by and knelt in front of him, lifting the man's head. Luxarn grasped at the wound, eyes wide and whole body shaking. It was a surface shot, just clipping the top of his skin, but Luxarn appeared ready to go into shock, like he'd never felt any pain whatsoever before in his whole pampered life.

Kale reached up to his ear as he scooted toward him. "We have Luxarn," he said to his men over the coms. "Send the package, then prepare the engine and have it ready for my return." He kneeled in front of Luxarn. "Your fleet will run, or the rest of them will die too. Earth will pay."

"Damn it, Kale," I said. "End this." I heard footsteps outside the door. Soon, Luxarn's guards would bring out the fusion cutters or worse and bust their way in.

"Don't do this, Graves," Luxarn sniveled. "Whatever he offered, I'll double it. Shoot him now."

"I wish I could, sir. I really do."

"You can!"

"He can't," Kale interrupted. "You see, you're not the only one who has a bastard child. Tell him, Malcolm. Tell him whose daughter my ambassador, Aria, really is."

My gaze turned toward the floor, and in my peripherals, I saw all the hope drain from Luxarn's eyes. Any smidge of faith that he could turn me, considering I was behind Kale with an open shot, died as soon as he saw my face and realized Kale was telling the truth. We collectors had a particular lifestyle, and siring kids outside the letter of the USF wasn't abnormal, but most got caught. They took their slap on the wrist and let their child go away. I never had.

"You really didn't know?" Kale laughed. "Isn't it wonderful to learn the secrets of the people we thought we could trust most? I wonder how many others he has."

"What do you want, Trass?" Luxarn growled.

"I want you to admit it."

"Admit what!"

"Everything. Admit the Great Plague that killed so many of my people was not an accident. That you planned the whole Great Reunion to take the Ring for yourself." Kale pushed the end of the gun into his fresh wound. Luxarn squirmed and kicked, but Kale managed to find the strength in his Ringer muscles to hold firm. "Admit you locked us up and watched us die just for the joy of it!"

"What do you expect him to say when you're torturing him, Kale?" I said. "Forcing a lie to make you happy is worthless."

"I want the truth."

"You want the truth?" Luxarn slid forward, wincing. "My father and I didn't even think about getting your people sick. All we cared about was the wealth of Saturn."

"That's a lie!" Kale cracked him across the face with the butt of his gun. Blood and two teeth spewed out as Luxarn toppled. Kale wrenched him back upright, and I was about to say something when I noticed my old employer cackling. Blood leaked through the new gaps in his mouth as he did.

"I wish it was. Though I can't say we complained about what happened. Darien Trass and you people fled Earth-like cowards while the rest of us faced judgment. But it came for you through us, didn't it? It always does."

"Liar!" Kale punched him again.

"Was it our fault you Ringers' pathetic attempt at a new civilization made you so weak? Children of Titan." Luxarn scoffed, a glob of red dripping from his lips. "We all came from the same rock. Your people just seemed to forget it, body and mind."

I heard more fidgeting at the door and glanced back. More Cogents were likely planting charges. "Kale, get on with it," I said. "We don't have long, and you are not dying here."

"Listen to the traitor, Trass," Luxarn said. "You've lost. You came here for an apology, but you'll never get one. We took the trash your people made on Titan and polished it. Made it something humanity could be proud of. The moment your people see that they'll toss you aside, I promise."

I could see Kale simmering inside. I'm not sure what he expected to hear, but Luxarn was once the wealthiest man in Sol for a reason. Even if what he was now paled in comparison, he'd always believed that the people of Sol were below him. That was the thing Kale and his followers failed to realize. Luxarn Pervenio didn't only step on the throats of Ringers to get what he wanted. He did it to everyone. He believed he was carrying out a grand vision for settling the solar system and beyond. For ushering humanity into the next age. Hell, after a while working for Pervenio Corp, I believed in that too, in making sure that humanity's reach was so vast we could never risk being wiped out again.

"So go ahead, Trass," Luxarn said. "Kill me and prove what

we've said about your kind from the beginning. That you're worthless. Because the only apology you'll ever get from me is that I cared enough to help your people survive after the Ring was already mine."

"Are you finished?" Kale questioned. "Good. You can lie all want, but I'm going to make sure you feel what we did. Malcolm, open the door."

"Do you want to die?" I said.

He shifted his aim towards me. "Open it, or Aria will suffer!"

"Fine! I'll let more of them in so you can get off on killing." I moved to the side of the door so I wouldn't be in the way of the guards outside, then extended my arm to open it. A Cogent strode in, and it only took me a step to realize it wasn't really one. The man wearing their outfit and eye-lens moved with too much character. I then saw the bodies of a few security officers lying in the hall.

The false cogent removed his eye-lens and tossed it to the side. "He's here, Lord Trass." He disappeared around the corner, then threw another man in.

Zhaff rolled once before slamming against the wall. His artificial left arm had been torn from its socket, loose wires dangling from just below his shoulder. His artificial left leg was mangled and twisted, broken open to reveal sparking parts. His eye lens had been ripped off, revealing a metallic jaw through his sinewy cheek and an eye socket that appeared like a hand terminal port.

All they'd left him with was the respirator latched over his mouth, but even it rattled like it had when he struggled for life on Titan. His human handed groped through the darkness as he tried to figure out where he was.

"I'll make sure nobody else gets in," Kale's guard said. "From ice to ashes." The man resealed the door.

Kale released Luxarn to run toward his battered son. "By

Earth. Zhaff, what did they do to you?" Luxarn asked as he helped Zhaff to his knees.

"Kale, you made a promise," I whispered. Seeing Zhaff had me feeling like I was going to choke.

"And I'm keeping it," Kale replied.

He stalked toward Luxarn and Zhaff, aiming at them. "You gave the order that got Cora killed," Kale said. "I've listened to it a thousand times. You didn't even pause."

"Who the hell is Cora!" Luxarn snapped. The volume of his voice startled Zhaff, and his artificial knee gave out. Luxarn scampered to lift him again.

"She was everything to me! And you ordered her to be spaced just because she was a Ringer. So before I pull the trigger, I'm going to make you see what it's like to lose everything. I know about Zhaff, Luxarn. I know how he was left to freeze on the surface of Titan. And I know who killed him."

"He's not dead," Luxarn said.

"He might as well be!" Kale shouted.

"Kale, don't," I said, teeth clenched.

Zhaff's head perked up upon now apparently recognizing my voice. He used Luxarn like a crutch to try and rise to his feet. His artificial leg wobbled, and his respirator hissed as he exerted himself. He turned his right ear toward me, and it was then that I realized his new eye-lens had also been hooked into an artificial right ear, which he also now lacked.

"Malcolm Graves," Zhaff said, his voice tinny and weak. "Why." He took a hard step at me with his human half. I instinctually raised my gun, and it felt like we were back on Titan all over again. Me and him, with Aria's life hanging in the balance. Then he took a second step on an artificial leg just like mine, and it gave out, causing him to collapse.

"It's him, my son," Luxarn said, grabbing his son, who dug

into the floor with his only hand to try and pull himself toward me. "Tell him to help us. He'll listen to you."

"I wish it was me who'd done it," Kale continued, ignoring my pleas. "Executing Sodervall felt good, but robbing you of your only son would have been so much better. Only I didn't have the pleasure. None of my people did."

"Kale, I'm warning you." I aimed at the back of Kale's head, even though I couldn't look away from Zhaff while his father struggled to stop him from crawling at me and wheezing. Kale didn't react to it at all.

"It was your own collector who put down the freak to save his daughter, my ambassador."

Luxarn's arresting grayish eyes spread wide, directed straight at me. I'd meant to shoot someone first to keep my secret, anyone, but I locked up again upon seeing his anguish. In that moment, my betrayal of Pervenio Corp was complete. I realized why Kale wanted me at his side for this more than anything else. He knew he couldn't break Luxarn without showing him the truth. And my expression had the truth written all over it, enough for Luxarn to know with his final breaths that Kale wasn't lying. That he'd won.

"Now he's going to finish the job," Kale said. "You're going to watch as your son dies, just like so many of my people. Shoot him, Malcolm."

I froze. Luxarn lost his grip of Zhaff, which allowed him to continue crawling toward me. Every breath he drew sounded like an air recycler failing. And the boy who could not show emotion for so long had rage inscribed upon his eyeless, half-missing face.

"Do it, Malcolm," Kale said. "I made you a promise, and now you get to make sure it's kept."

"Graves," Luxarn said, breathless. "Whatever he has on you,

I know you care for my boy. Shoot the Ringer bastard, and we'll forget about all of this."

Muted gunshots echoed outside in the hall, followed by screaming. There was a thud against the door, and somehow I doubted it was Kale's single guard mowing down Cogents and security officers. They'd break in soon.

"You did it once already," Kale said. "You saw my people beneath the Quarantine. You saw what he did to us. Your daughter gave everything to help, now you can do the same for her."

"Thirty years, Graves," Luxarn said. "Don't throw it all away!"

Zhaff's cold finger wrapped my artificial ankle and squeezed. He slowly drew himself to his knees, every part of him shaking.

"Family..." I swallowed the lump in my throat. "Right, Zhaff?"

"Malcolm, end this!" Luxarn screamed.

For months now, I'd allowed the Ringers to use me in the name of protecting my daughter. I let them force my finger around the trigger so I could end the life of a man who didn't deserve it and feed their lies. But even I had my limits. Luxarn earned plenty of pain for how ruthlessly he'd played his corporate game. He'd earned it for how he'd treated Zhaff. But no man deserved to watch those he loved be taken from them. If anybody should have understood that, it was Kale.

"Make him feel our pain!" Kale yelled.

So, I did. I lifted my gun, screamed, and fired. The back of Luxarn's head blew open, splattering blood and brains all over the wall.

"No!" Kale screamed.

He lunged to catch Luxarn's body, then stared into his eyes as the very glimmer of life fled them.

Luxarn Pervenio, the man who took control of the ring after the Great Reunion, used his riches to build a corporate machine the likes of which humanity had never seen. His relentless dedication to advancing humanity at any cost helped set up the foundation of our interplanetary civilization. And now he was dead.

Zhaff rose to his full height before me. He grabbed my arm to pull himself upright, but I let him, until his fingers wrapped around my throat. I stared into the face of death incarnate—of my friend Zhaff turned into a monster. I knew now that neither of us was getting off Undina alive.

"I trusted you..." he wheezed.

"I know." I craned my neck so his hand fit easier. I didn't fight it as he began to squeeze. "He should have done what's right and let you go." I imagined Zhaff as a child, being beaten by his classmates for being different. That was the reason his father pulled him out, created the Cogent Initiative, and turned him into a killing machine.

But the Zhaff I knew wouldn't have let life destroy him. Maybe, with someone better than Luxarn caring for him, he might have wound up using his brain to help an investor like Basaam change the world. Perhaps if I'd turned my daughter over to the USF, she'd been the head of some hospital somewhere saving lives.

"I should've too," I grated. Even broken as he was, Zhaff's grip was strong as iron. I let my gun fall from my grip and whispered, "Do it."

TWENTY-ONE

KALE

I watched the life drain from Luxarn Pervenio's eyes. I thought the sight of the man who'd spent a lifetime grinding my people under his heel dying would make me smile. I thought it'd make me feel something.

It didn't.

Luxarn's cold body slumped onto the floor, dipped in a pool of his own blood and excrement. I whipped around and saw Malcolm being choked by Luxarn's son. A twitch of regret plagued his features as his air was cut off. He looked like he'd aged years since he loaded me into the sleep pod and presented me to his former employer.

"He was supposed to watch just like I had to!" I roared. I charged across the room and smashed Zhaff across the side of his half-metallic head with all my might. The Cogent somehow remained choking Malcolm even as he fell unconscious, dragging the defiant collector to the ground with him. I pried Zhaff's cold fingers off Malcolm's throat, leaving him gasping for air. Then I aimed my pistol right between Malcolm's eyes.

"Do you know what you've done!" I screamed.

"The right thing, for once," Malcolm said, coughing.

"I should kill you right here."

"Go ahead. I said I'd help you deal with Luxarn, but you didn't say anything about this. He was already beaten. I don't care what he's done, nobody deserves to watch their child die. You should know that better than anybody. You're going to be a father, for Earth's sake!"

I pressed the barrel of my gun against his forehead, my finger itching to pull the trigger. Luxarn had made so many of us watch our families wither away in quarantine, unable to help them. I'd watched the footage of Cora dying at Luxarn's orders a thousand times, listened to him give them a thousand times more. Now he was dead, but he would never experience what we did. That crushing pain. I knew that was why I barely felt a thing as I watched the life flee his body.

Then I heard the commotion outside the door of his office. My guard had given his life, and now Luxarn's servants were preparing to breach the entry and take me down. Maybe I was going to die on Undina, but I refused to give Luxarn the satisfaction. Even in death.

"You're lucky I still need you, Collector," I said, pulling the gun away. He barely seemed relieved not to die. "Get up. We're getting out of here."

"He didn't have to know what happened," Malcolm growled, a harsh edge entering his tone.

"He deserved the truth," I replied.

"Not from you."

"Protecting your child is nothing to be ashamed of. He sent his to die in the name of credits."

Malcolm snatched his pulse pistol off the floor and leveled his aim at me. A film of tears glazed his eyes in a way I hadn't seen before. I knew he wasn't going to shoot.

"Zhaff was a good kid," he said. "His death didn't deserve to be used as a weapon."

"Well, it doesn't matter now, does it." I pointed at Luxarn's slumped body, the blood continuing to pool beneath it. "We made a deal, Collector. You get me in to kill Luxarn and out, and she walks."

"Yeah, well, me killing Zhaff in front of his father so you could prove a point didn't really figure into that."

"Consider us even for you taking Luxarn from me. Now you want Zhaff dead, you're free to take care of him. Then you're going to get me out of here."

He looked like he wanted to explode. He bit his lip, and his free hand squeezed so tight his knuckles went as white as a Titanborn's. He jumped to his feet, rushed over to Zhaff's unconscious body, and aimed at his head. He stared down at him, hand quaking, but he never fired.

"We don't have all day, Malcolm," I said. "They're coming."

His hand shook harder and harder, and then his gun-arm fell to his side. "We made you into this, Luxarn and me," he said. "But you're alive. I shouldn't get to choose where your story ends." He crouched and whispered something in Zhaff's ear.

"I won't ask again, Malcolm," I said.

He glared up at me, then he exhaled through his teeth. "I can't do it."

"That's your choice, then. I doubt he'll get off of here alive anyway."

"He tends to surprise you."

"Good for him. Now let's go, Collector. Think of Aria."

"Right, I need to get you out," he said, simmering. "Sure, why not. I've already come this far; why not keep helping a murderous psychopath who can't deal with a broken heart? What's a few more dead Cogents?"

Malcolm turned and positioned himself in front of the door, a mad look in his eye. Someone banged on it from the outside.

"What are you doing?" I asked.

"Don't worry!" Malcolm announced to whoever was on the other side of the door. "We're coming out now." He reared his artificial leg back with no warning and kicked the door with all his might. A group of Cogents was crushed against the wall on the other side. It partially missed one of them, squishing her arm only, but Malcolm plugged her between the eyes without hesitation.

"Let's go," he growled back at me. He moved into the corridor so fast that I had no choice but to follow. Another Cogent waited around the next corner.

"Malcolm Graves," the young man said. "What is happening?"

Malcolm blew the Cogent away without a second's hesitation. He passed a medical office, and a Cogent hiding inside wised up and shot Malcolm in the thigh. The force sent him into the wall hard, but his artificial leg absorbed the blast with barely a scratch. Malcolm rolled over and put a bullet through the shooter's eye lens. He was like a force of nature. A doctor inside squealed, but Malcolm shoved her onto the bed for her own safety.

"Keep up, kid," he glanced back at me and said.

A shot reverberated down the clean, metallic halls. Blood spurted as it clipped the top of Malcolm's shoulder, but he didn't go down. I fired around his hip and hit the Cogent in the leg. Malcolm finished the job. I'd never seen anyone recover from a pulse pistol shot so fast.

He wedged his artificial foot under the corpse of his most recent kill and hurled it at the shooter. It crushed the Cogent, and another one rounding the corner was knocked off his feet by the tumbling body.

Malcolm charged forward and barreled into him. By the time I caught up, he'd already shoved the Cogent against the doors of the lift out of the facility and was bashing him across the face with the butt of his gun. Once, then again, until his Earther strength had the young man's eye lens literally sunken into his eye socket.

Malcolm turned back to me, cheek doused in red. "Go," he rasped as he signaled the doors to open.

Zhaff appeared back down the hall, across Malcolm's swathe of death. He dragged his broken body along the floor with his elbow, and in his grip held a pulse pistol taken from one of his fallen brethren. He had no eyes, but the first shot he took missed us by a hair before clanging against the wall. I rushed into the lift to find cover.

Malcolm didn't move. He closed his eyes as if he hoped one of the rounds would blow out his skull. Like his job was finished. I grasped him by the back of the collar and had to push off the wall with my feet to haul his heavy body inside. The doors sealed, and somehow he remained unscathed, even though the back of the lift was riddled with holes. His legs started to give out.

I grabbed him. "Get up," I said.

"I got you out," he replied, panting. "Isn't that enough?"

"Not yet."

I slipped behind him and aimed the gun at his head. He didn't even bother to raise his. I wasn't sure he could. With his adrenaline waning, the wound through his shoulder had his arm hanging slack and his eyes bloodshot. Even my Ringer muscles were strong enough to keep him at bay.

"You won, kid," he said. "Is that what you want to hear? I don't have anything left." All the vim fled his voice. One final push to keep me alive for her sake, and now both his body and soul were failing.

"You have her."

"Thirty years. That's how long I worked for that man, and I

shot him. How many more have to die before your vengeance ends?"

"We don't get to choose when it ends."

"Tell that to the man you sent me to kill. You chose when Orson's ended. They chose when Cora's ended. Who's next, kid?"

The lift opened into the Undina Mining Facility proper, and I squeezed Malcolm's neck harder. A line of Pervenio security officers awaited us, rifles pressed against their shoulders and aimed at us.

"Step away from Mr. Graves!" their leader barked.

I ducked to make sure Malcolm's stout body covered most of mine and held my gun firmly against his head while we slowly trod forward. A Cogent could have made the shot, but not this lot of tired officers. There wasn't one of them that looked like he hadn't recently woken from a nap.

"Just put down your guns and get out of here," Malcolm grumbled. "This change has been coming a long time, and none of you are going to stop that."

"What are you talking about?" the officer said. "Don't move another step, or we will fire."

"Don't throw your lives away for him."

"Stop!"

Bullets tore into the officers from behind. Their bodies danced like they were being worked by invisible puppeteers before they dropped, blood pooling in all the air pockets mottling the rocky floor.

"Lord Trass, are you all right?" My guards rushed over to help me with Malcolm. They tore him from my arms and checked to make sure I wasn't wounded.

"Get your Ringer hands off me!" Malcolm snapped. One of my armored men punched him in the gut. He folded, but another kept him from going down so he could take another blow to the side of the face.

"Enough!" I ordered. "Luxarn is dead, thanks to him."

"He's gone?" The youngest of my guards could barely get the words out. There was a sense of relief to my guard's tone, like when the pressure exerted from a launch off Titan suddenly gives way to weightlessness, and all the fear of burning up goes away. It was then that I knew for sure I'd made the right call to chase Luxarn, and that Rin was wrong.

"For good this time," I said. The young man was so floored, even though the news was expected, that he dropped Malcolm. "It's time to go."

"What about the collector?" asked another Titanborn.

"Cuff him and bring him too."

"You made a promise, Kale," Malcolm snarled. "Remember that. You made a damn promise!"

I turned to him, grabbed the barrel of his pistol, and ripped it out of his hands. "And I intend to keep it, but you're not going to want to miss this." I waved more men over.

"Put a bullet in my head like a fucking man," Malcolm said.

Another bout of curses echoed through the mines when he was seized. With my men's powered armor on, his Earther strength was no match. They wrenched his arms behind his back and got him moving. His bullet wound had him moaning in pain, which only inspired my men to yank harder.

"The Fusion Pulse Engine has been installed," the youngest of the Titanborn addressed me as we turned and set off through Undina's barren tunnels. He had to raise his voice so I could hear him over Malcolm's incessant grousing. "The rest are back on board the *Cora,* and we have a clear path." Bodies were strewn haphazardly in our path, some armed like officers, others no more than miners. We couldn't risk anybody making a bold move.

"Any complications?" I asked.

"None. Basaam's instructions were all accurate. The coward gave in right away. It's anchored into the asteroid's crust just outside the hangar, and we used his equations to set it at the proper angle."

"Tell them to begin activating the engine and open a com channel from the *Cora* to the USF headquarters on New London. Now."

"Yes, Lord Trass."

We were halfway across the station's galley when my orders went through. A tremor shook Undina, like an earthquake, only from outside, not within. My bones chattered. Then another came, even more violent. It sent me stumbling into Malcolm and over an overturned table. My men were able to keep their balance in their armor and plucked me off him.

"What the hell was that?" Malcolm asked.

"M-Day," I said.

Before my men grabbed him again, I watched his eyelids go wide like he'd had an epiphany. I'd wondered how long it would take him to realize that every Earther's biggest fear was about to come true. That Basaam Venta's Fusion Pulse Engine, invented to propel an Ark Ship the size of a small asteroid across Sol, were being used to do it.

Three and a half centuries ago, a meteorite inspired Darien Trass to send thousands of Earth's finest men and women to Titan. He intended for them to start a new civilization. The most brilliant minds, free of all their worldly shackles—free to create a new paradise for man. Now a second meteorite would see my people freed from the survivors of Earth who refused to die and took that from us.

Acceleration from the engines third nuclear pulse had Malcolm's and my unarmored bodies soaring across the lobby like we were weightless. The pressure building up around my eyes was excruciating. My men snatched us out of the air before our spines cracked against the wall.

"Sorry, Lord Trass," the Titanborn guard who caught me said. "We have to go."

He slung me over his shoulder and took off across the lobby. Inertia fought him every step of the way, but with powered armor and mag boots, he got me to the hangar.

The *Cora*'s landing gear kept her planted firmly on the floor. The group trudged toward the ramp, struggling to battle the pressure despite their suits. I'd never endured sudden acceleration at this level. Even plummeting into the depths of Saturn on that luxury cruiser couldn't compare. I couldn't even part my lips to speak.

Pressure around my eye sockets built to the point to where they felt like they were going to burst. I could tell we were ascending the *Cora*'s ramp but was slowly losing vision.

"Get him in his suit, now!"

Hands fumbled across my body. I was tilted and bent until I heard the gentle hiss of a helmet sealing around my head. By the time I could focus my vision again, I found myself seated in the back of the *Cora*'s command deck. Judging by the stars through the viewport, we had departed Undina and were already in space.

Aria sat at the controls, two guns aimed at her head. I glanced back and saw Malcolm sat slumped against the wall in the corridor to the sleep pod chamber, cuffed and gritting his teeth. He too was under the gun. And last, in the copilot's chair, sat Basaam Venta, watching through the viewport for the first time as his beloved invention functioned.

A pulsating light as brilliant as the sun glowed on the back of Undina. Even though the asteroid was a furrowed sphere of rock, it was being propelled out of its orbit onto an unnatural course toward Earth like a ship accelerating faster and faster.

"It really works," Basaam marveled.

"Quiet!" One of my men smacked him.

I stood and made my way to the controls. "Aria," I said. "Are you all right flying?"

"We forced her to take two g-stims," one of my men said. "One for each of them."

She regarded me, tears filling her eyes, then looked to her injured father. "You have to help him, Kale," she said. "Please."

"Keep pace with Undina," I ordered. "If you do exactly as I say, we'll help. You two can leave together and be done with us."

"That wasn't the deal," Malcolm groaned. "Luxarn dies; she gets out. Nothing in between."

"And now you'll get to join her, Collector." I laid my hand on Aria's shoulder, but she squirmed out from under it. Even after everything, watching her reject me made my chest go tight. I fought so long defending her, pretending she understood our plight.

"Just fly, Aria," I growled.

"Coms are open to the USF Assembly, Lord Trass," one of my men said.

The face of Talos Gaveren, Voice of the Assembly, appeared on the center control panel. Others ran frantically around the room behind him, but the old man tried his best to seem composed. His lips parted as he prepared to speak, but I beat him to it.

"Luxarn Pervenio is dead," I said. "By now, you'll have realized the activity of the Undina Mining Facility is not natural. Utilizing the Fusion Pulse Engine invented by Basaam Venta for your Ark announcement ceremony today, we have affected its orbit. In a few hours, it will slam directly into New London."

Talos swallowed hard. "What do you want, Mr. Trass?"

"I want what we asked for on Mars. You will demand the full retreat of the PerVenia fleet back to Jupiter, along with the captives we so graciously handed over to them. Then you will formally sign over the properties of the Ring to the Children of Titan, with no ancillary conditions. No matter whose possession they are under."

"Mr. Trass, you have to understand. There are dozens of companies we will have to contact to gain legal permissions. It could take days. Weeks."

"Do as we ask, and the asteroid will miss your capital. Fail to meet our demands and you, and all the millions around New London, will know M-Day again. This will be our only conversation until you transmit the contracts. Goodbye, Earther."

I ended the transmission, and Basaam Venta immediately lunged at me.

"This isn't what they were made for, you lunatic!" he screamed. My men grabbed him before he could hit me, and slammed him to the floor. "This is insanity!"

"Get him out of here," I ordered. They obliged, and as they carried the flailing Earther out of the room, I heard Malcolm cackle.

"They've been preparing for another meteorite for centuries," he said. "They're going to blow Undina out the sky. Luxarn already hollowed her out for them with his mining. It'll be a cinch."

My men went to silence him, but I stopped them. "Do you ever feel like things happen for a reason, Malcolm?" I asked. "That this vessel, designed by the most brilliant visionary your people ever had, fell into our hands? And that you, for so many reasons, drove Aria to us, the most gifted pilot I've ever met?"

"Lord Trass," the Titanborn behind Aria said. "They didn't waste any time. They've targeted Undina with the full complement of their thermonuclear anti-meteor arsenal on Luna. It's enough to reduce Undina to pebbles before it hits."

"Earthers." I sighed. "Always in a rush. Aria, take us on a

full burn ahead of Undina. Use everything. Shoot their missiles down on approach so that they have no choice but to free us."

"No," Aria said, incensed. "No, I won't."

"You will." I drew my pulse pistol and aimed it at the top of Malcolm's head. "If any of those missiles get through, your father dies. If they don't, like I said, you'll both walk out of this together. This is what you brought us to Mars for, Aria. We'll get everything we wanted, and then you can be done with us like *you* wanted."

"I didn't want it like this."

"Then you didn't want peace at all!"

"I'm not worth it, Aria," Malcolm said. "Shoot the damn engine off of that rock and end this."

"Destroy the missiles, or I'll make him suffer like an Earther deserves." I knelt and wrapped my armored fingers around Malcolm's throat. As I did, I pressed my pistol into his wound. He writhed beneath me, but now I had my armor on, and putting the Earther in his place was even easier.

"Do it!" I bellowed.

"Fine!" Aria answered. "But I swear, this is it. I thought your people were worth helping. I thought you were worth it... but you're just as bad as they are."

She threw our engines into full burn, zipping over Undina. Based on Basaam's calculations, the Fusion Pulse Engine provided such powerful thrust using controlled nuclear explosions, it'd eventually be moving well beyond our ability to catch up, but Undina was massive in comparison, even for a relatively small asteroid. Engines had been used to generate faster spins for asteroid colonies to help with pseudo-gravity, but never to literally alter their trajectory at such a measure. Undina being almost entirely excavated by miners helped, but it was still incredible to see.

I raised Malcolm by the throat, planted him in one of the

chairs, and locked him in. Then I held on to the back of Aria's chair, magnetizing my boots so that the g-forces of our burn didn't throw me around the command deck. Dozens of thin blue trails raced away from Luna, an arsenal developed specifically to keep another meteorite from hitting Earth. We knew about it thanks to data found on Pervenio Station after we took over, and we also knew that the warheads, while immensely powerful, had been developed before the Great Reunion ever happened. They were intended to neutralize a rogue asteroid by using a drill on the tip to burrow into the crust before detonating, but they weren't prepared to stop an asteroid from being hurled at Earth on purpose, or a ship like the *Cora*.

"How do I operate the weapons systems?" the Titanborn who took the copilot's chair asked.

Aria smacked his hands. "I'll handle it." The sudden movement made her wince and grab at her bulging stomach. I couldn't imagine that handling these g-forces while in her condition was easy, even with g-stims in her system, but we needed her. Our son's future needed her, just this last time.

"Let her," I ordered.

The Titanborn leaned back, and Aria transferred all controls to her station. Her fingers darted across the screens with such grace, it was as if she were dancing. The *Cora* raced up over Undina, the rocky surface rushing beneath us. Aria targeted the first wave of thermo-nukes and hit one with a missile. It detonated in a flash of blue so dazzling, I had to shield my eyes, taking any other nukes in the vicinity with it.

The *Cora* quickly spiraled downward, the viewport coming within meters of scraped Undina as we escaped the glowing cloud of plasma from the explosion. Then Aria whipped us back around and took aim at another wave. All the vastness of space and her targeting abilities made it seem small. She was shooting only using scanners, no visual of the nukes—blind.

The warheads came from silos all over Luna, so they were staggered. Aria wove us in and out of nuclear shockwaves, just barely scraping by, with Undina barreling onward in our wake. With every nuke she disabled, she was forced to push the *Cora* faster. Basaam's engine had Undina accelerating exponentially.

We reached the same orbital range around Earth as the moon, closing fast. Aria fired all the *Cora*'s missiles in a perfect line, detonating them to form a wall of shrapnel. A handful of nukes got caught in it, releasing a destructive wave of energy like I'd never seen. She whipped the *Cora* downward, pushing our engines to their max.

Even my magnetized boots and armor couldn't hold, and I slid back across the floor. I nearly crushed Malcolm on my way toward thumping into the wall. Then Aria leveled us off, skirting beneath the wave of atomic death.

Two warheads continued their path toward Undina, closing fast. Aria's fingers trembled now as she worked the targeting array. I could hear her breathing heavily. She got a lock and fired. The missile clipped one in its engine and sent it sputtering on the wrong path, but she missed the other. A last-minute spray of flak wasn't enough to stop it. It struck Undina, burrowing through the surface before a brilliant flash of blue blew a chunk off the asteroid.

Aria held her breath as we watched the newly-hewn miniature asteroid spin off into the void. It was a sizable portion of Undina, but the rest of it remained intact, and now more warheads en route. It had enough mass left to level New London and nearly every settlement along the planet's Euro String out toward Old Russia.

"That's all of them," Aria exhaled.

She laid off the throttle, and I immediately got up and rushed forward. I craned my neck to look through the viewport at Earth, now front and center. The clouds coating its surface grew in detail. String-like settlements running across portions of the planet that remained above the ocean were now thin black lines extending for hundreds of kilometers. After the Meteorite, that was how Earthers built their cities, in long stretches rather than clumps so that they were safe from single explosions. Safety from extinction drove everything they did.

The largest protuberance in the Euro String was the city of New London, where the USF Assembly and so many other corporate headquarters sat. And if I could look down and see them now, it meant that all the millions of people gathered for celebration could look up and see Undina crashing toward them like a fireball. It meant that they feared judgment again.

TWENTY-TWO

MALCOLM

As I watched from my position at the back of the command deck, I couldn't help but be impressed with a man I'd grown to hate. Kale Trass was an insufferable freedom fighter with a weak constitution who couldn't see beyond his own nose to know what he already had. Yet he'd played his hand perfectly all the same.

He'd traveled to Mars to give a face to the rebellion and kidnap the genius they needed. He used Aria, Rylah, Orson Fring, me, and so many others to get exactly what he wanted, to fuel his people's anger or stoke Earth's fear. Maybe I'd lost a ton of blood and was disappointed he'd forced me off Undina alive, but a man like me, who'd spent his life chasing rebels, had to admire his relentlessness and curse myself for ever thinking his aunt was in control.

I remembered what I'd said to her once about kids like him getting creative when they go bad, and I knew this plot had his brokenhearted fingerprints all over it.

"Anything from the USF?" Kale asked.

"A transmission started coming through the moment the last

warhead went offline," Aria said reluctantly. She slowly synced the video message to the main screen.

"You win, Mr. Trass," Talo said, looking like he was ready to faint. "I've transmitted signed documents satisfying your demands, and I'll be dealing with the blowback until I die. The Ring belongs to you now, provided you divert the current course of Undina. I hope you do well with it alone. Goodbye, Mr. Trass. This is the last time Earth will ever deal with you."

As soon as the message ended, I clapped. Everyone turned to me so fast it was like I'd set off a bomb. "Well played," I said. "My whole life, I never saw Earth or the major corps blink, and you made them shit themselves in less than an hour."

"How do I divert it?" Aria asked, clearly eager to move on with the subject.

Kale didn't answer. He leaned toward the viewport, hands squeezing the backs of the seats on either side of him. Big, beautiful Earth hovered in the center. It'd been exactly a year now since I'd been there, the last M-Day when the Children of Titan made their existence known beyond their own world by blowing up a train platform in New London and robbing a hospital. They'd come far in a short time. Now Undina raced through space toward the very same city, a trail of blinding light at its back.

"You don't," Kale said, emotionless. Hearing his response made my heart feel like it'd plunged out of my chest. Again, it could've been the bullet wound, but I felt empty.

"What are you talking about?" Aria asked.

"Plot a course for Titan," Kale said. "We're going home."

"You made a deal to divert Undina."

"And now they'll learn how worthless deals with them truly are as they spend the next century recovering."

"They gave you want you wanted!" Aria went to shove him, but Kale grabbed her arm and squeezed. That snapped me out of a spell of lightheadedness, though, I couldn't manage much more than to sit up.

"Do you really think a signature makes Titan ours?" Kale asked. "They'll be back for us tomorrow, using trade and credits for leverage. They'll do what Earthers do, manipulate and corrupt. No, this M-Day will change everything. They take us seriously now, but after this is over, they will fear us. It won't matter if the deal is ruined, because they won't be able to touch us. They'll be stuck rebuilding their civilization for decades. Until our son is ruling over the Ring. That is how we win. Not with signed papers."

If there is one thing I've learned about rebels, the moment they're proficient enough to get you to respect them, they show their true colors. The moment you think they have an actual vision, they reveal their narcissism. Unable to fit in with the way the world works, they try to write it in their own image.

"There are millions of people down there, and you're just going to wipe them out?" I asked. "Innocent people. Good people." *And Zhaff,* I didn't say out loud. I'd left him behind for a chance to live his life, and thanks to Kale, he'd die anyway. Death indeed did follow in his wake.

I'd never cared a smidge for the rabble of Earth, but it was a collector's job, more than anything, to ensure they could live peacefully. The Amissum clan-family was down there, a few kilometers outside New London—that group of hardworking factory laborers I was born into before I ran to seek better things. They probably didn't know enough about Ringers to even care about looking down on them.

"Kale, don't do this," Aria begged. "I know I hurt you, but I've seen the good in you. I fell in love with that man. None of that was fake."

"You think this is about you?" Kale asked as he continued to stare at Earth. "Everyone always thinks it's about them."

I remembered how the Pervenio directors always looked after striking a solid deal or weaseling their way out of trouble thanks to a collector's talents. Like they were conquering heroes. Kale seemed neither proud nor solemn. He was relieved. I knew now, going back, that when Rylah came to my cell, I should have told them to stop and keep playing along in Kale's fantasy. Sure, he was always a deluded Ringer no thanks to his aunt, but Aria leaving him hadn't just broken his heart... it broke him.

"It's already done," he said. "Basaam knew. There is no way to communicate with the engine. The energy discharged in every pulse causes too much interference. Undina can't stop, and it can't turn."

"No... no!" Aria lunged for him and pounded on his chest plate. "I should have strangled you with your bed sheets, you fucking coward! They were all right about you. You *are* a monster!"

Kale's men went to stop her, but he ordered them to back down. I tried again to stand, but a firm hand on my shoulder sent me back into my seat without a fuss. I barely had enough energy left to keep my eyes open.

"I'm going to stop this. You need to be stopped." Aria sat back down, took control of the ship, and banked around so hard, it threw everyone off balance. She raced back toward the rear of Undina, making sure to keep the *Cora* corkscrewing so that nobody could keep their bearings.

"Let her," Kale instructed his men.

Aria targeted the pulsing engine stalk latched to the back of Undina and fired everything the *Cora* had left in her arsenal. Even if she knocked it out, the asteroid wouldn't stop. All she could hope would be that a few fusion pulses after it was knocked loose of its anchor in the rock redirected it into the planets vast ocean. The planet had already been half-drowned three hundred years prior, and Earthers were smart enough to resettle far from the new coastlines along high elevations.

It was a smart move by my daughter, a rash move, but futile. The plasma emitted by the engines nuclear propulsion vaporized every missile before even coming close to the surface. When Aria realized that, along with the rest of us, her jaw dropped and the *Cora* stopped spinning. One of Kale's men immediately grabbed her and yanked her out of the seat.

"No!" she howled. She reached back and ripped the man's sidearm out of its holster. Every rifle in the command deck swung to aim at her, I called out for her to stop, and that was when she did the unthinkable. Something she probably learned from the Children of Titan after so long at their side. She turned the gun on herself, aiming right through her belly button at Kale's son.

"Get your hands off me!" She shook free and backed slowly across the command deck, toward me. "I swear, if you don't stop it, I'll blow us both to hell."

"Aria, it's too late." Kale took a hard step toward her, but she fired once into the ceiling to stop him and then returned to aiming.

Kale raised his arms to get his men to lower their weapons, then took a different approach. He bit back his anger and tried to console her. "This is how we change Sol, Aria," he said softly. By Earth, the crazy kid really meant it too.

"By killing millions?" she replied.

"To ensure that millions of Titanborn will be born in control of their own lives for generations."

"If you do this, they don't deserve it."

"How many of us died in the Ringer Plague so Pervenio Corp could own the Ring? And he and his father let it happen. He told me himself. What do you think they'll try next?"

I snickered, and one of his men promptly wrapped a hand

around my throat as if they'd forgotten I was there. "You're really going to lie to her while I'm right here?" I asked.

"I swear it, Kale," Aria said. "Have Basaam find a way to redirect Undina, or we both die."

"Don't you dare touch my son!" his voice boomed. His features contorted, and all that sense of relief gave way to that heartsick rage, which allowed him to invent such a homicidal plot in the first place. "If you hurt him, your father won't know a day without torture. I'll freeze him piece by piece until there's nothing left."

"I should have never trusted you after I saw what you did on Mars."

"And I should have known you were too weak to be one of us."

"I thought your aunt was the crazy one, but I was way off," I chimed in, earning a glare from them both. "You set out to prove a Ringer was worth as much as an Earther; congratulations. We're all human. It's madmen like you Sol needs to be free of; doesn't matter where they're born."

Kale turned to me, his glower boring through me. "You don't get to turn noble when it suits you, Collector. You and your employer did the same thing for years. Self-preservation through killing. One or a million, it makes no difference."

"See now, that's where you're wrong. I told you before. You can kill Luxarn and millions of other Earthers, but it won't bring Cora back, and it won't make my daughter love you again. You'll never fill that great big hole inside you."

"I'm doing this for my people! For Titan," Kale shouted.

"Cora was a looker, that's for sure, but if I'm being honest, that girl's life wasn't worth a million anything."

"Stop using her name," Kale warned.

"I've seen just as pretty in the Martian sewers, without the baggage. The little half-Ringer couldn't have been too smart if she couldn't see you for the animal you are."

"Be quiet."

"Was Cora that good in the sack to make you lose your mind like this?"

"I said don't use her name!" Kale pushed off the pilot's chair and crashed into me, knocking me out of my chair and turning all the attention away from Aria. We tumbled down the corridor, spiraling, kicking, and punching. I snuck a few blows in too, though my fist crunched harmlessly against his armor. I didn't care. If he was going to ravage Earth just to fill his heart with something, then he was going to die with it. Now that I knew how far Aria was willing to go, I was done feeling helpless.

Kale and I crashed into a sleep pod so hard, the lid cracked. We bounced off, and I was able to raise my artificial knee up into his visor. He shrieked as it shattered and tiny shards stabbed his face. My fist punched through the opening and broke his nose. His flailing arm smashed my gun wound and had me seeing stars.

He pinned me against the wall and went for the pistol holstered on his hip, which I noticed was my own. I did the same. I wrestled his wrist to aim it away from me. My Earther muscles helped me stand a chance. I pushed him back and forced him to squeeze the trigger once. The bullet slashed through the neck-guard of his armor but didn't hit meat.

The recoil allowed him to regain control, and he fired repeatedly down into my fake leg at the joint. The alloy shredded away to reveal circuitry as complex as the human nervous system. It didn't hurt. Not even when the bullet sliced the thing's core structure and left it dangling off my hip like a loose air recycler vent. I spotted his men behind him, struggling to line up a shot at me. Then Kale switched on his armor's mag boots and gained footing. Weightlessness trapped me in his grip, with no chance to break free.

He held me against the wall with one hand and threw my gun aside. His other armored fist crashed into my jaw. "She was worth every goddamn Earther in Sol!" Kale roared. "Nothing like your whore, traitorous daughter!" He punched me again, jarring a few teeth loose. I couldn't even feel the pain, my body hurt so much all over, but my vision became spotted with black.

Focus, Malcolm, I told myself. I added in the lie that I'd been in worse scrapes before. Nobody else on the ship could get a shot at me, and I'd struck a nerve that had the boy king seeing red. But my pistol floated nearby, and as Kale beat my face to a pulp, I stretched my injured arm out. I couldn't even feel my fingers, so I had to watch as they threaded the trigger. Dazed as I was, I knew the weight of that gun like I knew my daughter. There was a single round left.

One last kill...

"Get off him!" Aria shouted suddenly.

She'd broken free of Kale's men and grabbed him by the shoulder. He whipped around out of reflex and struck her in the chest with his armored elbow. She was launched across the cabin into the wall. I got the shot off in the direction of Kale's head at the same time, but realizing it was Aria who gripped him had caused him to turn, and I missed my mark. He grabbed his ear and staggered backward. All he was missing was an earlobe.

Titanborn guards apprehended me and threw me to my knees, guns poking me from every angle. I didn't pay them any attention. I heard a cough that made my whole body go numb. Aria lay between two sleep pods on the other side of the cabin, just as Zhaff had after our failed escape. Her eyes gaped. Her mouth whistled faintly as air struggled to reach her lungs. The center of her chest was completely caved in, and the Ark-ship necklace I'd given to her so long ago lay in two pieces on the floor once again.

Kale's men rushed to him first, but he threw them aside and went to her. He tore off his helmet, droplets of blood streaming away from his nose and ear. He pressed his fully intact ear against her battered chest.

"What did you do?" I said. My mouth was so full of blood and broken teeth I could barely get the words out.

"Aria, breathe," Kale said. He tapped her face. "Aria."

Her arm quaked as she reached up and ran her fingers through his hair. I shouted and cursed, saying Earth knows what, but I couldn't break free to reach her. She stared straight into Kale's eyes and whispered something to him. Halfway through, she peered over at me. I couldn't hear her over my own ranting, but whatever she said made all the fury twisting Kale's features suddenly disappear.

TWENTY-THREE

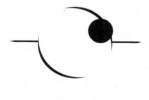

KALE

"Aria, breathe," I said. I pulled her close and stroked her cheek. "Aria."

With my other hand, I felt her ruptured chest. There was barely a heartbeat, and every time she breathed, I could hear her lungs rattling. Her fingers slid up around my neck, and she tried to pull my ear toward her mouth, but she was too weak. I had to help her by leaning forward myself.

"I know I'm not her," she whispered. "I'm sorry I couldn't be, but I shouldn't have run." Her voice was so fragile, it rattled like the rusty old air recyclers on the bottommost tier of the Darien Lowers.

"You don't—" She silenced me with a quaking finger over my lips.

"You're better than they are. I know it. Sol is filled with rotten parents... Don't be the monster they made you." Her gaze shifted to aim at Malcolm. "Be a father our son can be proud of, even if it makes his life hell. That's what I thought being Titan-born meant all along..."

Air whistled through her lips after those words. Her head drifted back slowly in zero G. I shook her by the shoulders, but her green eyes froze open. The brightness slowly drained from them.

"Aria?" I said softly.

"Aria!" I whipped around to see Malcolm slip out of my men's grasp, push off the wall, and soar toward me. If a look could kill, I'd be missing more than the tip of my ear. A Titanborn grabbed his foot and yanked him down, but Malcolm didn't stop. He clawed at the floor to reach her. One of my men pressed a pulse rifle to the back of his head. Before he could fire, I grabbed the man and flung him aside.

Malcolm raced by me to his daughter's side. "Aria!" he screamed again. Every time he did, it felt like a knife was being pushed deeper through my rib cage. I'd heard names screamed like that before, full of unbridled rage and anguish. I heard it every time a Titanborn child was dragged off by Pervenio Corp security to be placed in quarantine.

"Not you too," Malcolm whimpered. "Aria, wake up. Please. I can't lose you too."

I stared, dumbfounded. The *Cora* transformed around me, making me feel like I was back in that airlock cell on Pervenio Station where Cora was spaced. Where I found the recording of Director Sodervall hitting the commands that doomed her. Only, on this occasion, I stood where he'd been, watching. All that was different was that I wasn't smiling over executing someone only for being different than me, but I'd still killed her.

"Lord Trass!" One of my men shook me to snap me back to reality. "Lord Trass. Your son."

Malcolm huddled over Aria, in such a state of shock now he couldn't even cry. I noticed her stomach beneath him, protruding even more now that her upper body was crushed.

"Get her..." I swallowed the lump in my throat and gathered my breath. "Get her to medical," I ordered. I pointed to another of my men. "Wake Basaam. We need a doctor."

"*She* was our doctor," he replied.

"He's close enough."

Two of my men grabbed Malcolm, but he wouldn't let go. "No!" he snapped. "You don't get to touch her ever again."

I grabbed his hand and pried it free of her dress. He flailed and kicked, only one of his legs intact. His face was bloodied and bruised thanks to me, barely recognizable.

"I'll kill you, Kale!" he wheezed. "I swear on Earth you're going to die."

I shoved him against a sleep pod and held him secure while my men gently lifted Aria and carried her weightless body away. Another opened Basaam's sleep pod and pulled the confused Earther out.

"We have to save the child," I said.

Malcolm didn't answer at first. Instead, he stared daggers my way before spitting a glob of blood at my face. "Congratulations, kid," he then said. "You wanted to beat Luxarn Pervenio; you get to be him now. The most powerful man in Sol. All alone."

All I could manage to do was stare back at him. This Earther who'd likely presided over more crimes against my people than any man except for Luxarn, and I couldn't help but pity him. Was that how broken I'd looked after finding out about Cora?

It was then that I realized, no matter what Malcolm was, it didn't mean he loved any less. However many people he'd killed, however many lives he'd ruined, he still had a heart for Aria. All those Earthers waiting under the shadow of Undina loved and were loved by clan-families and friends. And they hated, Titanborn especially, but only because the screens surrounding them told them to. Perhaps many of them were related to those Earthers who tortured my people for so long, but it wasn't them.

I knew what I had to do. I only wished it didn't take seeing Aria like this for me to realize it.

I held Malcolm by the sides of his face and said, "You have to take care of him."

My response made his bloody brow furrow, but that was all I offered. I left him against the sleep pod, with his body so broken, he couldn't follow. I then rushed toward the command deck viewport. Undina was less than a half hour from hitting. Com messages from Earth popped up all over the display. Members of the USF begged me to stop, all those men and women who were so quick to sign off on Luxarn doing whatever was necessary to keep the Ring profitable, were now on their knees pleading with a Ringer.

Transport ships flitted across Earth away from New London. I knew it was those very same Assembly sycophants and schemers with a ride reserved for them, preserving their own lives while the civilians in New London filled the streets and watched their doom creep ever closer along the horizon.

They were Earthers, all of them—future collectors, security officers, assembly members, or corporate directors. Maybe there was a new Luxarn Pervenio down there ready to rise to power and get vengeance on us, but it took the dying words of a bastard daughter from the shit-covered sewers of Mars for me to remember what it meant to be Titanborn. What I'd forgotten in blind fury.

That we would stand against them together. That we'd taught my people how.

"One last ride, Cora," I whispered.

I leaned over the Cora's controls and accelerated toward the back of Undina as fast as the ship was able. Then I turned and headed back toward the cabin. Malcolm remained on his knees, wearing a thousand-meter stare, shattered. When he saw me, he didn't even try to attack. All the fight in him was gone.

"Why?" was all he could manage. I scooped him up and battled the g-forces from the *Cora*'s hard burn to carry him toward the med bay.

We stopped outside. All of my men surrounded the medical bed, bracing against the pressure. Two aimed weapons at Basaam Venta's head, forcing him to begin the procedure of removing my baby from Aria's stomach.

"He's s-still alive," the frightened Earther stuttered.

"Get him out!" a Titanborn ordered.

"It's not my area of expertise," Basaam said.

"No excuses."

"If my son lives, Basaam goes free," I said. My men regarded me, and I waved over the young blonde one I was most familiar with. The order buoyed Basaam's disposition. Nobody understood what the promise of freedom can do for a man better than me. He began requesting specific equipment at breakneck speed with the confidence of a genius.

"Lord Trass, what do you need?" the young soldier asked. His cheeks were still as soft as Luxarn's mattress in the home I stole.

"What's your name?" I said.

He seemed taken aback by the question at first, then shook his head and answered, "Geoff Parker."

"Geoff. Go to the command deck and make sure we don't crash."

"Crash?"

"Just go."

He glanced nervously back at Aria, then nodded and hurried by. I propped Malcolm up against the doorway. "Go to her," I told him.

"You don't get to walk away from this," he rasped.

"I'm not. She fought for us to have a world of our own. I'm going to go make sure we get it."

"Haven't you done enough?"

I stared at Aria's cold, impassive face, framed by strands of wavy hair as red as the surface of Mars. She wasn't Cora and never would be, but she was dead all the same because of this hatred between my people and her father's. I'm not sure if I ever really loved her or just told myself I did so I could feel something. I'm not sure if I could ever love again, but I was sure of one thing—she deserved better. All my people did. A king, and a father, they could be proud of.

"Not yet," I said. I turned away, but Malcolm grabbed my arm. His grip was weaker than an Earther's ever should be. The haggard old fool was on the cusp of death. Blood stained his mouth and shirt, and if he didn't get treated soon, he'd probably collapse.

"One day, I'm going to kill you," he said. "I don't care what it takes."

"If it had to be anyone." I lifted his chin. "Make sure Malcolm sees Sol as it truly is, just like she did."

"Malcolm?"

"Aria told me that was the name she wanted, before you both tried to run away."

I removed his hand and left him behind. Even his sharp wit couldn't produce a response before I was around the corner. For a moment, I worried that he'd follow me instead of doing the right thing, but he never came.

I entered the cargo bay alone. A rack of helmets on the far wall let me replace mine so I'd be able to breathe in space. I considered grabbing an oxygen tank, but what I was planning was a one-way journey, and there was enough woven into my suit's stores to get me there.

My mag boots switched off, and I steadied myself against the *Cora's* exit ramp while the ship's acceleration racked my body. It was sealed, like it should be during flight and without depressurization, but I tapped the control panel and overrode the system.

Then I waited. I closed my eyes and tried to clear my mind of everything, which was as impossible as it had been since the day Rin told me I was a Trass. All the awful things I'd done, I thought I did for my people, but it was clear now that wasn't always true. I did them because of those awful memories of an Earther security officer calling me Ringer like I wasn't worth a name. I did them for Cora and my mother. And most of all, I did them for me. To make me feel again.

I switched on my coms and set them to my and Rin's private line. "Rin," I said weakly. "Titan is yours. Tell my mother... Tell her I didn't die a monster." All this rebelling started with me trying to save her, so it felt fitting that my mother was the one who popped into my head as the end neared. I wished I'd have a chance to tell her myself, that I was sorry for letting her down, but Rin's word would have to do.

"From ice to ashes," I said staunchly, mustering all my courage. We were too far for me ever to receive her answer in time.

G-forces suddenly tugged on my body as the *Cora* turned hard. Geoff Parker, one of my Titanborn subjects whose name I'd finally cared enough to learn, did as I asked and kept us from crashing. My finger hovered over the controls to open the ramp. I waited until the wails of a newborn infant echoed down the halls of the *Cora*.

Then I set the inner door of the cargo bay to seal, closed my visor, and hit the command to open the ship's ramp. As soon as it cracked open, explosive decompression yanked me out into space. My body flew across the starry void at speeds that would have ripped me apart if not for my suit. One last flight without a g-stim so I could feel everything.

Undina filled my vision, surrounded by the glowing blue of

Earth. It was so close now. I was headed for the hangar nearest to the engine, where I wouldn't immediately burn up while it pulsed, like nuclear bombs over and over.

I didn't need my wings in space, so I held a straight line until the edge of the hangar was in reach. My elbow snapped as I struck, sending me tumbling along the surface until I was able to grab hold of a rocky outcrop with my good hand. That shoulder was nearly torn from its socket, but somehow held long enough for me to magnetize my boots.

Sweat started pouring down my forehead immediately, even through my visor. Everything around me was drowned in brightness from the Fusion Pulse Engine. It was as if I were walking on the surface of the sun. I crawled toward its base, anchored into the rock, and every meter closer made my armor feel like it was melting.

Earthers said that on their planet they were so near to the sun they could see it shine in the sky. That their retinas could burn if they stared. Now I understood. The engine was so blinding, I couldn't even look up.

I'm not sure how long I trudged along the wrinkled surface of Undina, but by the time I reached the base of the engine, I felt like I'd sweated all the water out of me. Even my powered armor couldn't help maintain the sensation in my limbs. My eyes were so watery, I could barely see.

I leaned against the base of the engine to catch my breath. Three massive, flexible arms extended from anchors dug into the crust, bending every time there was a propulsive blast from the fusion core and nozzle above. The whole contraption was slowly burrowing into the crust of the asteroid, but it would hold long enough.

I pulled myself around the structure, a wave of heat distortion making it difficult to tell how close I was to anything without touching it. I dug my fingers into the plating and tore a piece off to reveal the manual control panel.

Maybe it was the heat, or maybe Basaam's programming, but the whole screen was dark. This was the first field test for the drives, so nobody could be sure what would happen when they were attached to an asteroid, in space, without the proper housing and cooling an Ark could afford.

After a handful of failed attempts at activating the controls, I went to punch it out of frustration, but in the reflection, saw two lights. I turned around too late to get out of the way of a small transport ship, which had likely once been used to convey ore to the factories on Luna. It crashed into one of the engine's structural arms, pinning me against it. Without my armor on, I'd have been dead, but still, my entire rib cage felt like it'd been pulverized.

My lips were chapped, and my throat so dry, it hurt to inhale. I held my breath instead as I struggled to break free. I punched the ship in a Pervenio logo on its hull, again and again, screaming to help pour all my energy into every blow. I pictured Director Sodervall's smiling face when he spaced my people, and Luxarn's when I ended his reign for good.

After I lost count, I started to picture Aria's instead. She stood at my side on Mars when every Earther turned their nose up at us. I pictured my mother, frail and dying in the Pervenio Quarantine before I saved her. I pictured Rylah and Gareth, placing my first rifle in my hands and believing in some worthless Ringer pickpocket to lead Titan into the future. And then I saw Cora, gazing up at me with her brilliant blue eyes in that single night we spent alone together before she died.

I was thrust back to the present when the ship shifted enough for me to fall free. I would have laughed in relief if I could. I clung to one of the Fusion Pulse Engine's struts and tried to pull myself up. Then I felt a sudden, stinging sensation in my chest. I looked down. A hole cut through my chest plate. My suit was designed to automatically seal it upon exposure, but I'd been shot. I couldn't hear anything over the engine.

I fell to my knees, clutching my chest as I rolled over against the engine's support. I coughed, and blood sprayed the inside of my visor. Through it, I saw a shadowy figure topple out of the ship's cockpit. Whoever it was wore an exo-suit, but the sleeve for his left arm fluttered, and his left leg dragged behind him as he limped. Through the visor, I couldn't spot the whites of any eyes.

"Zhaff..." I rasped. "You have to stop it." I raised my arm to point at the locked engine controls, but Zhaff shot me through the bicep. It fell limp to my side, but my body remained too overwhelmed by heat to feel anything.

I groped through the darkness to find something to help me up while Zhaff holstered his firearm and limped over to the engine controls. I pushed against the ship with my knee and was able to get to my feet. I grabbed the first part I could find and tried to use it to pull myself at him until I realized that Zhaff had a hand terminal raised to the engine's emergency controls.

With only his single hand, he typed like only a Cogent could until the engine controls winked on and he moved to them. I felt the structural arm I was wrapped around shake, then lower. A wave of intense heat burned my cheek through my visor and made my insides feel like they were going to boil. I peered up and saw that the direction of the engine's pulses had changed, shifting Undina's direction.

I coughed up another gob of blood and fell back. As the plume of the engines shifted, I noticed the thin blue streak of the *Cora* far off in the darkness. I closed my eyelids and breathed in deep through my nose. My mouth tasted like rusting metal.

I'd leaped from the *Cora* to fix my mistake, I'd missed the birth of my son, and the future of our free world, yet it was Malcolm's mercy toward Luxarn's son that saved the people of Earth. Not me. And nobody would ever know.

A sound like crackling interrupted the steady pulsating of the engine as Undina entered Earth's upper atmosphere and its front began to burn up. A Ringer's body wasn't suited for Earth. That was one of the first things my people learned. The gravity was relentless on our bones and muscles, but most of all on our hearts. Without suits and proper medication, it would give out after a few days. My father learned that lesson when he came to Earth alongside Aria to steal medicine for my people.

Yet there I was, arriving at the cradle of humanity precisely one year later. I set out from Titan with the intention of destroying everything my enemies held dear, but as I opened my eyes and squinted at the dress of fire Undina wore around its horizon, I thought I could make out the shine of Sol.

We were all under the light of the same star. We were all humans. Sol-born. Maybe, now, the people of Earth would finally see that too.

"To ensure the safety of human propagation," a faint voice spoke. I lifted my heavy head and saw Zhaff towering over me. Despite being blind, his pulse pistol aimed directly between my eyes.

I opened my mouth to say something, but before I could, Zhaff's gun flashed, my head snapped back, and my world went black. And like Cora, I'd never be ashes upon the winds of Titan.

TWENTY-FOUR

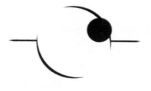

MALCOLM

It was M-Day, September 3, 2335. Exactly three hundred one years to the day after a meteorite struck Earth. Millions watched in horror from the streets of New London, torn from their celebration of survival. They waited to die, helpless as Ringers in quarantine, until Undina was redirected at the very last moment.

It landed in the middle of Earth's vast ocean instead. Tidal waves ripped across the planet, but Earth's tide had already been raised permanently by the last, much-larger meteorite, the coastal cities already toppled like dominoes. Earthers now stuck to the heart of the remaining landmasses, and so New London and all their strings of settlements remained mostly unharmed.

Earth's sky was painted a darker shade of gray from vapor and dust kicked up by the impact. Global temperatures chilled even further than they had since the first M-Day. It was nowhere near as cold as Titan, but every shiver of Earth's populace would be a reminder of Kale Trass's final act. His final "mercy," as his people called it.

I liked to tell myself, from time to time, that it wasn't Kale who'd redirected Basaam Venta's engine. But that maybe Zhaff had one ounce of the extraordinary left in him and found a way to redirect Undina himself, saving a planet and people who'd never given a damn about him. It was better than believing the man who'd killed my daughter was a hero merely for realizing his pain pushed him too far.

A handful of ships had ejected from Undina as it hurtled toward Earth and left me holding my breath that maybe I was right, though reports from the USF said they were all found empty. And the asteroid and everything in and on it had burned up in the atmosphere or been vaporized by the impact. Still, it didn't hurt to dream for once.

Presently, I limped along the docks in the Darien Uppers, still getting re-acquainted with my artificial leg after it required significant repairs. A sanitary mask covered my mouth. Rin Trass made me wear it after she spared my life upon our return. The Scarred Queen of Titan was now the legal ruler of all the Ring, until Kale's heir—my grandson—was old enough to take over.

It almost seemed fitting that out of the people in that hangar on Mars on that fateful day when I finally met Kale, Rin and I would be the only two to survive. The old wretches, burned out on living yet unable to die. Though I've always found that the best leaders are the ones who never wanted the crown, and wretched as Rin was, she was no Kale.

The Darien Uppers had become a place of commerce again. A Venta Co. trading vessel arrived in a nearby hangar, and although armed Ringers hounded it, the fact that it hadn't been shot down was a step in the right direction. Rin still refused to use credits throughout the Ring, but a man like me who'd seen all of Sol could always find a living.

For now, I had a full-time job. As I passed a statue being erected in Kale's memory in Darien outside the docks, I couldn't help but think about blowing it to bits. Every day I went by, my blood began to boil, but I kept my mouth shut and did as I was asked.

I rode the lift up one of the residential towers structuring Darien. The gardens at the top bloomed again now that the Ringers were done partying over rubble and celebrating their freedom. Maybe they'd finally remembered something life taught me—that hard work was the only way to control anything. As a collector or a grandfather.

The door to my dwelling unit opened as I approached. Rin strode out, not wearing her armor or her sanitary mask.

"Graves," she muttered as she passed.

The light caught her scarred face in just such a way that I could see through to the back of her throat. I tried not to stare and nodded in response, like I always did. It was her choice to let me live after we returned from Undina, so it was the least I could offer. We'd been through enough, I think, to have fostered a mutual respect for each other.

Rylah sat on the bed inside, and Kale's mother stood behind her at the back of the room, watching. I don't think I'd heard her speak ever since we returned without Kale.

Rylah cradled Aria's crying son with a synthetic hand she'd constructed after picking apart what was left of my leg. It was still mostly exposed circuits and joints, but it worked well enough, and she used it to repair my leg so I didn't need a chair like an old codger.

Real hands or not, Rylah was still the most gorgeous woman I'd ever seen besides my Aria. At least now that we were both missing limbs, I had a better chance. I limped over. She smiled and held out baby Alann for me.

Yeah, Aria's name choice for the kid didn't really stick with Kale's family, especially considering I was the only one alive who'd heard it. So, de facto Queen Rin got to choose while Kale's mother didn't seem to get a say in anything. Apparently,

Alann was Kale's dad's name, one of the founders of the Children of Titan.

I'm not sure that warranted having his legacy carried on, but it wasn't worth fighting over. Malcolm was a crappy name anyway—one I never cared to pass on. Not that I didn't appreciate the sentiment, but Aria wasn't thinking clearly whenever she had the idea. Always such a romantic. There was no reason to pretend we were closer than we really were and have me be reminded of it daily. My fault for being a shit dad, of course, but at least with Alann that could change.

"I can't get him to sleep," Rylah said.

"His mom never liked to sleep either," I said.

I took Alann and stroked his thin hair as he fussed. Then I lifted the cracked Ark-ship figurine hanging from his neck, which had belonged to my daughter. I'd been able to repair it again, though now a few small chunks didn't fit and the imperfections were noticeable. I closed my eyes and squeezed it, remembering the way Aria had stared at me on the *Cora* before she passed. Like, somehow, everything was going to be okay.

I looked back down at Alann. He had Aria's eyes, as green as the forests of Earth before the Meteorite. Every time I held him, I remembered why any time I was outside of that room being ridiculed by Ringers, I stayed quiet and lived among them. Rin decreed that the grandfather of Kale's heir couldn't be touched, but I endured my share of insults and spit-filled drinks every day, especially since they thought I'd killed Orson on my own.

Whatever they threw at me, I didn't care. Because as much as I hated Kale and his people for being behind the destruction of all the most important parts of my life—from leaving me in the position to have to shoot Zhaff twice for my daughter, to causing Aria's death—he'd given me something I never thought I'd get. Something that I damn well didn't deserve.

A second chance.

THANKS FOR READING!

To all you who made it this far, I hope you enjoyed the *Children of Titan Series*. Even if you didn't, please consider leaving an honest review wherever you prefer to leave your bookish thoughts online. Reviews are the lifeblood of newer authors like me, and they help more than you could possibly imagine.

If you enjoyed this story about the rebellion of Titan, consider checking out my *Circuit Trilogy* a Space Opera with a dark twist set in our solar system.

If you'd like to be updated about the series and its upcoming releases, as well as gain exclusive access to limited content, ARCs, and more, please subscribe to my monthly newsletter below.

Subscribe here: http://rhettbruno.com/newsletter

ABOUT THE AUTHOR

Rhett C Bruno is the USA Today Bestselling Author of 'The Circuit Saga' (Diversion Books, Podium Publishing), 'Bastards of the Ring Series' (Random House, Upcoming Audible Studios), and the 'Buried Goddess Saga' (Upcoming Audible Studios); among other works.

He has been writing since before he can remember, scribbling down what he thought were epic stories when he was young to show to his friends and family. He currently works at an Architecture firm in Connecticut after graduating from Syracuse University, but that hasn't stopped him from recording the tales bouncing around inside of his head.

Rhett resides in Stamford, Connecticut, with his wife and their dog, Raven.

**You can find out more about his work
at www.rhettbruno.com**

SPECIAL THANKS TO:

ADAWIA E. ASAD
BARDE PRESS
CALUM BEAULIEU
BEN
BECKY BEWERSDORF
BHAM
TANNER BLOTTER
ALFRED JOSEPH BOHNE IV
CHAD BOWDEN
ERREL BRAUDE
DAMIEN BROUSSARD
CATHERINE BULLINER
JUSTIN BURGESS
MATT BURNS
BERNIE CINKOSKE
MARTIN COOK
ALISTAIR DILWORTH
JAN DRAKE
BRET DULEY
RAY DUNN
ROB EDWARDS
RICHARD EYRES
MARK FERNANDEZ
CHARLES T FINCHER
SYLVIA FOIL
GAZELLE OF CAERBANNOG
DAVID GEARY
MICHEAL GREEN
BRIAN GRIFFIN

EDDIE HALLAHAN
JOSH HAYES
PAT HAYES
BILL HENDERSON
JEFF HOFFMAN
GODFREY HUEN
JOAN QUERALTÓ IBÁÑEZ
JONATHAN JOHNSON
MARCEL DE JONG
KABRINA
PETRI KANERVA
ROBERT KARALASH
VIKTOR KASPERSSON
TESLAN KIERINHAWK
ALEXANDER KIMBALL
JIM KOSMICKI
FRANKLIN KUZENSKI
MEENAZ LODHI
DAVID MACFARLANE
JAMIE MCFARLANE
HENRY MARIN
CRAIG MARTELLE
THOMAS MARTIN
ALAN D. MCDONALD
JAMES MCGLINCHEY
MICHAEL MCMURRAY
CHRISTIAN MEYER
SEBASTIAN MÜLLER
MARK NEWMAN
JULIAN NORTH

KYLE OATHOUT
LILY OMIDI
TROY OSGOOD
GEOFF PARKER
NICHOLAS (BUZ) PENNEY
JASON PENNOCK
THOMAS PETSCHAUER
JENNIFER PRIESTER
RHEL
JODY ROBERTS
JOHN BEAR ROSS
DONNA SANDERS
FABIAN SARAVIA
TERRY SCHOTT
SCOTT
ALLEN SIMMONS
KEVIN MICHAEL STEPHENS
MICHAEL J. SULLIVAN
PAUL SUMMERHAYES
JOHN TREADWELL
CHRISTOPHER J. VALIN
PHILIP VAN ITALLIE
JAAP VAN POELGEEST
FRANCK VAQUIER
VORTEX
DAVID WALTERS JR
MIKE A. WEBER
PAMELA WICKERT
JON WOODALL
BRUCE YOUNG

CPSIA information can be obtained
at www.ICGtesting.com
Printed in the USA
BVHW081100110220
572026BV00008B/1162